Book One of
The Lazuli Portals

The Cordello Quest

Joanna Gawn
With
Ron Dickerson

A catalogue record for this book is available from the
British Library

ISBN: 9781849142359

This novel is entirely a work of fiction. The names,
characters and incidents portrayed in it are either the
work of the authors' imaginations or are used fictitiously.

Joanna dedicates this book to

My husband, Walt - with love

Row & Tina - for your amazing friendship

Ron - for your unwavering belief

Ron dedicates this book to

My long-suffering wife, Mo

Nan – who gave me direction
and whom I still miss

The support of my family

Jo - for giving me the chance to
explore another part of me!

Book number ..2!....

of 44 numbered and signed
Paperback
copies of

The Cordello Quest

Part of
The Lazuli Portals
a trilogy being written by
Joanna Gawn & Ron Dickerson

Joanna's dedication

[signature: Joanna G]

Ron's Dedication

[signature]

IN THE BEGINNING

The tors and their stones
Peaked high on yon moor
Untouched and serene
Laid down far long past
They wait

Weathered and still
Under oft changing skies
Seen not noticed in time
Their awakening now due
They sit for her

Unknowing she comes
Her troubles bear down
To pass and evolve
To grow and renew
It is Now

PART ONE

AWAKENING

CHAPTER 1

The full moon slipped silently behind drifting silvered clouds grazing a dark velvet sky. I refused to recognise the quiet beauty of the night; I just wasn't ready to appreciate it. Weaving towards me through the wet grass, drink in hand, was Jason.

I glared at him. I was furious. How could he do this to me? To us?

Tears pricked at my eyes, and I wiped them away with the backs of my hands, angry that I felt so weak.

I turned my back on Jason, and contemplated the vastness of the moors. Even late at night, with the clouds backlit with mother–of–pearl moonlight, I could see the curves and contours of the hills and granite rocks, giant moonlit shadows playing across the sloping moorland.

By day, the scene was impressive, attracting walkers and day–trippers.

By night, it was lonely and utterly deserted.

I wanted to absorb the melancholy of the moorland into my soul; it echoed my mood perfectly.

This was *home*.

Torturing myself, I let my mind replay the events of the past few minutes. I'd come here with Jason tonight with expectations of some sort of commitment. I'd half-expected an engagement ring, a proposal.

Instead, Jason had announced that he'd received a plum job offer – a post based hundreds of miles away. He knew very well I never wanted to leave this mournful, beautiful, isolated landscape.

I tried to shrug aside my disappointment, but I couldn't seem to shake it. We'd obviously been on completely different wavelengths. On a different planet, even.

It hurt. It *really* hurt.

Jason, of course, was unaware of my scrambling, scattered thoughts. I had read far too much into his suggestion of this midnight picnic, thinking he was being romantic. Never believing – not for a moment – that he would be breaking us apart. He was celebrating; I was grieving for what I had thought was to be.

I hugged my arms to me as the breeze lifted. April nights on the moors can be cold, and I'd not brought a jacket with me. My mind had been humming with romantic visions of being wrapped in my fiancé's warm arms. I turned my head to see what Jason was doing.

Oh, great. Slumped against one of the low rocks, mouth open, snoring. It didn't get any better than that. He'd drunk too much. Again. Tears stung my eyes and I felt lost, disconnected from my surroundings.

The moon slid out from behind the swiftly–moving cloud, highlighting giant crags nearby. Without knowing why, I began walking towards the tall rocks. Jason and I had never visited this part of the moor, even in daylight. At least exploring the rocky outcrop would take my mind off how I was feeling. I reasoned that I had nothing better to do.

In the end, reason had nothing to do with it.

There was a magnetism, a pull, that drew me to the huge crags.

I could see my way clearly, the moon seeming to spotlight my path. Reaching the nearest crag, I stopped in front of it and raised a hand to the stone. I felt I might break in two, and I needed to lean on something older, permanent, solid. Connection to the natural rock might help me feel more stabilised, less fragile. The moon sympathetically cast its pale milky glow across the rock–face where my hand rested against the cool, rough surface. I could see different colours, grains of various minerals, flowing down the rock like ancient liquid frozen in time.

What happened next was unexpected.

My hand started to tingle, to vibrate, almost as if it was buzzing.

Alarmed, I tried to pull my hand away, but it was frozen in place. I was no longer touching the rock, but there was some kind of force keeping my hand locked to the ancient stone. I had no idea what was happening, let alone why. I was out of sight of Jason and the picnic remnants, and now I realised how very vulnerable I was; how very alone. I could feel fear bubbling inside me, threatening to overwhelm me. Something else was in control of me – and I hate being out of control!

Then, just as suddenly as it had risen, my fear subsided, and I felt instead an inexplicable, deep sense of peace. My breathing slowed, and I swallowed. I wasn't happy with this bizarre situation, but it looked as though I was trapped in it for the moment. I concentrated on my breathing, keeping myself calm.

A soft mist came from nowhere, creeping along the ground at the base of the crags. It started to gently rise, obscuring the bottom of each massive stone. The moon glided behind clouds again, leaving me in near–darkness.

The mist reached my waist. Surprisingly, I now felt excitement, a thrill of anticipation.

Quietly, secretly, the giant stones around me started to shift.

I watched, fascinated. I couldn't have moved, nor did I want to. Curiosity and awe conflicted with my dread of the unknown. Something special was happening, and I wanted to value every second of it.

There was no noise, no scraping or screeching. The enormous rocks just came to be somewhere else. I watched closely as the colossal stones silently and gracefully created a circle. I had been to Stonehenge and Avebury stone circles, and heard of many others, particularly here in Cornwall; but can honestly say I had never seen any of the vast stones *move*. However bizarre it sounds, I could see the crags moving with my own eyes, and I also seemed to be aware of it on some other level. I had no thought of calling to Jason, who'd probably be oblivious to everything, anyway.

In fact, I now had no thought of sharing this with anyone.

It felt for me alone.

Again, my awareness altered. I knew, even without looking, that the immense stones were changing again. Now in a perfect circle, stones in front of me, to the side and behind, the fabric of the rock seemed to waver, making my eyes water as they struggled to make sense of what I was seeing.

My arm dropped heavily to my side as the rock to which I'd been attached released its hold over me. For the moment, I was unsure of what to do, or where to go. I remained standing where I was, watching and waiting. My senses were totally alert, and I felt so incredibly and indescribably alive.

I felt *connected*. To this process, to the planet as a whole; a feeling of being adrift in space . . . but part of the Earth, too. I could feel the blood pulsing through my veins. Next, I detected a low hum in my ears, then a soft, gentle noise that I could not describe, except to say that it felt as if it was crafted by magic.

I remained transfixed.

I'm not sure when it happened, but I suddenly noticed that the mist had dissipated, leaving the stone circle empty but for me. I turned towards the stone to which I'd been joined, and saw that there was some sort of opening in the rock.

Something invited me to enter, something I was unable to resist.

With my back to the moon–silvered clouds, my shadow leaping in front of me, I tentatively stepped over the margin of the stone's entrance and into the blackness.

And found myself falling – tumbling, spinning, whirling downwards.

CHAPTER 2

How long I was falling, I do not know. There was no sense of time, or of place. No sound, no light. I was aware of no smell at all, and couldn't touch or feel anything; everything was completely neutral. I didn't understand why I did not feel scared.

In the absence of any sensation from my usual five senses, I slowly came to recognise that in fact I *could* feel something – I just wasn't sure how to interpret it. There was a kind of lightness around me, as if the air molecules were jiggling. I smiled; Jason would think I was cracking up. In my vacuum of space I cast a thought towards him, wondering whether he still slept, or whether he had now awakened and was wondering where I was. Would he worry? I felt sure he would. I missed him. I hoped he was warm enough!

The lightness around me began to coalesce into a visual phenomenon. I could now see sparkles of a soft golden light appearing in the void surrounding me. Gradually, these became more solid, larger, brighter. I felt as if I was watching a sunrise. *Feeling* a sunrise. The light grew yet brighter, my eyes conveniently adjusting at the same rate so that I was not blinded. Light shone at me, from all directions. I felt cradled and cared for – *safe*. I could not logically process what was happening to me; but it felt right, so I simply accepted that it *was* right. Perhaps reading my spiritual books (Jason just called them strange) had prepared me in some way, paving a pathway of acceptance.

Looking down, I was stunned to see that light was shining *into* me – through me. I was filled with light. I laughed. In the midst of this, the strangest experience of my life, with no idea where I was, I laughed. I couldn't stop. This was not hysteria, but pure, complete, blissful joy. I could feel it welling up, not just in my heart, but feeling aware of it in every cell of my body, and beyond it.

I was suffused with joy. It was the most incredible, amazing, awe–inspiring, exquisite feeling, and I let it flow over, through and into me. I still had no idea what was happening, but bring it on!

I felt a grin break across my face. I felt happy, so happy to just *be*. I was not happy *because* of something or someone – I just *was*. Wherever I was, in whatever place, having fallen so far into something I didn't understand, I felt on top of the world.

I could achieve anything.

I had unlimited potential, unrestrained happiness and unshakeable confidence. What a feeling!

The light started to dim a little, so that I could now see some colours and shapes. My feet felt warmer, and I became aware that I had stopped falling. Looking down again, I discovered that I was standing upon sand, a peach–gold ribbon of the softest sand I'd ever felt. I wiggled my toes, part of me delighting in the incredibly wonderful feeling of the sand, part of me wondering where my shoes had gone. The air was pleasantly warm.

More sights met my eyes – water so deeply sapphire–blue that it looked to be artificial; grass such a vivid bright green that it appeared to have been brushed straight from a child's paintbox. Colours here were remarkably strong; so much so that it was a little overwhelming. It felt as if I was looking at a photograph with the colour intensity turned up too high.

I could see no–one else . . . but I did not *feel* alone. I didn't have any expectations about what would happen next – each moment was so full, that I had no time or need to worry about the future. Already, I knew I had been altered; it was impossible not to be changed after being so completely absorbed by the light, or by simply being in this place.

My environment seemed to have stabilised. Colours now remained at a constant brightness and I was aware of movement, of silky grass–heads dancing elegantly in the soft light, of sand moving and sliding beneath my feet as I shifted my stance. Sounds were muted; soft and wistful, so that I felt soothed. Everything looked, sounded and smelled gentle and peaceful.

Instinctively I walked forward in the direction I faced. Ahead of me, purple–grey hills blocked the horizon, with apparently no way around them. I made no plans; I would just walk, and see what occurred, secure in this feeling of being safe and protected.

I continued walking, looking to neither left or right. It never entered my head to look behind. Forward was the only possible way.

The light had not left me completely. I kept catching sight of my hands as I walked; my skin shone as if I had been painted with a sparkly glaze. Had I fallen into a Twilight movie set? I had no problem with that, although I wasn't sure I wanted to be a vampire. So what was I, exactly? And where? A jolt went through me at my next thought – *how would I get home?*

~~~

I did not feel the time pass, but I was walking for what seemed to be hours – always forward, always directly headed for the purplish hills. As I got closer, I could see heathers in shades of violet and amethyst, spotted with prickly clumps of bright yellow gorse, and other shrubs and plants that I did not recognise. Again, the colours were so vivid that my eyes hurt. I felt more alive, more vital, than I had for – well, all of my life.

Cast adrift in this strange place, with the motion of walking acting on my brain like a meditation, I felt relaxed, yet still filled with a soft joy that I could virtually touch. As my mind slowed, it began to focus once again on Jason. I did not feel guilty that I had forgotten him for this period of time, for I knew that I was exactly where I was supposed to be, feeling how I was meant to feel. There was no judgement, not any more. I came to understand why he wanted to leave our little corner of the world, to seek new horizons and challenges. After all, what was I doing here, if not that? So in a matter of seconds, I forgave him and knew that all irritability and disappointment had dissolved into more helpful emotions. I began to look forward to seeing him again.

At that moment, I noticed a man resting upon a fallen tree ahead of me. I was nearing the base of the hills now, and had begun looking for a path that would take me up or through the hills to the other side. I could not take any alternative route or direction, as I was still being drawn to some place I did not yet know. As I came closer, I noticed his shock of dark hair, his tall build, and quirky smile. I stumbled as I realised with a jolt that it *was* Jason. I couldn't explain how he came to be there – so much in this situation could defy rational thought! – but it *was him*, I felt sure.

My mouth broke into a smile and I started to jog towards the huge log on which he was seated. He stood, a little stiff in his movements. I stopped in front of him and wondered why he was not smiling – in fact, he did

13

not seem to recognise me at all.

Confused, I waited for him to say or do something, to provide me with some lead on how to act. He grimaced, and I noticed that he held his left side, as if it was painful. A deep crimson stain covered the side of his shirt, and with horror I realised that he had been injured. Instinctively, I moved my hand forward – to soothe, offer comfort, anything to help him. His right arm shot towards me and deflected my arm. I let it drop to my side, feeling bewildered and upset.

What on earth was going on?

I hadn't spoken a word since my disagreement with Jason on the moor, after he had announced his decision to move away. My mouth was dry, and forming words felt unfamiliar and strange.

I started to speak, to ask what was wrong, whether I could help – but he placed his free hand over his mouth then over his ears, shaking his head. He was – apparently – unable to either speak or hear. Or perhaps we just did not speak the same language?

My mind fell into a dazed spin as it attempted to make sense of the situation. I knew I had left Jason asleep, snoring from the wine, and I knew he had not followed me, so how could he be here, in *front* of me, with no idea who I was, and with no capacity to understand me? I felt weak, drained, mentally confused. My lightness, my joy, had gone, and I really had no idea what to do next.

Exhausted, I sank down onto the log next to where Jason – no, not really Jason – had been seated such a short time ago. I needed some respite, some normality, something to hold onto. Perhaps I was going mad, and this was a delusion or a hallucination? Was I dreaming?

Well, whoever this man was, he wasn't *my* Jason, and I

realised that it was him that I wanted, not some substitute. Still, I couldn't exactly retrace my steps and find an escalator back to my stone circle entrance, so I resigned myself to making the best of the situation.

The man touched me on the shoulder, gesturing that I should rest. Yep, I could definitely do that.

I sat still, head bowed, hands limp in my lap, and tried to relax my breathing and my heart rate. Somehow, if I had faith and acceptance, I felt the answers would come. I just had to get back to that place so I would be able to recognise the answers when they arrived.

~~~

As my breathing slowed, and my head cleared, I started to feel more relaxed and less out of control. I was entering a zone of deep tranquillity, and felt my confidence return, just a little at a time. I raised my head and took a peek at the injured man who looked so like mine. He had his eyes closed, and I could hear that he was breathing deeply, as if meditating. Suddenly his eyes – so familiar to me – opened, and met mine in a direct, forthright gaze. I could not look away, although the eye–contact felt quite uncomfortable. There was some sense of a deep connection which I did not understand.

"You are fearful."

Wait – what? I heard the words, and understood them, but he had not spoken . . . how did he do that? I guess I looked like a startled animal, because he carefully reached for my hands, and softened his gaze.

His next words were more gentle. "We communicate by mental connection. We find it easier to communicate in this way, simply by using focused intention." He smiled, as if to reassure me that this was all quite normal. Of course it was. Telepathy, right?

I automatically opened my mouth to reply but he placed a hand in the air to signal me to stop. Okay, so he wanted me to do this telepathy thing, too. No harm in giving it a try. I willed myself to connect with him, then faltered. How did I do it?

He told me: "Just let yourself relax, and hold the intention to send me a mental message. That's all you need to do. Allow it to happen – don't force it. Release all preconceived ideas about speech, sound and thought, release all resistance to new ideas, experiences and beliefs. Your journey here has shown you that you can allow events without controlling them. Regain that trust, that faith, that openness." He nodded, which I took as permission to make another attempt.

I let my breathing slow, falling into that wonderful trance–like state of a few minutes before. I did as he suggested – intended to allow, intended to send this message. Before I could stop myself, I sent the thought: "How do you not know me, Jason? What happened?" My brain felt frazzled. I didn't understand what was going on.

The man looked puzzled, seemingly uncertain of how to react. Then he winced, and held his wounded side again. I jumped up and bent to examine the injury. He appeared to be still losing blood. Urgh. I'm not good with gory stuff.

Concentrating, I sent the thought: "Never mind, we need to attend to your injury. Do you have a doctor? Is there a village, or a city?"

"We all self–heal," he replied. "I have not been able to do so whilst focusing on you and your needs. I will need time alone to do this. Please follow me." He stood, and moved beyond a slab of rock that I had assumed was a sheer cliff. As he disappeared behind it, I realised there was a small opening leading to a tunnel. I entered, and followed carefully behind, making sure not to trip on the uneven surface. It was dry, but there was so little light, I continually felt as if I was on the verge of losing my balance. My eyes had not yet adjusted, and I could not touch the walls, feeling occasionally dizzy from almost total sight deprivation. The acoustics of the tunnel meant that sound was distorted, and no help in guiding me in the right direction. As before, I just kept going forward.

The man stopped a few paces ahead of me, and turned left into a sheltered nook, which had a faint light source – a gas lamp, perhaps. He smiled, and let me know by thought–communication that I should turn into the nook on my right, also faintly glowing with light. A curtain of some sort hung at the entrance to each little space, and he closed mine with a wave of this hand before entering his own little nook.

There was a roughly carved stone shelf–seat, which I sat down upon. It was neither cold nor warm. I was curious. How did self–healing work? Where did this tunnel lead? Were there more like this man, so similar in appearance to my almost–fiancé – but not him? I knew I'd have to take this minute by minute and wait for the answers.

The intensity of the light outside my little cave brightened, and I guessed the man had emerged. Cautiously – not wanting to invade his privacy – I lifted my hand to move my curtain an inch to the side. And got another shock when my hand went straight through it. I couldn't hold back a gasp. I quickly withdrew my hand, as if scalded.

The man's shape appeared blurrily outside my curtain, which vanished as he touched it. Even in the faint light, I could see that he was healthier. His shirt remained caked with dried blood, but he was walking without stiffness or pain. I wondered if self–healing could be learned as easily as telepathy? I directed that thought to him and he smiled wryly.

He sent back: "That usually takes a few years of training, which is started in childhood. I am glad that you are thinking of how you might develop your skills, Keira!"

Hmmm. So this was not my Jason, but he knew my name? How on earth did that work?

I asked; he frowned, again uncomfortable. I believed he was used to knowing the answers to pretty much everything, and I kept asking questions that were out of his reach. I touched his hand and let him know that it was fine; we'd sort these matters out some other time.

"One question I do have for you now, though." He waited for me to continue. "What do I call you? What is your name?"

"My name is Charls," he answered. I felt better having a name to address him by, even if he did look uncannily like Jason. One thing was for sure, I might be in a different world, but I wasn't going to be forgetting Jason anytime soon!

Since it looked like we were now moving on again, I stood, and awaited his lead.

CHAPTER 3

The change in the use of my calf muscles indicated that the tunnel sloped upwards for a short time. Although I was still effectively sightless, my other senses were more receptive as a result, and I felt that I was adapting quite well, all things considered. Charls remained a few steps ahead, walking confidently and with purpose.

"We are almost there," he sent. I stopped, not wanting to barge into him if he stopped suddenly.

Faintly, light started to glow in front of us. Charls became visible first as a soft silhouette, then his form took on sharper lines as the light brightened. I was starting to see him as a person separate from Jason, but his physical build and looks were so startlingly similar that sometimes I still got confused. To meet one person here, and for him to look like Jason, seemed more than a coincidence – more of a synchronicity.

However, I still didn't understand any of it, so gave a mental shrug and turned my attention back to what was happening.

Ahead, Charls had walked into the lighted space and waited for me to follow. The doorway was carved into the rock, and was surrounded by strange patterns that looked a little like hieroglyphics. I lifted my hand to touch them as I went past – they shimmered and became invisible. I blinked, but they had gone. Okay, one more unexplainable happening.

Realising that I was keeping Charls waiting, I hurried through the stone doorway towards the light.

And came to a sudden standstill.

The light illuminated a vast cavern – massive, as tall

as a cathedral, and more elegant than anything I had ever seen in my life. My mouth dropped open into an 'O' as I started to take in its immense size, the richness of the colours – were those precious stones? And gold? I was completely filled with awe, with wonder. I was moved to tears by the sight before me. The sides rose vertically towards a high dome, also encased in gold and precious stones, but also emanating a silvered glow– light of its own.

What *was* this marvellous place?

My telepathy had come on in leaps and bounds, as Charls caught my question. "It is a place where we fill ourselves with light and gratitude. That is how we live, and conduct all relationships; to remain at peace, we come here regularly to meditate, send peace and joy to each other, and remember our blessings. Your people may not understand this. They are used to competing, not co–operating. To taking lives, not spreading light. This is not true for all of you, of course – but in order to survive as a race, as a planet, you *must* learn to share light. There *is* no other way." He smiled as if to soften the lesson.

I tried to take on board what Charls had said. I recalled the feeling of bliss as I was filled with light during my journey between the stone circle and this world. I recalled the confidence in myself – not normal, I assure you – and the feeling of peace I had felt. I remember feeling that anything – *anything* – was possible, when in that state of perfect lightness.

So . . . perhaps that experience was meant as a marker, something to measure all future experiences against? To aim to re–create, even? Having had those wonderful sensations and emotions, I did rather feel inclined to regain that state if I could. I wasn't sure how me being here would result in the world changing its future, but I was willing to give it a try. I anticipated that I would be constantly learning throughout my time here.

I noticed mats of rush or a similar material bundled at the bases of the walls. Charls walked to gather two of the mats, handing one to me, and bending to place the other on the stone floor in the middle of the chamber, right under the glowing dome. Following his lead, I placed mine opposite, so that the mats were about a foot apart. He smiled, and sat, sending me the request to do the same. I emulated his pose – straight back, crossed legs, arms laying loosely on my knees. He closed his eyes, slowing his breathing, gaining a light meditative state.

I could hear that our breathing was matching rate and rhythm. There was a connection there, somehow. Perhaps he was willing it so?

"Not willing," Charls thought, eyes remaining closed. "More a case of lightly focused intention – which is *allowing*. Willing something to happen indicates that you are wishing for a particular outcome – and may incorporate some resistance. You have to release resistance; allow acceptance. Become the flow of life, rather than trying to direct it. Just *be*."

As his words reached me, I felt more and more relaxed. Not sleepy, though – I felt as if my mental capacity had been heightened, as well as my senses. I knew he was moving the index finger of his right hand. I peeked to check – yes, there it was, just waving up and down gently. I grinned. This stuff was cool!

Charls opened his eyes and sighed, although I felt it was an indulgent sigh rather than an annoyed huff. "Well done," he thought. "Your skills are improving rapidly; you are a quick student! But you lack concentration!" He closed his eyes again, so I did too. School lessons were never this much fun – or as interesting!

This time, I could feel some part of him touching me. Startled, I opened my eyes, but he remained seated on his mat, out of reach. I could feel his presence all around me simultaneously. I tried to concentrate, to keep my eyes closed, but felt my body tense – and I lost the sensation of Charls' nearness. I let my breathing slow again, relaxing my muscles, allowing myself to feel soft and aware. Slowly, gradually, I felt it again . . . a sensation of being lightly touched on all sides. It was gentle and supportive, and did not feel intrusive. It was not an invasion of my physical space; more like being wrapped in a loving hug without physically being held.

My curiosity got the better of me and I sent to Charls: "What is this? It feels wonderful, but I don't understand what I'm feeling!" He directed me to open my eyes. We remained seated on our mats and he started to explain what he'd been doing.

"Keira, I was consciously extending my auric field into yours. The auric field, which surrounds all living things, can be felt physically by those sensitive to it. I directed my aura to reach out to yours, and to fill it with light for the purposes of helping you as your soul wishes. That's perhaps an over–simplified explanation, but I don't want to overwhelm you with information."

This all sounded a little far–fetched to me, but it's not like it was the first odd thing to happen here. Still, in hindsight, I had *needed* a reassuring, friendly hug, so was glad of it! I felt uplifted, lighter, more positive, more alert. This was an amazing place . . . I wondered what was to come.

Charls rose, lifting his mat. I got to my feet and we

carried our mats back to their storage pile. Instinctively, I glanced up at the glowing dome above our heads. Its glow had softened, taking on a rose–peach hue. "Why has the light changed?" I asked.

Charls replied, "Boosting your aura with light has added what we term 'lovelight' to the cavern's store – for access by anyone else who comes here. The colour shows that energy from the heart, from the soul, has been shared for the benefit of others."

Wow.

I'd had no idea that love was – well, *visible*. Awesome just wasn't a strong enough word.

Charls stood in front of the cavern wall, hands in front of him just a few inches from the stone. You'd think I'd have got over being surprised, but when the stone in front of him vanished, I did blink in disbelief – just once! He turned towards me with a smile, then walked forward into the new opening. I caught him up and followed him through.

~~~

This tunnel was narrower than the one that had led into the magnificent domed chamber. I could feel the walls brushing my clothes occasionally as we walked. Again, there was no temperature, again no light to speak of. I was getting used to that. This passageway led slightly downhill, presumably deeper into the hills.

I realised that I was now living moment–by–moment, because so many things were unfamiliar to me that I had no expectations. Nothing to worry about, either, really. I had no idea where I was, or how I'd get back to my own life, so I'd switched off my worry circuit! I just had to take things as they came, accept them for what they were, and trust that it would all work out . . . somehow. After all, there must be a reason I had been drawn here. It could not be an accident.

Charls sent the thought to me that we would soon be meeting others. This could either be interesting or weird! Would they be similar to him? Or would there be many races? I was quite excited at the idea of making further discoveries. I was also curious about Charls' injury and wondered if any of the others we'd meet would raise the issue. I also wondered if I'd hear their thoughts as easily as I heard Charls'.

We continued walking for a short while, then stopped at another doorway. Again, this was framed by unfamiliar symbols, but I didn't attempt to touch them this time. I followed Charls through into a small, round chamber, quite ordinary in appearance compared to the previous grand cavern. This appeared to be a meeting room of some sort, as assorted mats, chairs and benches were placed around the circumference, with a couple of small tables set close by.

In the centre of the room, a tallish, gaunt man with long, plaited white hair sat on a larger, more ornately carved chair. He looked as if he had lived for at least a hundred years. His centrally–seated position indicated seniority, and he of course drew the eye towards him. Others were seated or standing, apparently communicating with each other – until they noticed me.

Everyone, without exception, turned to look at me. I felt my face colour; I'm never comfortable being the centre of attention. Charls invited me to sit at an empty bench next to him, and I sank down onto the old wooden seat gratefully, and did my best to become invisible.

The occupants of the room stilled, focused, and I

somehow knew that all heartbeats were slowing. Everyone except I had their eyes closed. Feeling like a child peeking at prayers when she shouldn't, I quickly shut my eyes, and began to slow my breathing. Were they all sending thoughts? Or just one, with the rest receiving? I intended to allow to receive, if anything was meant to reach me.

Initially, I was not aware of any thoughts or words, just a feeling that communication was taking place around me. Gradually, though, I could tune into this background awareness of 'static' and pick up the thought–sender, and was able to follow the telepathic conversation taking place in this silent cavern. It seemed that there was some discussion – almost a debate – about where I should go next, with whom, and when. So perhaps they had not been expecting me, after all? I decided that I would just go with the flow . . .

~~~

I was beginning to feel quite sleepy – jet lag, I thought with a weary attempt at humour. I allowed the thought–conversation to ebb and flow in my mind as I gave in to the drowsiness, knowing I was in that twilight zone just before sleep.

"She *must* stay with you, Charls – it is imperative that they do not know that she is here!"

I jolted awake at the shouting in my brain – things were getting heated! I was perfectly happy to remain with Charls – my surrogate Jason! But who were 'they'? And why was I to be kept secret from them? With some effort, I tried to refocus on the discussion, attempting to pick up threads that might tell me more of the situation. Charls looked grim; other faces looked pinched or worried.

Noting my concerned expression, he touched my hand in reassurance, then sent to the white–haired man: "Of course she should remain with me, Elder; but we must make plans to move her to a safer location if we know that they *are* moving towards us – losing Keira now is too great a risk; one we cannot afford to take." He squeezed my hand and smiled at me. I squeezed back but I wasn't feeling confident. I was frightened. My hands felt clammy, and I felt my heart–rate pick up. Charls reminded me to breathe, to allow, to relax.

I could feel tension throughout my body – adrenaline fighting with fatigue. I really just wanted to sleep, right here on this bench if need be. But I couldn't relax and sleep knowing that I was being hidden from 'something' or 'someone' and not knowing why, what or when. And it seemed that my safety was important to these people in some way. As if I was part of some mission in a place that I'd only become aware of merely hours ago. I struggled with that thought for a minute but felt too tired to pursue it. I let the thought drift away, finally; unable to fight the heaviness in my limbs any longer, I slept.

~~~

Jason woke with a start. His mouth was dry from the drink and the open–mouthed snoring; his body felt uncomfortably damp and cold. He looked around and saw nothing but the discarded picnic, the short, tussocky grass of the moorland, and the distant sea spattered by cloud shadows created by the bright moon.

His thoughts turned to panic – he could not see Keira anywhere. Turning to look around behind the rock, he could see their car in the distance – but no–one sitting inside. His sense of unease increased as he thought back to how he had misread Keira's understanding of tonight. He had thought that she had loved him enough to give up anything for him; it was certainly how he felt about her.

Well, maybe he had just put it badly, in his usual self–centred way. Whatever the cause, the result was the same: he'd had too much to drink – again – and Keira had wandered off.

More thoughts rushed into his head – stories of bogs and hounds and escaped prisoners. Keira was not capable of looking after herself. She was far too trusting and unworldly. She saw only the good in people, never believed they would cause her harm. She needed him to keep her safe. That was what he'd always thought, and felt. Part of his role as her boyfriend was to protect her. Another, he felt, was to provide for her; hence applying for a better–paid job. He wanted to give Keira everything she wanted. Didn't every man?

He stood up, cursing as he kicked an empty wine–glass. His head felt a bit woolly, but thankfully the cool, clear moor air was helping some clarity to return to his foggy brain. He really must start drinking less. Keira needed him – and he'd been asleep! Feeling helpless, he turned full circle, looking for any sign of which direction she'd gone in – or been taken . . . but who else would be out here, on a cold moor, in the middle of the night? Perhaps she'd just hidden behind a rock to take care of a call of nature.

Telling himself there was a rational explanation for Keira's absence – and that it was only temporary – he picked up a wind–up torch and decided to walk towards the large group of tall rocks nearby. The moonlight showed dew glistening on the grass, and he'd noticed that there was a hint of a trail where someone had flattened the grass as they had walked. Hoping it was Keira's footsteps he was following, he walked along the dark green path, keeping closely to the trail.

He reached a massive rock that looked as if someone had flung milk at it – trails of white flowed in rivulets down to the base of the rock. The moon caused the patterns to stand out boldly. Jason felt intuitively that Keira had been here. That she had stood here, waiting for – something. He turned the corner around the rock and came to an abrupt halt.

He'd had no idea that there was a stone circle close by – and this one was incredible! As magnificent as Stonehenge, so how come it was here in its natural state, without the usual barriers and 'Keep Out' signs?

He released the breath he'd been holding and walked slowly, almost reverently, into the stone circle.

CHAPTER 4

When I woke, the room was empty. My head had used Charls' chest as a pillow – how embarrassing was that! I blushed again, not sure how he would have felt about being trapped in such close proximity to me, someone he barely knew, and a female at that! For all I knew, he had a wife or girlfriend somewhere! I, of course, had Jason. I guess my oh–so–tired body and brain had simply turned to what it knew best – my Jason look-alike. Easily done, but I hoped that I hadn't offended Charls by dropping off practically into his arms.

I straightened, my neck stiff and a little sore from having been dipped at such an odd angle. As I manoeuvred myself upright, Charls extracted himself from me and stood. I thought he was going to walk away, but he turned to face me instead. His eyes looked so very caring and gentle, so familiar to me.

I again sensed that there was some sort of strong, unexplainable bond between us, leading to instant trust.

Charls reached out to help me upright, then stood back from me. "We need to move now. It would be best if you stay in my quarters. I have a spare room ready, as you have been expected, and everything has been arranged." He paused, then added: "Do not worry, Keira. Accept and allow, and be in the flow. Let your intuition lead the way; it is your keenest tool in any circumstance."

I managed a wobbly smile, and stepped back, then turned to follow him into yet another tunnel. I wished these pathways had better visibility so that I wasn't constantly worrying about bumping into Charls if he should stop suddenly.

This tunnel was level, and surprisingly short; in fact, I could already see a hint of light ahead. It looked like it might be daylight! My spirits lifted further at the prospect of fresh air and sunlight. I'd never been a huge fan of dark places or being underground. The tunnel widened and I saw Charls stop just on the verge of the exit to the outside. There was room to stand two abreast, so I moved to his side.

If the magnificent cavern had caused me astonishment and awe, then now I was completely dumbfounded. I think my brain stopped. Or perhaps it overloaded. The sight before me was . . . awesome, in the truest meaning of the word.

I looked out over a valley, and it literally took my breath away. From our elevated position, I could see down and across the valley. In one glance I took in the expanse of lush, vivid green foliage, punctuated by huge bell–shaped flowers in carmine, orange, purple and white, and many shades in between. The enormous flowering shrubs, when seen close–to, reminded me of rhododendrons. Their brilliant colours were beautifully offset by the glossy mid– and deep–green leaves; all of the plants looked incredibly healthy and vigorous.

Here and there, nestling shyly between the vast forests of glossy foliage, I could see signs of habitation – snippets of a curving path or road, an occasional hamlet or village peeking from its cradle of greenery. One wider pathway led down from where I stood, snaking its way through the valley.

And the *light*. It was pearly translucent opal white, and it felt *wonderful* simply to look upon it. It was tremendously uplifting and energizing. It reminded me of the dome in the decorated chamber. I felt myself draw in a deep breath, as if to internalise the quality of the air. Charls was smiling, and I felt that he was experiencing similar emotions, even though he'd no doubt seen it all many times.

"I don't know what to say!" I sent.

He grinned at me. "Welcome to Cordello. It is truly wonderful. The lovelight that you saw in the Grand Chamber is stored for all to use. The light here has the same quality. It can fail if we do not manage our resources in the right way. That is why we practice offering lovelight, in and for the Grand Chamber. It is a 'backup' if something should happen out here."

Slightly worrying – what could happen to this paradise? I must have thought it to Charls because he told me that the Cordellans were on the verge of a war. An army in a neighbouring country was making plans to invade, intending to rule Cordello and its resources for themselves, and to use the lovelight energy as a weapon against others.

Even I, as a visitor, could feel horror at the idea of this phenomenal lovelight energy being used for ill, and for the suffering that would no doubt be inflicted on the people that lived here peacefully and co–operatively. They were, to me, a model of how everyone *should* be living, and it was, without any doubt, so very wrong to want to destroy this – worse, to convert it into an instrument to harm others.

I felt my heart expand with compassion for Charls and his people. I knew with certainty that I did have a role to play here. I almost laughed – this was *so* not me! But the laugh never materialised. This was life or death for Charls' people. I knew that they would never survive living under conditions which used their lovelight for evil. I felt a little anxiety at the thought of any impending invasion or battle; my instinct is to run from trouble, not turn and fight it. But I hoped we might find a way to overcome this threat in some way, without resorting to fighting and death. I shuddered.

Charls thought to me: "Keira, the Cordellan strength is in working together and in working with our positive energies. In creating lovelight, in spreading it to raise the energy of all others. If we can raise it high enough, with sufficient focus and intention, it is possible that we can forestall any attack, and find a peaceful resolution. That is why you have come."

Okay, that got me. I was still learning this stuff; they were all experts! Where could I fit into this grand scheme? Stone circles, doorways in rock, blissful tubes of light, paradise, telepathy, lovelight, war. It was so much to take in over the space of just a few hours! I hadn't had enough sleep and I was running on empty. I told Charls I needed more rest before I could process anything else – if that was possible? He agreed, and we turned to follow the path leading down into the valley.

As we proceeded lower into the valley, I heard a muted roar of falling water, and glimpsed a rainbow out of the corner of my eye – a high waterfall. It was exquisite. Charls did not deviate from our path, which was lined with foliage, and soon the waterfall was hidden from view.

~~~

We continued walking, and I confess to being relieved that we were outside, and not in tunnels. I wondered what would happen if an army did come – would everyone retreat into the tunnels and caverns? Were there more caves and chambers inside the hill? Could they seal themselves in? My mind continued to wander along similar lines as we made our way to Charls' house. As we came to the first of the villages, I saw small, neat, brick and tile–roofed cottages, separated by narrow pathways. There was no litter; the whole place felt clean, cared for, loved, nurtured. It was quiet, though – no children playing outside, no animals either, although I heard distant birdsong and a hum–drone of insects.

I expected, at any moment, for Charls to stop, and lead us into one of the cottages. However we continued through this small hamlet, and from here the path became wider, more formal. Soft grasses edged the road, their wispy heads nodding and swaying in the light breeze. Poppy–like flowers dotted the grassed clumps, and I saw insects similar to butterflies darting, hovering and spinning among the flower–heads. Ahead, I saw more houses, each with a colourful flower–garden, and immaculately–kept herb and vegetable areas. This place *was* paradise!

I wondered how much further we had to go. I stifled another yawn, my feet feeling heavy and leaden. Charls, apparently, could walk for miles without fatigue; not so, me! And I had *already* walked for miles.

Now that I could walk side–by–side with Charls, I realised that the only building that I could see ahead of us was what I thought of as a manor house – it reminded me of a smaller version of Lanhydrock House in Cornwall, close to where I'd been brought up and continued to live.

I could see an arched gateway with a graceful driveway leading to the main entrance. The walls were built from a solid cream stone, and the house had imposing views in all directions. In the far distance, I could see animals similar to deer grazing in the grounds, and I caught sight of a flock of small birds swooping from trees placed around the edge of the fields. Just beyond the house, I glimpsed more gardens, and a large wooded area. The road followed the perimeter of the grounds for a short distance, then turned away to the left, winding into the cool shade of dense woodland. We bore right, making our way under the elegant archway, and along the gravelled drive to the main entrance of the house.

"You live here? Is the property yours?" I asked Charls, curiously.

"In a manner of speaking," he thought back. "My father owned this house when he was alive, but now it belongs to me. I am the Lord of this estate. There is plenty of room for guests!" he laughed. Then he sobered, remembering the threat laying over Cordello. He glanced at me, then thought: "But I forget. You need rest, urgently. Once you are refreshed, we can discuss how best we can protect you . . . and how best you can help us. That is okay, yes?"

Fighting yet another yawn, I agreed, my eyes instinctively feeling heavy with the promise of being able to sleep again soon. Charls led me to a room on the ground floor, and opened the door, before standing aside to let me enter. The room was beautifully furnished, although not as opulent as I would have expected. I spotted the bed, and sat down on it with a deep groan of relief. Teal–green silk pyjamas were laid out neatly on the pillows. Charls left, closing the door behind him.

I let myself fall back onto the bedcovers, ignored the pyjamas, curled up, and embraced the sleep of the utterly exhausted.

CHAPTER 5

When I awoke, the room was dim, crowded with unfamiliar silhouettes and shadows – the curtains remained open, letting the moonlight spill waves of soft light across the floor. This room was like any other in a grand house – normal bed and soft furnishings; lamps, rugs, and even a small en–suite bathroom. I wondered how this tallied with the unusual glow–light and fabrics in the tunnels and caverns. Perhaps those were in some way created through the use of lovelight. I had so many questions for Charls, but I knew I'd be unlikely to remember to ask them all.

I stretched to ease the kinks in my neck, and switched on the lamp, filling the room with a diffused golden glow which highlighted the rich colour of the burgundy curtains and bedcovers. I felt more like my normal self – rested, alert, optimistic. I was ready for information, planning, and doing my part to help these people. After a quick wash and a misguided attempt at pushing my hair into tidy chestnut waves (always a battle), I was keen to find Charls and discover what was to happen next. I brushed my clothes with damp hands in an attempt to smooth out the creases, making myself as presentable as I could in the circumstances.

Just as I reached for the brass doorknob, the door swung slowly inwards, revealing Charls with a tray of food – a savoury bread, fruit, bowls of nuts of some description, and a cup of a steaming drink. God, I hoped it was tea. I was dying for a cup. I stepped back to allow him and the tray safe passage, and he moved past me into the room. I sat back down upon the bed.

"How did you know I was ready for refreshments?" I

sent, with a smile.

"Telepathy can, in some cases, extend to a 'knowing' as well as sending and receiving words," he replied. Oh. So perhaps not all of my thoughts were totally private then . . . oops. Might be as well to be careful what I was thinking.

I looked again at the food. When had I last eaten? The picnic – however many hours ago that was. I fell upon the bread as if I'd not eaten for a week. These were mitigating circumstances – I felt as if I *had* been here a week already; I was starving. Charls watched me eat with some amusement. Washing the rest of the food down with the drink – it *was* tea, and it tasted wonderful – I brushed the crumbs from my hands, and decided to ask Charls a few questions.

"Charls . . . when I first met you, you had been injured. Was that related to the people who wish to invade Cordello?"

He frowned, and absently touched the area under his arm where I had first noticed he was bleeding.

"Keira, I think now is the right time to explain more of our history, our world, so that you can understand what we are facing. You already know the nature of the threat we face, but not from where it comes . . . or who leads it. Part of this involves my family.

"When my father died, my elder brother, Karn, was in line to run the estate, and to take over the responsibilities that come with this role. There are five such estates in Cordello – all overseen by the Elder. We work co–operatively and easily side–by–side. If one estate was ever to suffer, as they did once, many decades ago, then the others would assist by sending resources so that the failing estate could re–build. In turn, that estate may then have helped another which was in difficulty, in later years. It all worked very well for everyone."

Charls paused, chose a small blue grape–like fruit and popped it into his mouth. I remembered the sweet taste of it exploding in my mouth, my taste–buds zinging from the delicious citrus flavour, and making my tongue tingle. After swallowing his fruit, Charls continued with his history lesson.

"Unfortunately, for no reason that has ever come to light, Karn was unable to work co–operatively. He became greedy, increased taxes for those who could least afford it, and lined his own pockets. He failed to keep the estate in good repair. He did not fulfil any of his duties even adequately. When his exploits were discovered, he was given a chance to put things right, and to start over. He refused. He and our father fell out."

Charls took a deep breath, and I felt his pain and regret. He looked pale, and I wanted to comfort him. Again, I restrained myself from reaching out to him. *He was not Jason.* Thank goodness our telepathic connection did not include sensing each other's innermost feelings.

"Father gave Karn an ultimatum – repay the money, run the estate properly – or leave. Karn laughed, and said there was no money left, and he had no interest in playing at a mere lord of the manor. He wanted his own kingdom – and he didn't care whom he hurt to achieve his ambition. I remember Father losing his temper, which was almost unheard of, and Karn reacted violently. He carried a knife . . . he grabbed it from its sheath, aimed it at our father . . ."

Charls' eyes filled with grief. Oh, how I wished I could help him – my heart sank as I could guess how this story ended. It gave me no pleasure to find that I was right. Karn had murdered their father, then fled the estate and the kingdom, hiding with outlaws and renegades in neighbouring Vornen – it was a pity to realise that every world had such men – until Karn could grow his power and assume the leadership role he craved.

It was Karn who was coming to attack.

It was Karn, his own brother, who wanted lovelight, who wanted the power to create unlimited resources and weaponry . . . at any cost.

This time, I did reach out to Charls, touching his hand, empathizing with his sorrow. He gripped my fingers, giving them a brief squeeze before releasing them. He stood, and walked to the window, staring sightlessly at the deeply shadowed landscape.

"Karn sends scouts to check on our readiness, and perhaps our resolve to defend ourselves. I had been sent to meet you, but was ambushed shortly before you arrived. It seems Karn trains his scouts with knife skills, too. I didn't see him until it was too late; he stabbed me, then he was gone. I was watching for you, and it was necessary to wait until you were here. We could not risk you being taken, Keira. I had no time to focus on self–healing.

"So now you know that element of the story. But now we must make plans, work out how you and I, the Elder, and our people can work together, to retain peace here. We have created strategies – but until you were *here,* we were missing information that we needed to finalise our ideas."

Charls went onto explain that legend told of a young woman arriving from another timespace, who would gain enlightenment through her journey to and through their world – and who would, with their help and training, assist them in overcoming a great warrior with an evil heart. Wow. They had a legend and I was in it? I shivered – I really had never thought of myself in the 'girl who saves the day' role. But apparently, I had arrived at the time the legend foretold, so I guessed I was 'it'.

We continued talking through the rest of the night, he providing me with more information, fleshing out the bones of the story. I mostly listened, breaking in with an occasional question when I felt I needed clarification. Their history had been peaceful until the shock of Karn's betrayal and the beginning of his threats and harmful behaviour. At this point, Charls was the only one who had been injured, but it seemed as though scouts had been spying for some time, and it was only a matter of time before Karn decided to advance on Cordello, or before someone else was hurt, or even killed.

Charls reminded me that our strength had always been, and always would be, our lovelight. That we needed to continue to nurture and spread it, as often as possible. That we should visualise a positive outcome to all events, remain optimistic, and keep our energy 'high'. It would be the key to everything. It was still unclear quite how my presence would help Charls and his people, but we would work it out. We had to, for all of our sakes.

~~~

Dawn broke swiftly, shards of bright sunlight spearing the rugs in the bedroom. Surprised, I realised that we had been talking for hours, plotting, and throwing ideas around. Charls explained to me the general strategy that had been decided upon by the Elder together with the other estate holders. Each member of these would frequently and regularly add to the lovelight in the Grand Chamber, ensuring a greater backup store should the country's own supply be stolen, exhausted or otherwise reduced. In addition, the populace would also do their absolute best to each keep their thoughts and beliefs positive, to improve their already excellent co–operative actions; in short, to increase the 'vibration' (as Charls labelled it) of each person's energy.

I had visions of little molecules jiggling around happily – and Charls laughingly told me that my image wasn't that far from the truth. Energy could be sensed and seen by those whose own energy was 'high' enough.

He further described how such a high vibration, when held consistently and by many people simultaneously, could in fact help others to lift their own vibration, and even change their attitudes, their behaviours, to become more loving and co–operative ones. That, despite all of the threats from Karn, and the forays by his scouts, we might still be able to resolve matters peacefully. I really hoped so – I far preferred discussion and diplomacy to argument and war.

I explored the room further for a few minutes, then, as I placed a hand on my audibly growling stomach, Charls suggested that we adjourn to the morning room, where breakfast would be served.

I followed him from the bedroom into the beautifully wood–pannelled hall. Much like a manor house in my own world, the hall was decorated with portraits, presumably of Charls' ancestors. Across the hall, we entered the morning room, which was tastefully decorated in blues, greens and silvers. External doors led out onto a terrace and gravelled path, with views stretching towards the gardens.

My hunger temporarily overruled my desire to explore the grounds, to feel fresh air on my skin, but I was keen to explore them as soon as I could.

"Charls, is it safe to be outside? Only I really love gardens and plants, and would love to see what your gardens are like."

He thought for a brief moment, then decided that a wander within the grounds should be safe enough. After all, Karn did not know of my presence yet, and no spies could make it as far as the manor house or its grounds without detection.

I bolted the food, excited to see more of the external beauty of the place. Charls opened the doors and swung the doors wide. Cool morning air swept in, and I breathed in its refreshing purity.

Charls looked at me appraisingly. "Please walk with me, Keira, for there is much to show you." He held out his arm to me, and we stepped through the doors, down the steps onto a gravel path which led to the formal gardens. He released my hand so that he could walk ahead of me where the path narrowed.

Geometric planting that looked similar to clipped box had been filled with a mesmerising collection of flowering plants. The effect of the kaleidoscopic colour was uplifting and revitalizing. Some of the planting was Italianate in nature – with cypress, marble statuary, and citrus trees placed symmetrically either side of paved paths and squares. Other areas were filled with riotous colour and rambling white and softest–pink wild roses, whose scent stirred the senses and made me think of a Jane Austen novel – and Mr Darcy. Bee–like insects buzzed drowsily.

The heady scent of the roses, together with the artistic

41

designs of the garden's beds, lulled me into a fully relaxed state. The air was soft and sweet, small clouds backlit by lovelight so that they shone with a luminous silver–peach–white glow. Everything about this land was beautiful, and a small part of me yearned to stay here always.

I just had to remember that the man at my side, who looked like Jason, was someone separate from Jason, that Charls was an individual in his own right, in his own world. I resisted the urge to reach for his hand; it would have felt so right to wander these beautiful grounds hand–in–hand with Jason; it would be so wrong to confuse Charls with Jason, to give Charls false indication that I was interested in him romantically, when my heart would always belong to Jason.

Ironically, being separated from Jason – yet being with his 'double' – helped me to see Jason more clearly; I knew with certainty that I would willingly agree to live wherever Jason was. In the end, it was simple. I loved the man; I would do anything to be with him. How could I have ever considered otherwise?

Then I assessed my current situation. Would I even be able to return to my own world? Would I be trapped here in Cordello? Would Karn achieve his ambitions, desecrating and taking over Cordello? I frowned, as I remembered the reason for my being here. My feeling of well–being vanished in an instant, and as if Charls was tuned into my emotions, he turned to me, a quizzical expression on his familiar face.

"You are worried, Keira, are you not? Please – enjoy the gardens, and experience each moment fully. Allow such moments to lift you back to your natural state of optimism and happiness. Pleasure helps you to lift your vibration and to keep it high. You are helping us, in no small way, simply by being here – fulfilling your part in our legend gives our people hope. Never, ever underestimate the power of hope. Your presence will automatically expand the quantity and quality of lovelight that we can share and store. If you, too, can keep your energy high, that will spread to others, also."

Charls gently touched the petals of a golden–yellow rose as he passed. "Accept what might be, and feel the peace of the moment. You can become peaceful right now – just by intending so."

I made a conscious decision to relax my tensed muscles, including those in my face, neck and shoulders. I breathed in the glorious air, focused on the natural beauty surrounding me, letting myself absorb it with all my senses, tuning into the sweet, melodic birdsong. I felt my heart lighten, and my body loosen as I relaxed. Breathing slowly, I turned full circle to maximise the effect of the trees, shrubs and flowers. I felt I weighed about a stone lighter (hah! I wish!) and could not stop smiling. Not that I wanted to.

Charls was – as usual – absolutely right; decide to feel peaceful, and there it was . . . what a gift. I was learning so much here – I wondered if Jason and those I knew in my own world would recognise the New Me.

CHAPTER 6

We continued to wander leisurely through the grounds. Charls showed me a hidden grotto filled with tumbled ancient stones covered with vivid green mosses, complete with a natural spring tinkling into a basin. I saw a formal stone fountain, complete with an ornate dolphin sculpture (the dolphin was a sacred beast here in Cordello, valued for its energy and intelligence.) The falling water looked like liquid diamonds pounding into the pool at its base. There were so many areas of beauty that I couldn't help but keep my energy 'high' from feeling so good. This garden was perfect for this world – I loved it. Would that Jason and I could afford an estate like this, and re–create gardens to do it justice!

Feeling thoroughly buoyed up by my environment, I walked for miles with Charls before I started to feel some fatigue. It was coming up to mid–day, and I hoped I'd get food again soon.

Charls was amused. "Cordellans are not familiar with hunger in the same way that you are," he explained. "Lovelight can assist not only with resource production, but can also be used as an energiser, and helps us to reduce our need for food. We know that you have many meals a day in your world; we really only need one!"

I didn't feel three square meals a day was a lot of food, personally, but who was I to argue?

"We do however enjoy the taste, smell and texture of food, and continue to eat so that our bodies retain the ability to process it efficiently. Just in case we don't always have access to lovelight." It seemed that contingency plans had been made since Karn's first threats had been taken seriously.

Karn and his allies resided in Vornen, which adjoined Cordello along most of its length; it had proved difficult to patrol the border between the two lands. Cordellan guards vanished in mysterious circumstances; the missing men had not yet been found. I shuddered. I had never experienced conflict, and Charls' tales scared me – more so because I knew this was just the beginning. And I would not be able to turn tail and run and hide. I was part of this until it was resolved.

Taking a deep breath, re–focusing on some divine yellow blooms nudging my arm as I brushed past them, I concentrated on feeling positive, hopeful and peaceful. I was becoming better at this – it just took a bit of practice!

~~~

We reached the patio leading back up to the morning room; I was just about to place my foot on the lowest of the stone steps, when Charls decided to show me the orangery. We detoured around the front of the patio, and followed the path which headed towards the front corner of the manor house. Set back behind more topiary and another gorgeous fountain was a small, graceful building assembled from the same soft cream stone, with strong pillars and two–storey rectangular windows.

We entered by way of a door set into the side of the building. The orangery housed plants presumably too delicate for outdoors – vines with luscious pink fruits hanging heavily from the branches; other small shrubs and trees with delicate scents of almond, vanilla and orange. The whole room was filled with a heavenly aroma. Sunlight streamed in through the tall windows, casting soft, blurred shadows onto the stone paving.

Simple wooden benches were set at intervals so that visitors could sit and relax – and create lovelight, no doubt! The room was warmer than outside, thanks to the heat from the sun's rays, and the humidity caused by discreet sprinkler heads. It felt like being in an enchanted forest – although not quite as scary!

"Let's sit," thought Charls, indicating the bench closest to us. I was happy to do so – I guessed one could easily spend a lot of time here, drowsing in the heady scent, the comforting warmth, and the occasional hiss–sizzle of water sprinkling onto the plants. I sat, head resting on the warm wall behind our backs, and closed my eyes. It was so peaceful, I couldn't stop the smile breaking across my face. This was heavenly! It would be so easy to drift into sleep.

~~~

Jason felt as if he was picking up some sort of unusual vibe. He couldn't explain it, but he felt as if Keira was still close by. With a deep sense of relief, he spotted her settled in an awkward–looking position, slumped against one of the immense rocks at the far side of the stone circle. He jogged over to her, but dismay tugged at him as he reached her and became aware of her closed eyes and shallow breathing. Was she unconscious? Had she tripped, and hit her head in the dark? Frustration built – he should have been protecting her!

Jason hurriedly switched off the torch and stuffed it into his pocket, leaving both hands free. He reached out to Keira, thinking to wake or rouse her, to explore her head for any injury. He'd thought her skin pale in the torchlight – then noticed with a shock that her skin

46

appeared to be shimmering and glittering in the near–darkness. Hesitantly, he let his fingertips graze her cheek – and gasped as he felt the soft warmth of her skin. He was almost shivering with the cold; Keira was lightly dressed, yet was as warm as if she was sat in the glow of the midsummer sun. He lightly caressed her cheek, hoping for a response from her.

There was none.

Feeling a little panicky, Jason quickly shifted his fingers to explore her scalp, feeling first her forehead and then the sides of her head. No bumps, no wetness that might indicate that she'd cut her head. He gently lifted her head from her hard pillow of rock, and carefully examined the back of her head. Still nothing.

Bemused, he gently lowered her head against her rock 'pillow' and sat back on his heels. Now what? Common sense suggested he call for medical help, although he knew there was no mobile phone signal up here – he'd have to drive at least ten miles to be able to use the phone. And he'd had too much to drink. Strangely, Keira looked remarkably peaceful – healthy and normal, too, if you discounted the fact that she was glowing. There was even a slight lift to her lips, suggesting a hint of a smile.

Against his better judgement, Jason decided the best course of action was to sit with Keira, and to wait. He jogged back to the car, extracting his leather coat. He made his way back to Keira, and folding the jacket into a rough square, gently and carefully placed it behind her head. He sat next to her, laid a hand over hers, and closed his eyes.

47

CHAPTER 7

I woke from a dream, with moist eyes. I had dreamed of Jason. I had seen him awaken, watched him look for me, could see him following the same path that I'd taken, and knew with certainty that he had found the stone circle. Although I felt reassured that he was close – well, closer – to finding me, I also felt a stirring of anxiety that he might be heading into danger, if he was able to follow me here. What if a scout saw him? What if Jason was attacked!

No – I had to stop thinking like this. I *had* to keep my thoughts and expectations positive and hopeful. I suddenly remembered Charls, and turned my head to see if he was still seated next to me. He was, and his mouth was bent into a quizzical smile.

"Keira, did you dream?" he asked.

"Yes. I did dream – and I think it was one which was echoing reality back in my world."

He nodded. "You can expect that. Lovelight will enhance all of your special – you would call them psychic – skills. Among others, you will develop the gift of prophecy, and your dreams will assist you with this. These are skills which are latent within you – within everyone – and which are now being awakened. From now on, whatever you dream could be a reality which will occur if all other elements in your life remain unchanged."

He paused. "You can change your future, at any time, simply by being aware of your thoughts and ensuring that they are the best–feeling thoughts, the most hopeful thoughts that they can be. You do not yet understand the power of this, I realise. We Cordellans are well–

practiced at lovelight, and of manifesting the future we wish for. Sometimes, it is a little less simple – however, we do our best, always. No–one can ask more from you than that."

I understood. I had to keep all of my thoughts relating to Jason focused positively, and expect that only good things would happen. I would do my best to keep him safe. I didn't even know if it was physically possible for him to follow me. But if he did, how would he know where to go? There would be no–one waiting for him, no–one to guide him into the tunnels and through the caverns. I firmly placed my thoughts on Jason remaining safe, and on everything working out somehow.

In some ways, I was finding it easier to be positive, hopeful, raising my energy. But the realisation that Jason might now become involved in the war between Cordello and Vornen – in the vital battle for lovelight – well, that wasn't just a battle for survival, a war of good over evil.

Now it was personal.

~~~

Charls rose from the bench, and walked to the door at the far end of the orangery.

"We must go, Keira. We will be meeting with others soon."

Feeling some reluctance to leave the serenity of the orangery, I stood and followed him back into the garden. I hazarded a guess that this meeting was not a social event, but more likely to assist with planning, strategy and tactics. The garden and the soothing environment of the orangery had played their part in relaxing me, and in raising my energy – but now I could physically feel it falling at the prospect of returning to the 'real world' of the problems facing Cordello. It was an uncomfortable sensation, a heaviness that felt like a weight laying upon me.

I felt almost panicky as the familiar emotions of disquiet, fear, and worry crept back into my mind. I knew I *should* change my thoughts – but at this particular moment, I was unable to reach for any that were better. Charls was several steps ahead, and although we communicated by thought, he didn't always pick up on my feelings – perhaps I was blocking that aspect from him? Whatever, he did not show any sign of recognising the change in my frame of mind, and continued walking away from me, back towards the manor house.

I had not felt so low in mood since being made aware of Jason's intentions of leaving Cornwall. Not since that moment, staring unseeingly at the stars, the sea and the moorland, had I felt so disconnected. I felt as though I might lose everything that was dear to me, that if I lost Jason as a result of this 'situation', life really would not carry any meaning. Oh, I knew in theory that happiness should come from inside, that it should not be reliant on the presence or actions of another, but I was human – and right now, I felt as if me being here might just jeopardise everything.

For all I knew, Jason was still snoring on the picnic rug, not even aware of my absence. For all I knew, he might have assumed I'd stormed off in a temper, and was deliberately keeping out of his way. For all I knew, it was impossible for Jason to follow me here.

But – what if he could? What if he did?

Another thought brushed across my mind like a shiver.

What if I couldn't go home?

~~~

Fear bound me like a physical shackle; I felt sick and cold with apprehension, almost as if I had shrunk into myself. I didn't know what to do. So I did the only thing I could think of – I hurried after Charls and hoped he'd be able to 'lift' me. He'd reached the house by the time I'd caught up with him. He turned and started towards me, his face mirroring my own worry.

"Keira, what is wrong? You look – awful!" I knew he did not mean it to be unflattering, was merely concerned. I took a few seconds to get my breath back. He placed his hands upon my shoulders, and I could feel some sort of energy pouring into me. It felt like warm syrup flooding my veins from the shoulders down; pleasantly heavy, and soft and warm. I let out a deep sigh, and my eyes closed as all of my muscles began to relax. I felt light tingling sensations in my face and on my scalp. My head bowed, I felt the remaining tension literally drain from me. My feet were heavy, and felt rooted to the path. Was Charls giving me healing energy? This felt . . . wonderful. I felt connected to the earth below me, and a new sensation over my crown – like an opened funnel spiralling air into my head – led me to feel connected with the air above me; I knew I was somehow directly connected with the lovelight.

"Keira, are you feeling better?" Charls quietly asked.

I opened my eyes and raised them to meet his.

"Yes," I replied.

I really was. That lovelight – if that's what I'd received – was magic! I couldn't believe the transformation. Lovelight had extinguished my fear, worry, negative

51

thinking; it was all gone. I beamed at Charls. "That was incredible! It was lovelight, wasn't it?"

"Yes, Keira; my intuition guided me to provide you with a direct connection to lovelight, which is possible using my intention. I believe you may have been fearful?"

"Yes, I was; before I came here, to Cordello, I left someone behind in my own world. I think he has noticed that I've gone; I was really worried that he'd follow me here, and that he'd get into danger."

Charls thought for a moment. "Let's go in, and have tea and food. This will help you to continue feeling strong, and we can discuss the issue of your friend, and his safety."

Over a cup of piping hot tea, and a delicious seeded fruit cake which was baked to perfection, and had my taste buds dancing for joy, Charls shared his thoughts with me.

"Your part in our legend has always been clear. When you arrived, we knew, with complete confidence, that you were the young woman that we were waiting for, who we've all been reading and talking of for centuries."

A shiver passed across my back.

Charls continued. "What is also clear is that she comes alone. No–one else has ever been mentioned. I do not think your friend can pass into this world as you have, Keira. I think he is safe."

Relief rushed through me. Jason would be okay. I knew there was still the issue of me getting home again, after the story in the legend had played out, but at least I knew Jason would be unharmed. I hoped he was not too worried by my absence. I hoped he was still asleep. It would save him a lot of hassle!

CHAPTER 8

Jason woke periodically to check on Keira. Her smooth skin still glowed with a wholly ethereal quality. She looked amazing. He lightly tested the temperature of her cheek with his fingertips, finding a gentle, healthy–feeling warmth. Intuitively, he knew that she was fine. Yes, something very odd was going on, but there was no–one to give him any answers. He tilted his head back and gazed at the stars emerging from behind the high cloud. Somehow, seeing the stars, whose light had been emitted so many centuries ago, helped him to recognise his own small, but important, part of the process called Life.

To his surprise, he felt complete trust that everything would work out okay. He'd just stay with Keira until she was 'back' with him again. He wondered idly where her consciousness was, but having no idea how to follow that unusual thought to any conclusion, he let the unsolved riddle drift away.

Jason shifted his position so that he was resting against Keira without placing any of his weight on her. He caught her scent on the breeze, and, comforted that she was still with him in at least one way, he allowed himself to rest.

~~~

After we had finished tea, I returned to my room and washed, then did my best to make myself presentable again. A short battle with my hair showed me how fruitless any efforts to tidy my curly mop would be, so I abandoned that, and turned towards the bed.

Charls had shown some thought for my predicament – travelling spontaneously to another world generally meant that the traveller didn't have a bag of clothes with her – and had laid out some gorgeous deep red garments on the bed. Threaded through the red were beautiful, intricate designs of rose pink. The clothes – a fitted tunic with a v–neck, and a pair of comfortably wide trousers – were made of some material similar to heavy silk. I carefully dressed in them and sighed at the luxurious feel of the exotic fabrics against my skin.

We were due to attend the meeting in just a few minutes. I was nervous. I'm not generally comfortable around strangers, however this situation was forcing me into an environment where *everyone* was a stranger. I realised that I now categorised Charls as a friend. I trusted him with my life. So I would have to trust him now, to act for the benefit of everyone involved in the Cordello/Vornen dispute.

I closed my eyes, slowed my breathing and focused on its calming rhythm. It was so subtle that at first I didn't notice the change. Then, in my state of light focus, I noticed that my hands were very lightly tingling. I remained quiet, and accepted the new sensation.

I waited, and felt the tingle strengthen and spread. Now I could feel the same unusual feeling in my arms, feet, legs and face. I realised with excitement that this was how I'd felt when Charls had flowed lovelight energy after we'd left the orangery. Could I now self–heal? Or were these sensations the lovelight continuing the work from earlier? I'd ask Charls the next chance I got.

The bedroom door opened, and Charls entered, moving efficiently and, it seemed to me, in a business–like way. I'd leave my question until later.

"Good, you are ready. You look delightful!"

"A little flattery will get you everywhere," I replied with a grin.

He smiled back, then indicated that I should follow him. This time he led me to a small room beyond the main hall. As three of the walls were lined with shelves filled with books, I assumed we were in a library. Much of the fourth wall was taken up by a large window. Several comfortable chairs were placed conveniently near small tables containing reading lamps. Luxuriously thick rugs were placed on the wooden floor. There was no–one else in the room.

Charls continued walking to the far wall, selected a thick book from a low shelf, and reached his hand into the gap between the neighbouring books. He stood back, and glanced at me with an enigmatic half–smile. I watched as a section of the bookcase–wall swung inwards into the room. I had heard of such secret entrances to hidden passageways, but had never seen one, had never been behind such a doorway. Anticipation fizzed through me.

Charls invited me to enter first. I walked through, and stopped just inside the doorway. I didn't know which way to go. Charls replaced the book to hide the door mechanism, then followed me into the narrow corridor. He pressed a small lever on the wall to close the door behind us.

"Hold on, I'll create a light," Charls thought. A soft, pearlescent white glow began to appear in the air in front of him, so that I could see his face. Shadows danced on the walls as the light flickered, then stabilised to a gentle background glow. The light was about the size of a basketball and hovered a short distance in front of Charls.

"Did you make that from lovelight?" I asked. I was fascinated by the object.

"Yes, it's quite easy to do when you know how!" Charls said, moving the light with him as he turned away from me. The light cast enough illumination for us to see far enough ahead that neither of us would stumble or bump into each other.

Charls began to explain about the passageway. "We use this hidden route because it meets up with a concealed room which is only accessible from other manor houses. We can meet safely because the houses are secure, and we know that no scouts or spies can infiltrate. Thus we can hold meetings in the knowledge that no information will leak or be used against us."

Since the previous meeting that I had attended had been inside the hills, I had wondered about this second location. It made sense to have a backup venue, particularly if those attending the meeting were unable to make it to the chambers in the hills. We continued through the passageway until Charls came to solid–looking metal doorway. He withdrew a large, ornate key from a pocket somewhere in his tunic, inserted the key, and went inside. A moment later, I joined him.

~~~

We were standing in a small square room, barely large enough for the two of us and perhaps one other person. There was not much to see. Charls pocketed the key, and pressed a recessed button to the side of the door, which closed silently. I could feel the sensation of air moving, but could not see from where it came. A few seconds later the sensation stopped, and Charls pressed another button. The door opened, and we stepped into another passageway. Although not damp or cold, I felt that we were deep underground. Obviously, the meeting room would need to be below ground level if it was to remain secret.

Sending the globe of light ahead, Charls and I continued along the narrow tunnel. I was getting used to following him around like a puppy. This time our journey was longer, as we headed out beyond the perimeter of Charls' manor. I decided to put the time to good use, and told Charls about my earlier experience, recounting the feelings of tingling and energy in my body.

Charls was delighted. "Your intuition was correct, Keira; although energy does continue to flow after it is initially received, your account suggests that you were accessing the lovelight spontaneously, and through your own connection. I am proud of you – this will greatly assist Cordello in its endeavours."

I was pleased I was making progress. There was no point in me being here if I was not going to be helpful, was there?

"What is the purpose of this meeting? Who will be there?" I asked.

"The Elder will be present," Charls replied, "as well as each of the five manor lords. In addition, the other lords may each bring a trusted friend."

I thought for a moment. "But you're only bringing me – are you allowed to bring only one person?"

Charls stopped with a laugh, a deep resonant sound, then turned to face me. "Keira, *you* are my trusted friend! I trust you with my life. Why would I need anyone else?"

I was glad he saw me as a friend – and relieved I had told him that someone was waiting for me back in my world. I had seen no signs of a female companion at the manor, and presumed Charls was unattached. It would not be helpful if he formed an attachment to *me*. I hoped he realised we were friends – and no more. I felt we had a very deep bond, one that I could not explain, but I also knew that it was not meant to be a romantic relationship.

Finally, the light–sphere illuminated the end of the tunnel, which was filled with a hefty door built from a dark wood. It looked thick and impenetrable. Charls retrieved the large key he had used previously. Surely it would not fit this door, too? Wouldn't that be a security risk? No, he used it only to rap smartly on the door, in a sequence not unlike Morse code. We waited. I heard a muffled squeak and the door began to move inwards. The opening door revealed a large, intimidating man with a dark, sleek ponytail, high eyebrows, and a long thin moustache. I was glad he was on our side.

He stepped back to allow us to enter, closing the door with a thud once we were inside the room. He shot all of the heavy bolts closed, and, although I felt secure within the room, I had to suppress a shiver at the reason behind all of the secrecy and security.

Looking into the room, I recognised the Elder, with his ancient, lined face and long white plaited ponytail. He was seated in a normal wooden chair this time, with the four lords seated in a semi–circle, facing him. As Charls had indicated, each lord had brought an associate. Two chairs remained empty, placed at the left edge of the curve. We sat, and I waited to hear what would be said, or thought, next.

The Elder stood. His posture was erect for one so aged. This time, not being weary, I hoped I would be able to listen to the whole discussion, and not fall asleep. I was also now more practiced at thought–reading. The Elder began to send thoughts to the group.

"This is a time of crisis. Our country faces a threat unlike any before it. Working together, and with young Keira's help, I hope that we can end this difficulty with diplomacy. However, if left with no alternative, we will use our resources to defend ourselves and our people. I know with certainty that all of you here will commit yourselves, and your assets, to ensure that lovelight is protected and kept safe for the benefit of our future generations. There can be no mission more vital, no task more important, than this: to protect lovelight at any cost."

I could sense the gravity of feeling in the room. The Elder's low–key but impassioned 'speech' had affected me, too. I felt completely ready to provide the Elder with everything at my disposal so that the precious gift that was lovelight would be guarded from harm. He was an able and inspiring leader, and I could see from the expressions shown by the others present that he had their co–operation and commitment.

"Now I have some information for you. It was unexpected, and I must ask you to keep your energy high. It is natural that you will feel some disappointment, initially – but you are well trained in overcoming lower energies and recovering optimism and positivity."

Mentally, I braced myself, and I could see several pairs of shoulders straightening in preparation for the Elder's disclosure. One lord looked decidedly uncomfortable.

"Branay, a trusted friend of Lord Samarn, has deserted. He was caught spying, and despite Lord Samarn's best efforts, was able to escape. We believe that Branay has an accomplice in Cordello – but we do not know whom." All eyes turned to Lord Samarn, as did mine. He was looking at the floor.

"Lord Samarn's behaviour and actions are beyond reproach," the Elder continued. "No–one could have suspected Branay, who has been a valued associate for many years. So let us move beyond this, quickly, and evaluate the extent of Branay's knowledge, and its benefit to Karn. And I am sure I do not need to remind each of you to boost our store of lovelight at every opportunity. Remember: you can do this even if you do not have access to the Grand Chamber for any reason."

At this point, their conference shifted to a discussion focusing heavily on the location and quantity of various resources. I began to find it hard to follow the analysis, and I tuned out their thoughts, allowing mine to wander. Then I heard my name mentioned, and quickly refocused.

Lord Samarn noticed my renewed alertness, and repeated his thought for my benefit.

"Keira, I'm afraid that Branay knows that you are here in Cordello, and . . . he also knows that you are residing with Lord Charls."

Once again, everyone was looking at me, awaiting my reaction. I had not taken any part in the discussion prior to this point. However, I felt oddly confident, unnaturally courageous. "Lord Samarn, my role is to serve Cordello, and to protect lovelight. I will keep my energy high, and learn any skills needed quickly and efficiently; I will be as useful to you as I can be. I will not fail you."

I glanced at the Elder. He was nodding with, I think, satisfaction. The legendary Keira would fulfil her destiny and assist Cordello and the future of lovelight.

Since Branay knew a considerable quantity of information, relating both to Cordello itself, and also to my arrival and location, the Elder, his lords and their associates had a lot to discuss. However, they were clearly practiced at finding the positive aspects of any situation, and soon began to work out how they might turn the situation to their advantage.

The remainder of the meeting was used to finesse the details of this plan. The broad outline was this: Branay knew of my lodging at Lord Charls' manor. He would also assume that once his treachery had been discovered, I would be moved to a new location. It was a natural presumption that the safest route would be through the underground tunnels. Although the tunnels were thought to be securely sealed, it was clearly recognised by those present that Karn would stop at nothing to discontinue my role in fulfilling my part in the legend, and would find a way to ambush the tunnel routes.

It was therefore decided that I would remain with Charls, and that a decoy would be transported to one of the other manors. This decision would be quietly 'leaked' to Cordellans outside of those present, and we would prepare our own counter–ambush.

This seemed a risky proposal to me – who would be the decoy? What if the decoy was captured, or killed? What if the decoy was successfully relocated, but Karn attacked Charls' manor and found me? Would I have to remain indoors and out of sight from now on? I wasn't good at subterfuge; what if I gave it all away by simply popping my head up at the wrong time?

However, the Cordellan lords and their Elder were convinced that their proposition was sound. I trusted Charls' judgement the most – after all, Karn was his brother. I felt that he had the strength of character and intelligence to know how to outwit his own flesh and blood, without being blinded by that same blood–bond. The fact that both the Elder and Charls supported this strategy provided me with a small measure of comfort.

The decoy was a young woman whom I had not yet met – a distant cousin of Charls'. Tissa was of similar height and build to me, but well–equipped with ruthless combat skills. She sounded like a formidable warrior. I felt less apprehensive knowing that she would be capable of defending herself, but hoped that Tissa would not be overpowered if anything went wrong.

I knew that I would need to work harder than the others to keep my energetic vibration high, to remain optimistic. I was not as experienced at creating or using lovelight, had not their automatic understanding of the energy. I would need to practice accessing lovelight, and to be prepared to learn any other skills which were deemed necessary for this 'quest'.

I became aware that the thought–discussion had ceased. No–one had taken notes; I was unsure whether this was for security reasons, or because they had perfect recall. Perhaps it was a bit of both. The meeting was breaking up. Charls and I were the first to leave. On our journey back to the manor, retracing our steps of just a few hours ago, we both remained lost in our own thoughts.

Reaching the rear of the bookcase–door, Charls activated the lever to allow us access into the library, and extinguished the globe of light. It faded like a moon vanishing behind storm–clouds. I stepped out of the passageway and walked to the darkest corner of the room, trying to remain out of the light, out of sight. Charls closed the bookcase–door and walked to one of the small tables. With a click, a small drawer slid partly open. Charls gently pulled it open far enough to insert his hand.

He looked up at me, then down at the drawer. He removed his hand. I could not see what he was holding.

CHAPTER 9

Charls walked towards me, his hand concealing the object that he'd removed from the table drawer.

"Keira, I believe this will help you in your time here; I am sure that it will give you guidance on how to use your energy to its best advantage."

He handed the object to me. It was a small, thin book, about the size of a postcard, and I guessed it contained no more than forty to fifty pages.

"It is my great–grandmother's journal. She entrusted it to me when she moved on to her new life."

I was puzzled. "Sorry, Charls; I don't understand. Where did she go?"

"Ah. 'Move on' is the term we use when someone dies. We consider the process to be a transition to another place just as 'real' as this one."

"Oh! I see." Well, I thought I did. I waited for Charls to continue.

"This treasured little book has the capacity to teach you about lovelight, positive thinking, the power of prayer, belief, love and co–operation, and will help you to understand how best to develop your skills so that you can assist us."

I took the book as gently as I could. Feeling a reverence that I had not felt before, I carefully lifted the cover, faded now to a soft dove grey, and examined the first written page. The writing was clear and firm, despite its age. I read: "This journal belongs to Aida Charlotte Evangeline, Lady of Cordello."

As I read her name, a jolt of electricity pulsed through me. I felt the strangest, strongest connection with Aida, simply by touching her book and reading her words.

Charls noticed my reaction. "Keira? Is everything okay?"

A little shaken, I nodded my head. "I just had what felt like an electric shock. And I don't think it's static from your carpet," I joked. I stroked the aged paper and received a muted version of the same sensation. "It's like there's some sort of power in the book, which I access when I touch it." I looked up at Charls, wondering what his response would be. He had tears filming his eyes.

"Oh Keira . . . you are picking up Lady Aida's energetic vibration through your hands. You must have a natural affinity and skill for reading energy from objects. You could be more valuable to us in our mission than we first thought possible. At present, there is no–one in Cordello with this ability. This must be why my inner guidance prompted me to give you her book."

Oh, crikey. I could connect with dead people just by touching their things?

I tactfully enquired.

"Not just people who are in a new life," replied Charls with a wry grin. "People still with us, too. And perhaps also . . . people who have betrayed us, and are plotting against lovelight . . . Keira, this may be too soon to ask, and you may need some practice, but . . ."

Ah, I could see where he was going with this. "You would like me to handle a possession belonging to Karn?" I asked.

"Yes."

I thought about his request. Was this, then, the key to my being here? Having a skill with energy vibration that no–one else had? It seemed too much of a coincidence. I reframed my thoughts. This was a 'synchronicity' if ever there was one. In which case, I *had* to answer 'Yes'. You just couldn't say 'No' to synchronistic events.

~~~

It was the middle of the night, but Jason could not sleep. Yet he could not understand what was keeping him awake. He was not worried about Keira – yet. On some level that he could not comprehend, he knew she was okay. He was not on a high from the wine – if anything, he felt mellow and relaxed. So why was sleep so elusive?

And, despite his nap earlier, he did feel sleepy. Jason rubbed at his eyes, and yawned. He closed his eyelids again. Opened them mere seconds later. Watched as the white moon glided as silently as a wraith behind the next scrappy patch of cloud moving overhead. The sky darkened, the unclouded area becoming a sheet of black pierced with what seemed like a trillion silver–white stars. His eyes sought the only constellation that he knew, Orion; but he could not see it. He looked at Keira. Still asleep. Or whatever.

Jason sighed. He knew that he needed sleep, too – his body ached for it. Why was it always when you were this tired you couldn't get the rest you wanted? He noticed he had allowed some of his weight to press on Keira, and shifted slightly to ease it. As he repositioned himself, his peripheral vision caught movement to his right.

He turned his head sharply to see who – or what – was moving. He'd thought that only he and Keira were here. Even the sheep and ponies had kept clear of their picnic spot. Nothing had moved within the stone circle since he had arrived. His senses moved to alert, all tiredness disappearing in an instant as his protective and survival instincts kicked in.

He saw nothing. He shook his head to clear it. He was starting to hallucinate, or maybe he was seeing things that weren't there, in a half–asleep, half–awake state. Something told him, though, that this wasn't the case . . . he had seen something, he was certain. Carefully, he moved his body further away from Keira, and used the giant crag as a support to quietly heave himself upright. As silently as he could, he skimmed his head around the side of the great stone, looking intently into the darkness beyond the immense crags.

"You won't find me over there," a voice said from behind him.

Jason spun back round to face into the circle. What he saw took his breath away, and his legs felt as if they might crumple. He was glad he had rock behind him to support his body. His mouth went dry, his heart beat faster, and he felt utterly powerless to move. Thank God he knew that Keira was right beside him on the ground. He hoped that he could keep her safe.

~~~

I was well aware that time was of the essence, however I felt that I needed some time and space to practice this newly–discovered capability. I strongly felt the need to read Lady Aida's little book, to learn what she could teach me, before taking on the important task of connecting with any of Karn's possessions. I was here for a reason, and I had an unshakeable certainty that *this* was it. It could not be rushed.

I realised that I was learning to trust my intuition more. Well, that was the best guidance to rely on, wasn't it? And yes, because of that, I was beginning to have more confidence and trust in myself as a whole. This, in turn, was making it easier to remain positive, to have 'good–feeling thoughts', to be able to contribute to lovelight. It was like a cycle of self–growth, each small part triggering the next. It felt wonderful!

Charls was happy for me to head back to my room to read in peace. I was still receiving little electrical buzzy jolts from simply holding the book. This was slightly uncomfortable, but at the same time a reassurance that the connection was still there.

I seated myself on the bed, leaning against pillows, and made myself comfortable. Holding the journal, I turned again to the first page and re–read Lady Aida's first lines. Carefully, I turned the page and began to follow Lady Aida's journey with lovelight.

As I finished the final page, I noticed that I was squinting. I realised that daylight had faded, twilight had arrived and soon a soft darkness would fall. I stretched to ease my stiff limbs, and rose to switch on the lamp. In my mind, thoughts, impressions and ideas were swirling as if in a whirlpool, each rising momentarily to the surface before being sucked back into the maelstrom. I would give them time to settle, allow my mind to reflect, and re–position each new piece of the jigsaw into a picture. A picture which was forever changed, fusing new knowledge and insights with my own experience and history.

~~~

The tingles that I felt when holding Lady Aida's journal had become fainter and softer as I had read her book. Perhaps the connection was fading now that it had been initiated and recognised, or maybe I had absorbed its information energetically as well as mentally, and I no longer needed to sense the buzzing sensations from this specific object.

Charls respected my need for introspection whilst we ate a light evening meal. I made little attempt at small talk, nor did I taste the food, although I'm sure it was wonderful. I felt as if I was lost in my mind, and normal thought seemed a challenge too difficult to overcome. I returned to my room soon after our meal, and sat on the bed, contemplating.

My mind was adjusting, re–shaping, shifting, re–balancing. I couldn't remember anything that I'd read. It was as if I'd absorbed the meaning of the words without comprehending the language in which they'd been written. I knew that I would soon understand the sense of what I'd read, and that my intuition had been enhanced simply by reading the little volume. I was aware that I would 'know' a lot of things, without being aware of 'how' or 'why' I knew them. I felt a surge of confidence and self–awareness. I felt – brighter.

I knew that my being here in Cordello was increasing the lovelight energy. I knew that lovelight was increasing at an irregular rate. I knew that the trees were growing in tiny increments. I knew that the cloud was moving at a speed of three miles per hour in a south–westerly direction.

It was as if I had become attached to a network of energy outside of myself, and could sense its bearings in many different directions, as well as its strength, and even its potential. I could call on this energy at any time, without depleting it. I had all this information available to me, as if I was a super–computer. It felt incredible; I felt so *alive*. However, I also felt a great sense of responsibility and service.

The maelstrom in my brain was calming, and those pieces of information that were not immediately useful were stored in my mind for later retrieval. Really, the trees' growth rate was not my immediate concern. I could almost hear the information being sorted, then filed away. None of this seemed odd or uncomfortable – it was simply how it would be, from now on. I accepted it. I would be going with the flow on the largest wave.

I let Charls know that I would be having an early night, allowing my brain to complete its task of integrating the new knowledge and awareness that I had attained. And, tomorrow, we would begin working with Karn's belongings.

CHAPTER 10

I woke early to the sound of rain caressing the windows with soft, fat drops. It was a soothing sound but it had roused me from a dream filled with stairs, bridges, doorways, twists, turns, and unknown faces. I couldn't remember enough of the dream to make any sense of it, so I gave up on sleep, and started preparing for the day ahead.

My mind felt clear and sharp; I was probably more alert than I'd ever been in my life. We breakfasted efficiently, both Charls' and my thoughts on what we might learn from the day's events. As well as my reading of one of Karn's possessions, initial preparations would also be made by Charls and the other Cordellan lords for Tissa's decoy re–location.

We made our way up the elegant staircase to rooms on the second floor, my hand sliding up the smooth wooden bannister. I had no nervousness. I was completely comfortable with the task ahead. I knew that whatever occurred, I would have the resources to deal with it.

I waited as Charls unlocked the door to Karn's room. I supposed that he normally had no reason to enter the room. I wondered if he felt a sense of loss or betrayal each time he entered the space, or whether he avoided the room completely. The door opened inwards, and, at Charls' invitation, I entered first. The room was clean, tidy, and well–furnished. The bed, set centrally against the opposite wall, was understandably larger than the one that was in my room. A tall, dark wooden wardrobe dominated the wall to the right. Deep, solid chests filled the remaining wall. Floor–to–ceiling windows let in pale gold sunlight beaming from behind hovering rainclouds.

Charls' face was set impassively, neither frowning or smiling. He was all business. He flung open the wardrobe doors. My, this guy owned some clothes! All of exquisite quality – and so many of them! The space was filled with shirts, tunics, waistcoats, trousers, shoes. I expected the chests were just as full. I wondered if Karn missed his clothes!

"What do you think, Keira? Would a shirt be a good choice, do you think? Or a belt? Shoes? Or maybe it doesn't matter?"

I considered Charls' words for just a brief second. But I already knew the answer – it had come to me instantly. It was to be the soft brown leather belt hanging from a hook on the inside of the left wardrobe door. I couldn't take my attention from it. This was the item I would use.

~~~

Jason swallowed. Okay, so he must have fallen asleep, he reasoned, and now he was dreaming. Except he knew that he was dreaming – wasn't that called lucid dreaming, or something? He'd never had one. That was more Keira's sort of thing. He dug his thumbnail into the palm of his hand. Yep, felt that. So, not dreaming then? Yet, how to explain the vision standing just a few feet in front of him, inside the stone circle?

He refused to take his eyes from it. You couldn't do that with monsters in nightmares else they ended up right behind you, scaring the living daylights out of you and chasing you until you woke up. At least that's how his dreams usually went.

This phantom surpassed all of his previous dream–based characters. It – a she? – was around seven feet tall, and seemed to consist of white mist, a glowing, shifting, white light. A light that talked.

"It's okay, Jason; there's really no need to be scared," the apparition continued. Well, that sealed it; the thing knew his name, and that was impossible . . . so it must be a dream.

Jason felt safe enough to answer back. "I'm not scared. You just startled me. What do you want?"

"Want? To help, of course. That's what we do: help."

"Right . . . help with what, exactly?" Doubtfully, he glanced down at Keira. Was this spectre somehow connected with Keira's sparkling lack of consciousness?

"Jason – look at me."

He lifted his head, risking another glance at the shining figure.

"Am I really so frightful?" it queried softly.

"Well, no, but . . . I don't know what you are. Where you're from. What your intentions are. You'd be a bit off–balance if you'd just met you, as well."

"Quite," the figure responded. Was it laughing at him?

"Look," Jason continued, "my girlfriend wandered off and I found her here in some sort of deep sleep that I can't wake her from; I can't drive as I'm over the limit, and there's no mobile signal up here. So we're both stuck here. If you really want to help, get Keira to wake up so we can go back to the car and get some sleep."

"Keira can't be awakened just yet," the light–spectre told him. "It is very important that she is left where she is. That's one of the reasons I have been asked to present myself here. Keira must not – under any circumstances – be taken outside of these stones. It could do irreparable damage."

Jason suppressed a sigh. This character was being very inflexible. He was shattered. He just wanted Keira settled safely in the car, and to get some rest. It had been a long week, and he felt drained from the scene with Keira earlier.

"Jason!"

"What?"

"Do you understand me? Keira must not be removed from this sacred site. You could be risking her life."

Well, this was only a dream, so Jason guessed that it didn't really matter what he did. He might as well err on the side of caution and leave Keira where she was, at this 'sacred site'.

"Is that it, then?" he asked, a little defensively. Dream–characters shouldn't really tell you what to do, and he resented it. He had enough of that at work. Didn't they say lack of control over your work was one of the reasons there were so many stress–related illnesses?

"No, that is not 'it'," the figure retorted. Jason thought he sensed a barely–restrained impatience behind the words.

"Keira needs you to trust me. So much – far more than you will ever be aware of – depends on Keira right now. She has a vital role to play and it must not be interrupted. It would have grave ramifications beyond your own world –"

"Beyond my own world? This is the craziest dream I've ever had," Jason said. "We're the only human beings!"

The being remained silent for a moment. "Jason, your world is not the only one housing intelligent lifeforms. Did you not read the books that Keira has? Did you take nothing on board of what she tried to discuss with you? If your mind is really so closed, then my task will be harder than we expected."

Closed–minded? Who did this thing think it was? He

wasn't waiting around to be insulted further. He scrunched his eyes shut, and willed the circle to be empty when he re–opened his eyes. Counted to ten. Slowly. Opened his eyes. Ah, hell, the figure was still there. In fact it was closer to him now.

"Why won't I wake up?" he wondered aloud.

"Jason, you are not asleep. This is real. You have to get with the program."

He bit back a laugh.

~~~

The belt had an elaborate rectangular silver buckle, and I could see a design or pattern etched into the leather. Charls carefully lifted the belt from its hook, holding it out to me as if it was a tame snake. I was aware of my mind and body readying themselves for the task of connecting with the object. It was almost as if I could hear cogs and wheels turning at incredible speeds in my brain!

I reached out my hands to take the belt from Charls. As my fingers touched the soft leather, I felt a *zing* rush up my arms and into my head. A buzz spread throughout my body, and I trembled. As if seeing myself from a distance, I noticed my eyes flutter and close, and as my knees went weak, I sat down on the bed just behind me. I felt quite spaced out, as if my brain was temporarily somewhere else.

Behind my eyelids, I was aware of seeing shifting images, blurry and unfocused. I felt as if I was watching a movie whilst wearing a woven cloth over my eyes. The images were indistinct, and seemed to merge together. This was different from when I had picked up the journal. My new knowledge informed me that this was because Karn was still in this world, and had energetic 'cords' linking him to Charls, and to Cordello.

The buzzing settled down to a soft background fuzziness, and my body felt stronger. Keeping my eyes closed, so as to retain the 'vision' that I was seeing, I let my fingers run up and down the belt as if playing scales on a piano. I then let my fingers rest on the leather. Some of the images gained clarity, and I could see three men in a small room; no sound accompanied the vision, however I could see one man throw his head back and then slap another on the shoulder. Their body language suggested they were friends or colleagues, and I guessed they were laughing. The first man lifted something to his mouth – a tankard, or similar cup – and drank deeply. Perhaps they were in a bar?

I continued to concentrate on the images. Were they memories? Or were these events that were happening right now? Was I looking at Karn, or seeing things through Karn's eyes? I was surprised that my new awareness and skills had not provided an answer to these questions. Perhaps part of this task was a learning process for me. I felt a kind of energetic 'thumbs up' at that thought. Okay, so I would receive guidance, as long as I asked questions. Interesting.

The images shifted to another place, with a different set of people. From that, I guessed that these visions were possibly memories, as experienced by Karn, and seen through his eyes. Another 'Yes' from my subconscious. I hoped I wouldn't have a fierce, uncomfortable jolt if any question I asked had 'No' for an answer. Perhaps I should ask? I did – and felt no response. It seemed that I would have a tangible response if the answer was affirmative, and no response at all if the answer was negative. I just had to learn to ask the right questions.

I wondered how long ago these events had occurred. This time there was a group of four men and a woman standing outdoors, and I recognised the orangery positioned solidly in the background. The image became clear more quickly this time, as if my brain was becoming more adept at the task the more I practiced.

One of the men had his arm placed around the woman's waist; a sign of closeness or familiarity. The image sharpened further. With a small shock, I realised that the man was Charls. He looked a few years younger, and I saw him look into the woman's face with deep affection. He had never mentioned a sister, so . . . who was she? I couldn't find any way of altering my position to find a better perspective, I could only see what was presented to me. He leaned forward to kiss her gently on the mouth and she placed a hand on his cheek. Ah. Someone he cared deeply for. *Or had cared for. Where was she now?*

My perspective *did* shift – Karn was walking away from the group, towards the orangery. I saw him reach out to pull the door open, and walk inside. The vision started to stutter and lose focus, becoming almost foggy. It slipped from my grasp, and the movie screen behind my eyelids fell dark. The background tingle from holding the belt in my hands also finally faded to nothing, and I opened my eyes. The visions were over, for now. Charls was looking intently at me, concern etched on his face.

"Keira? What happened? Did you feel anything? Are you okay?"

"I am fine," I sent back. "I had visions – I was replaying memories; Karn's memories."

Charls look as if he'd been struck. "His memories?"

He sat down suddenly on the bed. "What did you see?"

I recounted the first series of images that I had been shown. My memory was now photographic and I could recall every detail, every nuance, every movement. When I began describing the second vision, the thoughts that I was sending to Charls started to stumble and falter. Instinctively, I felt that mentioning the woman he'd been with would cause him pain. I wanted to avoid that, but how?

Charls, however, had picked up on my hesitant delivery, and knew I was trying to hold something back. "Keira, please; it's really important that you tell me everything. We can not tell what small detail may result in being of vital importance. Karn hurt me very deeply, but I must know what you saw."

His face was grey, almost white, and I dreaded mentioning the woman he'd been so close to.

I took a deep breath, and related to him the details of the second vision, keeping my eyes on his face as I described the people present, and their gender. "You were there, Charls. You were standing next to a young woman –"

"Alaria," he replied, his eyes dropping to his hands. They were twisting in his lap. If only he had not asked . . . but I knew that every small event occurred for a reason, even if we were unable to understand why, at that moment.

I gave Charls time to collect himself. Eventually, he raised his head to look at me, grave sorrow evident in his eyes. Then they focused beyond me, as he recalled the beautiful young woman named Alaria.

"Of course, you want to know who she was. We were engaged to be married. I knew she was 'the one' from very early on in our relationship. Apart from our passion for each other, we also had much in common. Our few differences enabled us to support each other; one stronger where the other was weaker. We fitted together like the perfect jigsaw puzzle." Charls stopped, losing himself briefly in his memories. I felt so sorry that I had precipitated this pain. But I would not be able to control what the visions would show me, and he had pushed me into telling him the details of these first images.

Gently I asked, "What happened? Charls?"

His shoulders slumped; he was the picture of a man defeated, knocked down by loss.

"That day, Karn suddenly walked away from the group of us that you were shown in your vision. He walked back to the house, I think. We didn't see him again until the argument with . . . until he murdered our father." He sighed deeply.

"Alaria – she was there when it happened. She was horrified by what she'd seen – we all were – but she turned to run, was like a wild fawn trying to escape her hunter. She panicked. She tripped and fell – no–one could reach her before she hit the ground. Her head hit the foot of a marble pillar."

Oh Charls, I thought. You poor man.

"She – her skull was damaged. No–one could have survived that. She died, Keira. Karn as good as killed her, too."

I had really not imagined that it could be this bad. He'd lost his father and his wife–to–be on the same day. It was a wonder he had been able to carry on. It didn't take a psychic to reveal that he still loved Alaria – and always would.

I sensed him withdraw into his past. Alaria was suspended forever in her beauty and youth; her perfection would always be unspoiled. No–one would ever be able to replace her, in Charls' eyes. That probably explained why he lived alone.

There was nothing I could do to relieve his pain. In his current misery, he was beyond reach. My heart was full with compassion, but I could not live this torment for him. I could comfort, if he would allow; I sensed that he would not. He would drag his inner strength up and out, kicking and screaming, and deal with this alone, just as he always had.

"Charls, I am so, so sorry. I think it best I replace the belt, that we return downstairs. I'll make some tea?" My mother said tea was a panacea for all ills. I knew it would have no effect on his pain, but I thought that physical movement to a different room, reminding Charls that he was still living, breathing, might help. I replaced the belt on its hook, softly closed the wardrobe, and walked towards the bedroom door.

Charls remained seated on Karn's bed, his face buried in his hands. His shoulders were shaking, and I knew that he was crying, silently. What should I do? I moved outside of the bedroom door, offering him some semblance of privacy, but it felt heartless to walk away. I hovered at the top of the staircase, undecided. Finally coming to a decision, I sat near the top stair, resting my back against the wall dividing the upper hall from Karn's room. Minutes later, I heard a creak from the room; I guessed Charls had stood.

"Keira, please . . . would you come back in?"

I shot to my feet and rounded the doorway. Charls' face was tear–stained and pale. However, he had come through his grief, for the moment. He looked as he always did – strong, solid, resolute.

"Before we return downstairs, I want to thank you for telling me what you saw in the gentlest way possible. I needed to feel this grief and to allow it to flow through me, so that it is not blocked. This is part of self–healing. Blocked emotions lead to ill health. So I had to do this."

I nodded my understanding.

He continued: "I had not expected to feel Alaria's loss so deeply again. However, I now need to be strong, as befits my role as a lord of Cordello. I am ready to return to that role now. What happened here today, following your vision, I would prefer to remain private, between us. Would you do that for me, please?"

"Of course," I answered. His emotions, his reaction to my visions, were his private property, and I would not dream of sharing them with anyone else. He reached for my hand, squeezed it briefly, and managed a watery smile. Using willpower, the smile developed into a genuine one. Then he released my hand, and we walked side by side down the staircase, for tea.

CHAPTER 11

Respectful of Charls' feelings, I kept my chatter to a minimum whilst we sat, in the morning room, with hot cups of refreshing tea. My gaze strayed to the large doors leading to the garden. I longed for outdoor sights, sounds and fresh air. However, with Branay's betrayal, it was no longer considered safe for me to be 'out there'.

I sighed, staring into the teacup. Steam rose from the hot liquid, brushing the air around my face with a soft, comforting warmth. My eyes closed, and I had a startling, clear vision of Karn in the orangery. Looking through his eyes, I saw him lean forward and dig at one of the large pots, which housed a large fruiting tree. From my vantage point, I had clear sight of his actions. His left arm joined his right, and placed a small metal object into the hole that he'd created. He swept the dirt back over the object, so that no trace of his burial remained. He covered his tracks well.

The vision faded. I lifted my head with a start to find Charls staring at me.

"Keira, what's wrong? Did you see something else?"

"I did. Karn left your group, in my previous vision, and headed into the orangery. This latest vision . . . it looks as if he hid something in one of the trees' pots. I think it may be some sort of spy device."

Charls jumped up, slopping tea onto the carpet. He didn't notice. He placed the cup onto the table, then took mine from my hand. I took the hint, and stood quickly.

It looked as if I would be getting some fresh air after all. We almost ran to the orangery, Charls pulling the door open and rushing inside ahead of me. He looked back at me over his shoulder.

"Which one? Which pot did he place it in?"

I walked along the stone path, trying to overlay the perspective from my vision with what I could see now.

"Here," I said, stopping. "This one." I dropped into a crouch, and began to dig around in the dirt, eager to find the hidden object.

"WAIT!" shouted Charls. I froze.

He bent down beside me, and gently eased my hands back from the hole that I was making.

"It's possible that the device could be harmful. We can't risk injury to you, Keira. Let me."

"I'm sure it's nothing like that – it looked like a listening chip or something," I argued.

Charls fixed me with one of his authoritative stares. "Just let me do this, Keira. I'll take any risk. Not you."

I shuffled aside to allow him better access to the burial spot. Gently, oh so gently, he cleared the area with his elegant fingers, and then paused as something glinted with a soft bronze light.

"Here it is," he sent to me, lifting the object and holding it aloft. "Look. It is a listening device, as you surmised; thankfully it can't injure us in any other way than leaking information to Karn and his allies."

"How can it obtain information when we don't speak aloud? Surely it can't record anything, if all our communication is by thought? How can it possibly work?"

Charls replied, "It will pick up both sound and thought vibrations. So we must disarm or destroy it now, before more significant information is leaked."

He placed the tiny object onto the stone floor, then crushed it with the heel of his boot. Lifting his foot, I could see that the object had been smashed and split into hundreds of fragments.

"Won't he know now that we've found it and destroyed it?" I asked.

Charls replied, "Possibly, if anyone was monitoring it at that very instant. More likely, they'll just assume that it has a malfunction."

How much information had been passed to Karn from the hidden device? Would he know more than Branay had told him? We had no way of knowing. I wondered if I would have further visions helping us to locate additional devices; were there more?

"Charls, I had the vision – but was not holding any object of Karn's. Can you explain that?"

Charls' expression turned thoughtful as he considered the question.

"It is possible that when you enter a relaxed state, you might re–trigger the energetic connection that is normally only provided by holding a relevant object. What does your instinct tell you? You have Lady Aida's knowledge now; how do you feel about the question?"

I realised that he was right. I had forgotten to ask my intuition the relevant question; therefore I had not been made aware of the information I sought.

I needed to remember to check in with my all–knowing self, to ask and then to listen.

"Charls – do you want me to access Karn's belt again, sometime? I mean, not today, obviously – it's been a hard day –"

"Keira, we have to do whatever is necessary to retain peace in Cordello. I can deal with any unpleasant feelings that may arise in the course of these tasks. Please, do what you feel to be best, and I will support you in whatever way I can."

"I feel I need to connect with Karn again. Is now too soon?" I replied.

"No. Let's go back up to his room, if you feel ready."

Holding the belt again felt like returning to a well–known perfume or piece of music. There was a connection between the belt and me. This time, I was prepared for the visions, and my previous experiences had assisted the connection. The first image popped up onto my internal movie screen sharp and clear. I was looking down at a pair of shoes. They were light brown, made from a sturdy leather, with dark, square buckles at the outer edges. Two hands reached for the buckles and removed first the left shoe, then the right. The left shoe was placed on the floor in front of two feet dressed in finely woven socks.

My perspective shifted as the Karn in the memory–vision tilted his head to focus on the right shoe in his hands. He was removing the insole. Surely this vision had a purpose other than me watching a man fiddle with his footwear? After a slight struggle, the insole was successfully removed, and placed to one side out of my sight. Karn's fingers continued to investigate the inside of the shoe. Finally, he removed a tiny, circular disc. It was silver–grey, and very shiny, reflecting light so that it almost blinded me. What on earth was it?

My intuition gave me the answer. It was a communication module. This was confirmed for me as Karn's hands moved higher and held the little disc in front of his mouth. Holding it so that the whole circumference of the disc was facing him, he spoke quietly into the disc. I could not hear the words. Then he tilted it so that it was edge–on, barely visible. Was he listening? Yes. So this disc enabled him to contact others out of sight. Our mind–communication was only effective when those communicating were only a small distance apart. This device enabled communication across vast distances. Was he contacting someone in Vornen? My answer was Yes. However, I felt that further answers could only be obtained through future visions. That it was important that I kept re–connecting with Karn in this way. That I would only receive information in this piecemeal fashion.

I laid the belt to one side, and recounted the details of the images to Charls.

"Light brown shoes?" he queried, his voice muffled as he delved into the bottom of the open wardrobe.

"Yes, with a very dark brown buckle."

"He may have been wearing them, of course, but – ah, I think I may see – yes, here they are." Charls extracted himself from the forest of coats and trousers, holding the shoes that I'd seen in my vision. He discarded the left shoe, and proceeded to examine the right. As in my vision, removing the insole proved a fiddly task, but Charls eventually removed it, and allowed his fingers to explore the inside of the shoe.

"I can't find anything, Keira. You're sure this is the right shoe?"

"Let me," I suggested. I took the shoe from him, and dug around inside the shoe. I closed my eyes and allowed instinct to guide me. My fingers touched a rough piece of stitching which didn't quite conceal its treasure – I was able to wiggle my fingers and retrieve something small and hard. Triumphantly I produced the little disc.

CHAPTER 12

I held the disc out to Charls, wary of somehow activating it accidentally. He took it and held it up to the light streaming in through the window. It gleamed in the sun's rays. Charls tipped the disc sideways, in 'listening mode'. After a few seconds, he pocketed the disc. He sent to me: "I heard nothing. And this disc, thankfully, does only operate for spoken words, not telepathic thoughts. So it would not be able to pick up on our silent communications."

Well, that was a relief. I suppose that made sense; if the little disc could have collected telepathic thoughts, too, it could potentially receive and transmit the thought of every person that Karn passed when he wore those shoes. As Charls and I, along with other Cordellans, communicated silently, then our day–to–day words could not be leaked to Karn and his Vornen allies. Maybe we could use the disc to our advantage? Did it perhaps only work when someone with a similar disc activated his – or hers – simultaneously? My answer was again Yes.

"Charls – the disc needs another to communicate with. Either Branay had a disc, or Karn already had another contact in Vornen. Or maybe he was involved with someone else here . . ."

Charls looked at me for a long moment. "Of course. That makes perfect sense. Well, we can't really try to guess who it was – or is. We can only use what we have found, in the best way. Do you have any ideas?"

"Not fully formulated, no . . . but I do think we might be able to exploit the disc in some way. If that is the case, then I will know when to make use of it."

Charls began to move towards the door. "Meanwhile, I'll find a safe place to store it."

I wondered whether the plans to 'move' Tissa had been finalised. My intuition gave me a No as an answer. "Will Tissa's decoy transfer still go ahead?" I asked, as we returned downstairs.

"I will need to discuss our developments here with the others. But I think it likely that, yes, it will take place. We have to give the impression that we know nothing more than we did before. Your skills, Keira, need to be kept completely secret from Karn. They must not know about your abilities, about the receiver that I destroyed, or the silver communication disc. Those provide us with an advantage that we cannot risk losing."

Charls would contact the Elder in the usual way, which even I was not privy to. A meeting would be arranged. I would not be invited; Charls felt it better that I remain in the manor, and had decided that I need not know details of Tissa's transfer. I would not even know when it was taking place.

Charls vanished that evening, leaving me to my own devices. Obviously, I would have to remain indoors, and out of sight. As usual, staff on the estate would be guarding main approaches to the manor, to ensure that all within were safe. I did not feel scared. I felt that if anything potentially dangerous was in the offing, I would somehow know of it. More of Lady Aida's wisdom that had been absorbed into my mind, I realised. I would have a warning of danger to myself, but what of danger to others? To Charls? My answer was disappointing. Their safety was not part of my early warning system. I would have to remain vigilant and sensible.

I went to bed that night without seeing Charls again.

At breakfast, he was subdued and thoughtful. I kept quiet, allowing him time with his thoughts. He was a man used to his own space, and here I was, plonked in the middle of his life, and reminding him what it was like to have a woman around him. He disappeared again early in the morning, and I assumed he had opted for some quiet time in another room, to think, brood, or process his emotions – I didn't know which, and he hadn't told me his plans.

He had allowed me full use of the magnificently–stocked library, and I spent an idle morning randomly choosing books, and leafing through them. There were many fiction books, some plant and animal encyclopedias, which showed that Cordellan flora and fauna were not all that dissimilar to those in my own world. I found a map of Cordello, which showed boundaries with Vornen, and with one other country named Reika. With a shock, I realised that the name was an anagram of my own. That seemed to be – well, a synchronicity. I'd read The Celestine Prophecy and its sequels, and understood the general principles of the series, even though Jason thought it was all fantastical nonsense.

I carried the map to a larger table, which enabled me to unfold the document and weight it down on each corner. Reika was a small country by comparison with Cordello and Vornen. I knew with certainty that Reika was important, somehow. Its border with Cordello was – no, that couldn't be! If I was reading the map correctly, then I had 'arrived' in Reika. Charls had met me on the far side of the hills, here, before leading me into Cordello through the rock passageways. Tracing the map line with my finger, it indicated that the boundary between Reika and Cordello was at the point where we had left the tunnels. So the Grand Chamber, the meeting room, the tunnels . . . they were all *Reikan*. I desperately wanted to ask Charls about Reika; I felt so strongly that the country was of vital importance. Carefully, I re–folded the map and replaced it on the shelf where I had found it.

At that moment, the bookcase secret door opened into the room, and Charls rushed through, nearly bumping into me. I moved to one side to avoid him knocking me over, found myself slamming into a table and coming close to overturning the lamp. I steadied it, and looked at Charls. He looked harassed and stressed.

~~~

"Charls? What's wrong? Is everything okay?" I queried. Looking more closely at his ravaged face, I thought he looked shocked and upset.

"Tissa," he thought to me. "They've taken Tissa. And several of our men were injured. They were outnumbered and overpowered – many died." His face contorted with regret. He slumped into one of the comfy armchairs, and tipped his head back against the cushions, his eyes closed. He looked exhausted – from strain, or from physical exhaustion, or maybe a mixture of both.

I sat in the chair nearest to his, and ventured: "So the re–location was this morning? What happened? Can you tell me?" I wasn't sure if he was able to recount it; not sure I should have asked him, whilst in this state, to share anything with me at all. However, Charls opened his eyes and turned his face to mine, and began to explain what had happened.

"Yes, we carried out Tissa's re–location this morning.

Clearly our leaked information had reached its intended target, as they were ready for us. They had tunnelled underground from some point in Cordello – we don't know where, yet – and were hiding deep in the tunnel between here and our planned re–location site. Actually, knowing that they might try to breach the tunnel, they were waiting where we expected." He closed his eyes for a moment before continuing.

"But we badly under–estimated their numbers. They had *dozens* waiting – as we knocked one man down, so another came forward. We were forced to defend, of course, and they lost men, too . . . but they had more to sacrifice, and then more again. We never stood a chance."

Charls stood, and began pacing around the library. "Tissa put up a fight, but they were able to bind her wrists and ankles, and she was dragged off through their access tunnel. We had no–one left to follow, as we were all wounded at the time."

I jumped up and moved to check Charls for injuries, but he waved me away.

"It's okay; I was knocked unconscious, but we have all helped each other with preliminary healing; we are all recovering now. We were just incapable of doing more at the time. And now Tissa is captured."

He ran a hand distractedly through his hair, leaving it stuck up in haphazard spikes. "Once we've recovered fully, we'll try to follow the access tunnel to its source, but I expect Karn will have blocked off the entrance. Those of us involved are all too fatigued to think straight."

He stopped his pacing, and retook his seat. He looked at me, and said: "Keira, you need to help us, please. Not with visions; we're all too low on energy to process those right now. Please – would you help us to rebuild our positive intentions? We are all calling lovelight to us, but your additional input would help us further, and more quickly."

"What do you need from me?" I asked.

"Just access lovelight as you did before, and direct it with your mind to all of us Cordellans who were involved in the skirmish. And to Tissa, as well, please."

"Do I need to send it to you individually? Who should I start with – you?"

"No, you can send to us as a group. You don't even need names – your clear intentions are sufficient. Give it a try, and I'll let you know if I can feel my own energy boosted further."

I relaxed as best I could, breathing slowly and easily, letting my muscles relax. I found my connection to lovelight, and placed my intentions, like a prayer, for boosting the energy and health of all Cordellans who had been present in the clash. Immediately, I felt the air above my crown change, sensed a new space open up, and buzzing cool sensations rushing in, flowing down into my face and torso. With the intentions solidly in place, I felt the energies flowing into and then through me, as if I were merely a hosepipe channelling the energy . . . which I supposed I was. I resisted the temptation to open my eyes, to see if Charls was showing any reaction. I concentrated on my assigned task, doing my best to boost my energy, my connection, in order to help him and his alliance.

~~~

I felt very deeply relaxed; I sensed a continuous light buzz throughout my body; it was really quite soothing. I almost felt as if I was suspended in a bath filled with fuzzy energy molecules. My meditative state deepened, and I became aware of geometric shapes on the dark 'screen' behind my eyelids. They shimmered, spun, shifted, danced and some flashed rapidly on–and–off. It was amazing. I had not seen *these* the last time I connected with lovelight. Perhaps it was related to the fact that I was receiving lovelight and then transmitting it onwards? Yes, was the answer to that question. This was actually fun! I couldn't help a lazy grin spreading wide across my face.

I hoped the fun I was having was helping Charls and his friends. I continued sending forth the wonderful energy until I felt the buzzing slow to a soft tingle, and the energy seemed to fade. Feeling incredibly peaceful and filled with well–being, I opened my eyes to see how Charls was.

He was asleep. His face looked a healthier colour, and in repose, his face was softer, less authoritative; the lines of responsibility and regret had been erased in slumber. He deserved some decent rest after what he and the others had been through. I hoped that Tissa and the others were also feeling a benefit from my transfer of lovelight. I felt languorous from the infusion of lovelight – clearly it benefited the person calling on it, as well as those to whom it was being sent.

I concluded that if I moved, I might wake Charls. So I took the easy – okay, lazy – option, tilted my head back against the chair's headrest and slipped into a dreamless sleep.

CHAPTER 13

This dream–being was quite a character, Jason decided. It seemed to know just how to push all his buttons.

"Get with the program? You sound like my boss. I was right; this dream is just another nightmare!" Jason said bitterly. "I want to wake up. I want Keira safe, I want us to be warm, I want to sleep!" He knew that he sounded like a petulant child, but couldn't keep the frustration from showing.

"Jason, life is not always about what you want. I have already explained to you that Keira is involved in something way beyond your experience. What you want is not, at this moment, our top priority. I am here to ensure that you do not move Keira. I had not expected to meet so strong a resistance to this." The being fell silent again.

It gave Jason time to think for a minute.

He sighed. Of course he wanted what was best for Keira. He just didn't understand what was going on. He was too tired to work it out; it made his head hurt. He was too tired for mental gymnastics with – what, exactly? He rubbed his eyes again. He'd be needing matchsticks soon. So, he couldn't close out this dream; he was stuck in it for the moment. Okay, then, time for some answers. Maybe continuing communicating would be the easiest course of action, so that he could finish the 'story' and wake up.

"So tell me what you are. Who you are. What's going on? Why is Keira in this odd state?"

"You may as well make yourself comfortable, Jason; we'll be here for a while." The light–suffused figure moved yet closer. Jason could not retreat; his back was against the solid crag. He felt as if he would lose ground if he sat in the presence of this tall, glowing being. But fatigue won out over pride, and he allowed himself to sink to the ground, letting his knees bend in front of him. He placed an elbow on each knee to support his head, craning his neck to look at the being. It was so bright it made his tired eyes smart.

To his surprise, the light–being also changed position; he could only guess that it was somehow shifting into a seated position. It was now only four feet tall, much more manageable. Now he didn't feel quite so disadvantaged, height–wise. More equal adversaries. Well, maybe that was too strong a word, but they weren't exactly best buddies yet, were they?

"I am encouraged by the fact that you wish to discuss this situation. So I will try to answer your questions. Some of this you may not fully understand, but I will do my best to explain. Keira's 'mind' is in one of the parallel worlds. I am from that world."

Jason spluttered. Was this for real? He never had dreams with this much . . . imagination. Slowly, hesitantly, his mind began to consider the possibility that this spectral light–person was, in fact, real. That the words it spoke were truth. He couldn't explain it, but somehow what she said 'felt' right. He shivered as a chill marched across his back.

The being continued. "My name is Lady Aida. I am an ancestor of people living in a place in which Keira's consciousness currently 'resides'. I am no longer living on the visible plane in their world." Jason's eyes opened wide, all tiredness falling away. Had he heard that right?

"That's right, Jason," Lady Aida said. He sensed a smile. "There are many worlds in existence, and many 'peoples' on those worlds. Many are – for various reasons – simply not visible to you, as humans. I don't believe you would grasp my explanation for this – not yet. So please, for now, just accept what I tell you, and we can use that as a foundation for the rest of our discussion."

Jason thought on what she had told him. It all sounded so . . . fantastical. But a scrap of thought quietly rose in his mind, pushed its way to the forefront, clamouring for his attention. Something Keira had told him when she had excitedly told him about the Celestine Prophecy books. Something about vibration, and energy. At the time, he'd thought her ideas and explanations were wild and ridiculous. But – what if? *What if?*

~~~

When I awoke, the sun's reach had moved beyond the library windows and the room was cooling. Charls had gone. I felt so relaxed that it would have been easy to remain in my comfy chair, but I managed, with some effort, to rouse myself. After wandering the house without seeing any sign of Charls, I returned to the library and retrieved the map I had looked at just a few hours ago.

As I laid it out to examine further, I wondered idly why I felt no energetic connection with any objects that belonged to Charls, such as this map. The answer that I received was intriguing. Because Charls was here, and could work directly with me for the good of lovelight, and because he was able to teach me in person what I needed to learn from him, then I need receive no information from his possessions.

That was not the case with Lady Aida's special

journal, since she had moved on; and of course my connection with memories of the absent Karn were crucial in our crusade to save lovelight for the benefit of all. It all made perfect sense, as always.

Just trust, Keira!

I examined the detail of the map showing the border between Reika and Cordello. I confirmed that the area in which I had arrived was Reikan, and not Cordellan. I wished that Charls was here so that I could ask about relations between the two countries. The map gave only fairly sketchy pictorial information. Sighing, I re-folded the map and replaced it on the shelf. I wandered through the library, feeling suddenly restless. Maybe I felt the need for action, knowing what had transpired in the tunnel, knowing that Tissa was held captive somewhere.

I felt as if, at this moment, I had no function here, no role to play. I was used to following Charls' lead, working with him, talking with him. I realised that he had become a close and trusted friend. I was used to being in his company. I missed him. I noticed that my mood was turning melancholy, and would help no–one. I mentally squared my shoulders, and endeavoured to improve my state of mind to one of optimism and positive energy.

Charls would be back soon, I told myself. I would need to learn patience! And to respect the importance of 'good timing' for all events and circumstances. As long as I recognised synchronicity, and acted accordingly, then everything would fall into place. I remembered that much from the books that I had read.

Just at that moment, Charls entered the library via the bookcase door, thankfully looking a great deal better than before I'd sent him the lovelight energy. He was holding a large, flat, gold–coloured ornament in one hand. He held it out to me. It was a belt buckle shaped in a Celtic knot. It was beautifully designed and made, and crafted from a heavy, dense metal. I took the belt buckle and received an electrical jolt that almost knocked me off my feet. I staggered, using a nearby chair to steady myself.

"Tissa's," I sent with certainty. There was absolutely no doubt in my mind.

"Yes," Charls answered. "I found it in the tunnel. Can you . . .?"

"Yes, I can. I will."

I seated myself comfortably, and closed my eyes. The images rushed in like an incoming tide, overwhelming all other thoughts and images in my brain. This was so strong, I knew it was of vital importance to lovelight. I focused, and watched the images play.

The picture was, as always, shown from the perspective of the owner of the object. I saw what Tissa saw: a room with grey walls; they were hefty bricks, I thought. The floor was rough, brown, looked like dirt. I guessed she was seated on a bench or chair in a cell. There was a deep cut on her leg, raw and red, and untreated. It was weeping blood. She had been dressed in a shabby white garment not unlike a hospital gown. Her arms and legs were dirty. Knowing what I did of Tissa, I expected her to be determined to remain strong, and on the alert for any opportunity to escape.

I felt that the images I was seeing were in the past, not representing the current moment. I was right; as I watched, it was like seeing a recorded movie being fast–forwarded at twice normal speed. Tissa was looking down at the cut on her leg. As I let the images play, I could see the cut healing literally before my eyes. First, the bloodied area appeared to shrink, then I saw the two edges of the cut knit together, leaving a rough, nearly–black line. Still watching, I – and Tissa – observed the cut fade to a narrow, pale pink line. Lovelight had done this? I had no words!

In my world, this would be magic. If Jason could see this . . .

~~~

"Okay," Jason replied slowly. "Assuming that I believe what you've said – that part of Keira is in another world where you are not visible – that doesn't answer my question of Why Are You Here? And why can I see you, if . . . the 'others' can't?"

"One aspect of my purpose in being present here is to ensure that Keira remains here, inside the circle. Another part is to work with you so that you understand some of what Keira is doing. If all goes well, then once she has completed her mission, she will return to your world. If you are to stand any chance of remaining together as a couple, then you have to be able to understand her experiences. You will need to be on a similar wavelength. Not just mentally, or emotionally, but energetically, too."

Jason thought he understood. "Otherwise, she'll leave me behind; is that what you're saying? Share more of her thoughts with people who are on her wavelength?"

"Precisely!" said Lady Aida.

Hurrah, Jason thought. I'm getting with the program! He allowed himself a small smile at his tired attempt at humour. Then he backtracked down the path of Lady Aida's words.

"Wait! You said she'll return here if all goes well. Are you saying there's a chance she'll be . . . stuck there?"

He felt panic rise in him at the thought of losing Keira. Perhaps he should have asked her to marry him. If he had, this evening would have gone so differently. Now he had to face the fact that he could lose her. He felt slightly sick.

"I did not mean to alarm you, Jason. There is every chance that the legend will play out as expected, and that Keira will be absolutely fine."

"What legend?" Jason demanded. This was getting more complicated by the minute.

"Ah, that I cannot relate to you. It is not your place to know more." Catching Jason's sigh, Lady Aida added: "However, you asked why I am visible to you, yet not to others. The reason is very simple. I need you to see me. I knew that I stood more chance of having a sensible conversation with you if you could see me."

Jason laughed. "You're right. There's no way I'd have taken any notice of a disembodied voice. This is weird enough!"

"Indeed."

Now Jason was sure that Lady Aida was amused by his attitude. Well, it couldn't be helped. He was doing his best. Keira always said that was all that anyone could expect of anyone else.

~~~

The images slowed to normal speed. Tissa reached forward to smooth her fingers over the healed cut, her fingers coming away clean and dry. I saw her stand, then walk around the cell, examining the walls with her fingers, exploring ridges and bumps, perhaps hoping for some hidden exit mechanism. I guessed she had found nothing useful, as she then returned to the bench.

I saw her hands rise in front of her torso, and rapidly weave a globe of milky–white light. Unlike the creation that Charls had made, this light–object transformed into a globe of shifting, sparkling rainbow colours. It was breathtakingly beautiful; I was mesmerised by it. The globe moved up, away, across the room and rested, as if suspended, against the wall housing the only window in the room.

As I watched, the rainbow globe dilated, rose higher, wider, brighter. It expanded to encompass the entire window, which I had seen was barred. Just when I thought the sphere could not become any brighter, it flashed brilliantly, then collapsed like a dying star, leaving an open hole in place of the window.

Tissa leapt across the room and scrambled to the window ledge. The image shifted ahead in time, so that I saw her running through a dense wood of tall trees, crashing through boughs, branches, and leaves. I knew she was barefoot but Tissa wouldn't allow a small thing like a lack of footwear to hold her back. The next and final image was a snapshot of Charls' manor.

"She's here; I think Tissa's here!" I exclaimed, opening my eyes and nearly dropping the buckle.

"What?" Charls was astonished.

"The vision showed me her escape – using some kind of rainbow light – and the last image was of here. I think she's made it!"

"Wait here, Keira!" On that command, he whirled out of the room and was gone.

I stood up, needing to move around. I hadn't been able to tell whether Tissa was here, at the manor, or whether the vision had simply showed me her intended destination. I decided to ask my new knowledge and intuition. My answer: She *was* here!

Mere minutes later, a breathless Charls, together with an even more breathless Tissa, came through the door. Tissa's eyes were bight, her cheeks flushed, probably from her flight from captivity.

Then I spied Charls' eyes had a similar quality, and his normally straight–lined mouth was curving in a quirky smile that I sensed he was attempting to hide from me. Suspicion flared. Was there something going on between these two? If so, I was glad. Charls deserved every happiness. I tried to keep my own mouth from breaking into a smile, happy to allow him his secret. For now, at least!

Once he and Tissa had recovered their breath, and helped along by a light early–evening meal, Tissa explained how her leg had healed, and the means of her escape. Charls looked at me. "Does this match your visions, Keira?"

I confirmed that it did.

Tissa said, "I wondered how the cut had healed so quickly. Normally, with self–healing, that would have taken me several hours. Charls explained that you had been assisting with the energy–heal; do you know it took only a few minutes?" She smiled.

"I was pleased to be able to help." And I'd do it again in an instant, I thought.

"I will head up to a guest room; I feel in need of rest and time to myself." She stood, and turned to Charls. There was a long, slightly awkward silence. Then colour flooded her cheeks.

"Good night, Charls, Keira. I will see you in the morning." She walked gracefully from the room. I wondered how close her guest room was to Charls'? It was not my business, however, and stifling a grin, I also bade Charls goodnight and headed to my own room.

Next morning, I arrived downstairs to find that Tissa had already left for a secret location somewhere on the manor's estate. The fewer people who knew her location, the better. Charls would be assembling with the other lords, and the Elder, to discuss developments. Clearly, Karn and his Vornen allies would be aware that I had not been moved to a new location, since they had intercepted the subject of the transfer and found Tissa instead of me. So what would they do now?

CHAPTER 14

My newly acquired guidance provided no answer to that question; I had not expected one! I knew that the situation would play itself out, with each player acting their role. I hadn't been told the full, detailed story of the legend. No doubt Charls would inform me of any relevant aspects at the appropriate time.

He was subdued that day. Following the meeting with the other lords, he told me that I would remain here. Charls was well–versed in combat and battle, and his estate continued to be exceptionally well–guarded, despite the recent loss of men in the tunnel clash. His men had confirmed that the end of the tunnel, where Karn had entered, had collapsed. No–one could get out that way; conversely, no–one could gain entrance, either. The entry–point was also guarded night and day.

In other words, I was as safe here as I was anywhere. We now had the added bonus of Tissa's presence somewhere on the estate. She was, Charls told me, their top female warrior. So long as we had warning of an attack, he would trust her with his life. That meant that I had to trust her with mine, too.

In the midst of the threat of war, and death, I realised that I felt more alive than I had ever felt before. Yes, lovelight and my new abilities played their parts, too. It was more than that, though. It was a sense of being a part of something . . . of having something to fight for . . . something worthwhile, something important. I realised, too, that although I was playing my part here in Cordello, that back in my own world, Jason was waiting for me. *He* was my something worthwhile, my something important. I would fight for him, too. He was so very precious to me. He was not one for emotional words, for declaring deep feelings. But I knew, in my heart, that he had them, that he cared deeply for me. We'd make our life together, whatever it took.

~~~

Jason was curious about Lady Aida's apparent choice to be visible – or not. "So how do you become 'visible', then?"

"The full explanation for that is rather beyond your comprehension, my dear; at its most basic, I change my energy to a different density so that I appear to have physical form."

Right. Yeah, that didn't really tell him much, but Jason guessed that was as much as he'd be getting. At least for now. At least Lady Aida was trying to explain things to him. So far, everything she had said did fit with Keira being here: apparently unconscious, yet otherwise healthy. No way would he dream up this stuff himself. So . . . yes, he realised that he had subtly shifted into an acceptance of what he was seeing and hearing. If only Keira could see him now!

He glanced to his left and his features softened as he looked at the face he loved. He didn't tell her how much he loved her nearly often enough. He didn't feel all that comfortable expressing his feelings – especially the 'L' word. She was beautiful. His heart felt tight at the thought that he could still lose her. She made him laugh when he was grumpy. She comforted him when he felt sad. She lifted him when he felt stressed and fed up with work. He felt safe and right when he was with her. He wanted nothing more than to be with her for the rest of his life.

That was that decision made, then. He would propose to her as soon as she was conscious. It would be his first and most important question. His heart felt lighter at the prospect, as if he had already changed their future.

Looking back to Lady Aida, he thought he began to see more definition in her shape and features. "How is it that you look different to me now?" he asked, curious.

"I look different? In what way, Jason?"

"Well . . . I can almost see an outline of your face, now; and although you are still glowing and – well, a bit vague in your shape, if you'll pardon the expression – I just seem to be able to see you 'better' . . . sorry, I've not explained it very well –"

"You're doing fine, my dear! I needed you to be able to voice what you thought you were seeing."

"Which is . . .?"

"Which is that you have opened your heart and your mind – just a little – but enough that I have more substance to you now. If you had remained closed, then no matter how long I had been visible to you, you would have seen light, and light alone. Now you see me as a personality in my own right. If another like me was to join us –"

"There are more of you?" Jason was shocked. How much else did he not know? The thought panicked him a little. His safe world was changing into a vast, shifting maelstrom of unknowns.

"Of course! What I was going to say was that if another was to be with us now, then in time you would see this other being differently from the way that you see me. You would be able to see that we are each unique, just as humans are. Jason, you are doing well – please know that. Think how far you have expanded your horizons since Keira first left your picnic. Think on that."

He let his eyes fall shut as he replayed events from that time. Keira frustrated, disappointed, angry. Finding her gone. Discovering the stone circle. Making the decision to sit with Keira. The appearance of a glowing spectral being. All that Lady Aida had revealed to him since then. Yes, his horizons had widened and deepened. He still felt uneasy, though. He wasn't sure where his anchor was now. A thought fired through his head: that he was his own anchor. But he didn't feel strong enough!

~~~

I brought my mind and focus back to the present – always the best place to be – and returned to the map in the library. Charls was often absent, and I had not yet found a suitable moment to ask him more about Reika. This time, I learned no more than I had absorbed previously. A little frustrated, I replaced the map, and wandered idly through the library, examining the treasures that Charls had on display. I was particularly intrigued by a heavy, gold–metalled square paperweight that appeared, for a brief moment, to radiate a rainbow of light. I was on the verge of picking it up to study it further when I heard a voice upstairs.

My curiosity aroused, I tiptoed into the main hall. It was wrong of me, but I could not resist moving closer in order to eavesdrop. I moved nearer to the staircase, into a small walled archway containing a delicate rosewood table. There was just enough space for me to squeeze myself in next to it, and so remain out of sight of anyone upstairs. I kept quiet, breathing as softly as I could manage.

I've never eavesdropped in my life, so I have no idea what prompted me to start now. Let's call it intuition. Perhaps it was the fact that I could hear voices, which was so unusual in Cordello.

I was still – to my frustration – unable to make out the words being spoken. I could only hear one voice. Who was the man talking to? My patience paid off as I suddenly heard a shout of "No! We can't do that, it's too risky –" before the voice hurriedly reduced volume. My heart began to thud. One voice – talking somewhat furtively . . . was the person using a communication device similar to the one that Charls and I had retrieved?

I needed to know who was speaking. I knew, even from this distance, that it was not Charls, and clearly the voice was male. Charls' staff were so discreet that they were almost invisible, and I had never met any of them when I was in the house. Could I risk moving from my hidden location and exposing a possible traitor? I was literally in an agony of indecision. My muscles were tensed to 'fight', my mind said 'flight'. What to do?

In the end, my mind was made up for me, as the voice abruptly ceased, and I heard someone moving about at the top of the staircase. I attempted to wriggle further into my hiding place, knowing that anyone coming round to the morning room could not fail to see me. I did not have time to dash into the morning room; I knew the door to that room squeaked on opening and I could see that it was currently closed. I was sure that the corner of the rosewood table was creating a permanent dent in my thigh, but I didn't dare move. I was in shadow; I might get away with it as long as he went into the library, or to the kitchen.

I listened, heart beating loudly as I heard the man descending the stairs and stepping into the hall.

Footsteps came closer, crossing the hall, then to my relief, veered into the library. I ran as quickly and as silently as I could through the hall, towards my bedroom. Opening the door, I slipped inside, and closed the door silently behind me. I had not seen the man; but nor had he seen me. I would know the voice again, should I ever hear it. I had no proof that he was using a communication device, but I knew now that I would be wise to be more aware of those around me – even the near–invisible staff.

With my back against the door, heart still beating too fast, and nerves on edge, I heard the same rhythm of footsteps pass close by my door; they paused, then moved on. My heart pounded. Did he suspect? Or was he just checking that I was safely tucked up in my room, and sufficiently distant to be unaware of his communication? I would remember that walk, too. He seemed to have an uneven style of walking, as if placing his weight more on one foot than on the other.

I moved to the bed, and sat down on the covers, resting my head against the headboard. My mind was whirring and buzzing with thoughts, impressions, perceptions, and ideas. I guessed that the man, if he was a member of Charls' staff, would be familiar with the upper floor of the manor. Charls had an office next to his bedroom. Perhaps the man was a secretary? A valet? (Did Charls even have such a thing?) Or perhaps he had access to the bedrooms.

I didn't know whether to disclose what I had overheard to Charls. I had no evidence of wrong–doing, although, if I went by how I felt, I would say that it felt wrong. Something didn't add up, and I had a strong feeling that this little event was a key piece of the overall jigsaw. I had to trust my instincts, my intuition, my 'inner–knowing'. I would mention it to Charls the next time I saw him.

Meanwhile, I would remain in my room until Charls returned. I trusted Charls. I trusted Tissa. Everyone else would have to be considered a potential leak, or traitor, until I had identified the man with the uneven walk.

CHAPTER 15

I slept fitfully, with broken, hair–raising dreams of masked men hiding behind walls waiting to thrust a knife into me. This time, my dreams were of no help to me. They did not identify the man, nor did they provide me with any other useful information; they simply kept me feeling alert. I felt edgy, watched, and watchful. I made my way safely to the morning room for breakfast, and was relieved to see Charls seated at the table. On impulse, I decided to delay mentioning what I'd heard. However, instinct prompted me to mention the map that I had been studying. I waited until I had eaten some of the soft bread and a handful of the cherry–grape fruits before opening the subject with him.

"Charls, perhaps you can enlighten me about Reika."

He dropped his fork with a clatter. "Reika?"

"Yes," I confirmed. It's shown on the map adjoining Cordello, and –"

"What map?" he interrupted.

I was discomfited. Charls' expression towards me seemed to be projecting shock.

"Keira, who told you about Reika? What map are you talking of?"

"The one in the library. I only know what the map shows; that Reika borders Cordello, and that the border appears to be at the end of the lovelight passages and chambers."

Charls pushed his chair back. We had not finished breakfast, but his manner clearly indicated that I should accompany him. He walked so quickly that I was almost jogging to keep up with him.

In the library, he stood aside, and sent the thought:

111

"Please show me the map, Keira. I really need to see it urgently!"

I walked to the shelf and retrieved the map from its usual location, spreading it on one of the larger tables in the room. I weighted down the corners, and stood back to allow Charls to examine it. He leaned forward over the document, then stood back, waving his hands in frustration.

"Where, Keira? This map shows only Cordello and Vornen. Please show me what you see."

He moved to one side to allow me space to look at the map. I automatically moved my left hand to the area marking the lands of Reika – and stopped, puzzled.

"I'm sure this is the right map," I remarked. "It was right here, and it was marked clearly. It covered this whole area." I swept my hand across the empty space which, previously, had shown Reika.

I looked up at Charls, not knowing what else to say. I asked my intuition what had happened – had I taken a second map, showing different illustrations? No. Had the map of Reika disappeared? *Yes.* Why? No response.

"I believe that Reika has been erased from the map, Charls," I thought to him quietly.

He steepled his fingers, the tips tapping against his chin as he processed this information. He remained in thought for some moments, before looking directly at me.

"Let's sit," he said, "and I will tell you what I know of Reika." We made ourselves comfortable and I waited to hear more.

"Reika was once a great – no, a wondrous – civilisation. As you described, Reika adjoined Cordello on its Western border, with the boundary between our lands at the exit from the tunnels that I brought you through. Once, Reika was our ally, and assisted us greatly in repelling potential invaders, simply by their technology, and their efficient and creative use of lovelight."

I jerked in surprise.

"Yes, Keira, lovelight was . . . discovered, if you will, by Reikans. Some of my distant ancestors were Reikan – including Lady Aida, of course – and their story has been passed down through many generations. Back in the distant past, Reika was invincible, and our alliance with them deterred all threats; Cordello was safe. Reika had towers of a mineral that glowed like cut diamond, and they used crystals and other minerals to create almost everything that they needed. They healed with crystals, and used them to maintain wellbeing and harmony. They even had crystal 'farms' to ensure that they never stripped their lands of this valuable resource; everything was . . . perfect."

Charls closed his eyes with a sigh before continuing his tale. "Then, with no warning at all, the Reikan buildings and people simply disappeared overnight. Only empty space and the natural environment remained. One day Reika was there; the next, it had gone. Any Reikans in Cordello also vanished. It remained a great mystery. However, the legend – *your* legend – foretold that a young woman would approach Cordello through where Reika used to be."

Charls paused, his mind perhaps recalling our first meeting. Then he returned his focus to the current moment, to the map spread upon the table. "And now you tell me that you saw Reika on that map . . . to say I am amazed is an understatement. So what else can you tell me, Keira?"

I wasn't sure if there *was* anything else I could tell

him. I again asked my inner guidance and relayed it to Charls, with some degree of awe: "Reika and its people *still exist*. Not on this plane, but on the plane on which angels and the like reside. Reikans are now 'Ascended Beings' that can be called on for help, in a similar way to angels and lovelight. They can no longer be seen, and most people will not sense their presence. However, they will be present with anyone who calls for their help – as long as the request is for the 'highest good of all involved'."

I felt a shiver pass over my back, parading in a regular rhythm from left to right, and in my imagination, I perceived it to be an angel or Ascended Being trailing fingers from one side of my body to the other.

"Keira, I have learned to trust your guidance; even when it is as astounding as this. It may take a while for me to process this, even as I feel it to be true."

I knew exactly what he meant. I felt that it was a fairly easy leap of faith to believe in angels; they had been mentioned at points in my 'other life'; however I had not known that there were other Ascended Beings, let alone that people could call on them for help. Presumably the Ascended Reikans were only available in 'this world'. My answer was *Yes*. Did we have Ascended Beings back in my own world? *YES.*

My brain now adjusted to new beliefs, new *truths* very quickly, and within a few moments, all of my existing attitudes and beliefs had shuffled and reformed to take account of this new information. Great, so now our allies were back, it's just that no–one else knew they still existed, and no–one could see them. I knew that this information would be crucial to protecting lovelight, and was glad that I had remembered to mention the map to Charls.

Charls had risen from his chair, and had returned to examine the map. He did not question why I alone had seen Reika drawn on the document; we both knew that I had a unique role to play here, and that certain experiences would be synchronous and hold the key to future events. His trust in me was absolute, and I respected and was honoured by that trust.

~~~

On impulse, I moved to the table containing the heavy golden–coloured paperweight that I had previously seen projecting rainbow light. It was drawing me to it; I felt an almost irresistible urge to hold it. Following this overwhelming instinct, I picked it up. The cube was warm, and I felt that it was pulsing somehow, as if it was a living, breathing thing. My inner knowing guided me to place the paperweight on the map, right in the centre of where I had seen Reika drawn.

Charls and I gasped as rainbow light shot out from all four lateral sides simultaneously. It lit the map with shafts of glowing gold, white, and shifting rainbow colours.

"Keira! This is – incredible! Look! I can see Reika marked on the map! I can see it!"

Charls was like a small child finding his long–lost, favourite toy. I grinned at his excitement, and at my own.

I admit that I found it helpful that he could see what I had seen, and we could now see it *together.* The light and colours moving were incredible in their own right; their illumination of the mapped Reikan lands in the most literal sense was magnificent.

After spending a short time admiring the light and

using it to examine the map, Charls stood back.

"I think now is the time to remove the cube," he told me. I trusted his judgement, and reached forward to withdraw it. The lights contracted rapidly into the centre of the cube. Its exterior now looked dull and lifeless, and was feeling cool; I got the sense that it was camouflaging itself as an ordinary object. I replaced it where I had found it.

Charls' eyes were still sparkling with animation. We'd both enjoyed the light–show, and I guessed that Charls had felt honoured to see what no–one else would – apart from us. Reverently, he re–folded the map and handed it to me to replace on the shelf. I had just finished putting it back into place, and was moving back towards the chair in which I usually sat, when the library door was pushed open.

This was the first time that I had seen a member of Charls' staff. As the man walked towards Charls, I kept my expression neutral. *This* was the man with the uneven walk. I resisted the temptation to stare, to commit his face to memory. I feigned complete indifference. Charls and the man appeared to be in thought–communication, as the man's face looked harassed, with Charls' expression changing to one of puzzlement. The man made his exit, his walk–rhythm seeming to echo in my head.

Charls sent to me: "Symion tells me that Tissa has requested to see me urgently; for some reason she has not come here, and wishes me to go to her. I won't be long, I hope –"

"NO!" I sent back. "No, Charls – please trust me on this. I don't believe that Symion is on our side. I haven't had time to tell you what I heard earlier –"

"Keira, Symion has been in service at this manor for

over a decade! Of course I trust him!"

"Please, Charls; hear me out! Think of Branay!" I begged.

He walked towards the door.

I thought he was going to ignore me, to follow Symion's instructions heedless of my warning. I gave a sigh of relief when, reaching the door, he closed and locked it, then returned to me.

"What did you hear, Keira? Surely you can't mind–read Symion without his consent?"

"No, of course not! I literally heard him talking, speaking aloud. He was upstairs. I hid in the hall alcove, squeezed against the table. I know it was him because I recognised his walk. I couldn't hear actual words, but the conversation was all one–sided, so I guessed he was using a communication device. Charls, I was going to tell you about it sooner but my guidance indicated that the map was more important. You have to believe me; *he feels wrong to me.*"

~~~

Symion's arrival mere seconds after we had returned the map and the paperweight to their usual locations was, to me, another synchronicity. If he'd arrived just a few moments earlier . . .

Charls and I looked at each other, and I knew he believed everything I had told him. I guessed that he was going through a process of accepting that Symion could be – probably *was* – a traitor.

"Keira, if he is on Karn's side, if Symion had seen the map, or the cube –"

"I know! Your decision to put them both away at that moment was inspired."

I went on to tell Charls all that I could remember of my eavesdropping session. He agreed that Symion's behaviour was very suspicious.

"Once again, Keira, you were in the right place at the right time! I could almost believe that the Ascended Reikans are already working with you –"

"What is it?" I asked, as he hesitated.

"I've just realised – Reika is an anagram of Keira . . ."

"I noticed that, too!" I grinned. "No way is that a coincidence. Everything is coming together. As to the Reikans assisting, I believe they could be guiding our actions; such as your decision to pass me Lady Aida's journal; and to put the map away when we did. As long as we trust our instincts, we will be doing what is best . . . you agree, I think?"

"Yes. I do agree. Your spiritual– and self–growth are developing very well, Keira!"

"Life has certainly become very interesting of late!" I replied.

I thought of my 'other life' – and Jason. He was never far from my thoughts; but here, I was forced to concentrate on the here and now, on helping Charls and Cordello; I had little time to focus on Jason. I hoped that he was okay, and not in a panic because I had gone missing.

I brought my thoughts back to the present. I felt that it was time to elicit more information through Karn's belt. I turned to Charls to mention it, but from the thoughts he was sending me, it seemed he'd had the same idea. We were becoming attuned to each other.

In Karn's room, Charls retrieved the belt from the wardrobe, and handed it to me. I took the belt, and closed my eyes, running my hands along the belt's length. Immediately, the first vision began to play. I saw

118

a communication device poised in front of Karn's mouth, in the 'transmit' position. He was alone, outdoors, and speaking to someone, although I had no audible input in the visions. He turned the tiny disc into 'receive' mode and listened. Was he talking to Symion, I wondered? *Yes*, I was told. That confirmed Symion's treachery from yet another source. Could I find out what was being discussed? *No*. Ah, that was a shame. Knowing the subject of their conversation would have been pretty handy.

Communication ended, the disc was moved out of my sight, and I became aware that Karn was walking rapidly towards a small building – it looked like a modest house. He opened the door and entered into an untidy and cramped room, with books piled high in perilously crooked stacks, papers strewn across a desk, a chair set askew, a jacket thrust absent–mindedly over the back of it. Karn moved to the chair, lowered himself into it, and began to examine the messy assortment of papers.

Thrusting the top documents to one side, he seemed to be searching for one particular item. Using his eyes, I had a clear view of everything that he could see. His hands stilled as he found what he'd been looking for. It was a map. I recognised it as a copy of the one in Charls' library. The Reikan lands were not included, I was relieved to see. Did he know of their ancient location? *No*. Did he know of the Ascended Reikans. *No*. I was relieved.

I refocused on the view in the vision. His map contained subtle differences to Charls' document. Karn – or someone else – had drawn several new lines perpendicular to the border between Vornen and Cordello. Were these crossing points? *Yes*. Okay. So – in

119

theory, we might be able to increase our defences at those points; even plan ambushes. I tried to memorise the position of the new lines. I was grateful for my brain's enhanced capacity and function. At school, I'd been hopeless at memorising; now it could stop or win a war.

~~~

When Jason opened his eyes again, he was shocked to find that Lady Aida had gone. He felt short–changed, unfulfilled, as if he'd been left hanging. His muscles stiff, he awkwardly climbed to his feet, intending to go looking for her. But he could see that the stone circle was empty, and surely she could not . . . materialise . . . anywhere outside of it?

"Look up!" Hearing this faint command, he tipped his head back, gazing into the star–speckled sky above him. Like a comet, a white glowing shape blazed a trail across the dark sky. He watched as the shining figure flew closer to the ground, watched as Lady Aida came to a gentle stop in the centre of the ancient circle of stone. Wow, that was really cool! Would he ever get to do that?

"The answer to that, dear Jason, really depends on whether you believe that you will. On how well you open your heart and mind! But let us leave that thought alone for now. We have other matters to discuss and develop that are more time–critical in nature. Are you warm enough, by the way?" Lady Aida folded herself back into a seated position and Jason followed her example, hugging his knees to his chest to trap his body heat.

"Actually no, I'm still feeling pretty chilly. Sitting

against cold rock hasn't helped," he grinned.

Then his mouth fell open as a white glowing sphere materialised in front of Lady Aida. It swirled and shimmered, becoming larger and more transparent. It looked like a giant child had blown a massive bubble. It flexed and shifted, and Jason realised that it was coming closer. He managed not to flinch as the bubble reached him and moved into him . . . over him . . . behind his back. He noticed that he was completely enclosed in the bubble, whilst Keira and Lady Aida remained outside. He reached a hand out to touch the surface of the sphere. It had a slight resistance, but did not move; luckily his impulsive move hadn't popped the thing. He began to feel warmer almost immediately, a comfortable rise in temperature as if he was settled at just the right distance from a cheerful log fire.

"Better?" asked Lady Aida.

Great, he could still hear her. "This is fantastic! Can I take it home with me?" he joked.

He could now see Lady Aida even more clearly, could see her raise one eyebrow in amusement. He wished he could do that trick. Keira could, and it annoyed the hell out of him. Feeling pleasantly warm, he let his body unfold, stretching his legs out. Now that he was more comfortable, he was content to wait for Lady Aida to make the next move in their conversation.

~~~

The vision faded, and I opened my eyes, offering the belt to Charls to replace in Karn's wardrobe. Charls quickly fetched pencil and paper, together with our own copy of the map, so that I could create a new one to include of all of the lines that Karn – or his allies – had marked on their version. I sketched furiously, desperate to recall everything that I'd seen. My memory had improved, but I still felt concern that I *might* forget something . . . and that it could be *the* key piece of information that we needed to succeed.

Charls waited patiently until I'd finished, then took the drawing from me, studying it for some time. "I see what he has done. He has noted all areas where there are weaknesses in the boundary between Cordello and Vornen, which of course makes sense. There are some I was not aware of. I will suggest to the Elder that we increase our defences at all of these points." He looked up at me. "Well done, Keira. That is enough for today, I think. Shall we return downstairs?"

"I think we should, Charls; before we do, though, what are you going to do about Symion's message – he told you that Tissa had asked you to go and see her? Won't he be suspicious if you don't go?"

He froze. "I completely forgot about it! He may believe that I've left the house . . . but no doubt whatever mischief had been arranged is still awaiting my presence. If only I could get a message to Tissa. We are at a distinct disadvantage, not having our own communication devices to keep in touch with each other."

"We do have one, Charls, that you have hidden away . . . and presumably Symion has one secreted in his room, or perhaps on his person. So, that's two. That doesn't solve our current problem, though, as Tissa doesn't have one. Nor, I suppose, do any of your men guarding the estate?"

"Correct. I will have to go, Keira, and remain extremely alert. We don't have any idea of what they have in mind; it's tricky to predict what they'll try next."

"Before you do – I have an idea! How about asking the Ascended Reikans to support you, or protect you, whilst you are in this potentially dangerous situation?"

"Do you know how?" he asked, with not a little doubt.

"No," I replied, "but if we remember the importance of visualising and intending a safe, positive outcome, and make a request to them to help, I believe they will." Reminiscent of the sensation of earlier, I experienced another 'chill' marching across my back. This, I felt, was a sign that we were on the right track.

"Okay, Keira – I leave this to you. This is where your gifts and instincts seem to be better than my own."

"Let's sit on the floor, facing one another, as we did when we were in the Grand Chamber," I suggested. We settled ourselves as comfortably as we were able to, then closed our eyes. We both drew on lovelight, enveloping ourselves in a gentle, tingling shroud of the supportive, healing energy. I visualised images of both Tissa and Charls safe and healthy. When I felt that it was the right time, I called on the Ascended Reikans.

"Ascended Reikan Beings, I, Keira, and Charls, both wish to make a request of you, please. We are committed to protecting lovelight and the people of Cordello, both of which are currently under threat from Charls' brother Karn, and his allies, in Vornen. We understand that it is possible and appropriate to ask you for your support, protection and guidance in this matter." I was sending the words to Charls, as well as directing them to the Reikans. Hopefully he would approve of my words. I didn't want to upset the Ascended Beings by being too informal, or for them to think me rude.

I continued: "Charls has been asked to visit his cousin Tissa, who is located in the grounds here on the estate.

We believe this request to be a false one, made by those who wish to threaten lovelight and Cordello. We humbly ask for your help, for the best outcome for everyone involved, and of course for the safety of lovelight. Please enable Charls, on following this request, to remain safe, and to act in the best way for all. We are grateful for your assistance. Thank you."

I maintained the lovelight connection for a few minutes, then slowly released it, opening my eyes to look at Charls. His eyes remained closed for a moment, then he, too, opened his eyes. "That was perfect!" he thought to me. "Respectful, but not over the top. How will we know if they answer? Or if they help?"

"Well, I guess if everything turns out well, then we might assume they have helped. *Oh!*"

I clamped a hand over my mouth to stifle the scream that I knew would escape. Charls swivelled to follow my gaze, which was fixed on a point beside the wardrobe, and behind his head.

"Keira! What – ?"

Both of us were speechless – unable to form coherent thoughts. I lifted my other hand to shield my eyes.

Standing in a blaze of shimmering white–silver–gold light was what appeared to be a tall figure, at least eight feet tall, I estimated – but it was hard to be accurate, as the shape was in a state of flux. I felt as though I was swimming in lovelight; I had never imagined the energy could feel this strong, this powerful. It was as if it had flooded the entire room. I also felt incredibly emotional, was aware that tears were trickling down my face, and that I had begun to quiver.

The figure made no sound, but moved towards us. Charls manoeuvred himself into a kneeling position, so that he could more easily watch the figure. It reached out and placed a – was that a hand? – on Charls' head, as if blessing him. Light surrounded Charls, shifting and swirling, so that his physical form was obscured. This time, I could not hold in my gasp of awe.

The figure moved away from Charls and headed closer to me. The shaking intensified. I felt that I was in the presence of something – or someone – incredibly powerful, special, awe–inspiring . . . an exceptionally superior being.

The figure reached out to me and I felt a pleasant shock as it touched my head. My tears became a flood, my shaking became uncontrollable, and I felt as though my entire being, my soul, my spirit was being touched, cared for, supported, and held with an infinitely deep, loving and peaceful kindness. I was unaware of my physical form – it was no longer relevant; only this *oneness* with these feelings existed. I felt as if I were outside of time and space; *this* was all there is, all there was, all there would be.

Finally, the sensations eased, and I realised that I was in my physical body, seated on the carpet in Karn's room, with Charls kneeling opposite me. His face showed disbelief and awe. The amazing energy in the room slowly faded, the aftershocks of my body's reaction to the experience started to recede, and I dried my tears.

"What was *that?*" asked Charls, still quivering, with tears glistening on his cheeks. He wiped them away.

I paused to check in with my now–familiar guidance system. Had we been visited by an Ascended Reikan? *YES.*

"That," I replied, still finding it hard to think straight, "was one of the Beings we asked for help. I think we can safely assume that our request was heard."

We both shifted position so that our backs were resting against the foot of the bed – we needed some physical support for our bodies after that 'out–of–body' event. Charls put an arm around me, and held me close. We had shared an experience that perhaps no other people had ever had. It deepened the bond between us. Our physical closeness felt safe and real after our encounter with the Ascended Reikan.

CHAPTER 16

We allowed ourselves a few minutes to regain some equilibrium. Charls gave my shoulder a gentle squeeze, and rose to his feet. I followed.

He sent: "I should go now. I know that I am protected, and will be guided. As long as I check in with that guidance, I will be fine. Remember to hold that vision in your mind, too. Now, shall we head back downstairs?"

"Sounds like a good idea. Do you have an excuse ready if we should bump into Symion?"

"Oh . . . I'll just explain that I had needed you to help me with something, Keira. You return to your room; I'll feel happier knowing that you're in there, and I know you won't be disturbed by any of the staff."

He gave me a final glance and strode from the room and down the stairway. I gave myself a further moment, then followed a few steps behind. Charls threw me a reassuring smile as he moved through the hallway, then headed out through the front doors into the grounds. Since I had no idea of Tissa's whereabouts, I could not guess how long Charls would be – rather, how long he *should* be, if he was not waylaid by trouble.

I sat on the bed, in my usual spot. I decided to connect with lovelight. I made the link, then sat surrounded in the light tingling energies whilst I focused on seeing Charls strong, safe, and able to overcome any obstacles that he might encounter. I extended the visualisation to Tissa, willing her to be strong enough, quick enough, clever enough to deal with any problems that Karn or his men might direct towards her.

I was able to maintain concentration for a while, then found my thoughts drifting, until, finally, I fell into a doze. By the time I awakened, it was dusk. I jerked upright, remembering Charls' assignation. Was he back? What had happened? Would Charls come to find me once he was back, to reassure me that all was well?

I received no answers from my inner guidance, so jumped up from the bed and splashed water on my face to wake myself up. My hand on the doorknob, I twisted it as quietly as I could, then made my way softly across the hall to the library. All of the table–lamps were on, but the room was empty. I walked quietly to the morning room. The squeaky door was ajar and, again, all of the lights were on. I entered, finding this room empty, too. If Charls had returned, he could have gone up to his room. But I felt sure that he would let me know that he was okay, before doing so. Had I been tuned in to my intuition, I would have known that there was something wrong – we always switched all lights off *before* leaving a room – energy was precious!

But I was focusing on finding Charls . . . I was not paying attention to the niggling uneasiness that was trying to get my attention.

I was standing in front of the glass doors when they shattered.

I cried out, leaping back from the shower of falling glass. Three men dressed in grey, and wearing masks, stormed through the ruined glass doors into the morning room. I turned and ran towards the door that would take me to the hallway. I was frightened, but also frustrated. If only I had remained in my room! I had made myself a target by walking into a lighted room.

Stupid, *stupid.*

I was only halfway to the door when I felt a heavy weight hit me, pushing me to the floor. I couldn't breathe. The guy was flattening me. Two pairs of feet appeared in front of my eyes. The weight lifted from me, and I was dragged to my feet.

Two stern faces stared back at me. Their eyes were hard, devoid of emotion. The men were clearly combat–trained, and worked hard at their physical fitness. No wonder I had been crushed. My hands were pulled tightly behind my back, wrenching at my shoulders. I was too shocked, too shaken to focus mentally on any escape plan. Oh Keira, next time, do as you are told!

I was marched out of the morning room into the gardens, which were now completely dark. The man tugged me across the grass towards one of the formal areas. My balance was off, and I stumbled. The man holding my hands shoved me forwards. My eyes were only now acclimatising to the lack of light.

More walking.

I noticed that we were now heading into the woodland sector of the garden, where the towering, graceful trees loomed high above us. They looked menacing in the dark. I couldn't see anything in front of me, could only hear our breathing, and our footsteps on the gravel, along with the heavy tread of the two men walking a little way in front.

Suddenly the man escorting me fell against me, making a gurgling sound. My shoulders were wrenched again as he twisted, and I cried out. I found myself on the ground, this time with my head face down in grass and leaves. The tang of detritus filled my nostrils and I felt dirt on my tongue.

The man was laid awkwardly across me, pinning me to the ground. My arms were at uncomfortable angles, but I didn't feel any sprains or breaks. I wriggled, trying to shift his bulk.

"Keira?" came Charls' thought–voice into my mind. I

sighed audibly with relief. He was alive!

"Yes!" I replied. "I'm here!" I spat out tiny grains of soil.

"I know, I'm only a few feet away from you. Are you okay?"

I nearly giggled. "Well, I think so, but I have this guy slumped across me, and he's quite heavy . . ."

The weight lifted, and as the moon escaped the dark, heavy cloud, I saw Charls grinning at me, Tissa standing close by. She smiled. "Hi!"

I scrambled clumsily to my feet, my balance still a little off–centre. Tissa caught me by the arm, and I suppressed a groan. My muscles would ache for days; but if that was the extent of my injuries then I counted myself lucky.

With Charls and Tissa supporting me, I made my way back to the house. We entered through the disintegrated door–space since it was the most direct route, and continued through to the library. Charls disappeared and returned with several men, who were asked to clean up the mess in the morning room. Of course, the room was no longer secure from the outside. Charls locked the door and left several men on duty in the hall and in the grounds, their knives at the ready.

We had a welcome cup of tea in the library, where we began to bring each other up–to–date with the events of the last few hours. After I had recounted my own adventures to Charls and Tissa, Charls explained what had happened to them both.

"I was closely protected, Keira. The moon showed herself at the perfect moment, illuminating a man ready to knife me. I spotted him first, and was able to remove the threat. I had planned to reach Tissa using a lesser known route, but felt some hesitation. I felt strongly guided to use a path that has remained unused for many years, so utterly forgotten that even I had overlooked it. It was a circuitous route, but it enabled me to reach Tissa's location without being apprehended. I explained the problem to her, and we left by yet another little known path. Again, the moon helped us to see another man waiting in ambush. Tissa saw to it that he'll never walk again."

I looked at Tissa with respect. She was handy to have on side, that was for sure. Charls continued with his account. "I had the strangest sensation, then, that the whole fabrication had been concocted to leave you unprotected. So Tissa and I crept our way to the woodland. I somehow knew that you would be captured, and brought into and through the trees. We waited, and our opportunity came. The rest, you know."

I sent a brief thought of thanks to the Ascended Reikans for keeping Charls and Tissa safe, and assisting them in rescuing me. "Are you both unhurt?" I sent. They were both totally unharmed. "What of the two other men who were in front of me when you ambushed them?" I asked.

Charls looked at Tissa. Then he said: "Let's just say that Tissa can easily neutralize two men simultaneously. They won't cause any more trouble."

I considered that, sooner or later, news of his failed ambush would reach Karn, and that he would be really quite angry. Would he make another attempt? Tissa had escaped his cell. I had escaped his aggressors. Would he now give up? How badly did he want lovelight? Or me?

One thought crept quietly into my mind. Charls, Tissa and I were safe, virtually unharmed. In my lovelight visualisation, I had 'seen' Charls and Tissa as safe, guided, protected . . . I had not included myself in the intention. And from this evening's little drama, I had come off worst. I made a mental note to remember to include positive intentions for myself, next time. I was no good to anyone else if I didn't look after myself! And I had to remember to tune into my intuition if I wanted to hear it!

I realised that we also had to deal with the issue of Symion. Was he in the house, still? Or was he out in the grounds, waiting to stir up more trouble? Had he contacted Karn? I had no answers. I had no idea what Charls had planned for Symion. There were plenty of men acting as guards in the house, and Charls had posted two men outside my bedroom door, with another two standing outside my window. I closed the curtains for some privacy. It was now late, and I was exhausted. Sleep called to me, and I answered.

I dreamed of snakes, and of huge, angry lizards with razor–teeth and claws that sliced through flesh. I'd had nightmares after watching Jurassic Park. Now, I woke in the blackness, my body pulsing with adrenaline. I calmed my breathing, and called on some lovelight to help me to relax; the energy soothed me and I drifted easily into its calming embrace.

When I next awoke, it was close to breakfast–time, and I felt refreshed. The ordeal of the previous night had faded along with my bad dream. My bruises might take a little longer; although the lovelight had significantly eased the soreness, I still had some impressive markings in sulphur–yellow, purple and moss–green.

Tissa joined us for breakfast; in the circumstances it was perfectly natural that she had remained here overnight. Since Karn was now aware of Tissa's presence at the manor, Charls had suggested that Tissa reside here at the house. This was also beneficial because they would be able to plan and plot together, and it provided less opportunity for the opposition to set traps for either of them.

They both looked quite happy with the decision. In fact, now that I was paying attention, Charls was wearing a secret smile, a little one–sided tilt to his lips, that I had not seen him wear before. I sincerely hoped that he was happy with Tissa. He had been alone, and without love, for far too long. Their intimacy made me long to be back in the safety of Jason's arms.

We ate breakfast in the library, since the morning room was open to the elements, and eating in there posed an obvious security risk. I broached the subject of Symion. "What will you do, Charls? Is he still here, or . . .?"

"No, he's gone," Charls replied, draining his cup. "It appears that he took the opportunity to flee to Vornen. I've checked his room, and it's stripped of his personal items. He guessed that we knew about his treachery, that he'd no longer be of any use to Karn. In a way, I wish he had stayed; we could have plied him with false information."

"Presumably your extra defences are not yet in place at the border locations that Karn's map shows?"

He gave a wry smile. "You presume correctly, unfortunately. The timing was not to our advantage; however, we must play the cards with which we are dealt, and move forward as best we can. My men are moving into place this morning, and I will let the Elder know what I have done. I feel the need to move swiftly, to act now and talk later."

My mind drifted. My gaze floated towards the table containing the cube paperweight, and stopped.

"I have an idea!" I dropped my bread onto my plate,

moved to the table, retrieved the metal object, and returned quickly to the others. The cube felt cool, innocuous, a normal heavy object. No flashing lights; no pulsing; no warmth. Maybe it had only the one use – illustrating the Reikan territories on our map – but maybe, just maybe . . . it would help us in other ways? Charls looked expectantly intrigued; Tissa wore a puzzled expression.

"Charls, what is that?" she asked, as I placed it in the centre of the table, moving the assortment of cups, plates and cutlery to one side.

Charls looked at me, then said: "It's a metal paperweight, Tiss. However it hides a secret. And," he grinned at me, "I bet Keira thinks it hides a second secret. Don't you?" he challenged.

I smiled. "It's just a hunch. But – we are learning to accept our guidance as messages of truth, so here goes . . ." I took a breath, then placed my hand on the cube. If I was wrong, I'd look a fool. However, if I was right . . .

I spun the cube clockwise. I don't know how I expected a cubic object with a flat base to spin, but it did not disappoint. It spun faster and faster, until all we could see was a golden blur, the space around it appearing somehow distorted. The whirling paperweight emitted no light, and I held my breath, waiting to see what happened.

~~~

Still the cube spun; watching it made me feel slightly giddy. It was as if a force field of some sort was being generated. At least, that's what my inner knowing was telling me. Now I could see sparks literally flying from the rotating paperweight. Flashes of sapphire, ruby, and silver, as well as gold. We watched, silent and mesmerised. Still it spun.

Then suddenly, it stopped.

No slowing down, no wobbling – it simply ceased all movement. It sat, in the middle of the table, looking like a normal paperweight.

It was quite an anticlimax. What was the point of it all? Had something happened that we could not see? Or hear? I was puzzled, and I could see the same expressions of bafflement on Charls' and Tissa's faces. We looked at each other. Down at the cube. Back at each other.

"Okay . . ." said Tissa. "So what was the big secret, because I'm not really sure what that was all about!"

I bristled slightly; I felt Tissa's remark carried a sarcastic undertone.

"Nor I, Tiss," Charls answered with a wry smile. "But it's proven a very helpful cube thus far, and I'm certain that little exhibition wasn't just to show us its moves."

"No . . . there is something," I murmured. "I'm being given some information . . . just wait a second . . ."

Then it crystallised in my mind. I picked up the paperweight, and invited Charls and Tissa to accompany me as I led them to the morning room. The guards stood aside and Charls unlocked the door. "Why do you wish to enter, Keira?" Charls was bemused. He entered the room, with me on his heels, and Tissa behind us.

"Keira! Did you know this had happened?" Charls said, turning back to me, eyes sparkling.

"I was told to check the glass doors in the morning room," I confirmed with a wide smile.

Tissa moved forward to stand beside me. "Oh!" she breathed.

The glass doors were whole. It was as if they had never been shattered. We could not explain how they had become suddenly and miraculously fixed. However, we were in no doubt that the little golden cube had done this. What else might it do? It was clearly a device to value.

I felt a need to protect it. "Charls, do you think we should move it to a safer place? In case it gets – um, damaged?"

He considered the idea for a moment, then sent: "I understand your fears, Keira; however it might cause comment if it is moved – it has been in that position for so long."

"Would it matter?" I said. "Symion is gone – surely you do not suspect anyone else in the manor?"

"No, I don't; however we have had one violent and successful attempt to breach the manor's security, and I can't rule out another."

"Then surely it is wiser to remove it from one of the public rooms, and keep it with one of us, or hide it in one of our rooms?" I argued.

Tissa agreed with me, to my surprise.

"I think Keira is right," she said. "If it's important – and it seems that it is – then you should look after it, not leave it out for anyone to take."

"I think you should keep the cube with you, Charls. It's small enough to hide in a pocket. And I wonder if I should perhaps remove the map to my room?" I suggested.

"Let's go and get the map," Charls said.

We trooped back to the library, and I retrieved the map, tucking it under my arm. Charls took the paperweight from me, and slipped it into a zipped trouser pocket. I idly wondered if this beautiful manor house, Charls' home, contained any other useful devices? *Yes.* Oh – I hadn't really expected an answer! I bit back a laugh.

I asked: Where? What am I looking for? No answer. I was getting used to that. We would receive what we needed at the appropriate time, so long as we remained in touch with our intuition, and acted when we recognised a synchronicity. Lovelight, the Ascended Reikans, the extraordinary objects . . . and of course, us, the players in the game . . . we all had our part to play, like musicians in an orchestra. But – who was the conductor?

~~~

Jason checked on Keira again. Still glowing. Still unconscious. He shrugged. Well, he'd just have to trust that Keira would do whatever was needed, so that she could eventually return to him.

"Where exactly is Keira?" he asked of his spectral mentor. Might he at least know that?

"She is, as I have said, in a parallel world. No–one else from this world can enter it. No, not even you," she added, forestalling Jason's question. "Think of this stone circle as a portal, if you like; a locked portal, with the key being Keira's genetic code.

"The name of the place where she is currently located is Cordello. I come from a neighbouring, allied land named Reika. It's spelt R–e–i–k–a." Lady Aida watched him, waiting expectantly.

Jason waited, too. Was that supposed to mean something to him? Then it clicked. "It's an anagram! Of Keira's name!"

"So it is. Coincidence, isn't it?"

137

"Um. Well, Keira attempted to explain to me about coincidences. She said . . . I think I have this right . . . that if you see a coincidence in the right way, and treat it as something significant, then it becomes a synchronicity. And that can help guide you in your life. Does that make sense?"

"Perfect sense. You see, you were a reluctant student, but you have absorbed some of Keira's learning. It will help her. It will help you. So yes, Reika and Keira have been inextricably connected on many levels since long before her birth. What do you think about that?"

He considered the question. "Well, as if some things are 'arranged' for us before we are born, I suppose."

Lady Aida nodded. "Exactly. And once we are born, we mostly forget the decisions that we made. Some remember sooner than others. Keira has begun to remember. My race, the Reikans, awakened to our true destiny much earlier than other lands. There are none of us left living in their world now."

"Then how . . .?" asked Jason, feeling very confused.

"We had completed our learning on that plane. We are now in a different form of existence on a plane which the Cordellans and their neighbours cannot see. They would say that we have 'ascended'. I think it puzzled them a bit when we all vanished overnight, city and all."

Yikes. "So . . . does that mean angels and stuff are all real then?" he asked, feeling a bit out of his depth again. He could really do with Keira's help right about now!

"Oh yes." Lady Aida smiled gently at him, and that smile seemed to light him up inside. He felt all gooey and soft. He began to smile himself, unable to stop his lips curving upwards. He sighed, and closed his eyes, drinking in the sensation.

CHAPTER 17

Back in my room, I found the perfect hiding place for the map. No–one would find it, or have any idea of where to look. I felt a sense of relief knowing that the cube and the map were being concealed. After hiding it, I returned to the hall, intending to spend some time with Charls, hoping to relax and chat. I paused outside of the door leading to the morning room, as I could hear Tissa and Charls talking in low tones, then Tissa let out a sudden burst of laughter. More quiet talking. Then silence.

What was . . .? Oh. After hearing a long sigh from Tissa, followed by a low throaty giggle, I turned quickly away, feeling my face flush. I had no wish to intrude upon their private moments. I didn't know why they weren't communicating telepathically – perhaps they enjoyed listening to each other's voices? I moved away from the door, and hesitated in the middle of the hall.

Where to go? The library was free. But, perversely, I didn't feel like reading, I wanted to talk . . . or to walk. I felt frustrated from being cooped up in the manor, a third wheel to Charls' and Tissa's blossoming relationship. Guards remained on duty at all exit doors, so I was effectively trapped indoors. I let out a silent puff of irritation. Then I had an idea. Excitement bubbled in my chest.

Feeling like an errant schoolchild about to play truant, I returned to my bedroom, and cautiously peeked out of the window. The guards were patrolling some distance away. Watching, I saw them head around the back corner of the house. They were looking for intruders coming *towards* the manor, not trying to prevent me from getting *out*. On some level I knew what I did next was rash; I simply couldn't help myself.

I raised the sash window, grateful that it was kept in good condition, so did not squeak. Peering out, I saw a stubby stone ledge running the full width of the window, and, as I had suspected, only a short drop to the ground. Conveniently, short grass had been allowed to grow up to the walls of the house, so I even had a soft landing – and would leave no footprints on the dry turf.

I climbed out onto the ledge, jumped lightly to the ground, and ran as far as the corner leading around to the front of the manor. I heard heavy footsteps close by – the guards shuffling around near the front doors. Now where would I go? The other guards could return to my window at any moment, and I would be in plain view. My heart pounded with the urgency of having to move. The front guards fell silent. Maybe they had gone back inside? I risked a peek around the brickwork, was relieved to see my way clear.

I ran across the front of the house as quickly as I was able to, hoping my feet would make little noise on the gravel of the drive. I got away with it, to my relief. I ducked down as I reached the library window in case Charls and Tissa had migrated there from the morning room. I rounded the next corner, keen to avoid the front–of–house guards.

Still undetected, I arrived at the fountain, and then faced an open stretch of path into the gardens. The path was lined with the topiary trees . . . but I might still be spotted if I headed that way.

Wait. The orangery. That was close by, to my right, and provided better cover. I dashed to the door closest to me, the one located furthest from the morning room. Keeping low, I peered in through the glass set into the door, checking that the orangery was not already occupied. Good, it was empty. I cautiously tried the handle. It squeaked a little and I winced at the sound. The door opened, and I crept inside, still bending at the waist in case I could be seen through the door at the far end.

So far, so good. Apart from my forced sojourn to the woods last night, I had been hidden indoors for days. This was still inside, but at least I was now among leafy green plants, the scents of earth and citrus and wood, the musical soft patter of the water falling from the sprinkler heads. *Life.* I had needed to renew my connection to Nature.

I found a bench that was hidden from the other door by tall orange trees set in chunky square wooden tubs. With gratitude, I sat and let myself absorb the energies of the trees, water and earth. My eyes closed, I let myself drift, hearing only the steady hiss of the falling water. In my mind, I connected the sound with the waterfall that I'd seen on my walk from the caves to this house. I saw myself walking through the heavy curtain of white water, through rainbows, to a sacred and secret space behind the cascade. Giving my imagination free rein, I explored, finding a thick ledge of rock which led deeper into the hill to dry caves and tunnels.

~~~

I dreamed of dark secret passageways that twisted and turned under ageless rock; of ancient magical symbols that shifted and shimmered before my eyes; of mysterious people that I could not see or hear clearly. I woke with a start, feeling very foolish for having fallen asleep *here*, where I most definitely should *not* have

141

been. I relaxed slightly when I realised that the dream, although a figment of my imagination, may also be providing me with advance guidance, with information that I may need in the future. I filed the details away in my mind.

My last 'helpful' dream had been here, in the orangery, so maybe this calm, restful, green place was a source of inspiration for me. I would suggest to Charls that I be allowed to spend more time here.

Feeling a little shaky from having awakened so suddenly, I gave myself a couple of minutes to regroup and to feel properly back in my body. Then I turned my mind to the problem of how to return to my room. Oh yes, Keira, you fool – you acted first, and thought much, *much* later.

It was still bright daylight, not even lunchtime. I may not have even been missed yet. Particularly if Charls and Tissa were still lost in each other. I decided that the safest route was likely to be to retrace my steps. I should be able to manage the jump to my window–ledge . . . as long as the guards co–operated with my plan!

I bent double again and crept to the orangery door through which I had entered. The squeak sounded louder this time, but I had no choice but to open the door, and sneak through it.

I heard voices coming towards me. Panicking, I backed into the orangery, pulling the door to. I dared not risk fully closing it; that squeak would surely give me away.

My luck ran out like the final grains of trickling sand in an hourglass. Charls and Tissa were heading directly towards the orangery. They were deep in conversation, heads almost touching. Suddenly, a small bright bird, with wings coloured like rainbows, flapped noisily from a tree at the wood's edge. Tissa made an exclamation, pulling at Charls' arm, and they veered away from the house perimeter – and my hiding place – walking instead towards the wood. I silently thanked whatever had prompted the bird to take flight.

I released the breath I'd been holding, but I dared not move yet in case they heard me, or caught sight of my movement from their peripheral vision. When they had passed beyond the treeline, and had disappeared from view, I crept from the orangery, tiptoed around the corner of the house, and ducked under the library window. I would *never* do this again, I promised myself. Any future visits outdoors would be with Charls' knowledge; the adrenaline was taking my energy away from my muscles and I was running on unresponsive rubber legs.

I made it across the driveway to the next corner without being noticed. I would be so glad to get back into my room. And I was only scared of Charls' reaction if he found out. What would have happened if one of Karn's scouts had seen me, and taken a chance? I had been so childish, so thoughtless. I had been rescued last night and here I was running around in the open!

Hearing nothing, I poked my head around the edge of the brick, and pulled it back sharply. One guard was stood outside my window; he'd been looking the other way, but my brief glimpse had revealed that his head was swivelling in my direction. I had to move soon, in case the front door guards exited and saw me.

Oh come on, *move!* I willed him. My appeal had the effect I needed; the next time I checked, he was walking to the far corner. Now or never, Keira!

I dashed to my window, glad that the dense grass and my soft–soled shoes did not betray me with any noise.

Pumped with adrenaline, I leapt onto my window ledge, quickly raised the window and almost fell inside. I reached up to pull the window down, and collapsed in a breathless heap on the carpet below the window sill. I was exhausted. Muscles weary, I reached up to lock the window again, knowing that I'd forget if I didn't do it now. I closed the curtains.

I crawled to the bed, removed my clothes to allow my body to breathe and cool down, and curled up on the bedspread, as feelings of pure relief swept through me. Charls and Tissa could take care of themselves out in the open; I was no warrior, had no combat skills. Here, I was safe. I would only be going outside again when I had Charls or Tissa with me. Then I decided that continued self–blame would serve no useful purpose, and tried to forgive myself. Lesson learned; time to move on!

Later, when my rumbling stomach persuaded me that it was time for lunch, I dressed, and padded into the hall to see if my host had returned. I checked all of the downstairs rooms, but there was no sign of either Charls or Tissa.

I settled into the library to wait.

When they returned, Tissa was bubbling with excitement. The rainbow bird, known as the Cantura, was extremely rare, and only ever seen at times of great change; it was considered a good sign. I showed interest in all the right places as she described the magnificent plumage that I, too, had seen, even though only briefly.

I ate, and we drank more tea, before Charls suggested I might enjoy a trip outdoors, provided we were all vigilant. I nearly hung my head with shame. He didn't comment as my cheeks flushed with embarrassment. I had little option but to smile and agree that it was a lovely idea. We exited from the morning room, through the magically–replaced glass doors, and made our way down the steps leading from the patio to the gardens. I could see the orangery out of the corner of my left eye. I resolutely refused to look at it, keeping my eyes on the trees.

~~~

Jason allowed himself only a short moment to bask in the gentle, comforting energy before willing his eyes open. He knew that he could not selfishly doze off whilst Keira was off saving the world – well, one world, anyway. With a struggle, he brought his attention back to Lady Aida and their ongoing discussion.

"Is there any way that I can help Keira? From here, I mean," he added hastily, in case Lady Aida thought he hadn't been paying attention.

"Well, yes there is a way, Jason," Lady Aida replied. "Right now, it would be helpful if you think of Keira as being strong, successful, and positive. See her in your mind's eye, and in all of your thoughts, as if she is completely in tune with her intuition. It is that – her intuition – which is guiding her. We can pass insights to her as long as she remains attuned to her inner guidance system. We are protecting her and those working with her. But true success in her mission can only come if she trusts and acts upon her instincts."

"Okay. I can do that. Do I have to go into a trance or anything? Keira said I should learn to meditate, but it always seemed –" He stopped, feeling foolish.

"Seemed what, dear?"

"Well . . . a bit of a waste of time," he finished, sheepishly.

"Oh!" Lady Aida laughed, a beautiful melodic sound. "Many people think it's a waste of time. Until they practice it, and find themselves calmer, more relaxed, more in tune with their intuition; the benefits are so many. No, you do not need to meditate. Just try to keep your thoughts of her positive and upbeat. No fear, worry, or anger. Just 'good thoughts'. And don't worry, you will find that you slip up occasionally. You just do the best that you can, and you will find it gets easier."

"Keira always said my glass was half–empty, and hers half–full. She was always better at this stuff than me." He caught the warning look in Lady Aida's eye. "But I can catch up; from now on, I will be positive."

Lady Aida smiled and he felt happy that he'd pleased her. She had that effect on you. His boss could learn a thing or two from Lady Aida. Feeling negativity sneak up on him at the thought of his job, he mentally turned his back on it, and brought his focus back to Keira . . . and the wonderful ascended being seated in front of him.

~~~

Charls and Tissa were leading me towards the woods where they had walked earlier.

"The bird was truly amazing, Keira! You wouldn't believe how magnificent the Cantura's wings were. The Cantura has always been such a strong symbol of hope, hasn't it, Charls? And I so want you to see it!" Tissa's enthusiasm was infectious, and I found myself grinning. There was no guarantee we *would* see the almost legendary bird; however, it might have a nest or a mate nearby. Naturally, the colourful bird was a male, with the female being a smaller, dun–coloured creature.

Inside the wooded area, the air was cool and had a softer, moist quality to it. Breathing it in deeply, I decided to make the most of every outdoor moment, to literally drink it in, and absorb it on every level. Keeping me in sight, Charls and Tissa moved away to a seat carved into a large oak–like tree. They started to talk softly, and I saw Charls entwine his fingers with Tissa's. I perched on a small wooden seat a small distance away, turning away to give them privacy.

I wondered if Charls had told Tissa of our experience with the Ascended Reikan. I realised that I wanted him to keep it between us. Of course he would want to share things with Tissa, but I also felt the experience might be diminished by telling it to another; tarnished, even. I was not jealous of Tissa; but I did feel excluded. Charls was my friend, and since Tissa had moved into the manor, Charls and I had not been able to chat as we had before, just the two of us.

I missed him. My best friend in this world. I was lonely. Now that Charls and Tissa were a couple, *Charls did not need me as a friend.*

Noticing my slide into self–pity, I made an effort to lift my mood, to think more positively, to see the blessing in the situation. Charls was happy, after being lost and alone for too many years. Tissa was happy. They were a good match. How could I fail to be happy for them? At that point, my longing for Jason, my best friend in my own world, became so strong that I thought my heart would tear apart. I struggled to keep the tears at bay. I would *not* cry. I concentrated on my breathing, and connected with lovelight. I so needed the support at this moment.

I felt the familiar swirling, cool sensation above the top of my head, sensed the energy start to enter my body, flowing down into my arms and torso, then into my legs and feet. The tingling was comforting, but did not remove my loneliness, my feeling of *separateness*. I persisted with the connection, trusting that eventually it would bring me some feeling of consolation, a sense of peace, some measure of tranquillity. Finally, my slow and regular breathing allowed my body to relax a little, and my mind to follow its example. I *must* focus on keeping my energy high. I was here to do a job – to save lovelight. My own personal feelings were not important.

However, I remembered what Charls had said about suppressing feelings – which only caused blocks in the energy field, and potentially issues with health. Somehow I had to accept these feelings, not push them away. To allow them. To stop resisting them. I mentally asked lovelight to assist me with the process. Immediately, I felt the energy soften, almost as if it was soothing me. My body soon felt completely at ease, and I knew without any doubt that I was supported and cared for by this energy. I sensed that I would have to rely on my own resources to keep myself happy. I could not place the burden of that onto anyone else. It was my task, and mine alone.

Recognising that truth, I felt the weight on my chest lift, and could feel the area around my heart expand and open, like a box opening up to let the light inside. This felt an important moment for me. Self–reliance in its truest form. My happiness was down to me – always.

The tears had receded, and I felt strong again. I lifted my head and let my eyes take in the beauty of the trees around me, let myself absorb more energy from the ancient woodland and the earth.

Out of the corner of my eye, movement caught my attention. Very slowly, I turned my head, and looked directly into the eye of the rainbow–winged Cantura.

I held my breath. Would it fly away? It wasn't very big, about the size of a dove, but the colours were *incredible.* They sparkled, shimmered and shone, even here in the shade. No wonder it was such a spectacle in flight. The Cantura tilted its head to one side, focusing on me. I kept completely still. It chirruped, hopped closer. And again. When it reached my feet, it lowered its beak to the ground before meeting my gaze again. It gave another perky chirrup before flying back into the trees.

What a gift. No sooner had the thought been expressed, than I noticed a small glass object near my feet. I was certain that it had not been there before the Cantura had approached me. Carefully, reverently, I leaned forward to retrieve my 'gift'. I held it gently in the palm of my hand.

It wasn't glass. I'm not sure what it was made of, but it was heavy for its small size. It was shaped like a sphere. Perhaps it was crystal? *Had the Ascended Reikans sent this to me? Was it another object with extraordinary properties?* As the possibility hit me, I couldn't hold in a gasp. As I had surmised, gifts were being presented to me at *just* the right time. Ah, beautiful synchronicity.

CHAPTER 18

"Keira! *Keira!* KEIRA!"

I jumped up from my seat, turning towards Charls' voice as I got to my feet. He sounded agitated, even anxious. Tissa, too, had risen from their tree–seat, and looked unhappy about something. I hurried towards them. We didn't normally use voice communication; why now?

"KEIRA! KEIRA?" Charls called again..

"I'm here!" I said out loud, puzzled. I was only a few feet away from them. They were looking at me! I realised then that they were looking *through* me. Why couldn't they see me? Or hear me?

"Keira, we can't see where you are," Tissa called. "We think we heard your voice, but we can't actually see you . . . what's going on?"

Tissa *thought* she heard my voice? I was well within speaking range. I tried mentally communicating with Charls but could not seem to get a link. It was as if there was a barrier of thick fog between us. I tried sending my thoughts to Tissa, but experienced the same block. What on earth was disrupting it?

Then I remembered the crystal sphere clutched in my hand. I opened my hand, bending down to place the sphere carefully on the grass just in front of my shoe.

"There you are!" Charls exclaimed. Tissa visibly sighed with relief.

"I was here the whole time," I advised, "but I think this may have some helpful properties." I knelt down on the grass, Charls and Tissa crouching down opposite me. We stared at the little crystal object.

"What on earth is it?" said Tissa, reverting to mental

communication.

"Where did you get it?" asked Charls.

"One at a time!" I smiled. "The Cantura bird gave it to me."

"*Gave* it to you?" Charls sent.

"Yes! It hopped up to my feet, and dropped the sphere. Then it flew away."

"We didn't see the bird until just a moment ago," Tissa remarked.

Charls said, "Just like we didn't see Keira until she put the sphere down. I think this has invisibility properties. And some sound inhibition properties, too, I believe."

That made sense. "It also stops mind–communication," I added. I wondered if Charls was thinking along the same lines that I was . . .

He sent: "This could come in handy as a means of accessing information without being observed."

"My thoughts exactly!" I returned. "We'd need to be careful, though. You thought you could hear me when I spoke aloud."

"It *was* very faint," acknowledged Tissa. "As if you were calling out from a great distance or from the depths of a tunnel."

"Yes," agreed Charls. "We had no idea whatsoever that you were almost right in front of us. We could have walked right into you!"

I was thinking. "So how do we stop it from making us invisible – and inaudible – when we are carrying it?"

"I can solve that! Well, I think I can," Charls amended. "I have a small bag, made of a rare material. Such bags have reportedly been used in the past to transport objects thought to contain extraordinary properties. I had not expected to ever use it, but this seems like a good time. May I?" he said, as he reached

151

for the little sphere. I nodded. He picked the crystal globe up from the grass, and immediately vanished. Even though I was expecting it, I still felt surprise at his disappearance.

I looked at Tissa. "Let's go, then, since we can't see Charls."

We walked back to the house, each of us distracted by our own thoughts. The morning room doors ahead of us opened as if by unseen hands – which they were – and we followed through, Tissa securing them once we were inside the room.

"It's odd being unable to contact Charls with my thoughts," she sent to me.

"I know," I replied. "I felt as though a deep mist had come down and shut everyone out; it's a strange feeling!"

Charls re–entered the room, and took a chair opposite me. Tissa perched on the arm. "We'll have to come up with a plan to use that little device to our advantage," he stated. "Meanwhile, I have stored it somewhere very safe. And the bag works."

"How can you tell?" I queried, wondering how he had been able to test it.

"Because the sphere is somewhere on my person!" Charls grinned.

"Let's hope we can all remember where we've stored the rest of these precious items," I said. "Usually when I put something in a safe place, I forget where I put it! That was a joke," I added hastily, noticing Charls' startled reaction. Well, almost a joke. Perhaps it was just as well I'd only had the map to hide.

~~~

Jason found it was quite easy to envision Keira being strong and positive. It was her natural state of mind, although of course she dipped into sadness occasionally. She was philosophical about it; you take the downs with the ups and make the best of them that you can. The more that he thought about it, the more he realised that Keira was a good choice for any mission requiring positive thinking. She was certainly more upbeat and accepting of situations than he. She often found a good aspect to things that he had deemed as bad or worthless. Pride surged in his chest. His Keira, his beautiful girl, was acting out a legend in another world!

A smile playing on his lips, he saw her walking boldly, making good decisions, using both her common sense and her deep sense of compassion. He heard her giving instructions, putting people at their ease, discussing and resolving tense situations with her calm and peaceful manner. The more he thought of her in this role, the more he loved her, and the easier it became to see her continuing to act in tune with her intuition. He still believed that women's intuition was probably more sound than men's – at least in most cases – and most certainly in his. But he was learning, with Lady Aida's help, and when he and Keira were reunited, he would show Keira just how far he had come.

Then, unaccountably, he felt cold, a little dark, a little lost. Where did those feelings come from? The edge of a memory, the merest fragment, whispered to him. He shivered, despite the warm environment of his bubble. Then he connected the shard of the memory with The Nightmare.

"Jason," Lady Aida called softly, "how are you doing?"

He noticed that he had buried his head in his hands.

Now he dropped his hands and raised his head, meeting his guide's gaze directly. She still glowed an amazingly soft, luminous white, but now he could see her features quite clearly. She had that ageless beauty associated with some of the gracefully ageing women he saw on television. The ones who had kept away from cosmetic surgery, and looked like normal people, their facial lines an enhancement rather than a tragedy.

Lady Aida had fine cheekbones, beautiful warm, grey eyes, and curling silvered–blonde hair that fell behind her shoulders. The ethereal glow that suffused her helped, of course; it was like being cast in soft lighting. But she was lovely, and very easy on the eye. He knew that shouldn't be important – but somehow it helped. If she had looked like an old hag, maybe he'd now be finding it harder to trust her? Her smile was so full of warmth, and genuine compassion, that he couldn't help but feel comforted and safe in her presence.

Should he tell her?

~~~

Next morning, Charls and Tissa were to meet with the Elder and with the other lords. Charls and Tissa had a lot of new information to impart, and as I had resolved to remain indoors, and to behave sensibly, I remained in the library. As the bookcase–door closed behind them, I scanned the bookshelves for something to read until they returned. One book in particular caught my attention, one that I had not noticed before. There was, perhaps, a reason that I had noted it now.

It was a small volume, its cover and spine a faded dark red embossed with a gold–threaded pattern. I pulled the book gently from the shelf. The title read: "A History of

Cordello." As I had several hours to kill, I thought I may as well get some background to my temporary home. I made myself comfortable in my usual chair, and opened the front cover. An electric jolt coursed through my body as I made a connection with the book's owner. Karn. I recognised the signature of his energy. I closed my eyes and awaited the vision.

This time, I saw through Karn's eyes the very room in which I was now seated. Karn was standing near the window, his eyes looking out at, but not seeing, the garden. He – and my viewpoint – turned; I saw with surprise that Symion was standing just a short distance away. He looked worried, almost distraught.

I nearly jumped out of my skin when I heard Karn's thoughts to Symion. I had not previously been privy to the sent or spoken words in these visions.

"So. You agree to do this, Symion?"

"Y–yes, Lord Karn – but . . . what if Lord Charls –"

"Don't worry about Charls. Just keep out of sight whenever you use the device, and make sure you are not overheard. You know what will happen if you fail to report everything that you notice. I'm quite sure you don't want your dirty little secret to be . . . exposed . . .?"

Symion was visibly shaking. "Of course not, my lord. I will tell you everything that happens. But what if no lady comes? What if the legend is false? I cannot report to you of someone who doesn't exist."

What secret was Karn blackmailing him with? I wondered. Presumably, 'the lady' referred to me. *Yes.*

"Oh, she exists . . . our legends have never lied yet. I will not be here for much longer. Vornen is waiting for its new leader – and its new annexed Cordellan lands. With lovelight under my control, I can rule both territories without opposition. If you are discovered,

155

Symion, then you are on your own. Try to make your way to Vornen. I don't much care either way. You should be thoroughly ashamed of yourself." I could almost hear the sneer through the mental communication.

Symion averted his eyes; I thought that I – through Karn's eyes – had seen liquid glistening. Symion *was* ashamed, I felt. But of what?

"Lord Karn – please, let Sulla and Jenara go. They have done nothing wrong. The fault was all mine –"

"Indeed it was," Karn cut in. "And now you are being punished for your transgressions. They will continue to be held under house arrest until you have fulfilled your part. Don't worry, they are allowed a bath once a fortnight, and your little daughter has a toy to keep her amused. Your wife is fair to look at; I could be tempted by her myself." Karn laughed. Symion's tears finally fell.

"Oh, come. They are still alive. Remember that, and be grateful. Now. Keep the device safe, don't misplace it. This will be our last discussion on this matter – understood?"

"Yes, my lord."

"Get out of my sight. I have things to do."

Symion walked quickly from the library, closing the door behind him. I felt Karn sigh, and he turned again to look, unseeing, through the window. I doubt he'd notice the beauty of the Cantura bird if it flew right past the window. What a nasty piece of work he was!

The vision faded, and I let the book fall closed. I would catch up on Cordellan history later. For now, I was musing over what I had seen – and 'heard' – and wondering how it would fit in with the plans being made at the meeting. Innocent lives were at stake. Hostages. I somehow doubted that they would be freed when – if – Symion reached Vornen.

Feeling unaccountably tired after my vision, I dozed off, the book slipping from my hands into my lap.

I was awakened by the bookcase–door opening and Tissa's and Charls' return. Their eyes were bright, and Tissa looked as if she had been very thoroughly kissed. Hanky panky in the passageways, I thought with a grin. Well, why not?

Charls' face took on a sombre countenance as he related the outcome of the meeting. "The Elder and the Meeting were very pleased with your progress, Keira. You are proficient with lovelight, your connections with objects are providing us with valuable information, and your healing work is also excellent. Keira, I realise that our shared experience with the Reikan was . . . special . . . but clearly, I had to relate it to the Meeting. I hope you don't mind that I shared it?"

I shook my head. *Liar*, I thought.

"Charls had mentioned it to me previously," Tissa sent. "But he also let me know that he had only told me an outline of your encounter; he said that the details were too amazing to put into words. He hasn't shared those with anyone."

I was glad that she and Charls understood how strongly I felt about the Ascended Reikan's being with us, how sacred it had felt. I was grateful to Charls for respecting those feelings. Perhaps I had not lost my friend after all.

"Keira . . ." Charls began, then stopped. He looked at Tissa. Uh–oh. Something was up. I waited expectantly.

"What Charls is trying to say," Tissa continued, "is that we – all of us – think it's time that you played a greater role in what is happening. In what is to come. We believe that you have the courage, the strength, the

157

skills, and of course your place in the legend – we think that you are the best person –"

"The best person to do what?" I asked.

CHAPTER 19

Charls lowered himself into the chair facing me, and looked directly into my eyes. "We are all agreed that you should take custody of the Canturan sphere. That you should embark on a quest to Vornen."

My eyes widened. *Me?* I had assumed that my role was background support, not heroine. I felt uneasiness steal up through my legs and into my body.

Charls continued. "Under the protection of the Ascended Reikans, lovelight, and the properties of the sphere, we are hoping that you will agree to proceed to the border at Vornen. From there, you will be guided by your intuition. You will be able to glean information about scouts, soldiers, resources, and plans; information that we cannot otherwise ascertain, even through your visions. You will then return for debriefing, and we can prepare our soldiers and warriors for the battle for lovelight."

My uneasiness flared to horror in an instant. It sounded as if the Meeting had decided that combat was the only option through which Karn would be defeated. This felt wrong, so wrong. I could not agree to this. I stood up, feeling more resolute than I had ever felt in my life.

"No, Charls. I won't do this. I know with my heart, with my soul, that entering into battle is wrong. It could lead to the destruction of your people, Cordello, lovelight, and . . . you. My *instinct* is guiding me right now, and it is telling me very clearly not to go. *This is not the way.*"

Charls looked at me, astonished. Tissa touched Charls on the arm and sent, "I told you she would not agree. It is a dangerous assignment, and we must expect her to be fearful –"

"I am not a coward," I countered. "I just *know* that this plan is completely wrong. We need to think of something else. This is not what I am here for. I refuse to do this."

"But, Keira, how else can we win?" Charls responded. "We have already met with several combative episodes even since your arrival – scouting, which led to my injury if you recall? Then the tunnel fracas in which Tissa was captured and good lives were lost. Intruders in the morning room, which led to *your* capture. Karn quite obviously is upping the odds, is becoming more and more desperate for power, for Cordello, for lovelight. We are past diplomacy and negotiation. We need information, and we need to enter into battle to maintain our sovereignty."

"No, Charls. There will be a better way," I argued. I knew that I was right. Every cell in my body was screaming at me to prevent further bloodshed, to explore other opportunities, other ideas. I could only follow my heart in this. "We just need to use lovelight and the Ascended Reikans to help us to find that way."

I could sense Charls' disappointment in me, but I would not back down. I would not be part of it. I realised that I had not yet had a chance to relate to Charls the nature of my latest vision. Knowing the thoughts of both parties in a vision could be important.

"Before we continue, something else has happened; another vision," I began. I explained how the scene had played out, emphasising that I had 'heard' the entire mental conversation between Karn and Symion. "So, if I can hear conversations, I may be able to *get information* without going anywhere, or risking anyone's life. We

160

may be able to negotiate using the sphere . . . we don't know the full potential of it, yet!"

Charls interrupted. "I agree that it may be significant that you are now receiving words, but I don't see how that helps –"

"What I also believe," I broke in, "is that I may be able to contact Karn through the book, or perhaps his belt, and persuade him to give up this destructive ambition."

Charls was incredulous. "Even after hearing that he has Symion's wife and child held hostage? Keira, have you lost your mind? He's pure evil. He murdered our father – now we know that was premeditated! Now you tell us that he has taken hostages, is using blackmail! He wants to annexe Cordello! Have I missed anything out?"

"No," I replied. "No, you haven't. But there is some good in everyone. I believe I can find it, and bring him round."

Charls stood up. His face was thunderous. "You don't know him, Keira. You have seen him in action with Symion – and yet still want to give him a second chance. Well, I can't do it. Whatever plan you have, you'll have to do it alone. There is no longer any alternative to war. Strategies are already in place, and if you won't go to Vornen, then Tissa will."

Tissa's face flushed. "Me? But – I'm a warrior, not a spy. I don't hide behind invisibility spheres; I march with my head held high and my sword at the ready!" She shook her head proudly.

"Tissa, if Keira won't go – and we can't force her to – then you will have to take her place," Charls stated.

Tissa turned to look at me, her eyes hard, her lips clamped in a thin line.

Now I was on the wrong side of Tissa, a place I had no

161

wish to be. She turned her attention back to Charls. There was no love in her face now, no warmth in her voice.

"If you are ordering me to go to Vornen, my lord, then to Vornen I shall go. But I will go on my own terms. The Canturan sphere remains here. I will leave in the morning."

She stalked out of the room without another look at Charls.

He looked at me, his face a tight mask, then marched after her.

I was left alone. I *felt* alone. Had I done the right thing? Now Tissa would be heading to Vornen, unprotected by the sphere. I sighed. All I could do was raise my energy, ask lovelight and the Ascended Reikans to protect her, to protect lovelight, to assist us in whatever way would lead to the best outcome. I could do no more. But I didn't feel any sense of victory. I felt leaden, exhausted, and sad. I knew that however positive I managed to feel, there would likely be a loss of life.

And – for now, at least – it felt as if this house was divided three ways. We should be working together, not fighting each other. With a heavy heart, I returned to my room, and connected with lovelight. I had a lot of work to do.

~~~

I remained in my room until the next morning. What reason had I to leave it? My appetite had fled. The atmosphere of the manor house was edgy and prickly; it was a tangibly unpleasant sensation. I could virtually feel the animosity directed towards me from Tissa's room on the floor above. I could sense the cold disappointment that Charls was feeling. Now he had to send his lover to spy on Vornen, instead of risking 'just the girl from the other world'.

Well, he *did* have a choice, I reminded myself. He was *choosing* to believe that he had none. He had no perspective. His brother had murdered their father. His fiancée had died as a direct consequence. Cordello was under threat. Lovelight was the prize sought by his brother. Charls had not forgiven Karn – nor would he. With so much lost, and so much at stake, he was blinded to any other path.

But I – I had no such emotional baggage. The feeling that further combat should be avoided was so strong within me that I had no spirit to over–ride it; it was as though the power of peace consumed me. And I thought that to be a good thing.

I continued connecting with lovelight, keeping my energy as high as possible. I spent many hours in meditation, visualising a peaceful resolution. The fact that I had no idea how this was to be achieved was irrelevant, I knew. All I had to do was to keep the faith – keep intending and expecting matters to be solved through negotiation and peaceful means. No–one else had to die.

Maybe Charls' strong negative feelings towards me would moderate once Tissa had left. Then again, maybe he'd worry about her, and vent his anxiety towards me. I chose to believe the former, more positive option. I hoped I would be permitted to spend some time outdoors again. If Charls accompanied me, I felt it would be an uneasy companionship. But I also knew that time outdoors would help me with my quest for peace; I was not thinking simply of my own pleasure or comfort.

Hearing footsteps in the hall, I tensed. Tissa? The heavy front doors were slammed shut with considerable force.

She'd gone. I let out a quick sigh of relief. A minute later, I heard a tap at my bedroom door. I hesitated, then reluctantly rose to open it.

"Charls," I acknowledged. "Come in." I stood back to allow him to enter. He closed the door behind him, leaning against it. He looked uncomfortable, keeping distance between us. I probably looked on edge, too.

"Keira, I'm sorry I was so rude yesterday. I still can't agree with your policy of relying on negotiation, not at this late stage in the game. But . . . I do not wish to spend the remainder of your time here at odds with one another. We will need to find a way of being together without antipathy. I don't want to fight with *you.* "

Since I had already come to this conclusion myself, I did not hesitate in agreeing. "I don't want to fight with you, either, Charls. You are my only friend, here, remember? My stay here would be very lonely if we were antagonists, and not friends. You do respect my decision, though?"

"I respect it, even if I cannot agree with it. Do you, in turn, respect mine? Allow me to proceed with our plans?"

"I *do* honour your decision, Charls. But I will continue to work with the lighter forces in your world, and I will not stop until lovelight is safe. Can you also respect that? Please?"

He looked at me, and nodded. He held his arms out to me. I walked towards him and we had a brief, awkward hug to cement our renewed friendship. I just hoped our truce would last. We had some difficult times ahead, even *with* lovelight and positive thinking.

~~~

"Jason? My dear, you know that you can trust me. If something is bothering you, then accept it as a synchronicity. I am here to help you learn. So let's talk. What can I do?"

Where did he start? At the beginning, he supposed.

"I have a recurring dream. Well, a nightmare, really. Not about work, although I dream of that too, and that's never a good dream, either. But the recurring one –"

"Yes?" queried Lady Aida, very softly.

"It frightens me. Really frightens me. I wake up sweating, sometimes even crying. I can't always remember it. But the one theme that seems to run through them all is of me being blindfolded and bound, then moved to a dark place where there is not even a pinprick of light. It smells earthy, damp, as if I'm underground. I feel as if I'm being buried alive." He shivered again.

"I am left there for what seems like an eternity. It is . . . unbearably lonely. There is no light, no laughter, no sound, no joy. It's dark, silent, cold; there's nothing. Just me and the sound of my breathing. I feel like I'll go mad."

"And then?" asked Lady Aida, when Jason paused.

"And then I hear voices. Loads of them, all talking at once. None of them make any sense; I can't hear individual words or sentences. It's like they're all talking in languages that I don't understand. I only speak English and a bit of French, anyway. But they're all jabbering away, competing for attention. They get louder and louder until it feels like my head will burst.

165

After the silence, it's overwhelming – it's horrible. I just want it to stop."

"Have you told Keira of this dream, Jason?"

"Bits of it."

"And what was her response?"

"She wasn't sure, really. But she thought it might be a metaphor for something. I've had this dream since I was a kid, so it's nothing to do with work. I don't know where it came from, but it terrifies me."

"And why do you think you have remembered it now? On this night?" asked Lady Aida.

Jason thought. "Well, I guess it's because you're here, helping me. Working out the dream will help me progress in some way; do you think that's it?"

"Yes, I do. Keira is certainly right in that dreams are often metaphors for something we need to work through in our waking lives; although some dreams are prophetic or warning signs, most are the brain simply trying to make sense of life whilst your analytical mind is 'out of the way'."

That made sense. His mind was normally allowed to roam freely through work or money concerns, and mundane stuff like paying his credit card bill or remembering to buy washing powder. Not much soul–searching, it had to be said.

He allowed his mind to wander now into the edges of the dream, to pick at the periphery for any useful pearls of wisdom.

Gradually, smoothly, ideas slipped in and wound themselves together, becoming a thread that he could clutch onto.

"I'm fairly sure that being buried alive in silence is a metaphor for me feeling lost and forgotten, and unprotected and unloved," Jason pronounced, with quiet confidence. "I feel like a tiny, insignificant being, of no value. Worthless."

"And the voices?"

"They're telling me that I feel besieged by too many conflicting, worthless demands, with no chance of pleasing anybody." That's how it seemed to him, anyway, he thought, feeling a sense of wonder at these new insights.

"And how does the dream end?" Lady Aida gently probed.

"It just ends. I wake up – next to Keira. She's sleeping, her face soft, her hair tumbled across the pillow. I feel safe and secure, seeing her there. But I think I still need to work on being able to fend off the 'demons', the 'demands'. I feel as if I've always let people push me to do what they want me to do, without really working out what I want, or what I think is best. Keira's the only person who allows me to be myself."

"So," asked Lady Aida, "who are you at other times, Jason?"

He stared at her. What a strange question!

Lady Aida remained quiet, waiting. Clearly, she wasn't satisfied with his silence.

He reconsidered the question, discovered a new truth. "Perhaps not myself . . . it's as if I tried to be . . . I can't really explain it . . ."

"Who are you with your parents, Jason, if you are yourself only with Keira?" probed his light–filled guide.

"I'm who I think they want me to be . . ."

"And with your colleagues?"

"The same . . . I put on a mask to hide my true thoughts and feelings. I'm scared – that if they know what I really think and feel, that they'll reject me!"

"And there we have it," said Lady Aida, her tone firm.

"You are getting a very clear message, Jason: it is time for you to set aside your disguises and your masks, and to work out what is important to you, decide who you want to be, and how you want you live your life. This is your trigger to make the change – to live authentically, to own your 'self', and to stand with confidence in your own truth. Your life is your own, to be lived your way. Don't you agree?"

Jason's eyes began to film with tears. He never cried! But this felt like a moment of – well, a changing reality. A time of profound insight. Almost as if he was waking up from the nightmare. He felt lighter, could actually feel joy bubbling in his chest. This was amazing! He nodded his agreement, the tears spilling onto his cheeks. He let them flow; they felt like a release.

"Yes, it's an incredible feeling, dear, when a human being realises that he has value for simply being alive; the power he has in being able to make decisions, creating the life he wants, minute by minute. It is so very precious, Jason, your life; every life. Do not squander it. Make your choices, stand by them, and move forward without fear. You are protected. You are loved. I am only here as a transient guide. But there are others like me here in your own world. Once you begin working with them, you will find your path becomes easier. They will support you, help you find further insights into your life, assist you in moving forward on your journey of awakening."

Jason felt a lump lodge in his throat and the tell–tale pricking at the corners of his eyes as tears again threatened.

Lady Aida had not finished. "Each being is a tiny piece of the universe, Jason, but the universe can not function without each of you. Small, yes; like one drop of water in a vast ocean . . . but each drop is vitally important, Jason. Think how the ocean has the power to erode rocks, to shift sand, to harbour and sustain life. A being is never insignificant. I hope you'll always remember that. It's a crucial message."

CHAPTER 20

The next few days passed slowly for me. Charls was often absent, working with his men, training for battle. I knew it was happening; for my part, I used my solitude to regularly connect with lovelight, visualising Charls and Tissa and the Cordellans being watched over by lovelight and the Ascended Reikans, keeping them safe, guiding them to act in the best way.

I also placed intentions that the best outcome would be found, with minimal injuries or loss of life. I willed Karn to give up his plans for domination of Cordello and lovelight. I visualised Vornen and Cordello living together peaceably, overseen by the lovelight energies and the guidance and support of the Ascended Reikans.

However, I found that being alone most of the time brought its own issues. Despite lovelight lifting my mood whilst I was connected, and even for some time afterwards, there were times when it was difficult not to brood and worry. I was keenly aware of the plans being made by the Cordellans. I had an instinctive horror of war, whatever the apparent justification. Charls and I still 'talked' occasionally – when he was here, in the manor – but conversation now felt strained; we were both aware of topics best avoided. We were both aware of words unsaid, questions unasked. There was a new reticence in our friendship. I no longer felt that I could share everything with him, as I had before, and I mourned that loss.

One sunny morning, after he'd returned from a meeting, Charls invited me to walk in the gardens with him. Keen for a change of scenery, and particularly for some time outside, I agreed. We took a different walk this time, heading towards one of the rose gardens. This was an informal riot of blooms, which covered every vertical support imaginable. Insects were busy at the centres of the flowers, reminding me that life was continuing, even when I wasn't watching. A wooden seat placed in a pergola gave us a place to sit and absorb the colour, scent and sounds surrounding us. A cool breeze lifted my hair, playing with the strands. With a sigh, I dropped to the seat and rested my back against the rear of the wooden structure, closing my eyes and allowing myself to become part of the garden.

Charls seated himself next to me, remaining silent. Although this was not the easy companionship that we had once enjoyed, I was grateful for this time, for all that we *could* share. Perhaps, in time, if events went in our favour, we might regain our previous level of friendship and ease. I certainly hoped so. I had no–one else to turn to; we were both each other's sole companion at mealtimes and in the evenings. He continued to be my only real friend in this world.

My thoughts drifted, as they sometimes did, back to Jason. I no longer worried about him; at least in relation to Cordello and its quest to protect lovelight. I did worry that he was eating properly, getting enough exercise, not drinking too much, and not feeling too stressed by my disappearance or all that had happened as a result of it. All the usual stuff that people concerned themselves with in *my* world. Of course, I was assuming that time was passing here at the same rate as at home. That I had actually *been* missed. Well, I couldn't do anything about that, so I made an attempt to refocus my thoughts on the here and now.

And in the here and now, the bees and insects continued to buzz and drone; the flowers continued to engulf me with their scent; the sun continued to cast its warming rays on my skin; the light wind continued to flirt with the ends of my hair, blowing them against my neck and cheek. As I became more aware of the details in the outdoor life around me, my body began to relax.

I then understood the phrase 'being in the moment'. I let myself believe that this was all there is, was, would ever be. Much as when the Ascended Reikan had reached out to me, embracing me in light and that wonderful feeling of oneness, so being fully receptive to my senses in this one moment led me temporarily back to that blissful state.

I then recalled the awe that I had felt on my downward journey from the stone circle to Reika. Remembered the feeling of being a body of pure light. Of floating in joy. Of feeling capable of anything, everything. I let the memory of those feelings flow through my mind and body, tried – without effort – to record the sensations for recall later, when I might need fast access to ultimate self–belief and extraordinary joy.

The warmth and the soporific effect of the drowsy sound of the insects gave me a platform from which to doze. I slipped easily into a light sleep, and began a dream which would have far–reaching consequences.

~~~

I was aware that I was dreaming. However, I had no power to alter the events within the dreamscape; I remained an observer, as I did with the visions that I was given. I was running along the village road; running hard, out of breath. Beside and behind me, a number of Cordellans hurried with me. I sensed fear, panic, danger. I could not see Charls, nor did I recognise Tissa's face among those people running alongside and behind me. I realised that I was at the front of the group. Was I leading them?

I felt that we were being pursued, and those hunting us were getting closer. The houses had been vandalised; I noticed with sadness broken windows and doors, and some dwellings were belching out smoke. Gardens had been trampled, fences and walls knocked over or demolished. There was no time to grieve for lost homes. We had run out of time. I knew that the Cordellans were looking to me for the next move.

Suddenly, a vivid image of the waterfall appeared in my dreaming mind. The picture was so sharp, sounded and looked so real, it was as though I was already there. I knew that the waterfall would lead us to safety. I knew that the map that I carried would be crucial. I knew that Charls would join us – but not yet. We continued to run, feeling so tired, wishing we could stop and rest, knowing that to do so would be suicidal. And I, for one, would not give up my life easily. I had too much to live for.

Then the image started to fade and I felt myself begin to awaken. At first I could still see fragments of the dream–scene, but now it was falling away from me, disappearing too *fast*. Feeling frustration, I tried to hold onto the images, knowing their importance, but they had gone. I reluctantly opened my eyes. For now, the sequence of the dream was etched into my memory. I had to remember the map if we were forced to flee the manor. And I wouldn't mind betting that the golden paperweight and crystalline sphere would also be useful; I hoped Charls continued to keep them safe.

I quietly turned towards Charls, and noted that he too was sleeping. I was glad. He had not been getting enough rest, was quietly concerned about his country, his people, and Tissa. I hoped he would feel new energy when he woke. I connected with lovelight and directed a little towards him for an extra boost. I think he had been too preoccupied to do any self–healing. Well, I could pick up the slack, and give him the support he needed.

The sun had started its slide towards the horizon, losing some of its warmth. The light breeze had strengthened and I shivered as it grazed my arms, giving me goosebumps. I placed my hand lightly on Charls' sleeve, giving him a gentle shake. He grunted, then shifted position. He woke quickly as a thorn from a draping soft yellow rose pierced his arm. "Ow," he thought. "That hurt! Oh, you are sending me lovelight? It feels good!"

"I am," I replied. "I thought you could do with a top–up, and I bet you've been neglecting your self–healing, haven't you?"

He grinned. "Yes, I've had too much else to think about! Thank you, Keira, I do appreciate your support, especially when we – well, we've had some differences; I am grateful that you are helping me, helping us. Thank you."

"You're welcome," I said, fully meaning both words.

"Time to go," he said, looking at the sky, now filling with fast–moving grey cloud. We rose, and walked back to the house, feeling that things were a little easier between us. As we walked, I told Charls of the dream. He agreed that it was important.

"So, the map was featured, as well as the waterfall," he sent. "And that's the second time you've been guided to the waterfall, so clearly that is critical. I will keep the metal cube and the crystal sphere safe; they are always on me," he confirmed. We had no idea when the dream vision would become a reality, would need to ensure that we were prepared.

As soon as I returned to my room, I retrieved the map, and Charls provided me with a looped fabric pocket that would hang around my neck and underneath my clothes. It wasn't comfortable, but it fulfilled its purpose, as it had done for Cordellan guides and explorers over many years. Now our extraordinary objects would be kept with us at all times. And I wouldn't forget where the map was.

"Keira, I feel I should warn you that it is likely that war will begin very, very soon. We have had further incursions into Cordello from Vornen, injuring our guards – although we did cause some damage to Karn's men, too." He grimaced. "I know you would prefer a peaceful resolution, but we cannot just sit there and take what Karn is doing. We are defending ourselves. Karn has been increasing the frequency of his attacks, so it looks as if a formal declaration of war will be received – or made – sometime over the next day or so." He waited, gauging my reaction. I kept my expression calm. It was no good getting fired up about this; my role was to continue working with lovelight, at least for the time being.

"Thank you for telling me. Do you think you are ready?" I asked.

He considered the question for a moment. "I think we are as ready as we can be. Some of our troops will not be fully fit for action, and a few of those who are fit have never been tested in combat. We lost too many trained soldiers when Tissa was snatched in the tunnels. But they are strong, believe in themselves, and have trained hard and well. So – yes, we are ready." He took a deep breath. "And are *you* ready, Keira?"

I thought back to the dream. Felt a sensation of safety and protection surround me. The Reikans would assist. Lovelight would sustain. I knew that I would be guided, as long as I remembered to ask for help and to act on the information that I was given from the Ascended Beings.

Yes, I too was ready.

CHAPTER 21

Jason felt so alive, so energised, so filled with vitality; he felt like jumping up out of his warm bubble and running round and round in circles. Somehow that didn't feel appropriate in the presence of the elegant Lady Aida. But he felt like a child again, freed from restrictive bonds and limitations, released from expectations. He glanced at Keira, wondering whether she'd even recognise him now. He felt that he had changed, had an entirely new perspective on life. Then it dawned on him that this was exactly the feeling she had been trying to explain to him after she'd read her 'spiritual books', as he referred to them.

Oh Keira, I wish I'd experienced this when you did, so I could really understand how you were feeling! Jason felt guilty, recalling that he had waved off her excited chatter, and grumbled that she'd interrupted the football match he'd been watching.

"Jason, everyone walks their own path and at their own pace. Do not recriminate yourself for any blips in your learning along the way. Accept what was, and choose what will be. No–one can alter the past, but you have complete control over your present and your future."

"Is this really how Keira thinks?" he asked.

"Most of the time, yes," Lady Aida responded. "She is, after all, human. She has free will, has her own issues to work through; occasionally, she makes decisions that she is not happy with once she has used the benefit of hindsight. But again, that is part of her learning, her journey. She will put it behind her, do her best to learn the lesson, and move on. It is a new way of living,

177

Jason, a conscious way of living. Once you start, you can never go back to the way you were."

"I can see that," he answered. "Your perspective changes. Sometimes the new picture might blur, but it's always there, waiting for you to bring back into focus?"

"That's exactly right. Your life will feel a blessing from now on, because you will begin to see value in each experience, and in yourself. Isn't it wonderful?" Lady Aida enthused.

Jason grinned. "You bet it is! And this will make it even easier to think of Keira acting in the best way. I really can help her!"

~~~

Sleep was elusive. Rain battered at the window, and the breeze from the day had strengthened into a howling, tormented wind, screaming and sighing against the window–pane. I tossed and turned, the feeling of the unfamiliar map–bag against my skin both a distraction and a reminder of forthcoming events. The weather mirrored my emotions. Knowing what was to come, so soon, left me on edge and with a hollow feeling in the pit of my stomach. Knowing I should be lifting my mood and my energy, I lay in my bed, eyes wide open, connecting with lovelight.

I let the energy surround and fill me, relaxing slightly as I bathed in the familiar tingles and fizzing sensations. I asked the Ascended Reikans – again – for protection: to keep Charls and his people safe, to keep Tissa free from harm; to assist the Cordellan army in whatever ways were best. To assist me in keeping in tune with my guidance, in doing the right thing at the best time, in being courageous and strong and calm. In helping us protect lovelight with as little cost to human life as possible. Having done all I could, I allowed my eyes to close. Eventually sleep stole my last waking thought and my tired mind was allowed rest.

Waking early, I noticed that the rain had eased to a soft misty drizzle, and that the wind had dropped. The cloud was a heavy steely–grey, looking ominous and threatening. I shivered as I dressed. I double–checked that the map hadn't miraculously crept out of my neck–bag whilst I had been sleeping. I felt that today *would* be 'the day'.

Charls and I ate a quiet breakfast, both sensing a solemnity and gravity in each other's moods. He had packed knapsacks, filled them with food, water and anything else that he thought might be useful. I had no weapon; I had received no training in combat, and would probably do more damage to myself than to anyone else. And, of course, he was aware of my feelings about the impending battle. If I was to be captured, I would probably be safer being a 'harmless' unarmed woman, than if I was caught with a knife. Charls was fully kitted out with knives, his sword, and other equipment that looked like it would do damage, if only the bearer knew how to use it.

Then we waited.

An hour later, a messenger arrived and was brought to the morning room. He handed a small folded note to Charls.

Charls unfolded the paper, read it, then looked at me. His face was grave. I knew what was coming.

"Karn has formally declared war on Cordello, Keira. We must go to the people, make sure that we get them to safety. We can't wait for the other lords and their troops – they are not yet prepared for this."

179

We stood in the hall, just inside the front doors. Charls enfolded me in a hug, held me tight. He felt so safe. Against my hair, he spoke words aloud: telling me that I was brave and strong, a true legend, and that he trusted me to follow my heart and to do the right thing. I could feel his heart beating. I could feel the rumble of his words reverberating in his chest. Somehow, hearing the words spoken verbally rather than by mind–connection, they seemed to carry more intensity. I felt tears stinging my eyes and blinked them back.

We had to leave.

Charls released me, using his fingers to brush my misbehaving hair back from my face. He leaned close to me, whispered: "You are a dear friend, Keira. It is not our time to be more than that, but you must know that I care for you very, very much. *Please* stay alive, and make it home to your own world, to your Jason. If we are separated, do not wait for me; look out for yourself, okay?"

I nodded, not trusting myself to speak. Then he picked up his kit, and opened the doors.

It was time.

Doors closing behind us, we jogged to the estate boundary gates. I had not come this far from the house since I had arrived here. It felt like a lifetime ago. We made our way as quickly as we could to the archway and out onto the road. I had almost forgotten what this part of Cordello looked like. I hoped that I'd be able to find my way to the waterfall. My hand went to my chest, unconsciously checking that the map–bag was still safely held underneath my clothes.

As we progressed along the road back, coming closer to the village through which Charls had brought me only a few weeks ago, I felt a prickling at the back of my neck. Although this vista was not familiar to me, it somehow looked wrong. There was smoke . . . and noise.

I could see families running out of the doorways of their homes. I could hear women crying, a child screaming. Charls and I quickened our pace, conscious that we might yet need to keep energy in reserve. One man looked in our direction, recognised Charls, and began to stumble towards us. He had a knife stuck in his leg, blood trailing along the ground after him. I felt queasy.

"Lord Charls! Lord Charls! We've been attacked! Soldiers! They've destroyed our cottages, tried to smoke us out, they've been wrecking our homes! Please! Help us!" The man was sobbing, communicating aloud.

Charls reached forward and took the man's arm, attempting to calm him with softly spoken reassurances. Then he started barking out instructions. "You! Come and give healing to this man. Anyone who is unharmed, please help the others. You all need to be able to walk, if not run. Make sure everyone is mobile, and that the children have an adult to carry or accompany them. We need to evacuate you – when you are ready, you must *go with Keira.*"

Ah. So this was my little flock. This is where my dream–vision began.

I turned to see whether Charls would be coming with us – only to find that he was leading all of the men and two of the women back down the road towards the border with Vornen. He'd gone to fight, and I hadn't even noticed that he'd left. Then I realised that he'd probably picked a moment when I'd been busy so that we would not say any more goodbyes. I sincerely hoped our hug in the manor house hall had been an *Au Revoir,* not a *Farewell*. I allowed my eyes to follow him until he and the others were out of sight, then took a deep breath and turned back to the villagers.

They waited expectantly. I noticed that a few had left the group, and were now stealing like ghosts into the heavy forest beyond the cottages. A couple had small children. I hated to leave them behind – but there was no time to fetch them; they would have to look after themselves.

We had no idea when the invaders from Vornen would return. We had to assume it would be soon.

"Let's go," I said to those remaining with me.

They clustered around me and we set off along the road. One of the women offered to carry the heavy rucksack for me – she told me that her name was Roanne, and said, with pride, that she was a good fighter – she had four older brothers who had given her plenty of opportunities to learn defence techniques. I hoped she was as good as she thought she was. Just in case.

She seemed keen to assist, so I handed the bag over, my shoulders feeling the relief as I removed the straps.

I glanced briefly over my shoulder to check that everyone was still with me. They were. I trusted in lovelight. I had faith in the Ascended Reikans to protect us and to guide me. We continued along the road, my little band of villagers and I, until the path narrowed and I started to feel a little uncertain of my bearings. "Roanne, which path do we take to get to the waterfall?"

Her eyes widened. "The waterfall? Oh, my lady, we may not go *there*. It is a sacred place, villagers are forbidden entry."

How odd. My dream had left me in no doubt that I

was to lead them there. Well, that was where we were going, I thought firmly.

"That's as may be, Roanne, but that's our destination. So, please guide me there, quickly. We have to hurry."

~~~

Jason felt quite pleased with himself, as if he'd made an important breakthrough. Suddenly, the problems in his life felt less burdensome; they became less of a main event and more of a side issue. He felt that his world had somehow tilted on its axis, so that this time with Lady Aida in the stone circle was a prominent, important event. His work issues had shrunk and changed from a solid black mass to flimsy grey shadows, and these he would tackle using the light cast by his new perspective and understanding. Where once they had felt to him like anchors dragging him down, holding him captive in darkness and frustration, now they became challenges, problems with solutions just waiting to be found.

And it felt so easy, now, to allow his thoughts of Keira to be positive, bright and empowering. He was confident that she would succeed in whatever quest she had been assigned, simply because she was Keira; and, knowing what he knew now, he realised that she had the inner resources to create the synchronicities that she sought, and needed. He felt comforted and supported knowing that these light–beings were working with and for her, guiding her as Lady Aida was guiding him tonight.

He brought his attention back from his thoughts to the physical world before him. Cocooned in his warm bubble, he felt perfectly comfortable and at ease.

Until he noticed that the graceful Lady Aida seemed to be . . . fading . . . growing fainter, becoming dim, losing definition.

"NO!" he cried. "Please don't leave me, my lady! I need you here!"

The figure that was Lady Aida wavered and shimmered, but her light continued to recede. He heard a voice in his head, recognised it at once.

"I will return, Jason. But for now, I am needed in Cordello. You know what to do."

The sense of loss was indescribable. How could she go? He had so much still to ask her, to learn from her, so much still to discuss. He felt abandoned. A sense of being unprotected niggled at the edge of his awareness; the old familiar fear of being lost and alone. He tried to shake it off.

Persisting, it gathered strength, was threatening to consume him with loneliness and darkness. He fought it, determined to keep his thoughts light and bright. He would not – could not – go back to his old thinking patterns.

He would do this for Keira.

And for himself.

He sighed with relief when the dark sensation finally ebbed, subsided, faded away. The new Jason was stronger, had more purpose, more determination. He turned towards Keira, still glowing and sparkling in the darkness, still fighting in another world. His job was to keep Keira safely within the stone circle portal. So that is what he would do.

Our past, just gone, showed defence ideals
Of conflict, power and loss
The gain we thought was right and just
The future to secure

Yet now we fight on by distant plain
The truth cannot be seen
While both sides their just do proclaim
The real enemy stand by not seen

The conflict time of steel and fire
Causes all who touch to lose
The winner hides and bides the time
Awaiting our fall – lost and alone

Our power within we do not see,
Or see – and fail to join
With others who, like you, believe
The power of thought as one
Effect change to greater victory still

Your prayers you send to source divine
Must bear away from ask
But hold the charge that's in heart
Of right and love and care

The time is now to join and talk
To meet with others' minds
And send a prayer to hold and show
True strength that comes combined

Not closed to change; willing to look a'new
No fear, but trust you'll feel
Nor anger, but warmth to send
Not one, but one of many
In the real church of man.

© 2010 Ron Dickerson

PART TWO

BEYOND THE WATERFALL

CHAPTER 22

Roanne's blue eyes widened, but she perceived my urgency. Clearly, she still had misgivings about leading us to the waterfall, but she agreed to do as I asked without further argument. For a while, we continued along the path that led up to the tunnels and chambers, but then Roanne suddenly headed left, towards a wide thicket of golden bamboo. The villagers and I followed close behind.

Roanne pushed the crowded bamboo canes to one side, and stepped forward into the foliage. She vanished from sight. Without hesitation, I brushed the bamboo aside, and followed Roanne into the depths of the clump, holding the canes aside for the villagers on my heels. The rustling of the bamboo, together with the sight of the mass of tall golden stems, made me feel as though I was in a yellow–green jungle filled with constant whispering.

I was aware of muttered thoughts of disbelief being broadcast between some of the villagers, showing their concern that we were all heading into forbidden territory. I had no time to reassure them, could only lead by example, demonstrating my confidence in myself and in those advising me. The rustling ahead of and behind me continued. I could occasionally see my backpack moving in front of me as Roanne continued to forge a path through the bamboo 'forest'. The canes were about eight feet tall, so we could still see and feel the weak sun on our heads. The cloud was moving slowly across the sky, allowing the sun to peek through now and then. I was glad it was no longer raining – I wasn't overly keen on the whole tropical jungle experience.

Ahead, the bamboo was thinning, and I could see

191

Roanne step out into open space. I joined her, finding myself standing on a broad rocky ledge overlooking the far end of the pool. A high sheet of solid water fell gracefully, beautifully, noisily to our right. The rock soared into the sky, a natural cathedral of stone. The water was shot with multiple dancing rainbows, and the spray from the waterfall was reaching us even here, spattering our clothes with the cool water. A mist obscured the base of the centre of the falls.

I moved aside to let some of the villagers through; Roanne explained that none of them had ever been this close to the waterfall. They were as spellbound as I was.

Roanne said, "Well, here we are, my lady; what do we do now?" She remained by my side, but I recognised that leadership had subtly shifted back to me. I was fine with my new role – it was what I was here for. In my heart I *knew* that; but the occasional doubt reached up to threaten my confidence. I looked at Roanne, at the villagers watching me, and sent: "Now we go inside."

"Inside?" Roanne queried. "Surely we're not going through the waterfall?" She looked shocked at the very idea.

"Oh yes!" I replied, my eyes sparkling. I knew that our future began *beyond* the waterfall. I had full confidence that I was on the right path, both metaphorically and literally.

Looking to my right, I could see roughly–hewn rocks leading right up to the cascade itself. These would act as giant steps. The rock was damp, so I knew we'd all have to watch our footing. I didn't want to lose anyone through carelessness or accidents. I recalled a walk around a gorge some years ago, and repressed a shudder as I remembered my feet slipping on slick stone, with barely a handhold to keep me upright and safe from the rock–pierced maelstrom below.

I know I'd frightened Jason.

I'd been trying to impress him, those being early days in our relationship. I had no need to impress anyone, now, and I was the only person who could lead these people to safety.

Carefully, I walked towards the first of the 'steps' and lowered my foot onto the grey rock. It was smooth, ridged with a few narrow channels where the rock had been eroded by the water. Most of this slab was dry, the spray having drained into the channels, and I was able to move relatively quickly onto the next. This was wetter, and I had to will myself not to tense up as I placed my foot onto it. The steps ahead of me ascended in a gentle incline, and I hoped they might be fairly easy to navigate and cross.

On instinct, I stopped to look behind me, checking that everyone was following.

Oh *no*. One woman and her small boy were waiting back by the bamboo, apparently refusing to follow us. Everyone else was moving across the ledge and onto the slabs leading to the waterfall. I bit my lip. I tried to curb my impatience, knowing that whatever happened, there would be a reason for it.

I turned to Roanne. "I have to go back. That lady and her boy are holding back. They can't stay here alone."

Roanne followed my gaze. "That's Julianna and her son, Tobin. He is scared of water."

Ah. Houston, we have a problem! I took a calming breath.

"Roanne, please make sure everyone else remains safe, no jumping about on wet rocks, that sort of thing. I know it's common sense but . . . just be careful! I'll be back as soon as I can."

I retraced my steps as quickly as I dared, and walked back to Tobin and his mum.

"I'm so sorry," she thought to me. "I just can't get him to move closer to the waterfall!"

"Can I talk to Tobin?" I asked. She nodded her acquiescence.

I crouched down so that I was face–to–face with the boy. He looked to be about five or six years old.

"Hi, Tobin. I'm Keira." Gravely, I offered him my hand. The boy looked at me from wide, brown eyes, then his small, warm hand took mine and gave it a light shake. I continued to hold his hand in mine. Feeling a little uncertain of what to think next, I connected with lovelight, directing a gentle stream of it towards Tobin.

Inspiration arrived, as I'd hoped it would. "Tobin, tell me . . . do you like magic?"

His eyes widened still further, and he grinned at me. "Yes! I love magic! Do *you* do magic?"

I hesitated, then allowed my internal guidance to provide me with the words.

"Yes, I do. But, do you know, I can only do it in the magic caves that are hidden behind the waterfall over there?"

"Really?" he asked, his mouth forming an 'O'. I heard Julianna gasp.

"Yes, really," I replied, smiling. "So I can't show you the magic out here. We have to go – *in there*." I pointed to the waterfall. Tobin looked nervously at the cascading rush of falling water.

"But I don't like water!" he thought to me, his lower lip beginning to tremble. Uh–oh.

"But you *do* like magic – so that can be your reward for being really brave and fighting through the waterfall . . . can't it?" I looked at Julianna, who nodded her encouragement.

Suddenly Tobin released my hand. He put his small, bony shoulders back, looked up at Julianna, and then back at me, before saying aloud: "I am going to be a soldier when I've grown up, so I'd have to be brave for that, wouldn't I?"

"Oh yes, indeed," I remarked, my eyes holding his. "In fact, being so brave now, means you're already growing up *really* fast. Shall we go and see what magic we can find, now?"

He nodded, taking Julianna's hand in his small one, then determinedly led his mum to the first rock step. She helped him onto the slab, then up onto the next. And onto the next. I followed close behind. The other villagers were clustered on the broad final 'step' in front of the waterfall, some getting quite wet from the flashing spray and the droplets of mist.

Tobin and Julianna reached the final step, and I felt an upsurge of emotion as every single one of the villagers clapped Tobin's courage. I joined in. Until I remembered our reason for fleeing the village, for heading here towards safety.

"Shhhhh!" I sent. "We must not give away our location to anyone snooping around. Well done, Tobin," I thought, looking at the boy, "and now, onward." It was only afterwards that I realised that the sound of the water would drown the trumpeting of an elephant. But it would serve us well to remain cautious.

~~~

Charls had assembled those who would fight with him; the remainder would go with Keira. His 'soldiers' were pitifully few; a handful of men (the injured man

195

had been healed), and a couple of young women who had trained with Tissa. Guilt brushed his heart as he remembered that he'd sent her away, into probable danger. The guilt was strengthened by the realisation that he had felt relief when she'd left. He'd moved too far, too fast, and knew that he didn't love Tissa. He doubted she loved him, either.

For him, Tissa had been a welcome distraction from his confusing feelings for Keira; the girl from another world, a woman that he could never have. Not in *this* lifetime. If only Alaria . . . He banished the thought before it took shape. She was *gone*.

He could see that Keira was involved with the villagers, quickly getting ready for her trek to the waterfall. He gave her a long, final look, said a silent farewell, before deliberately turning from her – and then he and his little band of warriors moved quietly and swiftly away. They followed the road before heading across fields, angling towards the woodland beyond. He believed the marauding Vornen soldiers had retreated to their own country, that this morning's attack was just the first foray. Charls would need to keep his mind focused – he and his little army would have to do their best to keep Karn and his men at bay whilst Keira and the others followed their path – wherever *that* led.

He trusted that she would know what to do.

Charls wondered how this would all end. The legend foretold that the alien girl (how could he ever think of Keira as *alien?*) would return to her own world, once her part was complete. But what was her part? And what of him? What of the Cordellans? And, of course, lovelight? The legend had been narrated with many different endings, depending on who related the story. Which was the right one? Or was that still to be decided? He considered the possibility of lovelight being used as a weapon, felt the anger surge in his chest as a physical pain. He acknowledged it, let the energy of the emotion power his determination.

Arriving at the start of the woodland belt, they slowed and moved with stealth, doing their best to make no noise and leave no tracks. The woodland would grow thicker, becoming forest, before reaching one of the lesser–known parts of the Vornen border. Charls hoped that they could carry out their task without bloodshed or injury – on *either* side.

He could never forgive Karn for his treachery and murder – but he did not wish to become his brother's killer. He knew Symion's wife, and was determined to rescue her and the child. He had no idea as to how any of this would be accomplished, but he was ready to do battle *if* it was needed, *if* there was no alternative. Keira was so innocent, so trusting – so, for now, they would go their different ways, each with their own different role to play.

~~~

I made my way towards the front of the group, so that I was now the person closest to the waterfall. Julianna kept Tobin close beside her, reassuring him with her presence. Standing so near to the torrent of falling water was an almost overpowering sensation. This close, the rush of the water drowned out all other sound, and I felt a slight giddiness from the vibration of the relentless pounding of the water. The heavy cascade, beautiful as it may be, was still a very powerful force of nature, and one to be respected. How would we make it through without injury? We would be ferociously pelted by

197

several feet of water as we passed through. Tobin was so small. Now that we were *here*, I felt a momentary sense of doubt.

I had to trust the visions that I had seen – there was nothing else I could fall back on. Taking another deep breath, I sent a heartfelt request to the Ascended Reikans, asking for guidance. I closed my eyes to enhance my concentration, and waited for information to appear inside my mind.

Nothing.

Opening my eyes, I stared again at the deluge of water. There was so much of it.

The villagers were beginning to become restless. I had to do something – but it had to be the *right* thing. At that moment, the sun broke free from its cloudy embrace, and illuminated a thick black band in the rock that had previously been concealed by thick water vapour. I moved closer to investigate. Although still a part of the waterfall, the cascade seemed to have far less power at this location, and I wondered if the rock was in fact an opening. Watching my footing, being steadily rained upon by the rainbow–lit spray, I reached the cleft and found that I could easily stand upon the rock in front of it. I peered inside.

Of course, it was dark.

"Roanne," I sent, "do we have a torch in your backpack?"

This puzzled her. "What is a torch?"

"A flash–light! I need light! I can't see into this opening in the rock. I need to illuminate it."

"Oh. Well, then, create a light–sphere."

What? Of course. How did I do that, exactly? I didn't have time to waste.

"Roanne, please would you create one for me, so that I

can see? I'll explain later."

She shrugged her shoulders, and created a light, giving it a gentle push towards me. Presumably she intended that it would react to my instructions. I didn't know how it worked; I would need to learn.

The light reached me, then bobbed to my side. I silently asked that it move in front of me and into the break in the rock–face. It did so, its milky white glow more easily seen once it had penetrated the darkness beyond.

I peered into the fissure.

Now, *that* was interesting.

CHAPTER 23

The spherical light illuminated a narrow tunnel – a small space, yes; but wide enough for a person to ease through without too much trouble. The only thing that puzzled me was this: how would we get inside? The light, being fluid and . . . well, sort of magical, had been able to adjust its shape to move through the gap. I felt I didn't have time to spare, had to work out this conundrum quickly. I sent a further request to the Ascended Reikans – a cry for help.

Even as I finished the thought, I noticed something that I was sure had not previously been visible. A square was marked – engraved? – on the right–hand side of the fracture, at around shoulder–height. Just a simple square, no embellishments or fancy artwork.

Drawn to it, I placed my palm over the symbol and held my breath.

And waited.

I had followed my instincts . . . but nothing was happening! I forced myself to remain calm, to quell the feeling of anxiety bubbling up in me. I connected with lovelight and allowed it to flow into me. Then I *directed* it into my right arm, past my elbow, into the wrist, into the palm . . . and *out* into the square–shaped symbol. The energy flowed into and through and out of me, into the rock.

One moment, I was facing a cleft in the rock's face. The next, I had a clear entrance a good three feet wide. Slowly, I removed my hand. I could feel Tobin tugging at my sleeve, wanting to see his magic. Had he not seen *this?* Julianna pulled him back. The opening did not retract. I sensed that it was safe to enter. I knew I had to go inside first – and I had to trust that once we were all inside the tunnel, the access would close behind us, so that any Vornen soldiers finding this place could not follow. I hoped so.

"Roanne, I'm going in. Bring everyone through," I thought, casting a glance to her over my shoulder just before I dipped my head and proceeded into the tunnel. The sound of the waterfall was muted slightly once I was inside the rock. The stone beneath my feet was dry as there were channels to either side of the 'pathway', into which any water drained. The air was cool, but fresh, so I guessed there was an exit at some point. That would help!

The globe of light continued a short distance ahead of me, matching my pace. Then it started to lose brightness. I realised why; I was approaching daylight. I called the light back to me. How did I dismantle it? I let it know that it was no longer needed, and it shrank into a dense white ball, then allowed itself to be absorbed into my body as I stepped towards it. I felt a warmth around my chest, a bubbly feeling, and the emotion of peace. I felt strengthened, and revitalized. Much as I loved my own world, I acknowledged that Cordello was a pretty cool place to be.

Stepping out of the tunnel, I found a sheet of water falling across our path. It was comparatively light compared to the torrent that was the main waterfall. I hoped Tobin would be okay. I placed the intention that he would be fine. It would feel little different than standing under a powerful bathroom shower. Just in case, I took a deep breath, and held it.

Walking forward, I closed my eyes and stepped into the waterfall.

The first thing that hit me – apart from the water itself

– was the awareness that the water falling here was *warm*. I had no explanation for this, and so accepted it and enjoyed the sensation of being drenched in the balmy shower. Too soon, I was through to the other side, and turned to check on the progress of the others. Roanne and Julianna led Tobin through without difficulty, his face beaming a smile at his achievement. The other villagers followed, and everyone confirmed that we were all present.

Of course, we were all completely soaked. My hair hung around my face in dripping strands, but since everyone else was similarly dishevelled, it was easy to shrug off my sense of looking a mess. Our clothes were clinging to us, but the warmth of the water meant that we didn't feel cold.

The path beyond the mini–cascade was damp in places, but easily passable. We were now moving behind the main torrent, walking along a smooth stone ledge, with the falling water acting as an impassable rainbow–scattered white curtain on our left. I didn't think we were being pursued yet, but if we were, the falls would conceal our presence from anyone on the outside and the noise would mask any sounds we made as we traversed the ledge.

Suddenly, we reached a point where the image in front of us matched one in my vision. I realised – remembered – that we would have to turn away from this ledge, heading off to the right, and far into the depths of the rock.

~~~

The light began to fade as Charls and his companions moved gradually from woodland into deep forest.

202

Earlier they had passed trees of ash, sycamore, hornbeam and beech, with an under–planting of ferns and moss. Now they were mostly surrounded by intimidating firs, dark and silent and tall. The bird–sound and rustling of small animals quietened as they progressed further into the dark forest. His father had brought him hunting here a few times, once at night. He remembered the fear he'd felt when an owl had swooped silently in front of him, mere inches from his face. His father had reminded him that here in the forest he had no status, was an intruder. The forest was not a place to be at night. But this time, he had no choice.

It was so dark that, despite their training, the men were bumping into one another through lack of visibility. Charls created a dim globed–light, as soft and diaphanous as shafts of moonlight passing through silk.

It gave them enough light to see, yet would be faint enough to keep their presence here secret from any lurking scouts or retreating soldiers. He hoped.

Their pace was much slower as they crept through the undergrowth. It was so overgrown that Charls decided it was unlikely that anyone had passed this way for years. He heard the burble and chuckle of the brook that flowed to their right, letting him know that he was headed in the right direction. "Follow the stream into Vornen," his father had whispered to him all those years ago. Charls now owned this land, but Nature had reclaimed it many years before, indifferent to the ownership rights of the lord of the manor.

Absently, he fingered the pouch containing the Canturan sphere, hoping he'd remember to use it when it was needed. Then he felt for the golden cube paperweight, a solid shape bulging in his zipped pocket. He had two of the special objects. Had the map been of any use to Keira when she'd reached the waterfall? Where would they go, having reached the falls? Noticing his thoughts wandering, he pulled himself back to the present. He knew that they would need to continue moving through the forest at night; not an ideal scenario, but they would lose too much time if they did not keep going. He estimated that they would reach the Vornen border shortly before dawn. He sighed. It would be a long night.

~~~

I remained alert to any visible openings to our right. I let my fingers brush across the rock as we walked forward, wondering whether any opening would even be apparent. I recalled my journey with Charls from Reika to Cordello, the mysterious doorways that appeared as if by unseen forces. I could not assume that our entrance into these tunnels would be obvious.

I checked once again that all of 'my' villagers were still with me, noticing Tobin and Julianna close behind me. Tobin seemed keen to keep me in his sights, probably hoping that I would pull a rabbit of the hat. The magical metaphor turned to literal, as my fingers received an electric shock. It wasn't a harsh, painful sensation; more of a noticeable tingle, not unlike the sensation of absorbing lovelight. I paused, and peered at the rock. I slowly removed my hand, and there it was.

A diamond shape, carved into the rock, at about shoulder–height. This time, I knew what to do. Standing in front of the diamond, I connected with lovelight, and let it flow through me and out into the symbol. And the gap appeared.

"Roanne?" I thought.

"Yes, my lady?"

"May I have light, please?"

"Of course, my lady . . . and later I will teach you how to make your own!"

Roanne's new light sphere bobbed towards me, and I directed it into the shadowed gap. Illumination revealed another tunnel – I was used to them, by now – and without hesitation I began walking into the tunnel, the others following me.

This time the air had a slight mustiness to it, and I guessed that we would be underground for some considerable time. The tunnel curved first to the right, then the left, then back to the right, perhaps following the natural grain in the rock. Sometimes, our path led gently downhill. The tunnel seemed to go on for miles, but that may have been illusory.

I was surprised when the passage became wider, the walls smoother, the ceiling higher.

I was even more surprised when I stepped out into a cavern. The lighted sphere's glow enabled us to get a feel for the cavern's dimensions – enough to easily house all of us; we would be able to stop and catch our breath. Tobin had walked a long way on his short legs and I knew that Julianna had carried him for the last few minutes. No doubt the others were also fatigued.

I had not expected such an open space. I had assumed that the tunnels would remain narrow all the way to . . . wherever it was that we were going. In retrospect, knowing of the chambers under the Reikan hills, I might have guessed that we would discover more chambers buried deep inside this rock. I wondered if the Cordellan lords – or the Elder – knew of these? With the waterfall being sacred, clearly the villagers would never have seen any of this. It was new to all of *us*.

I allowed our spherical light to drift around the cavern, showing us its shape and height, then asked it to hang in the middle of the space, casting us all in a soft white glow.

"Let's sit and rest for a while," I sent. "Is everyone okay? Anyone need food? Water?"

Roanne replied, "We are fine for the moment, my lady, thank you."

"Roanne, please would you call me Keira?" I begged. "I am not a . . . a Lady of Cordello. I have no title."

Roanne met my gaze, and I knew she would be stubborn in this. "Lord Charls told us about you; you are the Lady in the Cordellan legend and deserve our greatest respect."

I met her half–way. "How about 'Lady Keira' then, if you feel that is acceptable?"

"It is, my lady. I mean – Lady Keira!"

Glad we got that sorted, I thought wryly. Okay, Lady Keira, now what?

My intuition provided the answer. *Check the map.*

I reached down inside my shirt for the protective map–bag, lifting it outside of my clothes. Opened the bag, withdrew the map. Unfolded it. The spherical light cast enough bright light by which to read the document.

I frowned. That couldn't be right. I turned the map upside–down. Then to the side. I was perplexed. The map no longer showed Cordello, or Vornen. It depicted shapes, lines, places that were all new. There was nothing on the map that I was familiar with.

With a shock, I realised that the colour of the paper had turned from old–white to pure white with . . . well, I wasn't sure how to describe it, but it looked as if the paper contained the essence of the rainbow. Just faint hints of the whole colour–spectrum, almost invisible, but definitely there. I thought of the golden paperweight sending out rainbow sparks and light. Of the waterfall and its rainbows reaching out from the base of the cascade. Of the mini–waterfall that I had passed through, map around my neck. The protective bag was waterproof and the document was dry . . . but I had to accept that there was a good chance that the waterfall had transformed this map – itself a special object – into a new document, one to help us on the next phase of our journey. In fact, now that I gave attention to that possibility, my inner guidance confirmed to me that I was right. The rainbow water had magically transformed the map.

I turned the map the right way up, with the lettering in the correct orientation. As I continued to study it, I realised that I could identify the waterfall's hidden ledge, as well as our detour into the tunnels. I could trace our route towards this cavern. I swallowed when I saw that we had covered only a tiny portion of the underground tunnels and caverns. The map clearly showed a myriad of dead–ends, and even some circular passageways. Even our cosy cavern had three exit tunnels. I was beginning to feel as if I was in a re–run of an adventure thriller.

Oh crikey, I hope we didn't meet rats or snakes. Or lowering ceilings covered with death–inducing spikes. I tried to keep my imagination under control. Our survival was up to me – I had to remain calm!

CHAPTER 24

Charls and his team reached the final belt of trees shortly before dawn, the indigo sky lightening and softening by degrees. Ahead of them was the border separating Cordello from Karn's Vornen.

They stopped, watchful.

Charls and his small group were dark shadows barely discernible from the tall columns of the firs. The area ahead looked deserted, with only an old, poorly–maintained wooden fence marking the boundary. Charls could see right through to the other side, to Vornen; the fence appeared purely decorative rather than defensive. Several of the horizontal posts had slipped from the fence, which was only about six feet high in any case; it would be child's play to cross.

Nevertheless, Charls mentally asked one of his contingent, a tall, muscular lad named Burron, to carefully scout the area of scrubby grassland to ensure that no–one was lying in wait. Recalling the map that Keira had compiled for him, he knew that this particular crossing had been unmarked. He thought Karn to be unaware of this access point, but Charls did not intend to lose any of his precious fighting force. His army was nowhere near the size he had envisioned.

The stream passed silently through the border a few feet away. Their canteens were already filled with fresh water.

"It's clear, m'lord," Burron sent to him a few minutes later. "No footprints, no sign of any human passing this way. Looks like deer knocked the posts askew as they jumped."

"Thank you, Burron. We'll proceed. Take the easiest

route; no sense in wasting energy."

One by one, Charls and the remainder of his team jogged quietly to the fence, keeping alert and listening for anything that might suggest that they were not alone. The fence breached, every person safely on the other side in Vornen, Charls stopped for a breath to get his bearings.

The scrubby grass continued a short distance up a gentle slope, leading to a worn gravelled path. Visualising the map in his mind, Charls knew that the road east led to Vornen's main square – and probably to Karn. Had the country not been under Karn's control, Charls might have requested permission to spend a few days touring the country, which was said to be abundant in water and fertile land. The country was clearly self–sufficient in food and fuel, and possibly in medicinal herbs, too; there was no need for Karn to annexe another country. Charls could not understand how any Cordellan could be motivated by such apparent greed and ambition.

Vornen welcomed Charls and his group with a spectacular sunrise. The light cloud diffused the emerging sun's colours so that the brightening sky was cast in streaks of peach and palest pink, a palette of colours similar to those seen when they boosted lovelight in the Grand Chamber. As they watched, a shaft of gold speared through an opening in the cloud, and Charls was struck by the idea that the Ascended Reikans were sending him a message of hope and reassurance. Taking merely a moment to appreciate the gift of the new day, they turned as one and headed east.

~~~

I made a quick connection with lovelight and sent a brief but sincere request to the Ascended Reikans, asking that they continue to work with me, so that I would lead the villagers safely to our eventual destination. I examined the map further, trying to see in the detailed drawings a way through, to plot the route that we should take.

Many of the handwritten markings made little sense to me, yet. I found the text difficult to decipher, unless I already knew what I was expecting to read. I could make out the words 'Waterfall' and 'Entrance Tunnel', then 'Cavern of ———'; but the final word in the phrase was unreadable.

So we were currently in the Cavern of *something* . . . the missing information taunted me, caused unease to nibble at my confidence, the little bites of misgiving soon merging into a larger chunk of apprehension, stealing my self–belief. Noticing this anxiety, this lower–energy, creeping into my mind, I mentally took a step back from it, so that it was if I was *watching* myself feeling that emotion. From that detached perspective, I could witness the emotion, then allow it to move through me. It passed, and my calm confidence returned.

Thank you, lovelight. Thank you, Ascended Reikans.

I took another calming breath, and attempted once more to decipher the map text relating to this cavern. As I did so, I felt a hand come to rest upon my shoulder, and looked up to see Roanne standing over me.

She crouched down, and sent: "So, Lady Keira, where do we go next?"

"I'm actually not certain, Roanne . . . I can work out where we've come from, and where we are, although the text is not fully readable. But I don't yet have a – a *feel* of where we go from here. I'm sorry, I just don't have the information as yet."

She sat down in front of me, and her blue eyes met mine in a frank gaze. "I think you are trying to do too much alone –"

"But –"

"*But* one of the reasons we are here as a group is so that we can help each other – as you did with Tobin, remember? Yes, Lady Keira, you are leading us, and no–one doubts your ability to do so, least of all me. But you do not need to take full responsibility all of the time. Allow me, at least, to help you."

She did have a point. I would soon become over–weary if I did not share some of the load, the decisions.

"Okay," I replied. "We'll work together."

"Don't worry," she reassured me, with a smile. "I understand that any final decision will always be yours – just use me as a sounding–board if you need to. I have things I can teach you; you have things you can teach me."

"Thanks, Roanne – that does help." I reached forward and wrapped her in a brief hug.

She hugged me back, then we drew apart, she re–positioning herself so that she was seated to my right, and able to see the map. I passed the document to her, allowing her to peruse it at length. We could not go anywhere until I – no, *we* – had worked out where we should go, and since I had not found – or received – any information to help us, I may as well invite Roanne's input. Maybe she could see something that I could not.

I closed my eyes, grateful to rest my brain for just a second. I let my mind drift, sought stillness. Perhaps I recognised, at a deep level, that I would need to be centred, that all hell was about to break loose.

211

"Lady Keira!" Roanne whispered aloud.

Startled by the sound, although she spoke so softly, I opened my eyes and looked at Roanne.

"What have you found?"

"I haven't . . . but look . . ." She was staring past me, pointing to the tunnel through which we had entered the cavern.

I could not make sense of what my eyes saw. It looked as if shadows were stealing into our cave.

Black shapes spread slowly from the tunnel and along the floor at the entrance to the cavern, rising up the walls. Some of the villagers had not, at first, noticed this. Then, panicked thoughts were passed from those who *had* seen, and the others became aware, jumping up, retreating to where Roanne and I were seated. The shadows, as dark as a moonless midnight sky, became *denser* – as if containing or giving birth to a malevolent energy.

Were these shadows protecting the underground world beyond the waterfall? Were we being mistaken as a threat?

Were we a threat?

I sat transfixed, unable to look away. Our spherical light seemed to bobble, then to lose structural integrity, wobbling, shifting, collapsing in on itself, its light simply absorbed – sucked in – by the dark form. We were enveloped in darkness; we were blind. I heard Tobin scream, the high, panicked sound abruptly cut off as his mother clamped her hand over his mouth. Roanne swiftly created a new light–orb, keeping it close to her, protecting it. Everyone was clustered around me – no, beyond me, close to the nearest of the three exit tunnels. Roanne and I had to make a decision: either stop or repel this threat, or get out of here *now.*

212

But if we fled, which tunnel should we take? And would the threatening shadow–form pursue us? Could we out–run it? Would it force us into dead–end tunnels? And then what?

Roanne grasped my upper arm. "I can read the words on the map. Cavern of Silent Shadows, it says."

Oh. Well that filled me with reassurance. That didn't sound at all bad, did it?

"Okay," I sent back, as the shadows crept towards us. "So, now what? What on earth do we do now?"

~~~

Despite the threatening darkness which had eclipsed our lighted sphere, and which was causing confusion and fear amongst the villagers, I somehow remained calm. Instantly, I realised that the Ascended Reikans were supporting me; I had clarity, knowledge, and decisiveness, all of which were needed.

I knew exactly what we had to do – all of us, together.

"Roanne, we are going to send these . . . *shadows* . . . lovelight."

"What?" She was shocked. "We're staying here?"

"Yes. And my inner guidance is telling me – very loudly – that the shadows will be dissolved by lovelight, and by our positive and hopeful and happy and light feelings."

"But – the globe! It was absorbed by the dark!"

"That's because we, individually and collectively, also felt fear, worry, anxiety. It is our consciousness which needs to surround and overcome the darkness, it needs to be a 'conscious decision'."

I could tell that she wasn't completely convinced, but knew also that Roanne would support me. I felt separate from my tribe of villagers – I think this was necessary so that I could tune in to my guidance. It was natural for Roanne to pass my decision to her people, to convey my total confidence in my plan. I had not taken my eyes from the creeping shadows, but I could see from my peripheral vision that everyone was slowly gathering around Roanne and me, some sitting, some remaining on their feet. Tobin and the older boy remained quiet, to my relief. Everyone was doing really well; it was a frightening and unusual situation for us all.

"Okay, everyone, just allow yourselves to relax, and connect with lovelight. Keep your eyes on the shadows, but don't be alarmed that they are getting closer. Just *see* them, and acknowledge their presence; maintain your connection. Then, intend that the lovelight flows out from you and towards and into the darkness. Just as if you were sending lovelight to another person. The darkness needs to know that we are of the light, that we are no threat, that we work together for the highest good." I hoped my thought–speech would calm, reassure and inspire them. Speeches were not my strong point, but I had done my best.

I was still connected to lovelight, but asked for a boost, intending that it was the perfect energy for the task. Directing the lovelight to the shadows, I felt a deep sense of peace fill me, and I knew that I had nothing to fear. I thought of fountains, sunlight, green grass, the ocean, of Jason, of my sisters and my parents. I felt love, peace, confidence, the essence of a smile. I knew, somehow, that the others were also connected to lovelight and sending the energy and their 'happy feelings' outwards; it was almost as if we formed a grid of energy, with lovelight humming along all of the wires, and then whooshing out into the darkness.

214

Silently, without movement, the energies flowed from each of us towards the shadows. At first, I thought nothing was happening. But then, although it was almost imperceptible, I sensed a shift. The darkness was no longer approaching – it had stalled. And Roanne's light–sphere was gaining in strength.

The formless black shapes at the entrance to the cavern seemed to lose depth and intensity; they were fading! We continued sending, continued thinking and feeling positively, continued focusing the lovelight. Have to keep going, *keep going*, came the thought.

The sense of interconnectedness, of connection to both lovelight and the others, was so strong; it was as if our combined intentions and energies and thoughts were multiplied beyond our numbers; it was a powerful feeling, and a humbling one. Our efforts were visible – the shadows continued to transform into ordinary air, to be absorbed into and uplifted by the powerful forces that we were sending. Finally the last remnant of the grey wispy energy melted away, and our cavern was back to normal. Only now, everyone was buoyed with lovelight energies; no–one appeared tired or weary; everyone was alert and rejuvenated.

Roanne and I grinned at one another. We'd done it! I remembered to thank my inner guidance, lovelight and our Ascended Reikan friends for their help, then turned my mind to the way forward.

~~~

Looking at the map, I knew instantly that we should take the central exit tunnel. On the map, the tunnels were tiny; but somehow – I had stopped questioning how all these insights functioned – the middle tunnel looked *brighter*. I asked my inner guidance – *is the middle tunnel the right one?* Heard a clear 'Yes'.

"Well done, everyone," I sent with the biggest, most confident smile I could manage. "What you have witnessed demonstrates the power of thought, and of lovelight. So long as we keep our energy high, and work together, we will be safe. I know that you know this; but now we're putting it into practice in a way that is new to us all. Now, I've determined from the map that we should leave this cavern through the middle of the three tunnels. So, if everyone's ready, shall we go?"

I was just about to walk to the tunnel's entrance when Tobin sent: "Was that the magic, Lady Keira?"

I gave his question due consideration. Then I looked at him with a solemn expression, and said, "Oh yes, Tobin, that was lovelight–magic. I think there will be more. Do you want to see more?"

"YES!" he shouted aloud, his high voice echoing around the chamber. This brought a few chuckles from the adults, and helped to keep the atmosphere buoyant and light–hearted.

The villagers stood aside, clearing the way to the tunnel's 'doorway'. Of course, it was pitch black inside, and even before I'd formed my thought–request, Roanne's orb–light was flowing in my direction. I smiled my thanks, and gave her a moment to create a new light for those who would be following behind me in the gloom.

I entered the tunnel, noting that it was considerably wider than the one that had led to the Cavern of Silent Shadows. That interested me; I wondered what lay at the end of *this* passageway? There was only one way to find out – keep walking! The light bobbed along in front of me. It was high time I learned how to make one myself – there just never seemed to be the right moment.

The floor of the tunnel undulated, but I noticed a trend of more downhills than uphills. The ground was dry, dusty even, and of course the mustiness in the air remained. It was good to have additional room between us and the sides of the tunnels; it felt less enclosing, less claustrophobic. The ceiling of this tunnel was higher, too. I wondered how long ago these passageways had been cut. And by whom. Who had drawn the map? My mind let these questions shift and slide, accepting that I probably wouldn't ever know the answers.

Then, a mental image of the Ascended Reikans entered my mind. I sent a silent query to my intuition. Did the Ascended Reikans create this underground tunnel–cavern system? *Yes.* And did they create the map? *Yes.* The answers had a rightness about them. I knew that if something *felt right* then it usually *was* right. It made sense, too. And perhaps explained why the waterfall was off–limits to all but the lords of Cordello, those who made decisions for the highest good of Cordello.

Well, they *had* done, until one of them had gone rogue . . .

My mind shifted to Charls. Was he okay? Was he in the midst of battle? I felt my heart–rate pick up pace, and felt the flickering of anxiety catch alight in my solar plexus. Before it could be fanned into a raging blaze of worry, I stopped my thoughts in their tracks, and again told myself to take a step back from them. I visualised my anxiety as a tiny flame, as if observing a small lighted candle. Then, resolutely, I chose not to allow the flame to grow, visualised extinguishing it with a single mighty puff. I pictured the smoke rising and swirling, drifting harmlessly away. Even the tunnel air felt clearer after that little turn of imagination.

My mind felt calm and centred again. Walking behind the globe–shaped light, with the silent villagers at the rear, it was too easy to let my mind control *me,* and to run amok with concern, worry, and all the other thoughts that would bring my energy down. It was my job, as leader, to ensure that I remained positive and allowed the others to lift their energy to the same – or higher – level. It was also my job to get us safely through this network–maze of tunnels and caves, to reach our destination (wherever that was) and to assist in the protection of lovelight for the current and future generations.

The tunnels continued – on and on, with no change except for floor slope, or wall curvature, the rock remaining the same dark grey colour throughout. The walls looked smooth, as if modern tools or machinery had been used to carve through the solid rock. Surely water had never flowed through the tunnels? Or ice? Noticing my thoughts rambling again, I focused on the spherical light ahead of me. It flickered. Perhaps that was what had brought my attention back to the present? I frowned. Shouldn't the light be stable? I could see no exit ahead, no daylight.

"Roanne," I thought.

"Yes, Lady Keira?"

"Are there any circumstances in which a spherical light would flicker when there is no exit close by?"

I waited for her response.

"Yes. There is one."

"Well?" I prompted patiently, when nothing further was forthcoming.

"Well, it's never *good* . . ."

Oh no. Another challenge so soon? What would it be this time?

Roanne continued: "If a globed–light begins to flicker, then it can mean that a darker energy is drawing its power. A bit like the shadows did back in the cavern, when we could see our light–sphere being sucked dry before it collapsed. Good things do not affect lovelight–spheres, only very bad things can." She paused. "Lady Keira, what do you think we face this time?"

"I don't know. I really have no idea. But the only way is forward, so whatever we come across, it is a situation that we have to accept, and deal with as best we can. As Lord Charls would say, 'This is the hand we have been dealt. These are the cards we must play.'"

I wished Charls was here. Roanne was, undoubtedly, a big help, but Charls and I had a strong, solid friendship; and I missed him: his support, his smile, his strength. I felt a twinge of guilt that I had immediately thought of Charls, not Jason; then I realised that was just how it was. Jason was not in this world with me and could offer no help. It was natural that I would think of turning to Charls for support. Guilt would do me no favours, would hold me back – would hold *all* of us back. Energy high, Keira!

~~~

Knowing only that something dark or challenging was probably not far ahead, it took some effort and focus to keep moving forward at our accustomed pace. I wondered briefly how many 'challenges' would be placed before us before we arrived at our destination. It was an idle thought, and I did not allow myself to dwell on it, and focused instead on Tobin's joy at seeing

219

magic, at the wonder of the waterfall, on the sound of our feet hitting the ground as we walked, on the way my now dry clothes felt as they moved against my skin, and on the smell of the air.

Was it in fact less musty? The atmosphere seemed sharper, clearer, somehow more defined. I was alert, and although a little wary of our next 'encounter', I trusted that with the support of lovelight, the villagers and the Ascended Reikans, I would continue to make decisions that would lead to the best outcome for Cordello and for lovelight.

We kept going, plodding onwards, each footfall one step closer to our goal. I tried to walk confidently, and not hold back when the rock walls curved away from me. I could not start envisioning malevolence hiding behind each bend in the tunnel walls – it would drain me of energy that would be needed. Somehow, I maintained a balance, almost dichotomous, between thoughts positive and happy, and of thoughts cautious and wary, ready to confront danger.

Still we walked, *still* we met nothing. The air had remained sweeter; how on earth did this reconcile with the threat of dark energy lurking and drawing on our lovelight–sphere?

Unless the darkness was disguised as something else . . .

CHAPTER 25

"Do you have a plan, m'lord?" Burron asked.

Charls did not immediately respond. He was not sure that this young warrior would feel comforted by the knowledge that his leader, his lord, was placing his faith in a population of beings that only he and Keira had seen. His companions would understand acting on instinct, though; those trained in combat understood the ability to make snap decisions. Angel–like figures appearing in front of you – or in your head – was a slightly different matter. It had been so easy to share those experiences with Keira; was it just easier to discuss spiritual matters with women? Or was it that Keira was special? He smiled at the question. It had only one possible answer.

He dragged his mind back to Burron's question, preparing his response.

"We head east, keeping to cover where we can. I alone, with the Canturan sphere, will go into the village and see if I can locate Tissa. As we have only one communication disc, I will have no way to communicate with you unless Tissa – or I – find another. So I will need to return before further decisions are taken. First, I want to know where Karn is. Then I want to locate Symion's family . . . I hope the old guy is still alive. After that, I will trust my gut."

Charls turned towards Burron. "I place you as my second–in–command, Burron; so if you become aware that I have been injured or killed, you should assume leadership of these warriors, and act as you think is best."

"My lord!" Burron was surprised, but Charls thought

he detected a gleam of pleasure in the younger man's face.

Fields to the side of the gravelled road gave way to copses of trees, and fences retaining deer and other livestock. Charls' keen eyesight noted the outskirts of the village, smoke rising from a distant chimney. Should he leave the others here? He thought so; there was good cover and the road seemed deserted. They headed quietly and carefully into the trees, leaving no tracks; some climbed into the branches for additional concealment.

Charls fingered the pouch containing the Canturan sphere, took a steadying breath. Then he placed his thumb and index finger inside the pouch, removed the little crystal globe.

And vanished from sight.

~~~

The tunnel floor started sloping downhill again, taking us deeper into the earth. Where was this clean air coming from? There was a sense, a feeling, a *knowing* of something familiar – something outdoorsy, fresh, rejuvenating. My nose and brain finally communicated with one another, and I recognised the scent of pine being carried towards us. *Trees.* But how was that even possible – we were deep underground!

My curiosity aroused, my steps picked up pace. I sent a thought to Roanne and the others, reminding us all to remain cautious. The spherical light continued to flicker occasionally, and was now fading, so either it was being drained, or we were approaching an area with more light.

And there it was.

222

After heading around a double–curved 'S'–bend in the tunnel, I walked out into the middle of a wide, open ledge. It overlooked a vast cavern with a lofty ceiling. The others gathered around me, being careful to stay back from the edge. Julianna gripped Tobin's hand. Even the older lad refrained from peering over the edge. It was a long, long way down, and it would be a very hard landing.

We stared at the unexpected sight before us.

The cavern was shaped like a wide, shallow bowl, with a high domed roof. There was no daylight here, but soft illumination was cast by a series of semi–spherical lighted objects suspended at regular intervals around the edges of the huge space. The colour and feel of the light reminded me of the gentle illumination that I'd seen at intervals in the tunnels leading from Reika into Cordello.

Set into the bowl was a dense cluster of pine trees, their trunks hidden by tightly–massed branches clothed in forest–green leaves. Almost cone–shaped, each tree was, I guessed, around fifty feet tall. The scent was not overpowering, simply fresh and clean.

I estimated that the little forest contained probably thirty or more trees. I could not hazard a guess as to their purpose, or who had planted them, or even how or when. Without sunlight and irrigation, how were they fed and watered? Who had placed the lights? Who maintained them? All questions that, for now, had no answers.

My pale sphere–light nudged my shoulder, as if asking whether it should dissolve. I asked it to remain as an orb; I never knew when we might need it in a hurry. It glided upwards to hover above my crown; I felt a tingling sensation prickling the top of my head. I looked

223

out over the vast forest, and the space surrounding it. The forest was encircled by a smooth stone walkway or path, which was accessed by a very long flight of stone steps. These steps led directly up to the far side of our ledge.

To continue, to move ahead on our journey, we would have to trek down and into this cavern, and find another way out. So, what place was this? I retrieved the map and tracked our journey from the Cavern of Silent Shadows . . . my finger traced the middle tunnel to . . . *here*. I found that I could read the name of this place. The Cavern of the Weeping Pines. *Weeping*? They looked perfectly upright to me! Healthy. Completely normal – if a little taller than I was used to.

The map appeared to furnish me with relevant information only when it felt like it. I could see no visible exit from this Cavern, although I supposed there must be one.

I let Roanne know what the map had revealed to me, allowing her to pass the information to the villagers whilst I let my thoughts roam on our current situation. There must be a way out. We just had to follow our intuition, and expect information to be provided as we needed it.

I moved towards the top step. Roanne caught my eye as I passed her, and gave me a reassuring nod. "It'll be okay, Lady Keira. *Trust.*"

I certainly hoped and intended so.

Placing my foot on the first step, I found the going to be easy as long as I leaned into the smooth rock wall to my left. We were still so high up; we couldn't risk anyone tumbling over the exposed edge of the stairway and falling to the ground far below. I refused to look too far ahead, keeping my eyes on the next two steps only.

Down, down, down we went. I counted to a hundred, then lost track. Checking back, I was relieved to see that everyone was following, and seemed safe. We were nearly at the bottom now, almost at the paved stones leading to the pines. There was no other clear way through; large boulders skirted the path, each huge rock smothered with a fiercely–prickled mossy plant. We were being persuaded to keep to the path.

At the point where the pathway joined the track circumventing the pines, I stopped. I don't know why – it was just an instinct. The air had changed. I felt a cool breeze. Perhaps it came from our exit doorway, wherever it was?

Then I became aware of a dull, creaking sound coming from above us.

I looked up, my eyes widening.

The trees' branches were bending, somehow flexing so that they were hanging over our walkway. Now they *were* weeping pines. The breeze strengthened – I know not how – and it seemed as though the trees were tossing their bodies about, as if in distress. Then, to my amazement, I felt droplets of water landing on my face and shoulders. It was raining. *Indoors.*

Tobin cried out: "Look, Mummy! The trees are crying!"

So they were. *The weeping pines.* So – what should we do about it? Were these apparently tormented trees any danger to us? *No,* came my answer. Why, then, this 'performance'?

"Lady Keira," Tobin voiced, tugging at my sleeve.

"Yes, love?" I said, looking down into his little face, which displayed his bafflement.

"Why are the trees sad? Can we make them better?"

Trust a child to get to the heart of the matter. *Trust,*

225

Roanne had told me.

"I don't know why they're sad," I told Tobin, as I let my eyes slide up the trunks towards their overhanging, dripping, anguished branches. The trees appeared to be utterly miserable. "But I think it might be a good idea to do some more magic, don't you?"

Tobin's eyes widened with excitement; he couldn't keep himself still. I communicated my thoughts to the others.

"Folks, I do not believe that these trees are any threat to us . . . I think they need our help. And our response to their distress may have an effect on what happens to us later on. 'You get back what you give out', that sort of thing. I know the trees look a bit *odd* . . . but my intuition is telling me that we need to support these trees, to send them our positive energies."

I suggested we spread ourselves out on the circular path around the trees, and again each connect with lovelight, sending its loving energy to the distressed trees, together with our happy feelings.

As I'd asked, the villagers made their way onto and around the path, ducking under the twisted, dripping branches. The creaking sounded ominous, but I didn't feel that it should worry us. The trees were simply displaying to us their need for support. Once we were spaced around the path (not that I could see anyone else), I began my connection to lovelight, and felt the villagers start linking themselves to the energy. I thought of Jason, of Charls, of sunshine and rainbows, of the Cantura bird and of eagles soaring high over fertile valleys, of cherry blossom and warm gentle summer rains.

And we poured out to the trees all the lovelight that we could channel.

I kept my eyes closed to help maintain a strong focus on my bright internal images. My sense of smell and hearing and touch were heightened, and I soon began to notice changes. First, I noticed that the pine scent was strengthening. A sweet, swishing noise replaced the cry of the wind and the pelt of the rain as the tears of the trees came to a stop. I opened my eyes and saw the trees slowly restoring their shape to that of normal pines. Their needles were bright and I could see a faint white glow surrounding the forest like a pale halo.

A sudden burst of thought flooded my mind. I *knew* that the trees had been in distress because of the deforestation taking place back in my own world. Somehow, the tree energies in both worlds were connected. This world *was* linked to mine . . . and not just by me coming here. Therefore, it could be that the saving of lovelight would have an impact in *my* world too.

And in restoring some energy, some love, some appreciation to this little forest, we had acknowledged that trees were valued, that they were worth saving, worth protecting.

"Look at their auras!" breathed Roanne.

Oh. So that's what the glow was! Roanne caught my look of surprise.

"All living things have energy fields and auras," she confirmed. "That's why Cordello is so rich in flora . . . lovelight creates a wonderful environment for growth and renewal. And now we've helped these trees regain their happiness!"

I felt liquid forming in my eyes. Trees had spirit; despite my love of plants, I had never known this. I would be much more careful how I treated my plants in future. They were *aware.*

227

Now that we had restored the trees to a loved, nurtured state, I wanted to ensure that they remained healthy and filled with vitality. If we were no longer here providing them with a continuous stream of lovelight, would their branches droop and the trees return to their misery? I genuinely felt a sense of regret – and of failure – at the thought of the trees returning to such low spirits.

"How can we keep them in this state, Roanne?" I asked.

"You mean: keep them happy? Energised?"

"Yes. Otherwise, everything we've done here is a waste of energy and effort."

"I agree. Well, we could create orbs of lovelight. Then we can program them to feed the energy to the pines as and when they need it."

"You can program them remotely? From a distance?" This seemed incredible. But lovelight *was* incredible!

"Oh yes! Energy spheres are highly responsive to our intention. We Cordellans can each create a special sphere just for the pines. Then we can tune in to our orbs each day, and draw on a little lovelight, which we then send on to the orbs to replace what they have used."

"That sounds like the perfect solution. Would you arrange it all, please? Get everyone to make this – orb?"

"Of course, Lady Keira. I'm glad to have a job to do!"

I smiled, and left her and the other Cordellans to their task.

I gave some thought to the next part of our journey. Several times, I walked the full circumference of the path around the miniature pine forest, looking for a way out. The rock walls were separated from the walkway by the giant, prickle–topped boulders, and I could not see – or think of – any way across these without sustaining injury. Aside from that, from my vantage point, there was no exit through the rock anyway. Nor could I see any symbols carved into the walls.

How on earth could we leave this cavern?

I checked the map again, but, frustratingly, the diagram showed the cavern as being surrounded by a blank space. So, I was not to know – yet – what was beyond the cavern. I would have to work it out. I folded the map and looked up at the vast space above me. The soft lighting on the rock–wall was located a good way above the height of the trees, and there appeared to be no way of accessing the lights.

I turned and looked at the trees. Tall, but only half as tall as the height of the cavern. Steps leading back to the ledge – our entrance. I could see no way out.

I spied several globes of lovelight hovering among the trees. Roanne and the villagers had finished creating their energy source for the forest.

"Roanne?"

"Lady Keira?"

"Do you see any exits?"

"No. I've been looking, but . . . no, nothing obvious."

She made her way around the circular path, stopping a few feet away from me. She, too, was looking at the trees. "Maybe, now that we've done them a favour, they could return it, so to speak?"

"I'd wondered the same thing, but I can't work out how they could help."

"Um . . . well, why not ask?"

"The Ascended Reikans?" I queried.

"Well, them too," Roanne stated, "but I meant: ask the

trees."

Oh. No, that thought hadn't occurred to me. I'd thought of climbing them . . . but asking for their help hadn't exactly been the first idea to pop into my head.

"Have you ever done that before?" I asked, looking at her quizzically.

"No!" she laughed. "But I've learned that nothing in here is as it seems. The rules have changed . . . or been broken; we need to be creative."

That was true. So . . . ask the trees. Right.

"Don't think, just do it!" Roanne whispered.

I sent to the trees an image–thought of us all trapped here, not knowing how to get out; I sent images of the new orbs and of lovelight flowing into the trees; of their glowing auras; of their tall, proud trunks and healthy deep–green needles. I asked for their help in finding a way out so that we could continue on our quest to protect lovelight.

Then I waited.

To begin with, I heard and felt nothing. Then I noticed that I could hear a faint rustling; my inner guidance told me that the trees were communicating. It was barely audible; I seemed to be aware of the hint of sound almost through a sixth sense. Out of the corner of my eye, I spotted Tobin pulling at Julianna's hand, so that she lowered her head to his. I watched as he cupped his small hands to her ear and whispered. The little boy seemed to prefer voice communication over telepathy.

Julianna straightened up and her eyes met mine. She walked towards me. She, too, on this occasion, chose voice over thought–communication.

"Lady Keira, this may sound ridiculous, but Tobin says that the trees have some information for you. He normally tells the truth, so I don't know where he's getting this story from –"

"It's okay," I reassured her. "I did ask the trees for help. They may have communicated by our youngest traveller for a reason. What did he say?"

"He said that we need to sit under the lowest branches of the pines, on the fallen pine needles, and then to wait."

"Is that all? Was there anything else?"

"Tobin!" his mother called. He came running over.

"Tell Lady Keira about the lights," she said to him.

"The trees said that the lights will carry us out to the tunnels."

"They'll *carry* us?" I clarified.

"Yes! Like Mummy carries me when I'm tired. But we have to wait under the branches, and we have to trust them."

Trust again. I asked the Ascended Reikans to confirm whether Tobin's suggestion – *information* – was correct. *Yes.* Well, it sounded bizarre, but as Roanne had said, things were different this side of the waterfall. In fact, things were different in this *world*, so why was I surprised that a bunch of trees were asking us to sit underneath them, so that we could be carried by light? We'd give it a try – we had no other bright ideas.

Roanne passed instructions to the villagers, and again we spread out on the circular path, then each crouched down and shuffled under the lower branches of the pines, our feet brushing through their soft straw. Roanne sat under the tree to my left, Julianna and Tobin off to my right. I sat with legs drawn in, my arms hugging my knees, and eyes closed. And we began our wait.

Suddenly, I began to feel dizzy, as if I had lost touch with the ground. I tried to open my eyes, to find a horizon to focus upon, but my eyelids seemed to be sealed shut. I felt my body shifting from side–to–side, as if I was no longer subject to the laws of gravity. Well, I supposed anything was possible! Tilted this way and that, I felt the beginnings of queasiness flare in my stomach. I held my legs tightly close within my wrapped arms. I had no idea what was going on! It was probably the same for Roanne and the others. Then, gradually, the motion–sickness eased, and I felt that I was still again. My eyes opened easily, and of their own volition.

I hoped no–one had a fear of heights. We – and the trees – had been lifted half–way up the centre of the cavern. We were at exactly the same height as the glowing lights on the rock–wall. That was *high*. I gulped.

Don't look down, I said to myself, over and over like a mantra. *Don't look down.*

Of course, I did.

Yikes. We were sat on a large opaque disc of white light, like a modern–day circular magic carpet. Ahead, I could see the ledge, and the steps. I looked down through the surface of the shimmering disc and spotted the ghostly outline of the circular walkway far beneath. The trees remained above us; the sheet of light held us *and* the forest up in the air, high above the ground. When I looked again at the wall–lights, I could see shimmering strands reaching out from each light–source to the disc. Perhaps the glowing lights were somehow powering this floating panel.

Casting a glance at Tobin, I was relieved to see that he wasn't frightened. He was having the time of his life – magic everywhere!

CHAPTER 26

Charls had taken the time to forewarn his little team that he would disappear so that no–one would panic when he became invisible. He knew that his band of warriors would stay put and wait – unless Burron heard that Charls would be unable to return.

Charls walked purposefully along the lane. He kept to the centre of the road so that any small noise his footsteps created would be as far from the houses as possible. He didn't trust the Canturan sphere to block all sound – he felt that he should proceed as cautiously as if he didn't have the special object. He hoped that any sound that he might produce in busier places would be covered by the general hubbub made by the Vornen people.

As he passed the last of the houses, he heard the sound of voices and shouts; the noise appeared to be coming from somewhere off to his left. Quietly, he made his way down the track towards the noise. He was entering the square. There were dozens of people, and they did not look happy. Arms and fists were raised, faces were grim and angry. What was going on? This sort of thing didn't happen in Cordello, and Charls found the atmosphere uncomfortably edgy and disharmonious.

Then he saw the cause of the disruption. A woman was tied to a thick stone post in the centre of the square. There was something familiar about her, but he couldn't quite grasp the fleeting impression before it melted away. The woman cried out and a chill ran down Charls' back, leaving him cold, filling him with the buzz of adrenaline. She shook her head as if in defiance – and then he had it. He felt as though someone had punched him in the stomach.

It was Tissa.

This was *his* fault. He should have stopped her from leaving. Persuaded her to take one of the special devices. Provided her with an escort, some protection. Then he remembered her pride, her insistence that she could do this alone. He realised that he'd never have been able to stop her.

Charls knew he had to do something. To free her, if he could. But how? She was surrounded on all sides by men and women screaming their rage, venting their frustration, spitting their *hatred*. And Tissa, strong and fierce and proud, would not have endeared herself to them in any way.

~~~

The strands flowing between the rock walls and our hovering disc wavered and twisted like malleable lightning. They flexed, turned, shifted and flipped. Somehow those tresses of light were keeping us, the disc and the trees at this elevated height – although I had not yet established how, or why.

As far as I could see, not one of us had moved from our seated position – possibly we were all worried that we'd affect the platform's centre of gravity, or stability. Yet, it held dozens of tall trees, as well as all of us, so surely it would be designed to take a little movement? Hesitantly, but feeling I had to make an attempt, I shifted position so that I was kneeling on the disc, my hands in the caramel pine needles. Slowly, I moved my left leg and placed my foot solidly onto the straw. Then, crouching under the low boughs of the pine, I moved my right leg and shuffled myself forward so that I could stand upright, beyond the trees' reach. I walked forward onto the white–light surface, and stopped about halfway across the whole diameter of the light–disc.

My eyes started to water, and I noticed that the air felt different up here. I squinted towards the edge of the disc. The area above the perimeter seemed also to shimmer, and I knew that I was looking at some kind of energy–field – perhaps it protected us? I felt a small hand in mine. Tobin had joined me.

"What d'you think, Tobin?" I whispered, looking down at him. "Are you liking all the magic?"

"Oh *yes*, Lady Keira . . . but the trees asked me to tell you something more."

"Something *more?*"

"Yes. They said that we'll be shown the way out."

"Oh. I don't suppose they said *when* this would happen?"

"Now. When I'd told you about it."

I looked up from his earnest little face. I now realised that the disc was slowly spinning. The rotation was hardly noticeable, but the view directly ahead of me had changed. Instead of facing the ledge, as I had been a few moments ago, I was now looking at a blank rock–face. The disc stopped rotating, and I watched, aware of Tobin's small hand still trustingly placed in mine.

I blinked. Had the rock pulsed – just for a moment? A chill ran across my back and I sensed the presence of the Ascended Reikans. *Trust.* I allowed my mind to play creatively. I could not reach out to touch the wall; it was still so far away. So I could not place my hand on the shimmering area, in order to channel lovelight into it.

But I could send the lovelight across a distance!

"Roanne!" I sent. She arrived moments later, several of the villagers also taking their first steps on this

235

strange device. "Let's get everyone together; the disc is stable enough. I think we need to send lovelight by distance into that point there," I said, pointing to the exact location at which I had seen a quivering ripple in the rock–face.

"Sounds good to me," she grinned, and began bringing everyone towards Tobin and me. I continued focusing on the area that I'd seen vibrate, quietly desperate not to lose my point of reference. I guessed Roanne would pass instructions to the others; they had not seen the pulse so would need to link their energies and intention with mine.

I reinforced my connection with lovelight, and intended that it flow through me towards that precise spot on the rock; and that all other lovelight energies being sent would hit that *exact* same spot. I knew intuitively that the energies would be allowed through the protective force–field. That was just the way it would be.

The energy felt strong and flowed well, the tingle on my scalp becoming more of a constant soft buzz as the lovelight poured into me and out towards the rock wall. I maintained the focus through my gaze, as Tobin's hand remained in mine. I knew I didn't need to beam the energy with my hands, just my intent.

Was it my imagination or was the wall getting closer to us? Of course, the disc must be moving *towards* the rock wall, transporting us over the spike–encrusted boulders below. The twisting light filaments were shortening on this side of the disc; presumably those on the far side were stretching to compensate. Well, this was an unusual way to travel, but then not much about my time here had been *normal*.

Closer and closer we came to the rock–face, until I

began to wonder whether the disc would crash into it. I visualised the platform stopping as a boat comes gently into its mooring . . . at least if the pilot knows what he is doing. The circular sheet stopped a few inches from the rock. I released Tobin's hand and walked forwards towards the rock–face, stopping about three feet away from it.

For some unexplainable reason – once again following my intuition – I did not step closer to the rock wall. I stretched out my right hand, allowing it to hover vertically in front of the spot that I had seen shimmering.

~~~

I had to trust that we'd done the right thing, that my tried and trusted tactic of sending lovelight would not fail us. As I continued to watch, the remaining force–field dissolved so that we could see the rock–face with complete clarity. I let my arm fall to my side.

What happened next took my remaining breath away.

The rock–face melted like grey lava, displaying creases and folds as if it was burning and melting from the other side. We could see it shifting and twisting. It made no sound. Next, the colour of the rock changed, by degrees, from a soft dove–grey to a pale toffee shade. I could sense the thoughts of the villagers, quiet admissions of awe, tinged now and then with an element of suspicion. The folds in the rock continued to meld and wrinkle. The rock's colour deepened to a beautiful russet, the colour of a crisp autumn leaf. We couldn't take our eyes from the metamorphosis – we had no exit yet, but this looked promising!

Roanne quietly moved next to me, and sent: "Do you

237

know what's happening, Lady Keira?"

"Not really," I confessed. "I saw things in the underground tunnels leading to the village – things that I could not explain. Shimmering symbols, and doorways that appeared from nowhere. But nothing that changed bit by bit, like we are seeing now."

"We were told that an ancient civilisation fashioned the magical elements of the tunnels of which you speak. So perhaps it is the same situation, here? It is likely that the Ascended beings had a hand in all of this, too . . ."

I agreed. "Their contribution certainly seems to have been a massive one; they are like a supportive framework for those of us left in human form." I thought for a moment, before continuing. "It's odd, you know – part of me is aware that the Cordellan lords and many others are out there, fighting for us and for lovelight, and I expected to feel a sense of urgency because of that. And yet –"

"And yet?"

"Yet inside this tunnel and cavern system, I feel as if time has held still, as if this under–world has been waiting for us to experience it. I feel no rush, just a sense of adventure, of exploration."

Roanne had an opinion on that. "It may be because we are cut off from the outside world; we have no way of knowing how they are faring. In *here*, our focus is on the current moment, there is no 'future', really, because it's completely unknown. There is only 'now'."

Letting our thoughts still, we continued to watch the rock flex and re–shape.

"Here it comes," I sent.

"How do you know?" Roanne was surprised.

"I just do . . ."

The rock vanished behind a screen of soft–pink and

white light, as if the lovelight that we had sent had reached a climax and exploded in one single burst. Thin drifting strands of peach–rose–white gossamer light obscured the rock. These finally evaporated.

I heard gasps of awe from those nearby. The opening in the rock wall was still not clearly visible – the edges of the opening were blurred, and the gap in the rock was sheathed in a veil of translucent peach–white light, as if lovelight continued to protect the doorway. What did this mean? Would only some of us be allowed access? That couldn't be right – we were all in this together. There was no other way to go!

I asked my intuition: Do we all go through? *Yes.* I sighed with relief. I would not have been able to leave anyone behind. Do I go first? *Yes.* That, I expected. This doorway was unusual, though – *more* unusual than those we had used before, anyway. And so I was a little nervous. Walking through waterfalls was one thing; a sheet of moving coloured light was . . . different.

CHAPTER 27

Then I remembered, just as if it had happened mere moments ago, my 'fall' through the light and into Reika. I knew that this could be very similar. There was no need to feel any fear or apprehension. I recalled the support available from the invisible Ascended Reikans, and felt a calm confidence descend upon me once again. My sphere of light remained above my head, and I asked it to remain close by me as I made my way slowly towards the shifting curtain of pastel–coloured light.

I sent a request to Roanne to send each person through one at a time once I had gone through, and before following herself; she readily agreed. This just felt to me to be the best way to proceed. In retrospect, perhaps it was not the best decision, but at the time, I could not have known that.

As I approached the light, it seemed to reach out towards me. I saw layers of light wrap around my body; felt as if I was enveloped in skeins of silk thread, like a chrysalis waiting to begin its transformation. Fully enclosed within a hemisphere of the beautiful flowing light, with the veil ahead of me hanging like a cascade of light strands, I reached the opening in the rock.

I took my first steps through the light–filled gap in the rock–face and felt indescribably peaceful – completely 'blissed out'. Time seemed to pause – I felt I could stay here in this amazing state forever. Tears streamed down my face; I felt so utterly safe and protected and supported and cherished. For a few moments, the emotions overwhelmed me.

Then I knew that I had to move forward again. It was time.

I lifted a hand to dry my tears, although I left my smile in place. In one further step, I was through the gap in the rock–face and out the other side. It was nothing like I expected. Although I was moving forward, walking on an apparently solid surface, all I could see was light and swirling rainbow and pastel threads of colour twisting in the air. I imagined that walking in the lovelight–charged clouds – if it were possible – would feel similar to this.

This felt like a kind of 'in–between world', a space between the underground cavern and – whatever came next. Should I keep going? Or wait? A *Yes* response came to my second question. I turned, and faced the direction from which I had come. I saw Julianna and Tobin emerge from the light–curtain into this space of light. Both were crying and looked a little dazed.

The other villagers followed, reappearing only seconds apart, and I waited for Roanne.

She didn't appear.

The teenager, Jos, confirmed that Roanne had been right behind him as he'd entered the light. Where was she? I tried connecting with her by thought, and felt a barrier. This was likely a result of the light–streams.

Come on, Roanne, I thought. *What's keeping you?*

Immediately, I had an image presented to my mind. She had stopped in the light–cascade, as we all had, but could not will herself forward, could not leave the bliss behind.

What should I do?

Without consciously deciding to do so, I began to walk back across the space to the entrance. I didn't even know if this 'portal' was one–way; would I dematerialise if I tried to go back in? Or would the fact that I was on a rescue mission keep me safe? I sent a brief, heartfelt request to the Ascended Reikans to support and protect me, knowing that they were wholly aware of the details of this situation.

I reached the gap and, taking a deep breath, placed my foot forward. I had a déjà vu moment, recalling stepping into the huge crag in the stone circle before finding I had no ground beneath my feet. I willed myself to push that memory aside, to feel confidence in my movement. And then, suddenly, I was back in the tunnel of bliss and light. Roanne stood just ahead of me, her eyes closed, her cheeks streaked with trails of slow tears. I reached for her, taking her hand and gently tugging her towards me.

"Roanne," I sent, "we have to go. You can't stay here."

"I want to, so badly," she sent back. "All my hurt is healed when I stand here, and I'm scared to leave, scared all the pain will return! I don't know if I can take it back!"

"I know . . . it feels wonderful, and healing, and supportive. But there is more light *outside*. This is a temporary state, Ro, this was never meant to be all there is. You have a choice, Ro. You can let the pain go any time you want."

"Please . . . " she whispered.

I was crying again, partly due to the energies in this space, partly with empathy for Roanne. I didn't know what hurts she wanted relieved, only that her pain was tangible, even in this high–energy place.

"Ro, we can heal this – together, if you want – back in the real world. This is not forever – how can it be? *You must come back with me.*" I gripped her hand more tightly, and turned, intending to drag her behind me if necessary. If she remained here, she would be isolated, would become lost, would die. I wouldn't let that

242

happen to her. Resolutely, I stepped forward, relief washing through me when I felt Roanne following close behind. I kept hold of her hand, not wanting to risk her turning back.

I breathed an audible sigh of deep relief when we passed into the outer light–world and joined the others. Only then did I release Roanne's hand. She looked at me as if in shock.

"I'm so sorry. I'm so sorry, Lady Keira! It just all became – too much –"

"It's okay," I said, giving her a hug. "It's okay."

She looked around her, taking in the space, the light, the colours. "Wow. Thanks for bringing me through that. This is spectacular!"

"Can you help me with the map, Roanne? Please?" I needed to remind her that she was important to me, to our journey, to lovelight. She had a role to play – as did we all – and I felt that jogging her mind back to the present was the right move. I retrieved the map from its pocket, and we studied it together.

~~~

To my surprise, the 'empty space' on the map had not been filled in. We still had no idea where we were now, or where to go next. Despite the seeming endlessness of the space, all of us were gathered in a loose group, none of us wanting to stray too far from the rest. Pastel light continued to swirl and move; there was nothing else to see but pale, gentle, soothing colour. It was very peaceful and uplifting, however it gave me no clue as to our next steps.

For once, I felt uncertain as to what questions I should ask of my inner guidance. This place felt like an intermediate staging post. It also felt safe. Since I could not acquire any new information from the map, I seated myself on the unusual soft–solid surface (this too, being obscured by light–threads of shell–pink and palest yellow), and invited Roanne to sit with me.

Tobin decided to join us, his little face beaming with delight at the swirling light–energy.

"Lady Keira!" he shouted joyfully.

"Yes, Tobin?" I replied, unable to stop a grin from breaking across my face. His good spirits were infectious.

"Have you seen the tower?"

Tower? There was a tower here? I looked around me, unable to see anything except the flexing light–strands.

"Not there!" he called, as I looked over my shoulder to see if I'd missed something behind me.

"Where, then, Tobin?" Roanne asked, as she too apparently saw no tower.

"*There!*" Tobin pointed into the distance straight ahead of us.

I peered into the light. Strained my eyes. Roanne and I looked at each other, bemused.

"Is he bothering you, Lady Keira?" Julianna sent, as she walked towards us, a frown creasing her forehead.

"No, of course not . . . he's fine. It's just that he says he sees a tower . . . but neither Ro nor I can see it!"

"Oh, Tobin often sees things that aren't yet visible to the rest of us," she clarified. "He seems to have a gift for seeing things that are not yet – *visually manifest* – in our world. He's not been wrong, yet. The tower is over there, yes?"

"That's right."

"Well, he's never seen a *tower* before, but I'd hazard a guess and say that it will be visible to you within a few days."

I laughed. "I hope we aren't here for a few *days!*" Then I received a nudge from Roanne.

"Look!" She raised her arm forwards, pointing at a spot about thirty feet ahead of us.

I gasped.

As we watched, an ethereal shape began to take form.

It began as just a vague gathering of light, very tall and just a few feet wide. Then it expanded and started to acquire depth. The pastel light began to become whiter, and the perimeter took on a silver hue. Everyone was paying serious attention to this . . . manifestation.

The image took on a clearer outline, becoming of substance, soaring upwards. Light–strands swirled around it. The tower – for it clearly *was* a tower – became more and more defined, until it stood before us, glittering and magnificent.

It looked like – crystal. Oh my God.

Was this the tower that Charls had told me of? From Reika? *Yes.*

The thrill of being shown this was immense. The honour that the Ascended Reikans accorded us was enormous. I was speechless and could not form thoughts. Everyone just looked at the crystal tower. None dared approach.

Then, as suddenly as it had come, it started to disintegrate. Tobin turned to me with sad eyes and said: "It's because the lovely energy is not safe, yet. We have to make sure it's okay before we'll be allowed to enter the tower."

I swallowed. I had given no thought to entering such a magical place. But if it were *possible* . . . then yes, I would be glad to have the privilege of seeing more of it. Tobin's message reminded me that we had not yet determined the next phase in our journey. Had the map now been updated? I pulled it from its safe pocket, unfolded it and laid it over my crossed legs.

Ahhh. Now we had information.

~~~

"Look, Ro!" I squeaked. She leaned close so that she, too, could see the detail of the map.

Now, the map displayed a name for our present location: 'The Light Portal of Bliss.' What a fantastic name. The euphoric pathway through from the Cavern of the Weeping Pines had been incredible, and would be unforgettable. The space we were in right now seemed to be a part of it. That possibly explained why the crystal tower had briefly appeared here; it could only reveal itself in an area flooded with an extremely high energetic vibration.

"So . . . where next?" Roanne sent to me. I tried to remain relaxed, whilst also concentrating on our desired outcome – finding the right way out. I intended that the information I needed would come to me easily.

I then felt the strongest urge to look up – and saw the light shear for just a few seconds, revealing a cream stone pathway leading off into the pastel light.

"There!" I pointed.

Roanne caught sight of it just before it vanished. I checked the map. Yes, there were four possible pathways set at right angles to each other. The one that we had seen was the second to the left after exiting the short passageway through the Light Portal of Bliss.

I jumped up, Roanne close beside me. Julianna had seen the path, too, and had already taken Tobin's hand. Jos and the others scrambled to their feet, ready to follow where we led.

Although the path had again disappeared from view, I knew exactly which way to go. I walked forwards, into the swirling coloured light, Roanne and the villagers behind me. Within moments, my feet left the odd solid–light surface and moved onto the firm stone. Still, the light filaments obscured my view of the way ahead, but I felt a deep sense of trust that I was on the right path.

I kept walking, wondering what lay ahead. It felt very strange to be moving on this narrow pathway, yet still enveloped by the light strands. Would we encounter another doorway? Or would the coloured light simply fade away, to be replaced by something more . . . normal?

My question was answered fairly soon after I gave voice to the thought. A gap in the light appeared. This time the break in the light strands remained open. Surrounded by the light, the gap appeared as a yawning black hole; not particularly inviting. But I knew we were in the right place at the right time, so we would just have to go with whatever presented itself.

Without hesitation, knowing that I was guided by the Ascended Relkans and by the pure energy of lovelight, I walked into the darkness, letting it swallow me whole. I trusted that my confidence would encourage the villagers to follow me without anxiety. Being inside the black space felt extremely odd after being surrounded by so much light; I requested my little orb–light to expand and cast a light–glow ahead, so that I could see what was in front of me. It did so, and I noticed with wry amusement that we had yet another tunnel to navigate. I didn't suppose that it would be the last.

The map had not indicated what lay at the end of this tunnel, so we would just keep going until another decision was required. After the open space of the Light Portal, I found the tunnel confining and claustrophobic. I curbed my impatience to be back in a spacious place, knowing that this phase of our journey would take as long as it took, and that I could not hurry it. Patience had never been one of my virtues – it seemed I would have to start practicing.

On we went, sometimes the path curving right or left, sometimes the ground taking us uphill, sometimes down. One step, then another, then another. It seemed to last for hours; maybe it did. The air was musty again, and I was almost tempted to turn around and retrace my steps to the Light Portal. That, though, was not the way forward, and would not save lovelight. Or Charls.

Wandering through monotonous tunnels seemed to jog my mind back into worry–mode, and I caught myself feeling anxiety for him and those fighting with him. I made myself stop that train of thought – and focused on counting my footsteps. I lost count at something over a thousand, and started again.

Then Tobin started to sing; I didn't understand the words, but the villagers seemed to know the song, as many of them joined in. What a great way to keep our spirits up, and to hold our focus on the 'here and now'! I hummed along. The tunnel acoustics played in our favour, giving our melody a slight echo that enhanced the overall sound. We started walking in time to the song, and time passed much more quickly. I wondered how singing became a part of their world, when most of their communication was through the mind–connection. Maybe it was a social activity? *Yes.*

Then, as it had done before, my little orb–light began to fade, and I guessed we were approaching another cavern or open space with its own light source. The tunnel became wider, and higher, and opened out.

~~~

Feeling helpless, watching Tissa writhe and cry out as she was bombarded with stones, followed by lashes from thin, whippy sticks, and then hard blows to her body by those closest to her, Charls tried to concentrate for long enough to form a plan. Hearing her scream was tearing his focus to shreds.

He backed away, edged around a corner out of the mêlée, attempted to work out a means of freeing his cousin. No, he didn't love her, not romantically – but she was family, and Cordellan, and in trouble. And he was the only one with a chance of setting her free from these barbaric people.

Charls found that his free hand had automatically taken hold of his knife. He tucked the Canturan sphere into a zipped pocket to keep it safe and allow him the use of both hands. An aura of calm descended upon him, and he recognised it for what it was – support from his Reikan helpers.

Feeling more centred, he remembered to create a link with lovelight, before asking for additional help and guidance from the Ascended Reikans. He knew that's what Keira would have done.

Moving quietly, balancing on the balls of his feet, he made his way back into the square, threading his way silently between the people that moved unknowingly across his path. The noise they made was both fantastic and horrific. Gradually, he created a path towards the stone post to which Tissa was bound. She was not as heavily surrounded as he'd thought; he could see her hands and ankles tied around and behind the post.

249

There was no–one standing behind her.

He crept forward, ducking as a heavyset man with a face like a gremlin swung a fat arm towards Tissa, catching his ring on her cheek, snarling with triumph as blood fell from the gash on her face. Charls struggled to contain his roar of rage, let it power him forwards. Reaching her bound hands, he held onto the join in the rope to protect Tissa's skin as he began to saw at the rough material with his blade. He felt Tissa jolt with surprise, but it was not she who gave him away.

It was the dog.

He'd cut more than halfway through the rope when a sandy mongrel snapped at his leg, before backing off and barking. At first no–one else took any notice, but then one or two of the Vornen rabble began to wonder why the dog was persisting in barking, snarling and leaping upwards near the post.

One of the guards watching Tissa – and provoking the crowd – bumped against Charls' arm and yelped in fear. The dog whined, sitting back on its haunches and baring its teeth.

Charls continued sawing at the rope, but his time was fast running out.

CHAPTER 28

My guiding light automatically pulled into a tight ball and resumed its earlier location above my head. The space that I led us into was cosy, and somewhat similar to the Cavern of Silent Shadows, but this place had spherical light–sources around the walls, casting an opal glow across the small area. I hoped that, this time, we really would be able to spend some time here in safety. To me, the space had a good feel to it, and Roanne's opinion of the 'energy' in the area was that it was light and happy.

The tunnel–walk had left my feet sore and weary, and my legs ached after all the walking of the day; I was sure the others felt tired, too. I sat on the dusty floor, my back against the smooth rock–wall. Roanne sat to my left, Julianna to my right, with Tobin snuggled up close to his mum. I sighed. My internal body–clock felt like its hands were swinging wildly in all directions – there was no sense of time inside this underground world. We shared some food and water, and rested, most of us too fatigued to even keep our eyes open.

Despite my intention to remain awake and alert – and on guard – I drifted into sleep, and did not wake even when Roanne spoke to me. She shook my arm to rouse me, and I woke with a start, feeling disoriented and bleary–eyed.

"Don't panic," she sent to me. "Nothing's wrong. It's just that you've slept for about an hour, and we think we'll probably need to move on soon."

"Thanks for waking me," I said, almost meaning it. I attempted to gather my wits and kick–start my brain into functioning. Still feeling slightly groggy, I drew on a little lovelight to help get myself back on track. I had been so tired, my sleep had been incredibly deep.

With a jolt, I remembered that I had dreamed of Charls. Had it only been a dream? *Yes.* I recalled nothing of the detail; only the vague knowledge that he was surrounded by others, knives and weapons drawn, and that he had lost men. Sadness folded me in its dark embrace; I knew that he would feel the loss of each and every man. He would know their wives, their children, would empathise with their grief. I hoped it *had* only been a dream – not a prophetic vision.

I felt that I needed to connect again with Charls, to get a clearer picture of what was going on in the 'outer world'. As soon as I got a chance, I would connect . . . and as soon as I got a chance, I would ask Roanne to teach me how to make the spherical lights.

But now, we did need to get moving again. The instinct to do so was strong within me, so I knew that I should follow whatever was pushing me on – or pulling me towards it. The others were ready to leave, so I hastily retrieved the map and sought the way ahead. Since there was only one tunnel leading from this cavern (which was unlabelled), then I assumed we should head into it, and on to the next one. I felt like a rabbit in a warren.

We crossed the short distance to the tunnel's entrance. With my intention, I expanded my light–globe and placed it just ahead of me, ready to light the way forward. I would be glad never to see another tunnel again, but I knew there would be many more . . . we had still covered only a short distance on the map. It would be helpful to know our destination, but that, too, was information beyond my reach.

What can I say about this tunnel? It was no different to

the others. There were no distinguishing features. We were inside it, we kept going, and this time the singing began earlier. Whether this was because everyone else was as bored by the tunnels as I felt, or simply because they'd enjoyed their singing so much in the last tunnel, I did not know, and did not ask. As long as their spirits were high, that was all that mattered.

I didn't immediately perceive the extra voice in the 'choir', but gradually awareness of the new sound made its way into my consciousness. The voice was clear, pure, as if light itself had found a voice. Once I became aware of it, I felt shivers run down my spine. The others noticed it, too, as their own voices dropped away, leaving the incredible vocal to float alone.

I slowed my pace without realising I had done so – the clarity and sparkle in the voice was like an angel's or siren's song, and I was not sure that I was ready to find out whether the vocalist would help or hinder us on our journey. Ahead of me was another curve in the tunnel, and I knew not what lay beyond.

The sweetly melodic song continued. It was beautiful but also strangely melancholy.

"Lady Keira?"

"Ro? What do you think? Good or bad?"

"What does your globe–light tell you?"

The light was steady, bright, and unwavering.

"It says we're fine . . . I'm going to proceed, okay?"

She sent her agreement, and I cautiously made my way around the bend, and approached the entrance to another open space.

~~~

The blasted dog would not leave Charls alone. The

canine knew that he smelled wrong – *Cordellan* – and did not fit in here. The man who had bumped him reached out, brushed Charls' sleeve, made a hasty grab. He called out and more men joined him, hands reaching and grasping until they had established the outline of his shape.

His knife was knocked from his hand, the dog was called off, he was surrounded, and there was no way out. He hadn't even finished cutting Tissa's hands free. In the confusion he could not see if she was still restrained, but he could not imagine how she could continue what he had begun.

Why was this happening? He'd thought the Ascended Reikans and lovelight were protecting him! This was *wrong!* Frustrated, he kicked out, making contact with a leg. The man howled, and threw a punch at where he imagined Charls' face to be. Charls saw the blow coming, threw his head to one side – catching a heavy blow to his left shoulder. It went numb then began to throb – a lot. The pain overcame his senses and he felt giddy.

That brief moment was all that was needed. The Vornen men had him bound within seconds, and he was dragged away from the centre of the square, over to an old cart, and bundled into it, his shoulder jarring and throwing myriad multicoloured stars across his vision. He lay on the hard surface, panting, hurting, and feeling utterly powerless. Several men climbed in alongside him, jeering and cursing at the space where he lay, unseen.

Something – a heavy piece of dark material – was thrown across him. All he could see was the dark weave letting through a close–hatched pattern of light. Now they would be able to see him, his shape delineated by

254

the fabric. He sighed. This was not going well at all. Tissa was still in trouble, and he had no idea where Symion or his wife and daughter were; Charls' men – and two women – were stuck in the copse, and he was trussed up like a pig on its way to market.

Feeling miserable, his energy plummeted, and he lost his connection with lovelight. Mentally he cursed the energy that he so respected and loved, feeling that he had been let down and abandoned.

Charls' teeth rattled in his skull as the cart bounced and bumped along a dirt track as it headed out of the village. His shoulder ached. His captors had left the thick fabric draped across him, and he felt overheated and claustrophobic, the cloth dipping into his mouth and making him cough.

He was relieved to finally sense the cart slowing, was aware of it making a sharp right turn before stopping. The horse whinnied and he heard the jangling of a harness as the animal and cart were separated.

~~~

The tunnel opened into another cavern, much as I'd expected. I did not, however, expect the sight that was to greet us. As the waves of music ebbed and flowed, I entered the cavern and stopped in my tracks. My light–sphere floated into the chamber, and stopped in the centre; Roanne's followed.

"Oh . . ." breathed Roanne, who had paused to stand next to me. My jaw dropped open.

Our eyes feasted on crystal. The cavern walls were thick with glittering and shining crystal stones – some small, others in great clumps with huge points thrusting from their sparkling, clustered bases. Our own spherical

255

lights cast a soft glow around the cavern, so that the glints of the crystals danced and flashed and twinkled. Only the cavern's floor, level with the base of the tunnel, was bare.

Every colour was present – from deep amethyst to sunny yellow, bright turquoise and fiery red and orange. Soft green, palest blue, clear quartz, lustrous brown, and glossy black – the stones decorated the walls and curved ceiling. I had the strongest desire to reach out and touch one of the crystals. I felt as if I was tingling from head to toe with the energies being shared by the stones.

The melody soared and dipped, filling us with rapture one moment, and leading us into melancholy the next.

But there was no–one in sight. So where was the music coming from?

Tobin, true to form, provided a clue.

"Lady Keira! Can you hear the crystals singing?"

Really? I confess to some scepticism. Tobin picked up on my doubtful facial expression and became quite indignant, his hands planted firmly on his hips.

"Lady Keira, the crystals *are* singing, I know it! Please believe me, please!"

"How do you know, Tobin?"

"The same way that *you* know things."

Well, that told me, I thought wryly. He was spot on, though – what right did I have to question his explanations, when I asked everyone to accept mine?

My eyes followed Roanne as she walked deeper into the chamber, examining the walls. She did not touch the crystals, but peered at them closely.

"Blue Lace Agate," she sent, standing before a translucent pale blue stone with indigo–coloured banding. "Amazonite. Red Jasper. Carnelian. Amethyst. Citrine. Hematite. Rose Quartz. This is *amazing,* Lady

256

Keira! Look at this glossy Tiger's Eye!"

"You know the names of all of these?" I asked, surprised.

"Most. I studied crystal healing for a while. Each has a different chemical composition, and hence a different energetic frequency. They can be utilised for healing and support."

She turned to me. "Reika was the place to study crystals. Until it vanished. They had built up such a wealth of knowledge and experience, and only some of it was written down for us to study."

"It's incredible," I murmured, wandering around the chamber, not daring to touch any of the glittering stones. "What's this one?" I asked, pointing to a black stone spotted with uneven white flecks.

"Snowflake obsidian," Roanne replied. "There are so many crystals, I really don't know them *all*. But I've had loved them ever since I saw my first quartz point."

I could understand her fascination. The crystals were beautiful.

"They don't normally . . . *sing,* though?" I queried.

"Oh no!" she laughed. "No, they're normally silent. But then this place has its own rules, don't forget. The singing must be significant, somehow. D'you have any ideas on that?"

"Nope." And I had no idea what we would need to do here – what our role would be. *Or how we would move forward.* I had seen no exit. Was this a dead end?

"Let me check the map," I suggested. I opened it out, spread it on my arm, and found our present position. "Roanne, this is the Cavern of the Crystal Song. There's no exit marked."

"More magical mystery?" she said, raising an eyebrow.

"Quite possibly. So, now what?"

We both stared at the incredible sight before us. The others were wandering about the cavern, peering at the stones, never touching. It seemed that we all felt hesitant about getting too close to the glittering rocks.

I put the map away, and recommenced my own ambling. The singing continued, although now, having been here for some time, it was finally feeling part of the scenery, was not evoking such strong emotion in me. What role did the music play? Was it healing our hurts? Lifting our hearts out of pain and regret, cycling into joy and acceptance? Where those thoughts came from, I was not sure – the Ascended Reikans, perhaps, or simply my own enhanced intuition.

Clearly, Roanne had some painful memories in her past; was she now feeling lighter?

"Ro, how are you feeling?"

She looked at me, her expression showing surprise. "Fine, I guess – why?"

"Just wondered," I shrugged.

"Ah, come on . . . wondered *what*, Lady Keira?"

"Okay. I wondered if you were feeling less . . . upset."

"That was ages ago!"

"Yes . . . but do those – difficult memories – do they seem easier, now?"

She considered my question. "Actually, yes . . . yes, they do. You think the singing crystals have worked on our emotions and memories, taking the sting out of them, as it were?"

"Perhaps. I'm just speculating."

She smiled. "I think you're right. *Again!*" And she did appear somehow lighter. As if a burden had been lifted, or at least eased. So perhaps that was our purpose in coming here? Or was there something else?

~~~

Roanne had been thinking about the Light Portal of Bliss. "I feel as if that place showed us just how amazingly good we *could* feel. And now the singing crystals are working on releasing all of our emotions and difficult memories, so that we are freer, and can more easily reach that state of peace and joy by ourselves. Once we've released the stuck feelings, we have space to invite new, better feelings and thoughts in."

I thought about her words. "I had been working on the premise that by thinking 'better thoughts', they would automatically overlay – transform – the not–so–good ones . . ."

"I think that, too. But sometimes memories are deeply painful and, despite our best intentions, they get locked away. We may not even realise they are there. Or they may be so deeply entrenched that something . . . *more* . . . is needed. I think this journey is helping us to access those deeply–held, traumatic feelings, and let go of them. I really do feel as if a weight has been lifted."

"Can I ask . . .?"

"Oh, it was a romance that went sour," Roanne replied. "I let myself get hung up on it, couldn't accept that the relationship was over. Now . . . I feel that I've done that, I've forgiven the man involved – and it really is in the past. I can move forward. Oh, this is a beauty!"

She was examining a large, deeply rich blue stone veined with sparkling gold. "Lapis lazuli, I think," she stated, "although of course there might be stones here that I have never heard of before! Isn't it gorgeous? I love it," she sighed.

The music stopped.

There was a light cracking noise, and the stone cleaved from the wall. Roanne's hand flew out reflexively, and caught the falling crystal. Everyone looked at everyone else. Thoughts flew: "Why has it gone quiet?" "Where's the music gone?" "Did you see that crystal fall?"

Roanne opened her clasped hand, staring at me. "What is it?" I asked. "Ro?"

She whispered aloud, "I've never held a crystal like this. My whole body is tingling, buzzing. I can feel my third eye chakra spinning madly. And as for my crown chakra . . . I think I might take off!"

She continued gazing at the beautiful crystal nestling in her palm. "Normally I might sense a crystal's energy when it rests in my hand, but this is . . . well, it's so strong, I feel like I *am* the crystal." Her eyes wide, she looked down at the crystal. "D'you think it's because I told the crystal I love it?" she joked.

Many a true word spoken in jest, I thought. "That is actually a possibility. Our journey here is based on sharing lovelight, and *love* and consideration for each other; it's not just positive feelings and thoughts that are important. Who knows just how powerful our emotions can be?"

Roanne closed her fingers over the crystal and tucked her hand in a trouser pocket. "It was a gift," she said. "I honestly feel that this crystal has asked to remain with me. And I can't stick it back on the wall, can I?" Her eyes danced with laughter.

Tobin laughed too, and said, "Miss Roanne, the crystal says that it was intended for you. You're meant to have it, and to take it with you, because it will be needed later."

260

"Thank you, Tobin," Roanne said gently, reaching down to place her free hand on his head, ruffling his hair with affection. "Your messages are very helpful, and we appreciate you passing them onto us."

The boy beamed at Roanne's praise, his eyes reflecting the light like little diamonds.

"Now what, Lady Keira?" she asked, leaving Tobin and walking past me into the centre of the cavern as she sent her thoughts to me. "No exit passage, no music; what happens next?"

~~~

"Interesting question," I sent back, wryly. As yet, I'd received no guidance on where we went next. The map was not giving up its secrets, this time. Perhaps a direct question would reveal something?

I intended to reach the Ascended Reikans, as well as my intuition, and asked: "Where do we go now?" I heard no response. I was expecting a visual sign rather than an audible one.

And, boy, did I get it!

At first, there was nothing.

Then, almost imperceptibly, I saw a shape begin to appear in the centre of the chamber's floor. Dust and dirt shook as something – energy? – created, no, *revealed,* a shape with straight edges marked out in dark grooves of stone.

"A hexagon," breathed Roanne, standing at my left shoulder.

"What do we do with it?" I whispered back. "Send it lovelight?"

"Just watch," she instructed. "I have a feeling that this time is different . . ."

261

We did watch; our eyes were transfixed as the shape became clearer and took its final form. It was indeed a hexagon.

And it began to rotate.

Very slowly, the edges shifted, inch by inch, gradually picking up speed. The movement made no sound. It seemed impossible that solid rock could rotate – and with no noise, at that; but then the giant crags in the stone circle and the spinning paperweight had already demonstrated that the conventional laws of physics did not seem to apply here. The Cavern of the Weeping Pines had proved that quite spectacularly.

So, I accepted what I was seeing, without further questions.

We stood silently in a circle around the hexagon, continued to watch as the hexagon spun yet faster still. Now it was a blur, with a faint white–gold aura visible around the design. Tobin reached to take my right hand, then said quietly, "Now it will stop."

The moving floor came to a standstill.

At first, the faint light obscured the area, then this dissipated and was absorbed into the air, leaving a black, hexagonal–shaped hole in the floor.

"Come on," said Tobin, dragging at my hand as he pulled me forward. Remaining a safe distance from the edge of the hole, I released Tobin's hand, and called to my orb–light to join me and illuminate my descent into the hole. To my relief, I saw that there was some sort of ladder attached to the under–lip of the hole. There were extending 'handles' which I lifted free of the hole; these would act as stabilising supports as each of us entered the hexagonal space.

I held onto the handles, and manoeuvred my body to place a foot onto the top rung. There was a thin wooden platform attached to each step, which felt more reassuring than stepping onto a simple narrow rung. Taking a deep breath, I brought my other leg onto the ladder, and began making my way down the steps. It was fairly easy–going; I just wished – not for the first time – that I knew where we were headed.

A small voice inside my head reminded me that I was always shown the next step on my path, and to trust the process. *Everything is perfect in this moment.*

Julianna and Tobin stepped onto the ladder above me, followed by Jos and the others. Roanne would ensure everyone else's safety, then follow last. I concentrated on not missing my footing, on my hand placements as I moved lower, and lower, and lower.

How much longer?

Then my light–globe showed me that I was approaching the bottom of the hole. It had been like descending into a deep well. I was glad to be on solid ground again. Turning away from the ladder, I followed my spherical light into yet another tunnel.

When would we smell fresh air again? Feel the sun? Hear rain – real droplets from clouds, as opposed to weeping trees? When would we feel the soft, warm breeze? Despite my best intentions, I was starting to feel edgy at being inside, away from the sky.

CHAPTER 29

Charls was dragged to his feet, the dark material slipping to one side. He winced as the movement jarred his injured shoulder – he needed time alone to concentrate on self–healing. The bright sunlight hurt his eyes, making them water, so he closed them. He was forced out of the cart, then the covering was thrown back over his frame. He managed a slight smile – they had no idea how to make him 'visible' through any other means. He opened his eyes, able to see only vague shadows and forms moving beyond the cloth.

"Well, what do we have here?" a voice spoke. Those few spoken words managed to convey a scathing mix of sarcasm, amusement, derision and leadership.

Karn.

Charls remained silent. Any speech would give him away. He could not reveal his presence to his renegade brother. The sphere should block any sound he made; but he was not willing to risk reliance upon that aspect of its power. Two of the men forced Charls' arms against his body, one man standing to each side of him. Pain shot through his shoulder, and he clamped his lips shut to stop himself crying out. It appeared that they and Karn were in thought–communication, excluding Charls from their conversation.

"So. It appears that you were attempting a *rescue.* How very *brave* of you. How *gallant.*"

Oh yes, the sarcasm of old was alive and well. Charls felt the familiar reactions of frustration and irritation arise, borne of long–held habits and childhood rivalries. Did families ever leave their past behind? He stifled a retort, willed himself to hold still, to keep quiet.

"Do you not speak? Are you an imbecile? No. I think not. To render oneself invisible takes a certain level of . . . intelligence. So how do we get you visible? What manner of deviousness are you using to remain hidden from me?"

Charls said nothing.

"Take him to the cells," Karn instructed. "And keep that cloak over him so you don't lose him. Don't give him even a hint of a chance to escape. I will interrogate him later; I am late for a meeting with Lady Maryn."

The men turned Charls and marched him towards a grim–looking building with barred windows.

Even the structure had a feeling of defeat and misery, as if the emotions of its occupants had impregnated the brickwork itself.

The cell which was to be Charls' new home was tiny, barely wide enough for the low iron–framed bed and its thin mattress. One high window cast a small square of light onto the stone floor. Charls was seated on the bed, the cloak over his shoulders for warmth. He would appear headless to the guards. He laughed bitterly.

How on earth had this *happened?* Should he have left Tissa when he'd discovered her situation? Gone straight to find Symion and his family? Or simply searched the small town, gathering information, then returning to his small band of warriors? Would Burron have taken command? Were they, even now, heading towards him? He had to believe that everything would somehow work out.

Charls attempted some self–healing, but found it hard to concentrate. Having nothing else to do except think and plan, but with no mental energy to attempt either, he rolled onto the thin bed and slept.

~~~

I mentally shook myself, reminding myself to keep to the task in hand – leading us to our eventual destination. The glow cast by my light–sphere revealed that this tunnel was much like the ones through which we had already come: fairly narrow, not all that high, and curving at intervals.

Nothing of interest.

I suppressed a sigh of boredom and frustration. Focus, Keira! One foot in front of the other. One step at a time. Keep the energy as high as you can!

This time, no–one started a song. Maybe everyone was still stunned after hearing the crystalline purity of the voice that had joined our own as we'd approached the Cavern of the Crystal Song. I certainly felt a bit vocally inadequate after that performance. Then again, maybe they, too, were feeling dispirited at navigating yet another tunnel.

On we trudged, seemingly for hours, although in reality it was probably far less. I connected with lovelight, asked for energy to lift our spirits. Suddenly, Tobin laughed aloud, and I smiled at his childish exuberance.

Julianna said, "Tobin's remembering what it's like to dance in the rain puddles!"

Thank you, lovelight.

What a great idea!" I acknowledged. "I'm going to think of my happy, fun things to make *me* smile . . . I need something to give me a bit of a boost!"

"Me too," sent Jos. "As I'm still just about categorised as a teenager, I'm sure I'm entitled to say that *I'm bored!*"

"I know, I know . . . tunnels are not much fun. We

could also try guessing what our next cavern will be."

"A meadow!" Roanne sent. I smiled, visualising long, slender grasses dotted with poppies and pimpernels.

" A flock of birds!" Jos sent. Hmm. Perhaps not. I had visions of being set upon by a flock of irritated crows.

"An indoor lake with a sandy beach!" said one of the other young women. I could almost feel soft, warm sand under the soles of my feet. *Almost.*

"A swing," said Tobin wistfully.

I let my mind come up with its own fantasy.

"The people that we miss," I sent. That startled me; I did not know where the thought had come from. I missed Jason. I missed Charls. My almost–fiancé. And my best friend. Both separated by the barrier between worlds, both connected by me.

My spherical light flickered once, then again.

My pace quickened; were we approaching the next cavern? I felt Tobin pushing at my back, was aware of Julianna attempting to hold him back.

"Lady Keira, I want to *see!*"

"See what, Tobin?" his mother asked.

"Our imagination!"

Our *what?*

Then I rounded the next 'bend' in the tunnel, and stopped dead as I found myself in a wide, open stone archway leading into a vast cavern. I was in danger of being over–awed by the sights in this underground world.

"*Wow*", breathed Roanne, moving to my side. "This is – just incredible!"

I'm not sure what part of the scene I noticed first. Directly ahead of us, a small brick pathway led to the lake's edge. The water, a rich teal, was amazingly beautiful; the depth of the colour was magnificent. The surface of the lake was perfectly calm and still. Narrow reeds and tall grasses surrounded most of it. The pathway continued into meadow–grass, with the inevitable poppies and pimpernels, as well as ox–eye daisies, plants similar to corncockles, and other flowers that I couldn't yet identify. I could see sand on the far side of the lake – a smooth, golden arc. My toes wiggled in anticipation.

To the right of the meadow, some shorter, emerald–green grass, with a couple of picnic tables and . . . Tobin's swing. He squealed when he caught sight of it. A light breeze rose from nowhere, riffling the surface of the lake, stirring the swing into motion. Poppies and grasses swayed.

Appearing from nowhere, small silver–white birds came into being, coasting on the light wind. Graceful and silent, they lowered to the lake's surface, each landing with a delicate splash before gliding across the surface towards us.

For the most part, we were silent, both vocally and in thought. We were taking in the sights before us. A gentle scent of lilacs reached me, and I instinctively turned my head to the right, towards the source. A beautiful, mature bush, fully in flower, sat close by, casting its scent on the air. And beyond it . . . I blinked.

Surely not?

The figure moved towards me, quite slowly, but with assurance. I recognised that walk.

Charls. My heart softened to see him. I had missed him. Was he really here? How *could* he be? The air beyond him seemed to shimmer and waver, and my eyes watered. Blinking again, I saw others taking form, coming towards us.

"Lady Keira . . ." Roanne breathed.

"I know . . . are they real?"

"Don't know. But Burron is there . . . what'll I say to him?" Her eyes were wide, and I sensed her anxiety.

"Who's Burron?" I sent.

"*Him*. The one I told you about. He broke up with me. I thought I would die from the heartbreak."

"Ro, all of this . . ." I waved an arm to encompass the cavern, "has manifested because of our imagination. Just as Tobin told us. Everything we mentioned – it's here. So, that means you wanted him here. Doesn't it?" I raised an eyebrow in query.

"Um. I want to be *with* him again, I guess. But I don't want the embarrassing conversation that would need to precede us being together again!"

"Well, play it by ear, and just take it –"

"One step at a time. Got it!" She threw me a quick, tense smile, and took a deep breath.

Looking back towards the advancing figures, Charls leading, I wondered what *I* would say to Charls. It felt like months since we'd last seen each other. I had no idea how long it had been. We didn't keep track of time – we walked, we stopped, we ate, we rested. It was at least a week, surely?

I searched for Jason, but did not see him. Perhaps he could not exist in this world, even in this magical place defined by our imagination and desires.

Charls stopped a short distance away from us. Then his shape flickered. Was he . . . a hologram? I groaned inwardly. Almost cruel, to show us our loved ones, yet not be able to communicate or touch.

~~~

Burron and the other holograms also stopped, letting

269

Charls remain at the head of their little group. There were five men in total, plus a young woman and a stunning girl of eighteen or nineteen.

"Oh . . . Leina," Jos muttered aloud, his face colouring a becoming shade of pink. I hid a smile. Young love – how long ago it seemed to me, now!

"Ro, can we go forward to greet them?" I took a step towards the group, hesitant and unsure.

"I'm not sure, Lady Keira. There must be a reason that they stopped where they did."

As we continued to watch and wait, that reason became clear.

The image of Charls disappeared for an instant, before reappearing a short distance to the right of his group. "They're not stable," I guessed, sending the thought to my group. "I think we should remain where we are."

Leina flickered, then reappeared next to Charls. I heard Jos stifle a shout. One by one, the other figures followed suit. All were now closer to the lake. The birds silently paddled to the farthest side of the water. The swing fell still.

The cavern held its breath.

Although I felt confident that these holographic visitors – if that's what they were – meant us no harm, and were likely here to bolster our motivation in continuing our quest, I realised that whatever force had brought them here might be imperfect. They might inadvertently cause us damage, so we needed to exercise caution. I needed to warn –

Jos had broken from the group and was racing towards Leina.

"NO! Jos! STOP!" I shouted, my heart pounding. I had an awful feeling that this wouldn't end well. Dread stole over me and lay upon me like an icy shroud. My legs were frozen in place; I could not move. I could only watch, helpless, knowing I would never reach him in time. "Jos!" I called, knowing that my plea would be in vain.

Jos ran directly towards the holographic group, reaching them just as they started to phase out and reappear yet closer to the lake. Jos skidded to a halt, trying to put the brakes on before he crashed into the figure wavering right in front of him.

He was too late.

Jos had touched the holographic image that was Leina, and as she had shifted to her new location, her energy had merged with his, and Jos had become . . . *part* of her.

I stared in horror, powerless to help, unable to stop the process. His physical body began to break up! I felt nauseous as I watched his arm simply evaporate. I was watching a nightmare unfold. His torso, merged with Leina's, became a veil of shifting shadows. I stuffed my fist against my mouth, trying not to scream as, piece by piece, Jos simply disintegrated.

One minute he was there; the next, he became a mass of floating specks which hovered for a moment and then dissipated like dust motes in the light. That was it? Jos was gone, just like that?

I became aware that Tobin was screaming, and had buried his head in Julianna's stomach. Tears poured down my face, and I felt as if I might crumple to my knees. Roanne clutched at me, her face white, her mouth open in shock. I felt her begin to shake, and placed an arm around her shoulders, providing her with what warmth and comfort I could. The whole scene suddenly felt so unreal, as if I only had to pinch myself to wake up. But my brain insisted that it was all very real. I had

271

to deal with it.

How did this happen? How could I have *let* it happen? My warning had not been strong enough, fast enough. I had let Jos down. I had let *everyone* down. I felt hollow in the pit of my stomach, and there was a thick ball of emotion lodged in my throat; I could not swallow. I felt sick. I felt cold. I felt utterly wretched.

One by one, we sat down. My legs felt simply too weak to support me. We had watched someone we cared about vanish in an instant. Jos was gone. His desire to be with Leina had taken him from us. I no longer felt any happiness or joy at seeing Charls' image. Just horror.

I stared blankly at the group as they moved yet again, Charls reappearing in the lake, only the upper half of his body visible above the water. If this was supposed to *support* us, to motivate us, it was having the opposite effect. We were all in shock. I did not know what to do. I wanted someone to revoke my mantle of leadership, my place in the legend. I was not ready to deal with it all. I wanted to be home. With Jason. *Right this minute.*

We sat grieving, feeling the loss, the waste, the stupidity of it all. I felt as if time had paused, holding us fixed in this state of disbelief and horror. They hadn't even been *real*. It was all so pointless.

Roanne had stopped shaking, was now sat with her eyes closed, rocking herself gently back and forth. I thought I knew how she felt. I wanted to be taken care of, rocked like a baby, confident of her safety and protectors. Looking around our little band of weary travellers, I noticed I was the only one with my eyes still open. Perhaps there was a sense of safety or comfort behind closed lids. I closed my eyes, seeking darkness, shutting out Charls and Burron and Leina and the other holograms as they moved still deeper into the lake.

"Why?" I silently asked the Ascended Reikans. "Why did this happen? Could I have prevented it? What else should I have done? What do we do now? *I can't do this! Help me!*"

"So many questions, dear Keira," came a loving, soothing, melodic voice; one that clearly belonged to a wise soul. I opened my eyes. A light–being similar to the one Charls and I had been privileged to encounter in Karn's room. A light–being with a benevolent, caring face, soft silver–blonde hair, and decades of wisdom and grace etched into her exquisite features.

"Who are you?" I sent. No–one else could see her; I was the only one of us, still, with opened eyes.

"I am Lady Aida. You have read my journal, my dear. We are strongly connected, energetically."

"Oh . . ."

"You have called for help from the stirrings of anguish deep in your heart; we are aware of your despair, your grief. I have come to assist you, to remind you of the greater plan. And I have news of Jason."

"Jason!"

"Yes, Keira; he is well, and he has come a long way, spiritually, since you left him and your picnic. I won't spoil the surprise he has for you. But he and I have been talking, and it is clear that he will protect you – with his life, if need be."

"But – surely, he's not still on the moor?" That seemed crazy.

"Keira, time in your world does not pass as time here passes. Trust me when I say that all is well. He is waiting for you to return. And he is safe. He is also aware that you have work to do here."

"Oh," I replied, again. It seemed that my capacity for

intelligent thought had deserted me.

"Keira, you *are* vital to this endeavour. So I am here to assist you in whatever way you need me to. This," she spread her brightly lit arms wide, "was supposed to bring you joy. Not death. Never that. We miscalculated, and I am sorry, so sorry, that it ended this way."

"Tobin hasn't even been on his swing," I sent irrelevantly.

"No," Lady Aida admitted. "But we will get past this before too long, you will all be able to let this go, and move forward with resolute hearts and a strong spirit. Just give yourselves a little time. Then, in the natural course of things, you will regroup, will find your buried determination and rediscover hope and optimism. We are flooding the cavern with lovelight, now, to assist you in your emotional healing."

And as I looked at her, she seemed to expand outwards, ever outwards, until the entire cavern was filled with a soft white pearly light. Hesitantly, I risked a glance towards the lake. The figures were gone. The birds glided gracefully on the surface of the water.

We were alone once more.

~~~

"So what do I do, now, Lady Aida? I really feel very low, very . . . lost. I can't seem to access any good thoughts or feelings at all."

"I realise that, my dear. And you should not block those feelings of distress. I know you know this. It was one of Charls' lessons for you, was it not?"

"Yes. I remember. I know I have to allow these feelings, then release them. But I just don't feel that I have the energy – the desire – to carry on. I am so tired.

274

I don't want to be a leader. I want to go home." My throat was so tight I couldn't have spoken if I'd wanted to. And my heart ached unbearably.

Lady Aida's figure glided closer to me and lowered to the ground so that she was facing me at my level. She reached out a light–infused hand and stroked my hair. Oh, that felt so comforting. I closed my eyes and let myself fully embrace the sensations. Then my head started tingling and warming, and I understood that Lady Aida was passing lovelight directly to me at the highest rate that I could handle. Unconsciously, I inhaled deeply, breathing in the lilac scent as it caressed the air. I breathed out with a heavy sigh.

My muscles felt less tense. I had felt as if I had been carrying the weight of the world – *two worlds* – on my narrow shoulders. I didn't feel ready to resume my leadership role just yet, but I did feel a little less overwhelmed. Lovelight continued to pour into and through me, and I gave into the soothing feeling of Lady Aida comforting her injured child.

After a while, I began to feel somewhat brighter; almost as if my life force had been restored. I felt more capable, had more strength; there was less of the heavy weight of weariness that had consumed me.

"Keira, I have taken the unusual step of hastening the process of your transition from grief to acceptance. I would not normally do this. However, your role is so very important, we – and Cordello – cannot afford the luxury of time. You need to be ready soon: not tomorrow, not next week. Within a few minutes, you must move forward again, leading your Cordellans as you have been so ably doing until now."

"I still don't feel ready. I feel I've lost my . . . *spark –*"

"You *are* ready. I have taken steps to ensure that you

are. There is no time to wallow."

How dare she! Then I understood. Lady Aida was cultivating my anger, to arouse strong emotion and get me back on my feet – literally.

I took another deep breath, allowing my heart rate to settle, and my mind to clear. Lady Aida finally removed her hand from my head, but I felt the lovelight energy continuing to course through me, and believed my own connection to be restored.

"Keira, know this: lovelight is energy from the Source of everything. Remember – it is always there, available to you and everyone else, ready to call on when you are in need. You are protecting Cordello's 'store' of the energy – but it can be replenished, given time."

"I do know that . . . I guess I was too upset to remember to call on it myself."

"Of course. That's understandable. I will be leaving shortly. But I will be here instantly should you need *me* – as opposed to Reikans in general, or lovelight. You are doing tremendously well, my dear. Everything is following its destiny. But now, it is time. I am needed elsewhere, and I have to respond to that call." She shifted to an upright position.

"Thank you. Thank you for helping me, for bringing 'me' back to myself."

"Any time. Now, you'll need to rouse the others and help them through their own distress. My time here with you has been outside of their time. They will not know of my presence. They will look to you, only." The glowing figure smiled. "Might I suggest some time on the beach and the swing? Consciously look for ways to lift your energy, until you're taken over with enjoying those ways, and naturally feeling better and brighter. It is for you to raise the vibration of those travelling with you. Your positive energy and light will transform their energies, too. That is the principle of resonance. And now, dear Keira, I leave you."

The light in the cavern slowly dimmed as the Ascended Reikan gathered her light into her being, and then she, too, slowly faded from sight. Now, it was just the Cordellans and me, and the water–birds.

CHAPTER 30

When Charls awoke his back was stiff from the hard bed, and the sun had set. The cell was cold and he shivered despite the cloak. He gingerly tested the mobility of his shoulder and was pleased to find that he could use it normally. His connection to lovelight had been maintained even as he had been sleeping.

When he heard his name spoken aloud, he looked wearily at the prison door. Seeing no–one, he rose stiffly to his feet and went to examine it more closely, peering warily through the observation slot set into the door.

No–one there. Who, then, had spoken? He heard it again: *Charls!*

Shaking his head to clear it, he realised that it was Tissa's voice. How . . .? Then he remembered. Before leaving the manor, he had retrieved the communication device that he and Keira had found in Karn's shoe, tucking it into a pocket. Karn's men had not yet searched him so he still had *three* of the special objects. Tissa was communicating through another device; she must have freed herself somehow.

Quickly, he fumbled his way into the pocket and brought the device to his lips. He placed the Canturan sphere into its special bag so that he could transmit. Speaking as loudly as he dared, he spoke his reply. "Tissa? Is that you?"

"Yes! Much has happened since your capture. I'll explain later, there's not much time. You are in the cells?"

"I am. One small high, barred window – no glass. And of course there is the door to the corridor."

He heard scuffling outside of his window, then: "We're

outside of the prison. There are several cells side by side. We can't identify which one you are in. Do you have anything you can throw at the window? A pebble?"

"I'll see what I can find. I'm *not* throwing the Canturan sphere!" He smiled, realised just how much his spirits had soared at the prospect of effecting an escape. Karn would be furious if he achieved it! He replaced the disc in his pocket.

Charls found a small stone, aimed at the window. His aim was true, the stone flying through the bars to fall to the ground outside. A few seconds passed. In the dim light, he became aware of a faint aura of pale moonlight at the window. It shimmered with rainbow colours. Keira had mentioned Tissa's use of a rainbow–coloured lovelight sphere to blast her way out of her own cell. But still, Charls had no means of reaching the window – it was simply too high.

But now his brain was working properly again, he was able to think tactically. With a triumphant smile, he extracted the golden paperweight from another pocket, and placed it on the ground in front of the window. Would it realise what he needed it to do? He sent a request to the Ascended Reikans to assist.

Then he waited. Instinctively, he stood back from the window and from the paperweight.

The golden cube emitted a soft glow of rainbow light, as if energetically connected with Tissa's sphere. The light at the window flared like a starburst, and Charls flung an arm across his eyes. When he looked again, the window bars had dissolved, and the window–space had been enlarged.

On the ground, the golden cube began to spin silently, the paperweight increasing in size and creating a solid, cubed step wide enough for a person to stand upon. It stopped spinning, began to pulse slowly as if inviting Charls to step aboard.

Charls flung the cloak aside. Maybe it would help confuse Karn and his guards. He hoped that they would think he was still there on their sorry excuse for a bed, would believe that he had only let the cloak fall from his body. He stepped onto the enlarged paperweight.

Like an elevator conjured from his imagination, the cube rose gently into the air.

~~~

I did not feel abandoned by Lady Aida's departure. She had strengthened me in all the ways that were most needed. Whilst I felt sorrow for Jos' meaningless loss, I had accepted it, and moved past the paralysis of overwhelming grief. Time was now the only ingredient needed to work through my remaining emotions, and move on. In the meantime, I was able to gather up my leader's mantle, and place its familiar weight over my shoulders. I was ready to encourage the Cordellans to move – as best they could – into the same state of acceptance, and to assist them in doing so.

I felt honoured that Lady Aida's visit had been witnessed by me alone. I was amazed that she had taken me into a separate slice of time, in which no other could participate. As I watched the group, they started to fidget and to open their eyes. Roanne's eyes met mine. They were deep wells of despair, and my heart ached in empathy. She shed no more tears; the wells were dry.

Intuitively, I sensed that action would need to be our first step in our recovery.

I stood, offering my hand to Roanne to help her up. She grasped it and remained standing next to me.

Following our lead, Julianna prised Tobin from her, and they rose to their feet. One by one, the other villagers stood, everyone appearing weary and heavy–hearted.

Speech time, Keira! I had their undivided attention. I let the words come from my heart.

"This has been a very difficult event for us to witness. I fully understand your sorrow, the whole medley of emotions swirling around within you. I have felt them, too. They were . . . overwhelming. Whilst we were seated, I was visited by an Ascended Reikan and was given support so that I am now ready to move onto the next phase of our journey. I won't pretend that it will be easy. Life isn't easy. It torments, teases, terrifies. It can also be joyful, amazing, and peaceful. Those good feelings will return, believe me. For now, I ask that you trust me, and come with me, and simply do your best."

Would my words be enough to inspire? To motivate? I held my breath.

"Can you do that?" I asked aloud, as gently as I could. Some nodded.

"Yes," whispered Roanne.

"Yes," said Julianna, her voice unsteady.

"Yes," said Tobin, his voice thick and wobbling.

Okay, then. "First, I think it would be a good idea to move about and explore more of this cavern. I'm going to walk by the lake, have a look at the wild–flower meadow, then maybe sit on the beach with my feet in the shallows. Ro, will you join me? Julianna?"

I made my way forward onto the path leading alongside the lake and towards the meadow.

Taking her cue, Roanne fell into step beside me; Julianna, with Tobin at her side, was right behind us.

Now that we were all up and moving, I felt that our momentum would keep us going. Everyone knew we couldn't go back. But I could not allow the shadow of grief to lead to apathy; we could not remain here for long, either. Too much depended upon us reaching our destination, wherever that was. I could not see that far ahead. I only knew – with absolute certainty – that what *we* did would be critical for the future of lovelight in Cordello.

The path was smooth, the air warm and fragrant with scents of lilac, water, grass, and some undefinable essence of Nature itself. It was easy to walk, to gaze at the impossibly teal–blue lake positioned to our left, even to smile at the little birds as they glided about. I recognised that the calm, graceful movement above water belied their hurried paddling beneath. A metaphor for my weary band of villagers, still fighting to rise courageously above their tumultuous emotions.

We entered the meadow, moving away from the lake. Unnoticed from the entrance archway, small azure butterflies skipped and tumbled among the poppies and daisies. Bumblebees zoomed and buzzed around us. They had inspired me since I had learned that, scientifically, they were too heavy to fly, but didn't let that limitation hold them back.

My eyes were drawn to the right, towards a huge yellow–striped dragonfly poised on top of a wide green leaf. Its large wings were virtually transparent, criss–crossed with a delicate network of fine dark lines. This place was paradise, and I intended and hoped that it worked its magic.

I felt a small body brush past me as Tobin rushed towards the swing. He clambered on, and within seconds he was part of the play–equipment, boy and swing blending into one, describing a wide arc as he gained speed and height. Julianna made sure she remained close to her child.

The grass here was short, ideal for sitting or lazing about on. I sat, leaning back on my elbows as I watched the longer grasses sway in the rising breeze. Some were vivid green, others wheat–coloured, glinting gold in the cavern's light. The meadow was a spectacular sight, but tranquil, too.

Roanne nudged me as she sat down. "This is lovely. It doesn't change what happened . . . but it helps remind us that there are good things in life to balance the difficulties. It's peaceful. Soothing. Some of us want to head to the beach at the lake; is that okay?"

"Of course! Do whatever brings each of you the most pleasure, the most comfort. I'll join you in a while."

Then she was up, and away. I smiled. Everything would work out. I had faith. We also had lovelight, Lady Aida and the other Ascended Reikans in our corner. *We would make it.*

~~~

I watched Tobin on the swing. Despite his earlier shock, he was bouncing back, as children sometimes do. He was fully focused on the activity of rising and falling on the swing, of flying through the air, of his short legs moving to propel him into the next arc. He envisioned no future, for his future was only in the moment right after this one. I stayed in the carefree childhood moment with him, appreciating him for reminding me what was important – right here, right now.

Eventually he tired, and Julianna took him to one of the picnic benches, where they snuggled together and watched the bees and the butterflies. Feeling a sudden urge to move, my toes reminding me that they wanted to bury themselves in soft sand, I rose and made my way, via the meadow, to the lake's beach. I removed my shoes, letting them dangle from my hand. I could have been at any quiet, peaceful beach, if I could ignore the cavern roof. Still, it would serve its purpose whilst we were here.

Several of the villagers had also removed their footwear and lifted trouser legs and long skirts to paddle in the still waters of the lake. Occasionally, gentle waves would run into the beach, spilling onto the sand, leaving a damp glossy band behind as the wave retreated. The sound of the water was soothing, almost hypnotic. I laid on the sand, cradling the back of my head in my hands, closed my eyes, and dreamed of the Bahamas. I'd never been there; but the air here was balmy, the water warm, and it was easy to pretend I was elsewhere – just for a while.

I felt as if time had no meaning, as if I was suspended between worlds. I needed the temporary escape.

~~~

Water splashed onto my closed eyelids, making me jump, and I scrambled to my knees, rubbing my eyes. Tobin! The little monkey had carried water from the lake and was flicking it at me. Two could play at that game! I pulled myself upright and ran to the lake, scooping up a handful of water, and chasing him with it. Julianna did the same, and Roanne, and soon we were all shrieking and running and darting across the sand. The cavern rang with the sound of laughter and squeals and we were all wet and out of breath when the game ended.

I couldn't erase the smile produced by our moments of

childish joy. After a few moments, though, I felt strongly that we needed to move on. We had lifted our spirits, and hopefully this would help us to continue on our journey without grief and sadness holding us back. The other adults sobered up, but I could feel that the energy of the group remained relatively light, and almost carefree. Considering the tragedy we had witnessed so recently, I was quietly amazed at the transformation.

I retrieved the map from its pocket, hoping that more information had now been added. Ah – a name. Cavern of Imagination. And the exit was . . . where? I studied the map intently. Nothing. I looked up, turned full circle, scanning the whole perimeter of the cavern. Nothing obvious . . . but then, the last two caverns had provided us with rather *unusual* exits.

Roanne approached and silently queried if I had found anything.

"Nope," I replied. "Only the name – Cavern of Imagination. Which is logical."

"And revealing."

"In what way? Ro, what are you thinking?"

"Cavern of Imagination. You said it. So perhaps we *imagine* the exit, this time."

For a moment, my brain rebelled against the idea; it sounded totally ridiculous. But my resistance lasted only for a moment. Then it all clicked into place and my mind felt clear and open. "Of course we do . . . it's so obvious when you think about it!"

"So what sort of exit do we want to 'create', Lady Keira? Preferably one that is quick and easy!"

I looked around me. Meadow, swing, picnic tables, path, reeds, lilacs, beach, lake.

Birds.

"Ro, how many of us are there?" I knew the answer. I wanted to see if she came to the same conclusion that I had.

"Fifteen. Um, no, fourteen; sorry."

I winced. Jos. "And how many birds?"

She took a moment to count them. "Fourteen . . ."

"And where did they come from?"

"Nowhere! I mean, they just appeared inside the cavern."

"So . . . can we imagine that they take us out, to where we should be going?"

"Yes, I suppose so. What exactly do you have in mind, Lady Keira?"

A plan was forming in my mind. A little vague as yet, but shapes, images, feelings, they were all coming together into what I hoped was a workable, cohesive idea.

CHAPTER 31

The water–birds suddenly paddled directly towards me. Of course, this was the Cavern of Imagination, so perhaps my thoughts were already being manifested even though I hadn't consciously formed them yet! Next, I'd think of a rainbow and one would appear.

And so it did.

Careful, Keira – instant manifestation! The beautiful rainbow seemed to begin at the far edge of the lake. It soared over our heads, and arched into the cavern wall far behind us, its peak meeting virtually the highest point on the wall. Right. I guessed that my idea needed to include birds and the rainbow.

And then I saw it, in my mind's eye. All fourteen of us, being carried by the small white birds and using the rainbow as a 'bridge' to the cavern wall . . . and beyond. It seemed a crazy, fantastical idea, but I assumed that it had previewed in my mind for a reason.

I let Roanne know what I was planning, just as the birds reached the wet sand where the small waves lipped onto dry land. The birds waded out onto the sand and headed up the beach directly towards Roanne and me. All fourteen of them.

The other villagers wandered closer, wondering what was going on. I didn't have time to warn them that something unexpected – something *else* unexpected – was about to happen. A mist descended over the birds, shielding them from our view. The cloud expanded – I presumed this was to allow the birds to undergo some form of transformation – then dissolved. Julianna gasped as the fourteen *large* birds stood facing us, watching us, waiting for us.

Tobin laughed. "Mummy, the birds have become carrier pigeons!"

Several of us laughed at his clever joke. "They really have, Tobin," I said aloud. "The birds are going to carry us. Where do you think they'll take us?"

"Over the rainbow," he said, with complete confidence. I knew then that my plan was the right one.

"That's right. Over the rainbow."

"Pot of gold at the end?" Roanne said to me, quietly, with a smirk on her face.

"You never know," I joked. Interesting that we had both been told similar fairy stories about rainbows. Did that mean there was some truth in them, even though the mere idea seemed ludicrous? Rainbows were not solid, had no real beginning and end. However, we were about to use one as a bridge, so I was open to finding something unexpected!

Now that the birds were the appropriate size to carry us, they were spreading out, one bird to each person. Even little Tobin would be travelling by himself. I could feel doubts bubbling up inside: how would we hold onto the creatures, to keep from sliding off? What would happen when we flew into the rock wall? I had many questions, but no way of answering them. I had to *trust*.

I suddenly noticed that 'my' bird was eyeing me very closely. I was keeping it – and everyone else – waiting. Okay, here goes. I lifted my left leg over the bird's snowy white back, and sat astride the creature, my fingers clasping tufts of silvery feathers at its neck. Surprisingly, I felt secure on my perch. The others followed my lead, Julianna helping Tobin aboard before mounting her own bird. Then, with barely any noticeable motion, we rose into the air.

Flying like this was amazing! We had a completely

different vantage point of the beautiful teal–coloured lake, and of the rest of the cavern. The birds circled so that we approached the rainbow from the lowest point above the lake. As we flew closer, the colours became brighter, and the bands wider, the distinct hues merging and coalescing into one massive ribbon of graduated colour. It truly was a magnificent sight. I had never seen a rainbow from such close quarters. This, being a product of our dreams and imagination, may have its own rules.

The colours were soft, but also dense, so that I felt that I would be absorbed by them as we flew. Hadn't Lady Aida's journal mentioned something about chakras? Yes . . . I recalled that the seven major chakras were linked to the rainbow colours, and that these colours could be used to boost health. There was so much I still wanted to learn, but, as usual, there was no time.

Then we were upon the rainbow. We glided upwards and onwards, over the red, orange and yellow bands, then the birds shifted their angle of direction a little and we were flying up and over emerald green, forest green, sky blue, denim blue, indigo, midnight blue, lilac and amethyst, before angling back towards the blues, greens and yellows. It was a spectacular ride. I would have been able to touch the coloured light with my hands, if I had not been using them to keep my balance. We must be close to the cavern wall now, as the ceiling was not far above our heads. Still we flew, never slowing, our elevation never dipping.

Then I saw it. The wall. It was directly ahead.

The birds dipped into the rainbow itself, surrounding us with coloured light. I felt warmth and tingling in my face and hands. Travelling unswervingly towards the wall, I desperately wanted to close my eyes, could almost feel the impact . . .

. . . but we were through! It was if the wall had never been there.

~~~

Looking around, it was difficult to say much about our new location. I knew that we *had* made our way through the rocky wall and were now outside of the Cavern of Imagination. We were still airborne. All around us was white light, and mist. *Cloud?* Then I was overtaken by dizziness and was forced to shut my eyes to keep from fainting. A gentle bump – almost unnoticeable – persuaded me to cautiously open one eye, then the other.

We were on the ground. All fourteen birds were positioned in an inward–facing circle, with all fourteen of us still aboard. We were in a small circular space which led directly into another tunnel. I groaned inwardly.

My spherical light bobbed in front of me; its movement reminded me to check the map before we headed into the next passageway. I dismounted from my 'carrier pigeon' and retrieved the map from its protective pocket. Within seconds, Roanne was beside me. I was aware of the others climbing down, of Tobin saying goodbye to his bird.

My attention was fully focused on the map.

Roanne sent, "The birds have gone."

"What? When?" I looked up and around the small space, seeing only Cordellans.

"Just now. We looked back and they'd just vanished. Products of our imagination, I guess."

"No rules, here, just as you said!" I smiled, and turned

my attention back to the map. A passageway, which led from this 'dead end' (only *we* knew better), led further into the deep underground network of tunnels, caverns, and heaven knew what else. Going by the map, and the locations left unnamed, we still had quite a way to go.

Did we just keep moving until we reached the 'end' of the map? *Yes.*

Better get moving, then. Lovelight needed us.

The Cordellans were already shuffling into line, ready to follow where I led next. I turned back to send a smile and a few words of gratitude, then headed into the tunnel, my spherical light leading the way. An ordinary tunnel, of normal size. One foot in front of the other. Tobin started to hum, and he was soon joined by Julianna and several of the villagers. I soon learned the melody of the chorus, and softly hummed along in all the right places.

It was a long tunnel. Nothing changed. We kept going. Kept humming. Kept our spirits up.

Surprisingly, I was able to keep my focus on the present moment, and away from worry and anxiety. Perhaps it was the act of humming, of paying attention to the tune. It worked, anyway. Very occasionally, my thoughts drifted to Jason, and to Charls, but the chorus soon brought me back to the present moment. There was absolutely no point in thinking ahead because we had no idea where we were going, what we would meet next, or how the whole trek would affect lovelight and Cordello. The present moment was all there was.

The tell–tale dimming of my globe–light indicated that we were probably approaching another cavern of some sort – or danger. After experiencing so many different sorts of caverns already, I really had no fixed expectations of what we'd behold in this one. Most of

291

the caverns had been beautiful and amazing, although I'd rather not repeat the Cavern of Silent Shadows again. I had a niggling feeling – an intuition – that this one might be more of a challenge than, say, the Cavern of the Crystal Song.

Instinctively, I called my spherical light closer to me, as if to protect it, and re–connected with lovelight. I felt that I would need the reassurance and strength that the loving energy provided to me. I sensed Roanne linking thoughts with the others and suggesting that they connect with lovelight, too. The energy in the tunnel lifted and lightened, and I took a deep breath, wondering what was around the next bend.

We soon found out.

The entrance to the vast cavern was filled with a plain of sharp, black rocks, lava–like and inhospitable. These continued as far as the eye could see. Tucked towards the left wall of the cavern, a row of haggard trees struggled from the ground, looking miserable and desolate, and with not a leaf in sight. But the main feature – and at this my heart sank – rushing, green–grey water pounding onto the rocks. The waves crashing onto the fierce shore were several feet high – how they were produced, I had no clue. The water looked heavy and lumpy, dense and glassy. What a contrast to the lake in the previous cavern! Even the sound of the waves – unheard until we had reached this entrance – was unpleasant. They heaved and sighed, crashed and moaned, sucked and slithered.

The wave sets rolled in without pause. Tobin whimpered, and from the corner of my eye I noticed Julianna pull him close. Not surprisingly, no–one else looked enamoured, either. I imagined that all of our faces showed the same expression: dismay. How on earth would we traverse this bleak, black environment without cutting ourselves to ribbons – or drowning?

Even the air was heavy, pregnant with ill–will it seemed; stormy grey tendrils of cloud swirled over and around us, lacing us with a hint of chilly moisture. This was going to be a cold, wet experience.

If we survived it.

We had to.

I pressed the map pocket closer to me, as if I could protect it with the rapidly cooling heat of my body. I knew that the pocket was waterproof – it had brought the map safely through the waterfall, after all. But *this* water was a far cry from the graceful cascade of the waterfall; this felt unwelcoming.

"Ro, any ideas?" I sent.

"Nope. Not one. We've never met water quite this *unpleasant.*"

"And look at the rocks . . ."

"They look lethal. Lady Keira, we'll have to think of something soon, it's so cool in here, we'll all be shivering if we don't move."

Roanne was right.

I asked of my intuitive self: *How do we get out of this one?*

And waited for an answer.

None came.

My mind was totally blank. No mental images, no visions, no words. Looking ahead at the gloomy, threatening scene, no solution miraculously presented itself. I was stuck. I didn't know what to do, where to go, or how to get there. I needed extra help.

"Ascended Reikans," I began silently. "We're in this cavern with evil–looking rocks and a few stunted, unhappy trees – and a *lot* of heavy waves. Help, please!

I don't know the way forward, and we're stuck here unless we can find a solution before we all get hypothermia."

I hoped they would not take umbrage at my informal manner. I was just explaining our predicament to them as quickly as I could. I was starting to shiver, and rubbed at my arms to warm them. My sleeves were wet, and rucked as I moved my hands over them. Where was a winter coat when you needed one? If we'd known that *this* was ahead, we might have been able to make contingency plans in the Cavern of Imagination!

The clammy air felt very uncomfortable. It was like standing just underneath a layer of mist. Still no ideas or answers came and I began to feel very small, very human, and a little bit worried. All my good–feeling thoughts had deserted me; all I could focus on was the plain of sharp rocks, the roaring sea, and the dripping cloud. Even the trees were ugly.

At that thought, I felt a zing through my skull. What? *The trees are ugly.* What a judgemental thought, Keira! The trees were doing their best, in very uninspiring circumstances. No wonder they looked as if they'd given up – with sharp rock and pounding waves, I'd felt close to giving up too.

But I wouldn't.

A mental image of the weeping pines entered my head for a fraction of time, barely long enough to register, yet somehow leaving an imprint in my mind.

We'd sent love to the pines.

As an experiment, I focused on the nearest emaciated tree, its branches clawing upwards as if in supplication to the clinging damp mist hanging above it. First of all, I sent it lovelight, and visualised a stream of loving energy flowing from my heart to the roots and trunk of the tree. Then I mentally directed emotions to the tree: acceptance, strength, joy, love, beauty, life. Nothing happened and I nearly gave up my test as a lost cause. Then, just as I was thinking that it wasn't working, the tree began to emit the palest golden light. My heart jumped with pleasure. It *was* working!

"Lady Keira?" Roanne sent, querying my stillness.

Startled, my concentration lapsed, and the tree's light faded. I looked at Roanne, and explained what I'd been doing. "So it seems that we might help the trees here, too . . . and maybe that's part of the key in finding our way through this cavern."

"It's no more far–fetched than what we found in the Weeping Pines Cavern," she acknowledged before continuing. "Okay, I'll tell the others what we're doing and we can all work together."

"Let's all focus on this one tree first, and see what sort of difference we can make by working together," I suggested.

As I'd hoped, our combined efforts caused the tree to glow quickly and to sustain its light. It now had an aura of soft gold encompassing its branches. Even from here, I could see that the tree was forming buds, and then – so quickly! – fresh, green leaves. Not moving, we turned our focus onto the next tree, which was farther away. This one, too, transformed before our eyes. And the next. And the one after that.

"Ro, can you all keep sending? I'm going to head to Tree One and see if I'm struck with inspiration."

"Of course."

Gingerly, I left the others, and moved towards the nearest black rock. It was slick with moisture and I knew I'd have to watch my footing. I scrambled onto the rock, one foot sliding backwards as I struggled to find a foothold. This would be a treacherous route; I did not want to ask the others to follow. Carefully, concentrating hard, I made my way across the layered rock, avoiding sharp slices of flint–like stone. My progress felt painfully slow, but I knew this might be our only chance.

Finally, my hands sore from little cuts where the rock had sliced my hands despite my caution, I was close to the first tree. I stood upright on the small area of dusty, flat ground at its base, letting my relief wash the tension from my muscles. I gazed at the tree – in this state it *was* beautiful. Like a spring cherry in full, cheerful bloom, pink and white aromatic flowers were suspended from its branches, covering almost every twig. Leaves thrust from in–between, bright green with narrow veins. The tree was vibrant. I sent it feelings of peace, love, gratitude, and a little dose of lovelight.

Responding, the leaves sparkled, and pulsed with inner light. The transformation had been incredible. I shook my head with amazement at the power of positive thoughts and feelings – of the change wrought by bestowing these feelings on plants that had looked like living skeletons. I reached out to stroke the petals of the blossom; impossibly velvety soft and smooth. And smelling of almonds.

However, I still had no idea how to use this to help *us*.

~~~

As I gently touched the tree, some part of me sensed its response. It was happy. It felt accepted and nurtured, supported and appreciated. "So what now, Tree One? Can you help us?" I sent.

The blossom flowers bobbed in the cool air. I

296

maintained my physical and mental connections with the tree, believing both to be important. I knew that the others were sending energy and positive feelings to the other trees, but dared not break my focus to look.

I gave everything to Tree One. All my appreciation and gratitude for its beauty and strength, despite the bleak environment it found itself in. It had always been beautiful; recognition of this enabled the tree to gracefully blossom in the most literal sense. But now it was changing again. The blossoms were curling and fading, transforming miraculously into seeds. Looking remarkably similar to sycamore seeds, with a central pod flanked by two wings, the seeds sprouted all over the tree.

I had forgotten the chill in the air until the wind lifted. This time – by accident or design – the cool breeze went in our favour. The seed–pods detached from their host and fluttered and skimmed in the air, dancing in spirals before drifting to the ground. Where they fell upon the harsh, black rock, they curled over the surface, as if becoming one with the sharp and slippery stone. Fascinated, I watched as the merging resulted in flat, smooth sand. The seeds continued to flow and skip, to fall and transform.

I looked back at Roanne and the villagers. Their attention remained focused on the other trees. I dared to turn my focus there, too, and saw trees heavy with blossom and fresh, green growth. Looking down at my feet, I let my eyes trace a route to the next tree. The ground linking the two trees was littered with seed–pods; hopefully the ground underneath was negotiable.

The path was as easy as I had hoped. Once there, I connected with the tree as I had done for Tree One. The same result – seed pods and a route to Tree Three. It seemed I would be able to create a safe route all the way from the first tree to – hopefully – the last.

But there was no safe route from the cavern entrance to Tree One. I really did not want the others lacerating their hands – or worse – trying to negotiate the evil black lava–rock. I thought of Tobin's tiny, soft hands and knew I'd need to find a better way.

Then, in my minds eye, a brief vision appeared. I was strewing 'spare' seeds from Tree One back to the cavern doorway. It was so obvious, I was stupid not to have seen the solution. I jogged back to Tree One, and saw that many seed–pods had fallen onto the ground under the tree, forming a soft pile. I stooped to collect handfuls of the light pods. Throwing them ahead of me, I waited for the rock to undergo its alteration and form the pathway, which I then followed. Having reached the others, I quietly gained Roanne's attention with a private thought, and hurriedly let her know what I had done. She nodded her understanding, then returned her attention to sending positivity, appreciation and lovelight to the remaining trees.

I made my way back to Tree One, and from there to the third tree, where I repeated the whole exercise again. I knew it would take a while to create a full–length pathway; there were at least two dozen trees between Tree One and the far end of the cavern. But it did not matter; I had a solution and it was being created, moment by moment. We would navigate this cavern safely and make our way to the next. One step closer to achieving our goal.

Tree by tree, seed by seed, the path was created. My connection with lovelight meant that I did not feel tired from the mental focus involved in working with the trees. I was surprised to find that I was already heading towards the penultimate tree. Both of the trees ahead of me were already blooming profusely, and I looked back to see that the Cordellans were following the path and were not far behind me.

The sea was kept back from the pathway by the fierce band of rocks on the 'shore'; they, at least, served our purpose whilst in their original, harsh state. All that was ahead of us now was the last tree. I moved towards it, and my eyes strayed beyond to a black opening in the rock.

The exit.

My body slumped a little as the last of the remaining tension dissolved away. We were nearly there. We all sent to the tree, which glowed, as I'd expected.

What I did not expect was that the sea would calm, or the air soften and warm. Stunned, I turned seawards and noted the astonishing transformation: the once–tumultuous, angry waters were now tranquil and still. Little wavelets lapped at the barrier of black rock, which now seemed benign. The trees had altered the environment of the whole cavern. *We* – together with lovelight – had caused this to happen. I felt a lump lodge in my throat – emotion. I let it through, allowed the tears to fall from my eyes.

I never ceased to be amazed by the power of our thoughts and feelings.

By the miracle that was lovelight – by the miracle that was *love*.

CHAPTER 32

Reference to the map revealed that this location was named the Cavern of the Dark Storm. I put the map away as Roanne moved to my side. We shared a smile of relief that we had made it through this latest test.

"I reckon the map should rename this cavern, now!" Roanne jested.

"Absolutely! I can't believe the transformation. All due to love . . ." I replied.

As with the weeping pines, I wondered how we could sustain this increased quantity of lovelight for the benefit of these trees. *How can we be of service?* I asked of the Ascended Reikans.

The cycle of life. Water. Use your imagination, dear Keira.

I thought on the words, let them pierce the fine membrane of my consciousness and sink down, lower, deep into my subconscious. I felt a shift in my awareness, a subtle change in the context of the words I'd been given. The words rose and fell, their sequence changing . . . their *meaning* changing.

I had it! *The life cycle of water.* Excitedly, I began to explain my plan to Roanne.

"We know the rules are different here, that we can be playful, creative – as long as our intentions are for the highest good. We intend that vapour from the waves rises as clouds. They hover in the cavern, dispersing lovelight to the trees as the rain or mist falls! If we trust that lovelight is sustained through the water–cycling process, then all we have to do is ensure that the energy from the trees can flow to the sea in the first place, then a 'lovelight loop' can be maintained!"

Roanne looked troubled. "But the rocks keep all the water back; there's no outlet – no stream or river, no way for the water to cycle back to the sea. It won't work!"

She had a point. Desperately, I looked around us. There had to be a way. We couldn't leave before we'd made provision for lovelight to be made available to the trees and their environment.

There *was* no solution. Our creativity would have to extend a little further. I allowed my brain to work on the problem, let my inner knowing and the information from the Ascended Reikans come up with an answer.

I spied Tobin hard at work behind the black rocks. He was digging into the ground, into the hard sand. His small hands burrowing into the surface, he was doing his best to create a lop–sided sand–castle.

"I've got it!" I beamed. "It's quite simple. We don't need to *do* anything, Ro! The moisture will seep down into the trees' roots, deep underground. There must be a – a water table, or something. Water returns to the sea through the usual underground process."

She grinned. "Even if that's not how it works at the moment, we can simply intend that it will do so from now on! Let's get everyone working on it, then we can move onto our next challenge!"

We formulated our group intention then stood quietly, visualising and placing our goals into the cavern's energetic memory, as Roanne referred to it. Our intentions were now part of the fabric of the cavern, and lovelight would cycle with the movement of the water. It was done.

Casting one last look at the peaceful scene, I turned again towards the exit, and walked towards it. Of course, it would lead into another tunnel. I was resigned to more tunnel–walking, but part of me – including my legs and feet – hoped we would not have to walk for too long before we could take further rest. This was no walk in the park.

I felt a flicker of frustration that I had no clue what was going on 'outside'. Was Charls okay? What of his men? Had my dream been in any way meaningful? I felt the need to connect with Charls – and soon. Despite my strong friendship with Roanne, despite trusting her, I still missed Charls. One friend does not replace another; I recognised that each of my friendships was special in its own way – each offering a unique perspective and benefit. I hoped that Charls and I would soon find a way to connect.

Pulling my thoughts back to *here* and *now*, I entered the dark shadow of the tunnel's entrance, and my trusty orb–light expanded and moved ahead of me, almost before I had finished forming the mental request. I guessed we were becoming attuned to each other's frequency.

To my relief, the tunnel was short – very short. It led to a small, empty cavern – I hoped it was a peaceful one – with lights high on the inward–curving walls. With a sigh of relief, I dropped to the ground and leaned against my backpack. I closed my eyes. It was bliss to stop for a moment. Lovelight had kept me going in the Cavern of the Dark Storm, but I did feel the need for respite now that it was over, and now that we were again trudging through tunnels.

Roanne seated herself to my right, Tobin and Julianna to my left. I knew I should stay awake, keep watch, but my body resisted my will and closed down, dragging me into a deep dreamless sleep.

I woke feeling groggy, and found myself slumped

against Roanne's shoulder. I struggled into a more upright position and met her eyes sheepishly.

"Sorry, Ro – I was completely exhausted. I hope you weren't uncomfortable?"

"Nope. Don't worry about it, you looked all in, so we let you sleep. Here, have some fruit, my lady."

I bit into the fruit – it looked, smelled, and tasted like a fresh red–green apple. It was refreshing. I felt suddenly alert. My globe–light bobbed above my head and I thought now might be a good time to learn how to make one myself. I asked Roanne if there was now time for me to learn.

"It won't take long for you to learn, as you're already greatly experienced with using lovelight, and you have learned a year's worth of skills in the few weeks you've been with us. But after that, we'd probably better get moving again."

I agreed. We had to rest now and then, else we would collapse – but we also had to keep our momentum going, needed to remember our long–range goal. However, I needed this skill; I had no idea if or when it would be needed.

"Right," she began. "Connect to lovelight, Lady Keira. Then visualise in the space in front of you an area into which the energy will coalesce."

I closed my eyes to improve my focus and did as Roanne advised. I felt the familiar lovelight tingles, and focused on the space that I would see just in front of me had my eyes been open.

"Next, place your intention that the lovelight streams towards that space. If you want a circular light, then see it forming a sphere. There are other enhancements that we'll discuss later, if we have time. We usually use a sphere because that form has an equal outwards

303

expansion from a single point of existence. For now, just let the energy flow to the space you are visualising."

I did so, pretended that there were filaments of lovelight pouring towards the spherical space I had 'created'. I pictured it about the size of a soccer ball. As I continued this visual in my mind, I could start to feel lovelight passing through me and out through my chest, as if I was a dry riverbed being flooded with rushing water.

"Then, just focus on that sphere becoming a complete, geometric shape . . . next, intend that the energy remain contained within . . . then intend that it is sealed."

I followed Roanne's instructions, creating in my mind a white ball of light, and, to finish it off, turning a pretend key in an imaginary padlock on the top of the globe.

"Now, open your eyes," Roanne said softly.

And there it was. My first light–sphere. Suspended in front of me, glowing steadily with its opal–white light. Just for fun, I visualised the sphere turning blue, and squeaked as my globe–light obeyed my instruction.

"Oh! Lady Keira, how did you know how to change its colour?"

"Um. I just asked it to, I think . . ."

"Mm. Well there's not much else I can teach you, really, because you so easily make the natural leap yourself without external guidance. There *are* more skills you can learn – how to make an exploding energy–sphere, for example, but that involves energy–weaving, and we don't really have time for that at the moment."

That sounded interesting, too. I had liked the look of the rainbow–coloured creation that I had seen Tissa fabricate in her cell; the sphere that had blown out her window! I wondered how she, too, was faring. Whether she had yet released her anger with Charls. She was feisty, and courageous, and I admired those qualities in her; but I was not sure we would ever truly be at ease with each other.

Now, it was time to move on again. There was only one exit from this safe little space, but I noticed with surprise that this next tunnel was wider than any of the previous ones. Did this have some significance?

~~~

The air felt cooler, too; fresher, somehow. My hopes rose, as I envisioned open skies and fresh air. Then rapidly fell as I recalled the map – still so far to go. I found myself wishing for some kind of time–and–space machine. Of course, our quest was as much about what we learned on the journey as it was reaching the final destination. Logically, I knew that; emotionally I wanted the 'quick fix'. I let out a soft sigh and refocused on our current location.

My newly–created globe–light travelled alongside the light that Roanne had made for me so many caverns ago. They bobbed together like a pair of gauzy white balloons in the lightest of breezes. I sent instructions for my new light to change from white to silver, and then to shell–pink. Experimenting with my new spherical–light helped to pass the time and kept me alert. We were all tunnel–weary, and despite our recent rest–break, it seemed no–one had the energy to sing or hum.

We might not have seen it at all had we not had the extra light–sphere.

A shape had been lightly carved into the tunnel wall, located just as we approached a slight bend to the left. I stopped suddenly, Tobin knocking into me with a muffled 'oof'.

"Sorry, Tobin," I sent absently. My mind was focused on the carving. My two lights obediently illuminated the cavern wall from either side, so that the shape was perfectly and clearly defined.

"A dolphin!" cried Tobin softly.

Yes, a dolphin. Charls had explained to me that dolphins were sacred to the Cordellans, appreciated for their wisdom and intelligence as well as for their beauty, their playfulness and their curving 'smile'. I was glad that the dolphin was well–cared for here. But what was it doing on a wall deep inside this underground network of passages and caverns? Surely its presence had some meaning – gave us some message? I knew it was no coincidence and we had to take notice of the carving.

No answers were forthcoming from my intuition, so I decided to seek Tobin's advice.

"Tobin, do you know why the dolphin is here?"

His little face formed an exaggerated frown. "No, Lady Keira, I don't know why. I think you need to ask somebody else." He looked pointedly at Roanne. Who said children couldn't 'do subtle'?

"Ro?" I sent.

She shrugged her shoulders. "Honestly, nothing comes to mind. Maybe it's not important?"

"I was drawn to examine it more closely – I believe it *is* important," I replied, gazing again at the drawing.

Roanne leaned forward to study it. "It has a deep blue eye," she pronounced. "The same colour as . . . oh!" She broke off and delved into her pocket, producing the lapis lazuli crystal.

"You think this has a role in this?" I asked.

"It's the only 'answer' I can give," she sent. "Here, take

it. See if it leads to anything."

I took the dark blue striated stone from her, held it in the palm of my left hand, and turned it over with my fingers. The crystal was warm from being stored in Roanne's trouser pocket. I let it rest in my hand, staring at it. Then I looked back at the dolphin. The eye was a deep, midnight blue. And it was flashing. So the stone and the carving were linked, somehow.

~~~

As Roanne had mentioned on first holding the crystal, it gave off a powerful tingling energy. My hand was almost uncomfortably buzzing from its frequency. The vibration spread along my arm and into my shoulder, and before long I felt as if my scalp was being tickled with a feather. I resisted the urge to scratch at my head. This crystal had *attitude*. But what could it possibly have to do with the carved dolphin?

Then I remembered that dolphins communicate using sonar. I wondered if the lapis lazuli crystal was able to vibrate at the same frequency . . . and communicate in some way with the carving. An utterly fantastic idea of course, but . . . *Yes*, came the answer. Okay. So why would they need to communicate? And why was the dolphin's eye blue? So that Roanne would make the connection between the carving and the crystal? Again: *Yes*.

I felt my forehead wrinkle in concentration. Why would they *need* to communicate? I felt a tug at my sleeve and automatically closed my fingers over the crystal to keep it safe. Tobin was trying to get my attention.

"What is it, Tobin?" I asked, aloud.

"Lady Keira, I have some information now. I don't really know where it came from. But I was told to tell you that you already know the answer."

"Thank you, Tobin. I don't feel that I do –"

"You do," he replied, his certainty making his little face appear very solemn. I smiled at him, then looked again at the crystal captured in my hand.

The deep blue colour was fading . . . then deepening . . . it was *pulsing*. Okay. The cube paperweight had pulsed, and it had proved to be a 'special object'. We had already guessed that this crystal was such an object. I just didn't know what I was supposed to *do* with it. Frustration rose as I tried to manually scan my brain, to find some answer that may have been assimilated from reading Lady Aida's journal.

Still nothing came to me.

Everyone was waiting.

I cleared my mind, stopped thinking, and created space for insights to rise from my inner guidance. Instinctively, I connected with the lovelight energy.

Clarity suddenly arrived, illuminating my thinking process like the warm sun after a summer downpour. Of course. We three – the dolphin, the crystal and I – were designed to function as a trio. The stone was trying to connect with me, so that the dolphin's message could be received, and translated. Not exactly obvious; but, once the thought was conscious, I knew that this *was* the answer. The ancient Reikans had programmed a message within the dolphin; everything had waited for this precise set of circumstances to occur.

Perfect timing.

"Roanne, I know what to do. I just don't know what will happen after I do it – so it might be best if you all move back a little way . . . keep Tobin safe." As I spoke, she and Julianna were already retreating up the tunnel, Tobin tucked behind them both. It was just a precaution; I had faith that everything would be fine.

I stood with my back to the tunnel wall, facing the dolphin.

Closing my eyes to focus, I mentally connected with the crystal. Then I opened my eyes, gazing directly at the sparkling blue eye of the dolphin. "What message do you have for us?" I asked silently.

The air around me seemed to change, and my ears felt as if they needed to pop – the air pressure had altered, and I guessed that the dolphin's message was being transmitted through me to the crystal. I felt very faintly dizzy, as if gravity had lessened, as if I might suddenly fall to the side and hit the floor. I felt, too, another strange sensation in my ears: a fullness, as if they contained water. I shook my head, trying to make my ears clear. The pressure changed and my ears began to ring, a high–pitched regular toning taking the place of the fullness. It sounded like a percussion triangle being struck repeatedly, and at close range. It was a little uncomfortable.

Then, with no warning, the pressure returned to normal, the toning stopped, and the air felt as it had done before. It was quite a relief. That was only half of the task completed, though, wasn't it? The dolphin had transmitted, but as yet, I had received no translated message.

I unfolded my fingers from their protective shield, revealing the lapis lazuli resting in my palm.

The crystal continued to pulse.

CHAPTER 33

Instinctively, I again let my eyelids fall closed, knowing that I would need to concentrate on what happened next. I was startled when an image zoomed onto my mind's black movie–screen. The background colours were over–bright, similar to my perception of saturated colour on first arriving in Reika. Once my 'mind's eye' adjusted, I could see the central image with more clarity.

It was a pattern of some sort, endlessly–repeating blazing white shapes growing smaller and smaller, then the image pulled away and I could see that the recurring shapes were unfolding on an ever-increasing scale. I recognised the nature of the pattern – *fractals*. The building blocks of the universe, weren't they? I had seen some pretty amazing videos on YouTube. I knew that they had been preparing me for this moment, for this recognition.

The fractal images were beautiful beyond belief – but I wasn't sure *why* I was seeing them. Standing here with these images playing inside my mind, I felt as if I had tumbled into a kaleidoscope. It was like being in another world – which was itself inside another world. This could get complicated!

I waited patiently, knowing that I either already had the answers, or would be given them, just as Tobin had said. The next step, the next thought, all would unfold in the right way, and at the right time. I had so much faith, now, that I would be guided. As long as I remembered to ask . . . and to watch and listen and feel for the answers.

Still I waited. I was acutely aware that I was the only

one of our group who was seeing these images. I tried to curb my mounting impatience, allowing events to unfold in their own timing.

Then, the frantic expansion of patterns slowed down, and I could see a larger, still image forming, something recognizable, something every child would be able to identify.

A snowflake hung inside my mind, sparkling white on a deep blue background. I could see incredible detail. It literally took my breath. The image panned out slowly, and I saw hundreds, thousands, millions of tiny snowflakes falling, each unique, each a triumphant representation of nature's artistic flair, the whirling flakes together forming a flurry of white.

And I understood the message.

Each tiny snowflake, so perfect and amazing, was also part of a larger entity, capable of forming drifts and banks and storms. Like each drop of water becoming, en masse, a lake, a river, an ocean. Grains of sand on a beach. Water vapour droplets forming clouds.

Human beings forming families, communities and countries.

And my understanding expanded again. This was a message about humanity. About the innate perfection of each person, and about the function of each human as a single point in the world population. I was being shown how each of us was inextricably a part of a far greater whole. About each of us being embraced and accepted as unique, celebrating our diversity whilst also working together in a cooperative role for all of mankind.

About how we were a *part* of nature, and could never escape it.

The image of snow spun away, to be replaced by a picture of the Earth, as seen from space. Blue, green, and white, our only home. Tears filmed my eyes as I gazed on the familiar sight, and I felt homesick for my own world, for everyone that I knew . . . and for everyone that I didn't and wouldn't know. For humanity. Without being shown images of destruction and war and anger, I knew that the focus of this message was to find a way for humanity to work together to protect our planet – before it was too late.

Compassion for all beings filled my heart, and overflowed. I didn't know what to do with all this emotion! It was too much to contain.

The thought came to me to direct this tender feeling to the planet that I could see hanging on my movie–screen. I poured the emotion into the planet, intending peace, harmony and healing to every part of the oceans, the rivers, the mountains, the deserts, the jungles, the cities . . . I let the energy flow out of me, from my heart into the Earth's. Finally, I was spent, my legs feeling weak. The image of Earth began to fade and I was on the verge of opening my eyes, when I hesitated.

I heard the eerie song of a dolphin. A flash of silver upon blue brushed my mind's eye before disappearing. I heard a distant series of clicks and whistles, then all was quiet. A few seconds of silence passed before I dared to open my eyes.

I let my gaze come to rest on the dolphin carving.

The eye was no longer blue. It was blazing white, like a diamond refracting light. Or perhaps it was the sun reflecting on newly–fallen snow. I might have imagined it, but I thought the carving flickered. A narrow ray of rainbow–coloured light flitted across my vision; I blinked and it was gone.

My sleeve was tugged again, and I looked down to see that Tobin and Julianna had returned to my side.

"Lady Keira?" Tobin sent silently.

"Yes, Tobin?" I sent back.

"Don't tell anyone else, but that dolphin moved! It's happy now. It knows that you'll do your best to pass its message on when you get back to your own world."

"Really?" I was surprised. What role could I have in world affairs? My job was mundane and underpaid. Well, I hoped I would make it back to my own world, then I would see what happened from that point.

~~~

It was time to move on, and I absently pocketed the crystal to keep it safe. Why I didn't hand it back to Roanne, I don't know. As I started to make my way forward through the tunnel, I considered what information I should pass to Roanne and the others. For some reason, I felt that this message had been sent to me, personally. Most Cordellans were already fully aware of the benefits of living peacefully and cooperatively.

But surely they wondered why I had been connected with the dolphin? And Tobin – his silent message to me indicated that this particular event was not for general understanding. So, I chose to say nothing until I was guided to.

From this point on, the tunnel was like all of the others. I returned my focus to the rhythm of my walk, my breath, how my body felt. I was fully in the 'now', with no thought of any future or past. It was soothing and calming.

The tunnel broadened further, and I felt a warm, small hand push its way into mine. "Hi Tobin," I sent, angling my head briefly to smile at the boy. He smiled back, his

313

trusting child's smile, his faith in me and his mother absolute. Adults always had the answers, didn't they? I rather thought that Tobin had more 'answers' than most adults in my own world.

So it was that I reached the end of the tunnel with Tobin at my side, Roanne and Julianna mere steps behind. We came upon it without warning, turning a corner and finding we had nowhere to go. Tobin and I stopped suddenly, Julianna tripping slightly as she stumbled to a halt immediately behind us.

"Lady Keira?" Roanne asked silently. "Have we taken a wrong turning?"

"How could we have, Ro? We've come here directly from the dolphin . . . there was no other way to go except backwards!" I was puzzled. I had been so certain we were on the right path. I picked the map from its pocket, frowning as I examined it. It now showed this tunnel, and a blue dot which presumably represented the dolphin's location. From that landmark, I could see the tunnel continuing into the underground network, with no dead end being shown.

So . . . did that mean that there was a way through? Either ahead, or to one side? The map, of course, did not – would not – reveal the answer yet. It was up to us to work it out. I packed it away.

"Any ideas, Tobin?" I whispered softly.

His huge eyes looked at me, his head shaking slowly from side to side.

"Not this time, Lady Keira!" he sent.

Okay. So this one would be up to me.

I scanned the wall ahead of us. The rock was uniformly smooth, very similar to the walls arching in on either side of us. I reached my right hand out in front me, letting my palm gently come to rest upon the cool

314

surface of the rock. I did not connect with lovelight; I simply let my hand connect with the stone, and waited. I had a déjà vu moment, the briefest shard of a memory, a vision of being connected with the huge crag before the massive stones had become a circle.

As if acknowledging my recall of the memory, the wall ahead of us glided silently aside, revealing darkness beyond the doorway. My globe–lights, bobbing near my shoulders, moved forward at my instruction, and onwards into the secret passageway.

This part of the tunnel was smaller, narrower. Tobin fell behind me as the spherical lights and I walked forward into the passage. It felt different, though . . . then I realised that the air was sharper. Surely we weren't at the end of our journey, yet? My hopes rose, my mind instinctively presenting me with images of blue sky, puffed white clouds, and wide open spaces.

Well, the wide open space was bang on target. The tunnel suddenly deviated left and we found ourselves at another large doorway, and beyond . . .

Beyond lay a massive chamber – I could not see the far end of it. The space was not completely open, however. Towering white stalagmites thrust from the ground, their points reaching high into the air. Perhaps to maintain a balanced environment, correspondingly long stalactites hung from the roof of the cavern, some lazily dripping liquid onto the floor below. Here and there, columns had formed, where the two formations had met halfway. The cavern was crowded with the structures, but I could still see that the space extended for a considerable distance.

To the side of us, rimming the cavern walls, ran a narrow stream. It seemed at first glance to form a circular rill, and I wondered if it looped around the

315

whole cavern.. It was almost perfectly still, just a few slow ripples marring its calm surface.

Standing here, at the entrance, I could not plot a clear route through the statuesque formations. I also felt that we needed to ensure that we did not touch these magnificent natural creations. It felt wrong to interfere in any way with these incredible structures; they had been here for thousands of years, and we were merely travellers who were privileged to witness this magnificent sight. I passed a request to the Cordellans to keep clear of the formations as we passed.

Roanne slipped to my side. "Can we get through, my lady?"

"I think so. I'm sure we must be able to. We just have to be careful – respectful. Surprisingly the floor in this area is only wet near the rill, so I hope our footing will be secure. I feel it's really important that we don't touch anything except with our feet, don't you?"

"I agree," she said. "They're different from crystals, but still formed from minerals. I think human contact might affect their growth, or something."

"I think we have to tread carefully, and take it –"

"One step at a time!" She threw her head back and laughed, the sound echoing around the chamber. I grinned, glad of her friendship and support.

"C'mon then, let's make a start and see what happens." I took off my backpack and held it close to my chest. I walked slowly forward to a space between two giant stalagmites, their smooth surfaces reaching up merely a few feet apart. The floor was dry. I turned sideways just to make sure I cleared the gap, and shuffled through to the other side. Once on the other side, I analysed my next steps.

I felt as if I was in a forest of white statues, a silent

tableau of characters frozen in space and time. I shivered, and vowed to curb my imagination. Next, I'd be imagining souls trapped inside each of them. I focused upon my feet, making very sure that I did not slip or stumble. To damage one of these . . . it didn't bear thinking about.

I could see a possible way through, and walked carefully towards it. My route was not as it had first appeared. In front of me, a thick column rose from floor to roof, and to either side the ground was wet, slick with shallow inclines of puddled mineralised solution. It might not be passable. But no way could I walk through a column of limestone, or whatever it was. I didn't have many options.

~~~

I sent to Roanne: "I'm going to try to make my way around this column. It's the only option I have . . . unless you can think of another?"

"No, I think you have to try, Lady Keira. Please be careful."

"I will."

There was nothing to hold onto if I should slip. Even if I made it past the column, would the Cordellans also be able to find their way without harming themselves or the statues? How would Tobin manage? I bit my lip, and took a deep breath. I knew my footsteps needed to be sure – hesitancy could be worse than confidence in icy conditions, and this glossy frozen liquid turned the dry cavern into a similar environment.

I moved forward and placed first one foot directly onto the flattest area of the slick surface, followed by the other. I still had my backpack clutched to my chest.

There was not enough room between this column and the neighbouring stalactite to extend my arms for balance. Displaying far more confidence than I felt, I kept moving forward, making my way slowly and carefully around the left side of the enormous white column.

"Lady Keira? We can no longer see you. Everything okay?" I heard from Roanne.

"I'm fine!" I sent back. "There are more formations beyond the column. Dozens of them." Realising that I had reached 'dry land', I stopped and turned, retracing my steps with my eyes.

"Ro!" I sent. Were my eyes deceiving me? "It looks as if you might have a way past, after all."

I could clearly see outlines of my footsteps in the mineralised puddle. Somehow – inexplicably – the steps that I'd taken had dissolved the glossy substance. As long as the others placed their feet inside the traces of my steps, they would have a clear route through.

I waited as Julianna proceeded carefully around the column, her small feet easily fitting within my footprints. As expected, Tobin was close behind, followed by the others, with Roanne coming last.

Once we were all standing in the clearing, we took in our surroundings. We seemed to be surrounded on all sides by pale columns and statuesque formations. I felt as if we were lost in a cold, white forest, caught in a perpetual winter.

I wondered whether this cavern had any purpose for us – or if it was purely an obstacle course that we must cross before finding an exit to yet another tunnel. I consulted the map and found nothing of use. Frustrated, I looked around me again, sure that there must be *something* that would point the way, help us through, guide our path.

The answers are within, Keira. Startled, I looked around, expecting to see Lady Aida right behind me, but there was no–one.

"Lady Keira?" questioned Roanne, no doubt noticing my expression.

"I thought I heard someone speak . . . I think it must have been internal guidance," I replied absently. Now Lady Aida was in my head; I hoped she would stay there. Right now she was my guiding North Star, my safe place, my guiding light . . . the one person to whom I could reach out, hold onto, and follow home.

"Lady Aida?" I sent. "What can you tell me? How do we get through this?"

Within, Keira.

Back to intuition, then. Of course, all my guidance would come to me in that way; Lady Aida had merely been sending reassurance, and the reminder to trust myself. I wondered how many times I would need to take the 'trust' lesson before I learned it properly? Well, I am only human, I thought; all I can do is my best.

~~~

Despite Lady Aida's reassurance, I still felt a little lost and alone. I was doing my best to trust; but I realised that I was finding this particular cavern, so cluttered and crowded with the statuesque columns and stalagmites, more challenging than any of the previous ones. I was feeling tired from all of our challenges. I didn't know what was being asked of me, of us. It felt like it was simply eating away at time – time that we didn't have.

I could think of no way of utilising lovelight here. We'd moved rock and walls but I just couldn't visualise us moving a giant column of ancient limestone. The idea didn't *feel* right. The whole journey seemed, suddenly, so unreal.

And what resources did I have left to draw upon? I'd had all the help Lady Aida was offering; Charls was not here; none of the Cordellans had any ideas. And neither did I. We had already lost one member of our party, and we still seemed miles from the end of our trek.

Not for the first time, I wished I was home, safe in bed, dreaming, snuggled close with Jason.

Within.

The answers are within, I repeated, like a mantra. Another thought followed it, one that crystallised Lady Aida's words into real meaning: The *resources* are within.

Of course! This cavern could well be nothing more than a test of our resolve, our stubborn refusal to give in or to give up; our determination to protect lovelight from a tyrannical egomaniac. We simply had to keep going – no matter how far we had come – until we reached the end. That was all. It was about perseverance. It was all within. So be it.

One step at a time, we kept telling each other. So do it, Keira!

"Stay here until I let you know I've found a way through," I instructed the others with a quick smile. I turned back to the statuesque formations blocking my path. The ground was dry to either side of us, so I began investigating whether there was a pathway around this clump of overgrown mineral. My exploration to the right revealed only a narrow gap separating the huge off-white stalagmite from the cavern wall; there was just enough room for the water–filled rill to pass through. Even Tobin would have trouble squeezing

320

through that gap.

Retracing my steps, I examined the area at the far left of the cluster. Ah, now this showed some promise. The stalagtite here ended a short distance off the ground, which was – miraculously – bone dry. As long as we were very, very careful, I thought we would be able to crawl – or slither – underneath the blunt point of the stalagtite. I passed my backpack to Roanne, and laid down on my tummy. After sending my spherical lights ahead, I shuffled forward until my head was almost level with the stalagtite, then dipped it and kept my eyes fixed on the ground just beneath me. I crawled slowly forward on my elbows, keeping my head and body low. My clothes would be filthy after this. I felt like a child again, only more ungainly; this would be easy for Tobin!

Finally, I felt I was a full body–length past the stalagtite, and carefully rolled myself onto my back. Looking up, I saw that I was well clear of the structure, and that there was plenty of room for everyone in the space beyond. I moved back to the gap and knelt down, sending to Roanne to pass my backpack through. It arrived face down, its webbed material covered in dust. Looking down at my clothes, I could see that I was coated in the same dull, stony colour. Where was a hot shower – or a waterfall – when you needed one!

It took a seemingly endless time for everyone to make their way through the low gap, but eventually we were all reunited, although we looked as if we'd been rolling in a massive bag of wholemeal flour. I tried brushing myself down, but it made no difference as my hands were just as dusty. I gave up, and turned full circle in an attempt to find our next path.

There! Triumphantly, I spied a rough sequence of

steps carved into the rock adjoining a floor–to–ceiling column. Who had created them, I did not know, although the obvious answer was the Ascended Reikans. But why? Purely to help *us* through this cavern? They rose only a short height before descending on the other side, like a small up–and–down staircase. The remaining width of the cavern, at this point, was taken up by impenetrable columns of limestone, which left us no alternative way through. Backpack in hand, I made my way up and over the large steps. It was a relief to have an easy way through, for once. From the apex, I followed the rocky steps down onto more dry ground.

I almost tripped, as I was not looking at where I was placing my feet.

I was looking at something else entirely.

CHAPTER 34

Charls was level with the cell's open window–space and was able to clamber onto the rough stone framework and heave himself through the space, before dropping to the ground. Looking up towards the window frame, he waited whilst the expanded paperweight glided silently through the window–frame, shrinking as it fell, spinning, dropping into his hand. He tucked it back into his pocket.

From the darkness, Tissa stepped forward and gave him a brief hug.

"Come on," she sent. "We have to leave. I'll bring you up–to–date on the way back to the others."

As they walked along the deserted road, Tissa explained that Charls' work on the ropes binding her hands had meant she had been able to free herself. Creating a tiny, dense sphere of heated lovelight, she had directed it towards the remaining strands of rope, and intended that they burn through. Charls' capture provided sufficient distraction for her to then drop to her feet and tackle the ropes there. Within seconds, she was on her way out of the square.

Tissa then disclosed that, prior to her capture, she had been able to locate – and free – Symion, Sulla and Jenara, who had been held captive together in the same cells from which Charls had so recently escaped. Unwisely, they had been left unguarded, as Karn had called all of his men together to fire them up against Cordello. The family had been sent back to the copse, and one of the female warriors was now escorting them back to Cordello.

"Did you find out what Symion's 'crime' was?" Charls

asked.

"Oh yes," Tissa said, raising her eyebrows. "He had injured a man in a brawl many years ago. Defending Sulla's honour. He was being blackmailed by Karn."

"Is that all," Charls said softly. Poor Symion, being punished for an accident that had not been his fault. Charls had been quietly informed of that incident, had heard from trustworthy sources of the unreasonable provocation by the so–called injured party. He might well have thumped the guy himself, if the man had spoken of Alaria in that way. Perhaps Charls should have told Symion that he knew of the incident, that he did not judge or condemn him for it. He sighed.

"So what circumstances led to your capture, Tissa?" he asked quietly.

"I took a risk; I thought I would try to find Karn, and . . . immobilise him. Unfortunately, my gamble went in their favour, and not mine. I couldn't hold back a cough, and practically announced my arrival to Karn and his army as they began to assemble in the square for their practice drills. I couldn't believe how bad the timing was. I guess I could have used the Canturan sphere, after all."

"I'm sorry, Tissa." He should not have allowed her to come to Vornen alone.

"No matter, Charls, we're back together now. Do you have a strategy for battle with Karn?"

"I don't feel there's much use for strategy, Tissa. We're outnumbered until the other lords arrive – *if* they arrive. We may be better trained than Karn's men. And maybe we are more determined? You also have a great command of lovelight. I'm not happy about using it as a weapon – that's exactly what we're trying to *avoid* – but in this case perhaps the end justifies the means."

Charls was silent for a moment. "We will rest for a while then make our way back to the village at dawn. Set fire to the houses, have every weapon ready, and fight as hard as we can. We will have the element of surprise, at least. Our tactics won't win any prizes for the best battle campaign, however to a certain extent we will just have to make decisions on the fly. Do you agree?"

"Yes, I do, surprisingly. I also agree that we need rest – it is only three hours until dawn. Ah, here we are. Burron, all is well?"

Burron was on his feet in an instant. "Yes, m'lady. We're ready to go when you are." He nodded to Charls. "My lord! Good to see you!"

Charls grinned, then he and Tissa sat down under the trees to rest, awaiting the dawn.

Awaiting the start of battle.

~~~

As I placed my feet safely onto the dry ground just beyond the miniature staircase, I belatedly remembered to let Roanne know that she and the others could follow. My mind was taken up with the sight immediately in front of me; I thought of several questions – none of which I could answer.

My spherical lights bobbed ahead, further illuminating the space in front of me.

Water. And lots of it.

A few feet ahead of me, the floor ended abruptly at a stone ledge, giving way to a wide water–filled expanse. It was dark and still, and looked deep. The water was, I guessed, about fifteen feet across, and stretched the whole width of this immense cavern – and beyond. To

325

my left, the blackness yawned, apparently endless. The cavern appeared to extend deep into some unknown space, the water filling its breadth. How would Tobin manage this?

Beyond the stretch of water I saw dry ground, more stalactites and stalagmites, and beyond *that*, I hoped, an exit. But there was no boat, no rope bridge, no obvious way to cross the water. I almost stamped my foot with frustration. We'd come so far! My initial reaction was a little flicker of fear, of anxiety – a sense that we were, finally, beaten. I was tired of challenges and difficulty.

Then my fighting spirit overpowered my feeling of powerlessness. Of course we would find a way! That's what we did! It was simply another *small* challenge, and part of a much bigger picture. The fact that I had not one spark of an idea yet was irrelevant. I had to keep a helpful perspective. A solution would present itself; we just had to intend that it did so, and remain open–minded so that we recognised it when it appeared.

Instinctively, I connected with lovelight. Roanne came to stand to my left, and said nothing.

"Speechless, Ro?"

"Mm. I guessed we had more statues to work through, but I hadn't expected water . . ."

"Nor me. But here it is. So, thinking caps on again. I've reconnected with lovelight."

"Good idea; I think we all should. Let's get everyone else connected, too."

Julianna glided to my right, Tobin's hand in hers.

I connected with Julianna. "How is he?"

"I actually think he's okay, Lady Keira. His triumph at the waterfall seems to have made a big difference to his approach to water. But I'll keep an eye on him!"

I looked at the water. It wasn't so far, was it?

"Can we all swim?" I queried. I did not know of an outdoor pool in Cordello other than the sacred lake at the foot of the waterfall.

Julianna said, "There is a small, shallow pool not far from the cottages. Many of us learned there. Of course, back then, Tobin refused to enter the water, so he can't swim."

Roanne looked at me sheepishly. "I can't, either. I don't know how."

"I think we can manage between us," I said, still thinking. "We don't know how deep the water is, but if the rest of us can swim, or tread water, we should be able to help you across without any problem."

Then Tobin's face fell.

"What is it?" I asked gently.

"What if there are monsters?" he almost whispered. "Ones that pull us under, so we drown?"

"Oh, that's just fairy–tales, sweetheart," Julianna laughed, although her eyes, meeting mine, were devoid of mirth. I appreciated her attempt to keep our plan on track – however, Tobin did have a point. We didn't know whether there was anything under the surface. Should we take the risk, anyway?

It really was quite a short distance – wasn't it?

~~~

The atmosphere in the cavern seemed a little darker. It was the idea of monsters, creating an undercurrent of unease in each of us. I tamped my burgeoning anxiety down into a place where it was hidden and locked away, and not able to interfere with my need to think – and considered again the water before us. Something about it didn't look right. Thoughtfully, I made my way to the

327

edge of the dark expanse, and dropped to my knees, lowering a hand to the liquid surface, allowing my fingers to break through to the depths underneath.

I touched solid ground. In surprise, I pulled my hand back, then tried again.

Yes, I was right. I extended my arm further and tested the depth a little further out.

"Ro! I think the water is only a few inches deep!"

"Oh!" she laughed, bringing a hand to her heart in relief.

So why had it been made to appear deep, bottomless; a difficulty? What challenge, really, did this present to us? I was relieved that it was not a barrier after all – but baffled as to the reason for its existence.

I got to my feet, and experimentally moved my foot towards the surface of the water. The top of the water dissolved into ripples as my foot broke through, and I planted it firmly onto the solid sub–surface. I shifted my weight forward; would it crack? Break? It held, and I threw my backpack to the ground before bringing my other foot forward to join the first. Now I was standing fully in the water. It reached a short way above my ankles. I almost laughed at the unnecessary problems that I'd tried to solve.

Moving forward one pace, then another, and another. Probably a quarter of the way across already. Another step.

Then I froze.

I could hear a roaring and squealing, like a train approaching through a tunnel. Although I looked left into the darkness, towards the source of the sound, I could not see anything. The noise gained in volume, becoming louder and louder, closer and closer.

Any moment now, it would be upon me. I squeezed

my eyes shut, feeling powerless to move from this vulnerable position. My legs were rigid and I could not force myself to get out of harm's way. I clamped my hands over my ears to drown out the noise. It was unbearably loud, overwhelming, threatening. I couldn't bear it.

Panic had filled my chest, lodging in my throat as an unexpressed sob. My stomach had twisted into a knot.

I started to hyperventilate.

Sinking to my knees, I became distantly aware of the water slinking around my calves. I heard a low moan, realised it was my own voice.

"Lady Keira! Lady Keira!" Someone was calling me, but I had no control over my limbs, or my thoughts. I was as trapped within my fear as a body bound to a railway track in an old movie.

I knew the end was coming. I had so many regrets.

I had not told Jason that I wanted to spend the rest of my life with him.

The rest of my life was passing *now*, in a flash, and I waited fatalistically for the impact; for the very last moment of consciousness.

"*Keira!*" came the cry again.

Locked in my immobile state, a glimmer of thought rose in my mind, clawing its way to the surface, clamouring to make itself heard above the noise: *I was still alive.*

How could that be?

Then, I realised that the deafening sound was not getting any louder. It had reached a climax; why wasn't it increasing? Why wasn't I dead already?

The urge to keep my eyes and ears closed to the sound was powerful; but somehow, the self–preservation instinct was still kicking in, over–riding it. Taking a deep breath to slow my fast–beating heart, I opened my eyes, and looked about me.

There was no threat.

No train, nothing.

I didn't understand. What was happening? Slowly, I removed my hands from my ears. As I did so, the sound stopped in an instant. What was *that* all about? Bewildered and shaken, my legs useless, I crawled through the shallow water on my hands and knees, keeping my sight fixed on the ledge at the far side of the watery expanse.

Trembling, I pulled myself onto the ledge, and turned to face the others, hugging my legs to me for warmth and self–comfort. I couldn't stop shaking.

"Ro, what the heck just happened?" I sent. My teeth were chattering too much to speak aloud.

"We don't *know*, my lady! You just seemed to lose control; you looked to be in the grip of some terror, and would not respond. I was really scared for you."

"You're not the only one," I replied with feeling. "So you didn't hear it, then?"

"We heard nothing, saw nothing, felt nothing. We had no idea what you were seeing or hearing."

My shaking slowed, then ceased. I was recovering from the shock.

The water had not been the challenge, for me.

Overcoming my fear was.

"Ro, I think this is a test of our reaction to what we fear most. In my case, I have an instinctive horror of being run over, as I was in an accident as a kid; and I also have a fear of loud noise that I can't escape from. I think each of you needs to be prepared to face your . . . *demons* . . . in order to cross the water."

"Okay," she replied, slowly. "I'll pass the information

on. Who should come over next?"

"Julianna," I said. "Tell her to bring Tobin at the same time. I believe they'll both find it easier together."

"Should we all come in pairs, do you think?"

"To be honest, Ro, nothing helped me until I stood up to my fear and faced it down. It probably doesn't matter one way or the other."

Julianna elected to carry Tobin as she crossed. She, too, made it to less than the halfway point before her fear confronted her. She clutched her child to her, as tears poured down her face. Tobin was screeching; I knew nothing of his nightmare, only felt my heart squeeze tightly at hearing his distress. My own face was wet with tears as I watched, helpless, as Julianna and Tobin battled.

This was horrible. Could we bear the torment of this? Of watching those we cared about – loved, even – as they experienced pain and terror and despair? Would my heart break?

We called to her, willing her on, directing lovelight to both Julianna and Tobin. Finally, both mother and child appeared to become more peaceful. Julianna released her tight hold on Tobin, his little face red and hot from being buried in her neck. Julianna opened her eyes, and I saw pain flash there, briefly, before softening. She stroked Tobin's head, murmuring words of comfort, then was able to move forward and join me. I felt enormous respect for her. She had continued to protect her son, had not fallen to her knees as I had done. She sat beside me, Tobin in her lap, and I squeezed her hand.

"I hope I never repeat that experience," she sent to me. "I saw Tobin being taken from me, bundled away by savage men, whilst they threatened me . . ." She gulped, her eyes filming with tears again.

"You don't have to tell me," I sent, understanding a little of her anguish.

"No, I must. I faced it alone, I need to share it now. The – *vision* – that presented to me was one of Tobin being hurt; it was unbearable. But somehow, I fought back, and we're through."

"And Tobin? His vision?" The boy was still clinging to his mother, face buried in her neck.

"He sent me the images. He was lost, knew I had moved on, he said there was no–one to care for him, no–one for him to *love* . . ." She bunched a fist to her mouth, her other hand holding Tobin tightly around his waist.

My heart heavy, I returned my focus to the other Cordellans. I was not looking forward to watching the others cross. A young woman named Willa was next, She, too, fell to her knees, her face a tortured mask of fear and panic. She had closed her eyes. We called to her, hoped that our voices would help her to find her way through her fear. Lovelight flowed in a constant stream.

As with those of us who had already crossed, she finally found her core of inner strength, battled her demons, and made her way to sit with us. Shaking, she positioned herself next to me, and I wrapped an arm around her shoulders, imparting whatever warmth and reassurance I could.

"Bats," she said, her teeth chattering. "Can't stand them. They were in my hair . . . but I'm okay, now."

I murmured some words of comfort, and watched as the next Cordellan crossed. As each person ventured onto the water and met with their terror, we called to them and sent the energy, doing our best to assist each with their trial. Finally it was Roanne's turn. She gave us a courageous smile then began her crossing. Her smile faded as she reached the halfway point; she had got further than the rest of us; was this significant? I willed her on, sending as much lovelight as I could channel.

Then her vision hit.

She cried out, and crumpled into the water. Her arms flailed, but she did not rise.

Her mouth and nose were *underwater*. I leapt to my feet, knocking Willa aside in my haste, and ran back into the water. Whatever panic gripped her, she was taking in water and would drown if she did not move. I clutched at her shoulders, but her fear had taken over her body; she was rigid, heavy, immovable.

I dropped to her side, took hold of her head and angled it so that the left side of her mouth rose clear of the water. She spluttered. Her arms continued to writhe. I could hear the Cordellans calling to her.

I couldn't lift her!

~~~

"Ro!" I sent, pleading with her to get up. Still she flailed, fighting me at every turn. A shadow fell across her body, and I looked up to see Willa. She had understood the urgency of this situation. Together, we heaved and lifted Roanne clear of the water. She coughed up water, the fluid dribbling down her chin and onto her soaked clothing. She was trembling like a leaf in a storm, and I knew she would need longer to recover. Her eyes were glazed and unfocused, and I began to worry that she had gone into a catatonic state.

"We need to move her, *now*," I said to Willa.

We dragged her forward, her legs unresponsive; she felt as heavy as a bag of wet cement. My muscles were burning but I would not leave her. We struggled to heft Roanne up onto the ledge, and it became easier as the others – even little Tobin – grabbed hold of her and manoeuvred her onto solid, dry ground.

Roanne retched and coughed, then sat shaking and silent.

Now what did I do?

I saw a vision in my mind. Roanne was seated in the centre of a circle; all of us directing lovelight to her. Quickly, I arranged us in a ring around Roanne, and we directed the energy towards her, with intentions of reviving, comforting, healing, or whatever else was best for her.

Another thought flashed through my mind, and without thinking what I was doing, my hands moved of their own accord, drawing on and weaving lovelight into a sphere. The globe I coloured orange and yellow, the colour of warming flames. I directed gentle warmth into the ball, and sent my creation into the centre of the circle towards Roanne. I heard Julianna gasp; I had not been taught this, was not expected to know how to do it. This was high–level lovelight work!

On reaching her, the sphere appeared to expand and envelop her entirely. She was enclosed within a ball of warm, healing lovelight. We continued to send Roanne the energy. My hands were hot and tingly, my feet buzzing, and I knew that Roanne would receive more than the sum total of what we were sending, that the group energy would be amplified beyond its constituent parts.

She would need it all.

I almost felt Roanne's body relax as the soothing energy flowed through every microscopic element of her energy system and physical body. Finally, I felt the rate of the flow of lovelight slow down, and knew that the fiery–tinted sphere would soon have completed its task. The colours faded to a soft peach–pink before the orb dissolved and the coloured strands floated aimlessly on the air surrounding us. Roanne's clothes and hair were completely dry. Her eyes were soft and warm, her cheeks a healthy light pink.

"I'm okay," she said, and I leapt up to wrap her in a hug. She held on tight, as if feeling fragile, still, and so I kept her close to me for a little longer before releasing her, willing my own strength into her. One by one, the other Cordellans hugged her, lending her their warmth and support; then she bent down so that Tobin could kiss her cheek.

"Really! I am okay now. Thank you, Lady Keira, Willa, *all* of you," she said, turning to us with a well of gratitude in her eyes.

"Any time," I replied. I meant it. She was my best friend here in Charls' absence. I didn't want to lose her, nor was it easy to see her hurt or in pain. I was relieved we'd all made it through the water, won the battle against our fears. I'd left the backpack behind, but I wasn't going back for it; I felt a shudder pass through me at the thought of another trial by water.

Before approaching the statuesque formations behind us – between us and the cavern's exit – I checked the map. Very apt, I thought, without a trace of humour. This space was named Cavern of the Lost. And we very nearly had been.

Now, it was time to move onward again.

Roanne was back to her normal self. I wondered what she had seen that had caused her such panic and grief. I looked at her, raising my right eyebrow in query.

"Drowning," she said succinctly, looking at me as I

packed the map away.

I nodded in understanding, sensing she wanted to put the experience behind her.

Turning, I could see – to my relief – a relatively clear path between the forest of stalagmites. On this side of the water, there was more space between each structure, and the ground was drier too.

I set off along the 'path' that we could follow, winding my way between each pillar, stalactite or stalagmite. This part of the trek felt remarkably easy. Perhaps it was just the profound sense of freedom and relief following our fearful experiences. I was quietly pleased with the heated–sphere of lovelight that I'd conjured up. I felt that I deserved to be here with the Cordellans.

I felt a renewed sense of *rightness,* as if I had demonstrated to *myself* that I was, indeed, the 'girl in the legend', that my place was here, and now.

We were now able to make good progress, as the going was easy, the path smooth and clear to follow.

Coming to end of the path, I saw a blank cavern wall in front of me, with no doorway, no exit.

We stopped.

I caught sight of a momentary shimmer in the rock. Before my eyes, a symbol caught the light from my sphere, glinted, then faded. I fixed my eyes on the spot, watched for it to happen again.

There.

It was no simple square or hexagon this time; instead, the shape was a circle inscribed within a triangle.

I continued to watch as the shape took on three–dimensional form. It presented as a sphere inside a pyramid, the sphere spinning lazily, the pyramid pulsing with golden light. It was beautiful, mesmerising. I felt that the symbol contained ancient meaning, but was unable to locate any relevant information in the expanded memory–bank of my mind.

"Lady Keira?" Roanne asked.

"Yes . . ." I breathed.

"This is a symbol that I have seen in the Grand Chamber. I know the map said we had a way to go, yet, but –"

"But you think we're at the Grand Chamber?" I sent silently.

"Yes," she replied, with a nod.

Gravely, I watched as the symbol shimmered and glinted in the light. I could see in my mind's eye a vision of Tobin and I working together, but I had not needed the visual cue. I knew in my soul what needed to be done.

"Tobin," I said. "Would you come here, please?"

I felt his little body nudge mine as he moved forward to stand beside me.

"Place your hand on the circle, on the sphere," I prompted.

His small arm reached up to the symbol, then he placed his hand flat against the stone. I reached out, placing my hand over his smaller one, combining the energetic lifeblood of my own world with that of Cordello's future, and its ancient past.

CHAPTER 35

Shortly before dawn, Charls and his company moved silently onto the road and headed back to the village. Charls had changed his mind about destroying the villagers' houses – he remembered the terror on his own people's faces as their cottages had been vandalised. His argument was with Karn and his soldiers, not innocent villagers.

"Charls! *Look!*" Tissa hissed, as they rounded the corner towards the square. It was filled with people.

Soldiers.

Karn, standing at the forefront, stared directly at Charls. A young woman was standing at his side, sword drawn. They were ready for battle. Charls cursed; he had lost his element of surprise. They would have to fight it out, here and now. He felt sorrow for his little band of warriors, knowing they were hopelessly outnumbered.

How many would make it home, this day?

His eyes not leaving Karn's for a moment, Charls withdrew his sword and his knife, both weapons having been loaned to him from Tissa's plentiful supply. Burron stood to his right, weapon–ready, Tissa at his left. He could feel her bristling with anticipation and adrenaline, could sense the waves of hostility and aggression pouring from her.

This was it.

"So here you are. My baby brother. The Invisible Man, no doubt. We meet again, Charls."

"Karn." Charls kept his voice steady. "You have to give this up. Lovelight is not a resource to be plundered and stolen, to be fought over. It is a gift, it is precious –"

"What would you know of precious, brother? You've never had desire for money, for beautiful objects. Yet you ended up with the manor and its treasures anyway, and I with nothing! How ironic!"

"Karn, you brought your troubles upon yourself. You cheated, you abused your position. That is not the Cordellan way."

"The Cordellan way? There was no place for me there. I would never have had a position of leadership, of command! You were in the way! *Father* was in the way!"

Charls had taken an angry step forward, paused as he felt Tissa's hand upon his arm. She gripped him fiercely, restraining him from any foolishness. "I will never forgive you for what you did," he answered softly.

"Alaria wasn't my fault," Karn said sharply.

"Alaria's death was an accident; part of a chain reaction – caused by you."

"So what now, Charls? Do we fight? You can see that I am ready. My people are ready."

"They are not *your people*, Karn. You are Cordellan!"

"Cordello never provided for my needs, brother. I can fight you and your sorry band of men. Oh, a couple of females, as well, I see. Where are the other lords? Could you not raise a proper army?"

Charls willed himself to remain calm. It would be easy to be swept away by emotion, to react rather than act.

~~~

Our hands glowed with sparkling golden light, as if shards of diamond were shining from the centre of the symbol and out through our hands. Tobin's and my hands felt hot, and they were vibrating with the power flowing from the symbol. With a flash of light so bright that I was astonished that we were not blinded, the rock wall in front of us vanished, revealing a space through which we could walk.

Into the Grand Chamber. I instantly recognised its amazing beauty, its cathedral–like grandeur. The precious metals and stones glinted and glowed. The chamber was empty of people. Tobin and I walked through the doorway and continued moving forward until we reached the centre of the room. I was aware of the others following, and very soon we were all standing in a loose group, feeling somewhat awkward, waiting for – something.

The trouble was, I had no idea why we were here. It had taken us so long to reach this place; it seemed like 'home' of sorts; certainly a place of safety. I could hardly believe we had made it. But – now what? Would Charls come? Had he already been here, and left? Were we expected to wait? Or to do something? What? I felt as lacking in direction as a sailboat without a breeze. Just drifting. And waiting.

I decided to sit. Fetching some of the rush mats, I plopped them down on the floor, and sat down with my knees raised against my chest, hugging them to me. My clothes and hair were still damp from the water; the fiery orb had dried Roanne's clothes and hair, but the rest of us remained wet and cold. Julianna, Tobin, and Roanne followed my lead, sitting to either side of me, and Willa came to sit close by. The remaining villagers clustered together a short distance away.

I decided to check the map. Thankfully, it had remained dry, and was still legible. The distance between the Cavern of the Lost and the Grand Chamber – which was now marked – had shrunk drastically. I wondered if the special sphere–within–pyramid symbol had acted as some sort of short–cut? Tobin had wanted magic; I hoped he had been suitably impressed on his journey beyond the waterfall. It had certainly not been without interest!

Now that we were in familiar territory, and presumably near the end of our trek, my body began to relax and I felt the weight of exhaustion settle into my limbs. I was so tired that I thought I might sleep for a month. I was also hungry, but we'd used the last of our supplies several hours ago. My stomach gurgled.

I tried to sit quietly and relax, but, despite my fatigue, I felt restless. It was as if I was waiting for a climax. Something important was coming, I could almost taste it. Anticipation was humming in every vein, and this waiting, this inaction, was causing me to fidget.

Still I had no idea of events outside, of Charls' progress. A chill stole through me . . . was Charls even alive? Would I ever see him again? I felt pain in my chest at the thought that we'd had our last laugh together, our last hug, our last *everything*.

I was so tired I was letting my emotions get the better of me. I hugged my damp knees closer, letting my head and neck drop forward, resting my forehead on the top of my knees. I closed my eyes, willing myself to feel calm and peaceful, for my body to follow suit.

Sighing deeply, I breathed into the dark space bounded by my head, knees and arms, and concentrated on the rhythm of my breathing. In. Out. In. Out. Letting the simple meditation work on easing my tension, relaxing my shoulder and neck muscles, feeling the relief as my neck muscles lengthened.

Letting myself just *be*.

It worked. The silence, the darkness, the privacy: all

341

restored my core balance and peace. My mind cleared, and I knew that I should connect with Karn as soon as possible.

I raised my head, and looked around me, as if an object owned by the rebel would appear out of thin air. Then I recalled that I'd had visions from Karn purely as an effect of the steam from a hot drink. Well, we had no hot drinks . . . but perhaps I would now be able to connect by intention alone?

I let my head drop once again into the dark sanctuary created by the curves of my own body. Regulating my breathing, entering a relaxed and meditative state, I closed my eyelids, and placed the intention to connect with Karn. Of course, this was a 'real–time, live connection' that I sought, not a past–memory vision.

I had no idea if it would work. Just in case, I boosted my connection with lovelight.

I almost jumped when I felt myself on the periphery of another mind. Could I enter? *Should* I? What was the protocol for this sort of thing? The energy of the mind felt angry, prickly, aggressive, and I felt a brush of fear touch the back of my neck. Was this a really foolish idea?

I didn't know how to make progress. I knew I was close – but didn't know if I was protected from Karn pushing his way into my mind, into my memories – what if he could locate us through our mind–connection? Should I instead try connecting with Charls first? The idea flirted with my mind, and I felt an strong instinct to follow it. The decision felt right.

Trust, Keira.

~~~

I felt a rush of emotion move swiftly up through my body – my intuition seemed to be suggesting that Charls was still alive! And I was to meet with him – in his mind. I expected it to be a much more pleasant experience than communicating with his brother, although I felt a little reluctance to enter my dearest friend's head.

I stepped back from Karn's mind and turned my thoughts instead to Charls. Gently, sweetly, I felt for the periphery of his mind, recognised the sure strength and firm morality of his consciousness. I intended the connection, and, almost reverently, climbed into his mind. I knew that I was being accorded a great honour, could feel the complete trust that Charls was placing in me. He had given me permission to enter.

He knew that I was with him, in his mind.

I was not here to peek at memories and had no wish to invade his innermost thoughts; this time, my task was simply to pass on a vital message. To send lovelight to Karn's troops. To send, send, and then send some more. To remind him that force was unnecessary. To advise that the energy should be *allowed* to flow, gently, that it would be accepted by the right people at the right time, and that the right outcome would be reached.

My message given, I began my retreat, pulling away as gently as I could. Before I reached the edge of his consciousness, I received a response. I halted my departure so that I could receive the information. The message he sent me was not in words, not in thought, even.

It was purely a feeling, but I had no doubt at all that it was from Charls – either consciously, or direct from his fine spirit. The message filled with me joy and light and hope and peace. It was a message of unconditional love,

343

letting me know that he would always be with me, wherever I was. Tears spilled from my closed eyelids, hot and salty, running slowly down my cheeks as the emotion overwhelmed me.

I gave myself time to absorb the message, to appreciate the loving gift that I had received, to honour Charls and his trust in me. I lifted my head and dried my tears, my eyes watering again as they adjusted to the light in the Grand Chamber. Awestruck, I realised that everyone was meditating and sending lovelight. The chamber was filled to bursting with the peach–rose energy, the air was light and sparkly and soft. I added my own intention, and felt myself lifted even higher in joy and love as I became interconnected with the energy and those sending it.

This was, I believed, more powerful even than my experience in the Light Portal of Bliss.

I felt as if I would burst from the wonder of the feeling, from the clarity and purity of the energy.

Our experiences had strengthened us, heightened our connection with lovelight and even bolstered lovelight itself until it was love made tangible.

CHAPTER 36

Karn sneered, the expression turning his face ugly. He took a step towards Charls, the woman next to him only a heartbeat behind. Charls remained perfectly still. His mind flicked to Keira, who wanted no war, no bloodshed. Charls was disappointed that he had not been able to reach Karn, had not been able to reason with him.

Sorry, Keira. I have failed.

Then he felt an odd sensation on his scalp. As if a flower bud was slowly, gently unfurling, opening to the sun. He smelled lilacs. Time seemed to come to a standstill, the figures around him motionless.

Complete silence.

Complete stillness.

He could see the unpleasant expression stamped like a brand onto his brother's face, looked down to see Tissa's hand frozen on his arm, her fingers curled into his wrist.

He felt as if he alone was living this moment.

The strange feeling on his scalp continued, crept over his skin like a butterfly's kiss; it felt as if his head was being opened to another dimension, another life.

The square remained utterly silent.

His head began to tingle, as if he had connected with lovelight.

He waited, knowing that whatever was happening could not be rushed – that time had no meaning.

He felt – an *essence* – of someone.

Keira.

The scent of lilacs grew stronger and he breathed it in, filling his lungs with the sweet, perfumed air.

"*Charls,*" he heard. A whisper, a breath, inside his

head. Or had he imagined it?

Connect with lovelight.

It sounded like Keira – the voice had her rhythm. The presence inside his mind *felt* like her. But how could they be connected in this way when no communication devices were being used? Had Keira been able to directly access his mind? He felt her there, welcomed her presence, hoped that she could feel his warmth and his joy at her closeness.

You can avoid conflict. Send lovelight to Karn's army. All of you must do this!

Charls felt impatience tug at him, at Keira's insistence on solving this through peaceful means. There were no peaceful means left; Karn had seen to that! Here they were bearing arms against one another, his little band facing off against Karn's army. He swallowed his impatience and took a deep breath, knew that Keira would only be doing what she felt was right.

Please try, Charls. It's really important.

The palm of his right hand started to itch, then to heat and burn. Surprised, Charls saw that his fingers were folded into his palm. He opened them, saw a blue stone reveal itself. A deep blue crystal. As he watched, the crystal began to pulse with light. How on earth . . .?

~~~

He felt Keira withdraw from his mind, a coolness taking her place. Charls was tempted to try to hold on to her presence, to call her back. But he knew that she was leaving for a reason. Time could not stand still forever.

Tissa's hand flexed on his arm, and she withdrew her hold. Burron shuffled his feet. The others in his little troop stirred, too.

But Karn and his men remained immobile, locked into a fixed point in time.

"What's going on, Charls?" Tissa said, quietly.

"I'm not certain. But Keira has given me a message. And this."

He showed Tissa the crystal.

"Lapis lazuli," she declared. "How did you get it?"

"I have no idea," he answered, with complete honesty. "But it is important. And Keira also said that it is important that we send lovelight to Karn and his men."

"Lovelight?" Tissa was sceptical. "Instead of *fighting?*"

"Yes - instead of fighting," Charls affirmed. He looked again at the crystal beating its pulse in his hand. "Pass the word. Send lovelight. All of us, together. Now." He secreted the crystal in his pocket, next to the golden paperweight.

Each of them connected with lovelight, let it pour into them and outward, directed it without force towards the Vornen people and to Karn. Standing stock still, they sent the energy, together with their focused intention of resolving the conflict smoothly and with the best outcome for *everyone*. There was no plan, no strategy, no forcing of their will. The energy simply flowed . . . and flowed. Where it was accepted, it permeated energy fields, made changes. Others rejected the lovelight, which bent away and flowed onwards. Not a drop of the precious energy was wasted.

Charls realised that the energy in the square had shifted.

And that time was flowing again.

~~~

Now it was time to connect with Karn. My breathing had become fast and shallow with dread, and I worked on restoring my meditative state. Again, I asked to make the connection, let my mind reach out expectantly. It brushed the other mind like a feather's caress, so soft and delicate that the touch was barely noticeable. But I knew that it had happened. My mind tiptoed back and made the pass again. My knowing told me that the mind was Karn's. His energy remained defensive and sharp, but this time I sought a way in, trusting that I was protected by lovelight and the Ascended Reikans.

Like a spider extending one long leg to search for its prey, I let my consciousness flow outwards and, like water, find the easiest way inside.

There. I knew that I was in.

Next, I searched quietly and invisibly for his memories . . . creeping around until I located one relating to the killing of his – and Charls' – father. Surprised, I sensed regret co–existing with tamped–down rage and hatred. I didn't like the way his mind felt; it had no firm foundation, seemed to tilt and wobble. So many mixed emotions, none of them acknowledged. Unstable. I knew, though, that I must do this.

I concentrated on replaying the scene where Karn had committed the murder, and had then watched coldly as Alaria had fallen, her life ending as tragically as his father's. I retrieved the memory, bringing it to the forefront of Karn's conscious mind. I felt my eyes swim with tears as I watched the scene unfold. Not knowing how I was doing this, I placed the intention that Karn's crime become known to those who needed to know it.

Immediately, I felt his emotions surge, was aware of his rage . . . and also his feeling of profound puzzlement. Although I could not see his current

348

existence, his memories–in–the–making, I sensed that something was changing. The memory itself had a different quality.

It is done.

I had no wish to remain in Karn's mind longer than was necessary. I withdrew my consciousness from his memories one careful, quiet step at at time, until I felt that I was outside. It was a relief to be free from his mind; it was not an easy or comfortable place to be. I began to bring my mind back to myself, then to integrate myself back into the group.

Together, we flowed the energy into the Chamber, into the tunnels, directed it with our intention towards Charls and his troops, offered it to Karn and his own men and women.

I also sensed the presence of a woman who would be a catalyst for change. I knew that she would unite Cordello and Vornen.

~~~

Some of the Vornen warriors were fidgeting, others appeared to be in confused communication. The woman next to Karn, apparently his deputy, seemed to be deep in conversation with Karn. Her body language indicated that she disagreed with him about something. Something *major.*

Charls and his company continued to send the energy, hoping that Keira was right, that her intuition was sound. She'd got this far by trusting it, Charls thought, so he should trust it – and her.

The woman arguing with Karn now turned to the men waiting with them. She was speaking aloud, but she had her back to Charls so that he could not hear her words.

He detected passion and purpose from her body language, was shocked to notice himself admiring the grace and lines of her body, the way the long strands of her mahogany hair moved in the light breeze, turning to burnished copper as they captured the sunlight.

Charls had not expected to be distracted by a woman. He had reconciled his feelings for Keira, knowing that they were worlds apart. Maybe she had been a bridge to help him move forward, to finally, completely, leave Alaria in the past, where she belonged? Maybe Tissa had been a stepping stone, enabling him to remember what it was to feel like a man again. Maybe now he could again feel genuine, deep emotion for another woman. Even if she was apparently a warrior from Vornen . . . and on the wrong side of this conflict.

Tissa touched his arm again, a brief contact that carried no meaning for him other than to gain his attention. He dragged himself back to the situation at hand, allowing his thoughts of the female warrior from Vornen to drift away like vapour.

"What is it?" he asked silently.

"It looks like there's some sort of revolt, don't you think?"

"It certainly looks that way. I wonder why? And who *is* that woman?"

"That *woman* is in fact a *Lady*, cousin. Lady Maryn, highly respected and, I heard, very fair–minded too. It's a shame she's not Cordellan."

Indeed, Charls thought to himself. *Indeed.*

Still watching the performance play out in the square, Charls was surprised when Lady Maryn turned on her heel and marched directly towards him. Something deep inside him altered; this creature was beautiful, and he knew, in his gut, in his soul, that she was special. He could not take his eyes from her.

Her eyes met his, held. He could almost sense sparks arcing between them. She was very close now, and he saw her pupils flare in some kind of recognition. *She had this knowing, too.*

He lowered his weapons.

"Lord Charls," she said, aloud.

"Lady Maryn, I believe."

"Indeed. We have not had the pleasure of meeting, and I am sorry that the circumstances are as they are. I have a question – just one – and ask that you answer it honestly, please."

"Of course."

"Did Lord Karn kill your father?"

Charls maintained the eye contact, finding himself unequal to the task of looking away. The connection with her was so strong, he wanted to hold it, to deepen it, to drown in it.

"Yes," he said softly, remembering.

"And it was not an accident?" she queried, her eyes softening in response to the pain reflected in his.

"No. It was not an accident."

"I see. In that case, he is unfit to lead and I, as his deputy, am stripping him of command. My soldiers will stand with me."

Charls was astonished. *Keira, you are a miracle,* he thought, hoping somehow she would connect with his emotion and understand the enormity of what she had done.

CHAPTER 37

Lady Maryn stalked back towards Karn and their army. Charls and his band watched as she had an intense discussion with Karn, which ended abruptly as he shoved Lady Maryn. Charls gritted his teeth, allowed the scene to play out as it would. Tissa caught his expression, knew that things had irrevocably changed between them.

Lady Maryn clearly had support within the men standing with Karn, as several moved swiftly to keep their Lady from harm. Charls saw her sword arm flash upwards to Karn's neck, the sunlight glancing off the sharp blade.

He knew perfectly well that she needed no such protection.

Karn struggled and twisted against those holding him. Lady Maryn's sword nicked his throat, a single drop of blood spilling, a scarlet rivulet bisecting his neck.

With an enraged snarl and a roar of defeat, Karn's anger fuelled his strength.

He broke free and began to run towards Charls.

Charls stood his ground, raising his own sword in defence. He felt the air around him change as his people again raised their own weapons, slicing the air with silver.

"Charls . . ." Tissa warned.

"It's okay. Just wait."

Karn continued towards his brother, fury contorting his face into a hideous mask. He held his sword horizontally in front of him, as if hoping to run it straight through Charls' belly. Charls' stomach muscles tensed in anticipation, although he knew – somehow –

352

that it could not end in such a way.

He was right.

Karn had been fast.

Lady Maryn was faster.

She swerved to a stop between Charls and Karn, her body barely an inch from the sharp point of Karn's sword.

"No. No, Karn, you will not do this. You *will not*."

"He's taken everything from me! My manor, my people, everyone! This is my chance to lead, to run a country *my* way, without interference from Cordellans! I can make Vornen great! With lovelight we can conquer every land around us! We can be great!"

Lady Maryn waited as two of her men silently approached Karn from behind, cuffing him and ensuring their bindings were tight and sure. This one could not escape.

"No, Karn. That is not what we have been working for. You had us take up arms against Cordello – under false pretences. You told us that your brother had committed murder."

Charls took an involuntary step towards her, fire rising from his belly, his whole body tensed. Lady Maryn turned and raised a hand to stop him, then let it drop to his arm, a gesture of compassion and peace. She let it remain there. He felt her warmth through the fabric of his clothing, the feel of her hand seeming to pass through his skin, affect his blood, his nerves.

"Take him away and lock him up," she instructed her officers. They moved away, Karn muttering and cursing. Lady Maryn turned back to Charls, resuming eye contact.

"Lord Charls, your brother also told us that *you* and your Cordellans planned to create a weapon from your

353

lovelight, that you planned to make war on us. I know now that this is not true."

"You are correct," he replied, his mouth curving into a smile. He felt as if they were the only two people in the world, had forgotten the soldiers standing, waiting, wondering why their commander was being led away, ranting like a madman.

"He gave himself away," she advised. "Something happened to him; he suddenly blurted out that he had killed your father, that he was a liar, a fraud, a murderer. It was most odd. I could see from the wild expression in his eyes that he understood what he was saying . . . but he was unable to stop himself."

"The truth always comes out," Charls said. "Not always straight away. But eventually. I am glad that you know him for what he is, *who* he is."

"Shall we send the soldiers home?" Lady Maryn whispered to Charls, leaning close so that strands of her hair tickled his cheek.

"I think we should."

"I also think that you and I should discuss further the future of Cordello and Vornen. You have other Lords in Cordello, yes?"

"Yes, but –"

Her eyes sparkled with mirth. "Good. I have several sisters who are looking for husbands."

"Are you . . .?" Charls had not considered that she might already be wed. He held his breath, awaiting her answer.

"No. It would appear that I have been waiting for *you*, my Lord Charls."

He felt his heart open and fill. This felt right.

CHAPTER 38

The Vornen soldiers dispersed, most appearing relieved that bloodshed had been averted, although a few faces seemed to express disappointment or puzzlement.

Tissa gave Charls a searching look, then nodded once before walking away, the Cordellans following her out of the square and heading back towards Cordello.

Only Charls and Lady Maryn remained.

She seemed surprised to see that her hand remained in place on Charls' arm. She withdrew it slowly, Charls thought, as if she could not bring herself to let go. He resisted the impulse to reach for her, to regain the unusual intimacy created by such a normal action.

They walked slowly around the square as they talked.

So began the process of truce, and of moving forward. Charls enthusiastically described to Lady Maryn the wonder that was lovelight: its power, its joy, and how it engendered cooperation between the Cordellans, who had committed to work with the energy for the greater good. Maryn readily confirmed that no citizen of Vornen would ever agree to using a precious resource such as lovelight in any harmful way. The safety of lovelight was procured, initiating a new future for both countries.

As for Karn, Lady Maryn had come to a decision.

"He will be exiled," she announced. "All of Vornen knows him for what he is. He will be trusted by no–one. His treachery will not be forgotten; even now, stories and songs are being written that will immortalise him."

"Not quite in the way that he had intended," Charls murmured.

"No, I suppose not. However, that is how life works –

355

you get back what you give out."

"How will he live, in exile?" Charls wondered. Despite all that Karn had done, he was still his brother. It surprised him to feel this concern, to feel again grief at the loss of his sibling.

"He will need to become self–sufficient. And to be able to defend himself against the predators, the wild animals here. He may not be helped, that is the way of our exile. His life will likely be – shortened." Lady Maryn was watching Charls, gauging his reaction. Charls closed his eyes, mentally saying a final 'goodbye' to Karn. He allowed himself to feel the complex mix of emotions swirling through him: disappointment, grief, concern, relief. A memory of Karn as a small boy rose into his mind. Karn, smiling, happy. What had changed him into the cruel, mean egomaniac that he had become? He would never know, never understand.

~~~

Charls and Lady Maryn made their way back to Cordello, she leaving Vornen in the hands of a trusted associate – one of her sisters. They talked on their journey, finding that they shared a similar philosophy for managing resources and working with people. Charls was relieved; lovelight was safe and its breadth would be expanded to encompass Vornen. There had been minimal loss of life. It would do no harm to Charls' reputation to have achieved this. The Elder – and, of course, the other lords – would be pleased. In leading the bid to defend lovelight, Charls had proved himself to have qualities that might, in time, result in him assuming the mantle of Elder.

Charls was looking forward to seeing Keira again.

Although the majority of his thoughts were taken up with his new companion, he knew how valuable Keira had been to Cordello, and to lovelight. He truly loved her – as much as he'd love a sister. He firmly believed that he and Keira might cross paths in some future lifetime. Their bond was too strong to simply fall away.

Once back in Cordello, he led Lady Maryn along the main pathway and up the hill towards the Reikan tunnel. The other soldiers – including Tissa – had been instructed to remain in the village. He wanted to greet Keira alone, introduce her to Lady Maryn.

Reaching the entrance to the tunnel, he paused, letting himself absorb the relief, the pleasure, the joy of having lovelight safe. Then he entered, Lady Maryn following a step behind.

To his surprise, the tunnels were filled with light . . . *lovelight.* He had never understood why it had been impossible to create lovelight spheres in these tunnels, why the only illumination had been indistinct flares of faint light dotted here and there. Now that they had achieved protection for lovelight, it seemed that the energy was joyfully spreading as far as it could. Or was it something that Keira, herself, had done?

There she was. Walking towards him. Her top was smothered in dust and her trousers looked wet. Her face displayed a bewildering array of emotions. He saw exhaustion, relief, joy, surprise, confusion. Love. He realised that she had noted that he was not alone, that a beautiful woman stood at his shoulder.

"You are the one," Keira said.

"The one?" Lady Maryn questioned.

"I apologise. That was a little blunt!" Keira laughed. "I sometimes have information flit into my mind, but I don't always have time to process it before I speak or send the thought on. I was told that you . . . Charls, would you help me out, here?" Keira looked embarrassed.

Charls read Keira's face. *She knew.*

He reached for Lady Maryn's arm and gently brought her forward to his side, before turning to face her, to look again into those marvellous eyes.

"I think what Keira means to say is that I am very much in love with you, and I would be honoured – and the happiest man in Cordello – if you would agree to be my wife."

Stunned, Lady Maryn looked from Charls to Keira, back again.

"Well, really!"

Charls felt ill. She was turning down his proposal? Was it too soon?

"I should think you could have got down on one knee!" Lady Maryn chuckled. "Charls, of *course* I will marry you – there was never any doubt of it, not after we met in the square!"

Grinning sheepishly, Charls gathered her to him, holding her close, inhaling her scent, her essence. He didn't want to let her go.

"Just say where and when," he muttered into her glorious hair. "I'll be there."

~~~

Like coloured snowflakes, tiny shapes of rose, blue and yellow confetti–paper fell on Charls and his new wife, Maryn. I was bursting with happiness for them both. I could see that Charls, at last, was truly happy; and their union was helpful to seal the truce between their two countries. All of Cordello and Vornen seemed to be here – except for Karn, of course. He was long gone. Maybe he had already moved on. I could not be sorry for that.

Maryn's beautiful, elegant dress had long sleeves of delicate lace, a high, softly curved neckline, and a full skirt that draped perfectly. The material was the colour of lovelight, which now seemed to permeate every molecule in Cordello, casting a rose hue over everything, as if a sunset was laying in wait around every corner and behind every cloud.

I was happy to be outside in the fresh air, far away from tunnels and caves. I saw everything around me in a new light – and not just because of the subtle tones of lovelight. My perception had been altered; every single part of my vision had more clarity, more depth, was more vivid. It was as if I was now more alive than I had ever been. My energy was high; I felt *more* than I had been when I had arrived in Reika. I hoped I would be able to retain this new awareness – this new level of understanding – when I returned to my own world.

Lovelight was safe. Charls was loved – and in love – and blissfully happy. The Cordellans had avoided war. Everything was rosy. As for me, my time here was coming rapidly to a close. I knew it, could feel it. Curbing my restlessness to leave (I didn't yet know how or where I would go), I smiled as Charls led his beloved Maryn in a graceful dance across the gravel driveway, and towards the trees. They had created hundreds of small, golden flickering lovelight orbs, placed them at the edge of the woodland and in the air above the guests, and in the trees surrounding the orangery; now that dusk was falling, the lights twinkled and glittered like the stars against the indigo blue sky. The manor house and its grounds had been transformed into a magical, romantic fairyland.

I saw Roanne dancing slowly with Burron, being held close; they were barely moving, simply holding one another and re–connecting. He held her gently, but with a strength that suggested he would not let her go, this time. I felt that there was love there, still, and hoped that my dear Ro would be happy.

Leina had not come; I was not all that surprised.

Symion was dancing with his wife, his odd cadence hampering him a little as he moved with her; she did not notice, was glowing with happiness at being free, at having her husband safely returned.

Tissa remained aloof and alone; but I saw from her eyes that she had no regrets.

I felt someone tap me lightly on the shoulder, turned to see Charls. He could tell from the expression on my face that it was time for me to go, that I was saying my mental farewells.

His eyes filmed with tears and he took hold of me in a tight hug that left me breathless. I gripped him hard, knowing this parting could be nothing but painful. I did not want to let him go, and I sensed the same desperation in him.

These were our last few minutes together, then our incredible friendship would be nothing more than a memory. It all felt so *final*.

I knew that the moment had come, and could not be delayed.

I pulled away, Charls reluctant to release me, knowing that he would never see me again. *Not in this lifetime*, the words whispered through my mind.

But you will meet again.

I kissed him briefly, tenderly, on one cheek and then the other. He dropped a light kiss into my hair, then loosened his hold on me, letting me go. I turned and walked away. My goodbyes to Roanne and to Tobin and the others had taken place earlier, knowing that it would be easier to leave quietly. I had known that Charls would be the last person that I would have contact with in Cordello, just as he had been the first when I had arrived in his country – when I had come to play my part in their legend.

Now the circle was complete, and my place was outside of it.

I walked away, not looking back, made my way unseen to the road. Walked on through the deserted village, on up the dusty path to the tunnel leading to the Grand Chamber. And to Reika.

CHAPTER 39

It felt strange to be returning alone to the Grand Chamber and to the other caverns inside the hills. Charls had offered to accompany me, but I felt his place now was with his bride. I knew the route to take, and I also had a strong intuition that I should do this alone.

It was quiet; I heard no sound except my soft footsteps. The sky darkened moment by moment, and I entered the tunnel as the last hint of rose–pink sky slipped away, leaving a dark canvas for the stars to paint.

The tunnel had a different atmosphere now that lovelight shone into every crevice and crack. Now, the walls gleamed, and the space felt homely, happy, loving. I wondered what would happen to the underground network of tunnels and caverns between the waterfall and the Grand Chamber.

There were some things that I would never know. It was not my place to. I was a transient, a visitor, a guest, and I was going home.

I walked past the nook where I had waited while Charls had been self–healing. I let my hand fall into the curtain, seeing it shimmer and disappear, recognised the lovelight quality of the ethereal fabric.

Before I knew it, I was back at the hidden cleft in the rock. A full moon was rising, showing me the way ahead, illuminating my Reikan surroundings with her bright light.

I passed the tree stump on which Charls had been seated when I'd first approached the purple–heathered and gorse–clad Reikan hills. I let my hand drape over the rough bark, remembering our strange conversation, my first introduction to telepathy. I recalled my astonishment on first seeing Charls, so very like Jason . . . yet not Jason. I still failed to understand why he and Jason looked so similar.

Leaving these landmarks behind, I set my eyes forward, gazing at the sea, and began walking towards the sand, stained almost white in the moonlight.

My return journey seemed somehow shorter. Perhaps my familiarity with Reika as a separate entity from Cordello gave the space more . . . depth? Maybe my knowledge of this place helped me to connect with their history, their energy. I could imagine the Reikans busily and lovingly growing and using their crystals. I had briefly laid eyes upon their fabulous crystal tower – something only a handful of Cordellans had ever witnessed.

I could envision the tower quite clearly in my mind's eye. The clarity of my memories continued to surprise me. It was as if the crystal tower had re–materialised ahead of me. As I walked, I cast a glance to my right, towards the sea. Moonlight laid a shimmering silver–white channel across the water.

The air was soft, and there was a hint of lovelight in the few light clouds passing slowly above me. I stopped walking for a few moments, letting my eyes shut, absorbing the moonlight on my eyelids, on my face, my neck. The light felt cool and kind, soothing.

The crystal tower remained prominent in my mind. As I opened my eyes and looked ahead, the tower seemed to rise brightly from the sand. This was nonsense. Surely the tower was in the Light Portal of Bliss? Frowning with puzzlement, I continued walking straight ahead, a path which would lead me directly to the tower's door. The crystal was a clear, strong white, yet it emanated a soft glow which prevented the crystal from blinding me.

As each step took me closer, I could feel energy – lovelight – radiating from the elegant building. It was real – it had to be. I couldn't explain how, or why, the tower was now *here*, just as I was walking through Reika, on my way back home, but I knew this was no vision. Tobin had said that the energy needed to be high for the tower to materialise . . . and now lovelight was present and tangible everywhere.

Synchronicity at work, again.

I asked my intuition: Am I to go inside? *Yes.*

Unaccountably, I felt nervous at the prospect. I would have felt more confident with Charls or Roanne at my side. Once again, I felt adrift and alone, uncertain. My mouth was dry; I licked my lips, tried to slow my pounding heart as I reached the door, lifted a hand to the ornate crystal handle. It was warm to the touch.

Slowly, reverently, I turned the handle, and let the door open.

~~~

Inside, the air was cool, refreshing. The walls and floor were a soft–white marble, the ceiling high and slightly curved. There were no windows, yet the place was flooded with light, as if the day's sunlight had been absorbed and then trapped within. I was standing in a large circular room, with a sparkling spiral staircase off to my right. Ahead, towards the far end of the round room, was a large ornate chair. A crystal throne.

Someone was seated in it, someone tall, glowing silver–white, pulsing gently with lovelight. I thought I knew who it might be.

"Keira. Welcome."

"Lady Aida. It's lovely to see you again. I wasn't expecting . . ."

"I know. But we have to get you home, don't we? You can not return in the manner in which you arrived."

"So how . . .?"

"All in good time, my dear. How are you?"

I hesitated. I had so many emotions, it was hard to separate let alone label them.

"I am relieved that lovelight is safe. I am happy that Charls and Maryn have found each other, that Cordello and Vornen are at peace. I am a little sad to leave it all . . . but I have missed Jason and am looking forward to seeing him, getting back to normal life."

"Ah, Keira! Your life will never be normal, my love. I do know that Jason is eager to have you back."

"I hope so!"

"So. How would you like to travel home?"

"I didn't realise I had a choice!" I replied.

An unexpected vision arose in my mind – the blue planet suspended in space.

"I thought you'd pick that one," Lady Aida remarked, as she rose gracefully from her crystal seat. She held out her arm as she made her way towards me. I reached up to take it.

It was odd seeing my hand and wrist vanish into the lightbody that was Lady Aida's form. I took hold, and she guided us towards the immensely beautiful staircase. We ascended with wings beneath our feet, barely touching the gleaming treads of the staircase as we rose. At the top, we entered another fabulous room, bare except for a small table, which looked to be fashioned from a pale pink crystal. *Rose Quartz,* I could hear Roanne say. I saw a small silver cube placed in the

365

centre of the table. It looked remarkably similar to Charls' paperweight.

Lady Aida reached for the cube, and as her hand laid hold of the object, we were both enveloped in a silver light that obscured everything else from view. Again we rose from the floor, and I guessed we were ascending, although I had no marker against which to judge the height.

The air become cooler, sharper, and the light slowly, slowly began to fade.

I gasped. We were *flying*. Lady Aida and I were still upright, but we were moving through the night sky, way off the ground, the sea and sand and the magnificent crystal tower below us.

How . . .?

"Trust, Keira," Lady Aida sent.

I trusted.

Higher we went, until the tower, the sand, the sea, all of Reika were distant images. I could see beyond the hills into Cordello, saw tiny pinpricks of light as the Cordellans celebrated Charls' and Maryn's marriage. A wisp of sadness fluttered across my heart.

I am leaving. Goodbye.

"Be in the now, Keira." Lady Aida suggested. "Make the most of what I am showing you."

I looked around me, feeling so much wonder that I lost the ability to speak or think. I simply absorbed. We had left the world far behind now, were in space. The darkness surrounded us – yet, paradoxically, there was light everywhere. From distant stars, from nebulae. This was impossible, and yet . . . I could see whole galaxies, spirals of stars and dust. I felt disconnected from it all – how could I even *be* here? Yet, simultaneously, I felt profoundly interconnected with the life present here. I was made from stardust, from the elements which created the stars and the planets. I would return to dust. I felt one with the stars birthing in the nebulae, and, to my surprise, with the 'nothingness' around me.

"Not nothingness, my dear. How can it be *nothing* when we are moving through it?"

I didn't have an answer. I was not an astronomer, had no training in astrophysics. Although now, I was very tempted to learn more about this incredible environment.

"What is it then?" I asked.

"It is potential. What can be. Do you understand, Keira?"

I thought I did. I shivered as the impact of this new understanding hit me.

We can do anything. The universe is waiting for us to co–create.

Life is limitless.

~~~

The sights I saw, the images, were breathtaking and astounding. I wanted to spend more time here.

"Not now, dear. When you move on, when you die, you will see this again."

"*I will?*"

"Yes. But it is not my place to say any more than that. You have much to do before that moment comes, and your Jason is waiting for you. Shall we?"

I nodded, and we began to descend. I was glad the pace seemed slow, not wanting to experience motion sickness. Jumping out of aeroplanes and the like was not my sort of thing, I have never fallen from the sky towards the ground. Until this moment.

Our speed was faster than I had realised, as I noted that Earth – my home – was now in view, and approaching faster than seemed possible. This was part of the vision that the dolphin had offered to me. We swept past the moon, and I gasped at the immense size of the ancient craters. Then only the glorious blue planet was ahead. A lump lodged in my throat as we headed into the atmosphere.

How could we be doing this?

"It doesn't matter how, Keira, only that you *are*. Enjoy the journey."

Oh, I was. It was . . . incredible. I saw the continents growing larger: the Americas and Canada, Africa, then Europe. Finally Britain came into focus, my home country. The lump in my throat seemed to expand. I wanted to cry. Lady Aida, right on target, flew us towards South West England, and far ahead, I could see the River Tamar snaking in from the sea, a thin silver strand. Now I could see roads, and the contours of the land: the browns, greys and greens of the high moorland and the rocky tors as we came closer, closer.

Then I could see the stone circle, just as I had left it. With a strangled cry, I saw a transparent white sphere, with a figure inside.

Jason.

Beside him, I could see – me.

"Lady Aida!" I cried, panicking.

"It's okay. He can't see you or me. You have remained there whilst part of you was in Cordello. *Trust me.*"

It was all very well for her to say. She wasn't the one in two places at the same time!

CHAPTER 40

We slowed almost to a stop, hovering mere inches above the ground. Jason appeared to be sleeping, his hand stretched out towards me – the *other* me.

"He was cold, poor dear," Lady Aida advised. "The bubble keeps him warm. He is protecting you, ensuring that your physical body remains within the circle."

"The stones are sacred, I suppose?" I asked.

"Yes. The circle of stone has acted as an energetic portal through which you – and only you – could be transported to Reika. Once you leave it, there will be no returning. The Cordellan stage of your life is complete."

"That sounds cryptic."

"You would not want to know what happens next, Keira, surely? Where would be the surprise? The anticipation? The growth? That is not the way of Life."

I knew that she was right; but I was intrigued nonetheless.

We were now standing upright on the grass in the centre of the circle of tall stones.

Lady Aida kept my hand tucked in her arm. It was just as well; I was trembling. How did the two of me reconcile to become just one? Would it hurt? Was it dangerous? We began walking very slowly towards Jason. My stomach felt as if a thousand butterflies had taken flight within. Absently, I touched the lapis lazuli crystal in my pocket. I had forgotten it was there. I had not meant to bring it with me from Cordello – had not meant to bring it *home.*

"Keira, stop worrying! Trust in the best outcome, as you have learned."

I took a deep breath and did as she asked. I found

myself automatically seeking the connection to lovelight – then remembered that it was not present here.

When my crown began tingling, I stopped walking, amazed that I had somehow connected with the energy. Was lovelight everywhere?

"It has different names in different worlds, Keira. You may think of it as universal energy, there for all to access – so long as it is intended to be used for a good outcome. It is limitless."

Just like the nothingness of space. They are one and the same.

I stepped towards Jason again, feeling the comfort of the lovelight – the universal energy – flowing down through my body like a shower of light, supporting and assisting me. I vowed never to take this energy – this potential – for granted.

The energy might be limitless, but it had great value, was precious.

The shape in the bubble shifted. Jason was waking.

"He can't see us, yet. Our vibration is too high. It will remain so until you are fully re–integrated into your physical body."

"How do I . . ."

"Hold the vision of yourself complete, integrated, and let yourself flow back," Lady Aida advised. "I will remove Jason's bubble now," she continued.

I visualised as she had instructed. I had a moment of slight dizziness as if my head had been separated from my body; I felt as if I was shifting between realities. Then I sensed, rather than heard, a quiet *pop* – and suddenly I was looking at Lady Aida from my other vantage point. Jason was beside me.

He yawned, his eyes opening blearily. I watched him as he remembered where he was, his eyes immediately flicking across to me to check that I was okay. Bless him.

He saw me watching him. I have never seen him smile so widely. He quickly closed the short distance between us, enveloped me in a hug; he was holding me so tightly, I thought he might crack my ribs. I could feel his heart beating against my chest, a steady, safe, reassuring beat.

Real.

"You're back, you're back, you're back . . . I thought I was going to lose you, Keira!" he spoke into my hair. Although his voice was muffled, I could hear his relief.

"Well you haven't lost me; I'm here, and I'm fine. Lady Aida brought me home."

He released me, turning towards the light–filled Ascended Reikan standing patiently before us.

"Thank you, my lady. For everything. But mostly, for looking after Keira –"

"I didn't need looking after!" I insisted, glaring at him. Jason's head spun back towards me, his expression one of amazement.

"Yes you did, Keira! You disappear whilst I'm sleeping and I find you slumped unconscious against a rock –"

"But I was fine! I did what was expected of me, and my quest is complete, and I'm back safe and sound!"

"Lady Aida told me I had to protect you. Didn't you?" he asked her, his head turning to get her reaction.

She had gone. We no longer needed her. I would have liked to have said a goodbye.

Goodbye Keira. Live well. Be happy. And good luck. With . . . everything.

"Goodbye, Lady Aida, and thank you. I will miss you," I thought.

I turned my attention to Jason. "I can't believe we're

arguing within minutes of me being back!"

"Oh, Keira . . . that's an old pattern, one we'll change once we've adapted to our new 'selves'. Actually, I have *loads* to tell you! I think you'll be surprised by what's been happening!"

"Actually," I replied, lifting one eyebrow, "I have quite a bit to tell *you*, too!"

Jason got to his feet, pulling me to mine. He looked me over critically, then smiled. "You're not sparkling anymore. You had a shimmery golden glaze on your skin."

"That was make–up," I jested. "God, it's cold. No wonder you needed a warm bubble."

Jason picked up his jacket, unfolding it and placing it around my shoulders.

"I missed you, Keira. I really was worried that I was losing you. Let's get back to the car," he suggested. I caught a hint of excitement in his face, in his voice. "There's some champagne in the boot. I packed it, just in case . . . You see, there's something important I really want to ask you . . ."

EPILOGUE

Silently, the mist rose within the stone circle, and crept stealthily over the grass. It curled around each of the immense crags, cold white fingers enveloping them in an impenetrable, dense vapour.

The stone circle became completely hidden from view.

One by one, the giant crags slipped into their original positions, as if the ring of stones had never existed.

The moves were soundless . . . out of space, and out of time.

This portal had closed. It would not re–open.

Time would pass.

Waiting for the perfect moment.

The moment when the players would be summoned.

For the opening of the next portal.

~~~ The End ~~~

Visit the website:

www.lazuli-portals.com

and register for updates

for the remaining books in

The Lazuli Portals series.

If you enjoyed this book,

Ron and Joanna would greatly appreciate

you leaving a review on Amazon

or recommending this book to a friend.

Thank you!

Where it all began
www.winterjasminereiki.co.uk

Cover design & illustration by
Stuart Cooper, Illustrator and Concept Artist
http://gladiatorsc.deviantart.com/
http://stuartcooper.cghub.com/

Lightning Source UK Ltd.
Milton Keynes UK
UKOW022256291211

184508UK00002B/47/P